LOST LOVE

The Zankli Chronicles
Book One

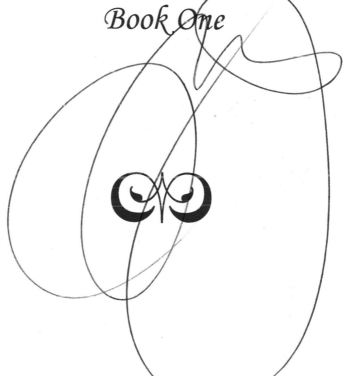

M. J. Duffy

ISBN: 1449520073
ISBN-13: 9781449520076

ACKNOWLEDGMENTS

I could never have written this book without the help of four wonderful women, Kai El Zabar, Kenya Williams, Rene Woods, and Cynthia Tollette. Kai, thank you for the countless hours you spent with me, quietly listening as I read my manuscript. Your editorial support, feedback, and boundless faith in the Zankli Chronicle was a cornerstone in finishing this book.

And to you Kenya, my fellow book lover and critic. I will be forever grateful to you for your companionship in this journey. I never wrote a word or developed a plot, without thinking, will she find this believable. Thank you.

To Rene, my loyal fan and exuberant cheerleader, the Lost Love characters are as real to me as they are to you. I have enjoyed discussing Andre, Hara, and Tyler with you, and your feedback has been invaluable.

Finally, Cynthia your friendship is without question, one of my most precious assets. Thank you for your relentless nudging and disregard for any excuse I had for not finishing this book.

To My Sons
Because you always believed in me,

Kyle, Laté, Tete

And because you never doubted
I would publish
the Zankli Chronicle.

I love you

For My Wonderful Siblings
with much love

Charmaine
Janis
Pinky
Arthur

for your patience, encouragement, and
support

To Moza, Bob and Sylvia
Thank You

For My Readers

Be sure to go to www.mjduffy.net for the latest on
The Zankli Chronicles, book signings, book announcements,
and web broadcast readings.
Please feel free to email me at mj@mjduffy.net.
I would love to hear from you.

The Zankli
Sacred Prayer

Oh God, I bring before you your children who you have gifted with the light. Bring unto them what is yours to give, yours to provide, and yours to understand. Bless them with the joy of goodness, and deliver unto them longevity, wisdom, and foresight.

They are the Chosen, offspring of your heart and a testament to your supremacy. They pledge eternal devotion to you and through you, they irrevocably vow life and honor and everlasting unity.

The Legacy

Welcome to the world of the Zankli, an extraordinary people of ancient lineage from sub-Saharan Africa who are the descendants of indigenous tribesmen and a band of celestial beings who have amazing physical and spiritual powers. At the dawn of time, in the lush and fertile land of modern-day Togo, the Zankli celestials interbred with the local natives for ten decades before their departure. Their parting instructions to their numerous offspring were that they should join with each other for five generations before branching out and linking with other tribes.

The earthly Zankli inherit their sires' celestial gifts, some more than others, and enjoy youthful longevity—aging slower than fellow humans—into their seventies and eighties. Some Zankli can mind merge—speaking and hearing telepathically—others have extraordinary healing powers, exceptional ones can move through time and space, and the truly blessed have all of the gifts combined. Known as the Chosen Ones, the truly blessed are prophesized leaders, purebred, and the bearers of future princes of Zankli and rulers of humankind.

PROLOGUE

LOS ANGELES ~ 1980

The hallway echoed with piercing wails. The baby was crying again, but the night nurse lounged comfortably in the oversized chair and ignored its cries. She blocked out the wails for hours. Shifting her weight in the chair to better distribute her well-endowed hips, the nurse continued to slowly flip the pages in the grocery section of the *Valley Times*.

Resentment was a large part of Ethel Mae Matthews' personality. She resented working the graveyard shift. She resented reporting to the charge nurse. She resented her cramped apartment in the smelly, overcrowded building where she lived. Most of all, she resented being assigned to the Pediatric AIDS Ward at Olive View County Hospital.

Moistening the pudgy index finger on her right hand, the large woman's lethargic motions portrayed extreme boredom as she eyed the coupons in the sundry section of the newspaper.

The baby's bed was in an isolated section of the ward, and the persistent cries held a desperate air that the nurse could no longer ignore. Ethel Mae slapped the newspaper on the table, released a frustrated sigh and angrily shot out of the chair.

Muttering under her breath, she crossed the hall to the nursery. But before she reached the bawling infant, the charge nurse pushed past her and, rushing over to the bed, grabbed the child. Nestling her cheek on the tot's head, she hugged and shushed the baby simultaneously.

"What's the matter with you? Didn't you hear this child crying?" Sophie Tyler impatiently asked the night nurse.

"I heard her, but she has been going on that way all night. What am I supposed to do?"

Looking at the heavyset woman disbelievingly, Sophie Tyler flipped, "Well you would cry too, if you had this in your diaper." The child's diaper reeked of urine and was sagging and puffy. It was obvious that it had not been changed in hours.

The wails stopped the moment the charge nurse scooped up the baby. Carrying her over to the changing table, the nurse removed the disposable diaper as she wiped her bottom. The odor of urine permeating the room was soon replaced by the sweet smell of baby powder.

"How could anyone abandon something this precious?" Nurse Tyler mused. "She is truly one of the prettiest babies I've ever seen. Look at her eyes, aren't they beautiful?"

Turning back toward the night nurse, Sophie Tyler was surprised to see a flicker of disgust flash on the nurse's face.

Sophie was even more startled when the nurse replied, "It wouldn't be hard for me to leave if I thought my child was HIV positive. I mean, she's gonna die anyway. Why go through the heartache?"

Leaning against the doorjamb, the night nurse gazed down at the floor and then back up again. "Listen, if I were you, I wouldn't let any fluids from that child get on me."

Looking down into the child's uniquely colored eyes, Sophie Tyler ignored the words spewing from the night nurse and spoke more to herself than to the unsympathetic woman lazing in the doorway.

"She doesn't even have a name," Sophie muttered under her breath. "Who would do that to a child?"

Sophie was aware of this particular nurse's HIV phobia. It was pretty much the attitude of all of the private agency nurses. And the charge nurse feared the instant she left the room, Ethel Mae would leave the child and scurry back to the nurses' lounge.

On impulse, the charge nurse, still cradling the baby, walked across the room to the rocking chair. Humming softly, the petite woman, her long blonde hair hidden under the crisp nurse cap, eased down gently lifting her feet off the floor and pushed the chair into a soft swing.

Her melodic hum mingled with the raindrops splashing on the patio. The dual sounds blended into a soothing rhythm. The baby slept peacefully, unaware that her fate was intertwined and dependent upon the two caregivers.

BEVERLY HILLS ~ 1991

Rachel Mueller placed the cordless phone on the desk. Her hand unconsciously rubbed the receiver with a repetitive rhythmic motion as she looked out the large bay window framing the luxurious office. The view was spectacular. It was a wondrous clear morning, and the landscape beyond the office window was breathtaking. Any other day, Rachel would have taken pleasure in the snow-peaked San Bernardino Mountains flanking the Los Angeles basin, but today Rachel was oblivious to the cinematic scenes revolving outside the spotless window panes.

She stared sightlessly into the plush furnished office as she considered her next move. Rachel was not really surprised by the lab results. In fact, if Rachel felt anything at all it was numb; and she sat in a state of dreamlike detachment. Although three specialists had confirmed the original prognosis, she was not prepared for the finality of Dr. Joseph's diagnosis. She had terminal, inoperable cancer. All three doctors agreed. The tumors had spread from her ovaries to her lungs. If Rachel lived another three months, it would be a miracle.

"*Man proposes,* and the *God of your great-grandfathers will dispose.*" Nanny Peters' favorite prophecy reverberated in Rachel's mind. *Man proposes and life disposes.* The stunned woman repeated the prophecy over and over with silent resolve.

Not by as much as a finger's twitch did the elegant woman reveal the turmoil behind her practiced calm, but her mind raced in the eerily quiet office.

At thirty-four, Rachel was the picture of quiet chic. Her thick dark locks were stylishly groomed into a sleek bob, which covered her ears and framed a face that could easily grace the cover of *Vogue*. She was not what one would describe as a classic beauty, but her high cheekbones, strangely colored eyes, and generous mouth made Rachel a stunning package. Still it was her hourglass figure that captured the attention of most men.

She was not the rail-thin stuff of a fashion model. What distinguished Rachel was she that had what many referred to as Marilyn Monroe sex appeal. Her palm-sized breasts, tiny waist, and gorgeous ass proved a lustful magnet to both sexes. No matter how conservative her dress, her curves beckoned. But the unsolicited attention was never returned by Rachel, and her lack of interest in either sex had earned her the title of ice maiden.

Today she wore the five thousand dollar pink and black St. John knit suit, accessorized by a pair of ebony Prada pumps, with the casual grace of the truly privileged, and with what her best friend Angie laughingly called, "the pomp of the rich and shameless."

Swiveling in the chair, pointing it toward the shelves, which held priceless rare edition books from ceiling to floor, Rachel lifted one shoulder in a philosophical shrug, and thought, *a real kick in the ass this time.*

A loud laugh exploded in the room. Startled, then realizing the outburst was her own; Rachel shook her head, and with a lopsided smile exposed perfectly veneered teeth. It would be ludicrous if the entire situation was not so tragic, and with that thought, a brief wave of despair flashed across her face. Her colleagues would have been floored by the revealing crack in her legendary cool.

Self-mockery had given way to panic. She was unnerved. Stumped. Overwhelmed. She was not ready to die, was not prepared, and had no faith in a higher power. To her way of thinking, God had forsaken her when her father died, and, as far as she was concerned, confirmed his desertion years later when she was taken hostage by brutal kidnappers.

Prayer, Rachel privately argued, *was for the weak and cowardly. But what should I do?* She queried silently.

Unconsciously, Rachel's hands formed in a prayerful steeple under her chin. Lowering her head, she rested her brow on her towered fingers. In deep thought, the indomitable woman contemplated her next move.

With the same resolve she employed when confronted by a business crisis, she examined the facts. She had terminal cancer. She was unmarried and without legal issue. It was a complex truth that bore cruel realities for her family and the love of her life—Mueller International—the main reason she remained sane in the years following her abduction. Mueller was her cherished legacy, but it meant nothing without a successor.

What a cruel twist of faith, Rachel lamented.

Under the terms of her father's Will, if she died without a blood heir, all of the holdings of Mueller International would be liquidated and funneled into a nonprofit foundation. The prospect was unthinkable.

As little as she cared for her mother, Mercedes, and as frequently as she fought with her half brother Simon, she would not like to see them destitute. In the 1970s, her brother had lost most of his trust in bad Mexican loans. Mercedes, poor soul, had never been wise with her money. Rachel doubted if they had one million dollars between them. If she died without a legal heir, her half brother and mother would be turned out with little more than the clothes on their backs.

Rachel sat silently for hours, playing chess with her options. Finally, she settled on a plan. With calm resolve, she turned and picked up the telephone. Her perfectly manicured, tapered, cherry nails pressed the intercom button. Sherri Masters' cool voice answered immediately.

"Yes, Ms. Mueller."

"Ask my mother's secretary to schedule a breakfast meeting for tomorrow morning." Rachel's gentle, cultured tones had been honed over years of practice and personal restraint.

"Let her know that I would like to have breakfast with my mother on my patio at nine o'clock."

"Yes, Ms. Mueller." Sherri's crisp, professional manner made Rachel smile. In nine years, Sherri had never called Rachel by her first name. Her executive assistant exercised a professional code, which discouraged overt familiarity. And truth be told, the formal relationship was exactly as Rachel liked it. Their interaction demanded high levels of performance from Sherri with no excuses. Rachel had no doubt that she would be meeting with her mother the following morning, because Sherri rarely failed to deliver on one of Rachel's requests.

"Also, would you get Al Rosenthal on the phone and let him know that I would like him to leave his evening free for a special project. Tell him I'll call him with a briefing around two o'clock."

Rachel had not realized how tense she was until she released the intercom button. The knuckles on her left hand had turned white as she clinched her fist into a tight ball. Disturbed by her lack of control, Rachel released her fingers and stretched. She took a deep breath and let it out slowly; and her hand automatically lifted to the right side of her face where her ear was supposed to be. The pat at her hair was a comforting habit developed years before to assure the empty space was covered. Closing her eyes, she leaned back, her head resting against the soft leather of the executive chair.

She dreaded the thought of tomorrow's meeting. At that moment, Rachel would have gladly traded places with a Palestinian hostage, if by doing so, she could have postponed the upcoming talk with her mother.

Where would she begin? Rachel mused. She and her mother were not close. There was no love and little fondness between them. Their relationship was like a bad cell phone connection, impossible to hear clearly. Thoughtfully, Rachel stared into the bookshelf unseeing and smiled ironically, as she pictured the scenario playing out like a slow-motion movie.

The phone rings. She answers. It's Mercedes. Her mother's voice is unintelligible, garbled, being filtered through a receiver with heavy static. Mercedes is shouting, but Rachel can barely hear her. The conversation is stilted. There are gaps, blank spots, and voids at frequent intervals. Before long, there is a complete break in the connection. Then the line goes dead.

Rachel could not recall a time that she had spoken with her mother when that scenario had not played out, not even when she returned home after eighteen months of captivity. A deep shudder shook Rachel's body as she recalled Karl and her months of imprisonment. She felt her stomach churn; the memory was nauseating.

She picked up the phone and dialed Angela. Tears pooled in the corners of her eyes. The call was one of the most difficult she had ever made.

Flipping through the thick stack of papers, Rachel initialed and signed her name on three sets of legal documents. Then she handed them to Al Rosenthal. Pausing, her violet eyes captured Al in a steady gaze.

"I'm sure I don't have to remind you that this," Rachel waved the documents above his hand, "should be kept in strict confidence."

Reaching for the documents, Al tucked the neat stack of papers in his briefcase, carefully closing it as he snapped the twin locks in place. The soft click resonated in the room communicating the finality of the moment. Al's eyes acknowledged her request, and he responded grimly.

"Have I ever betrayed your trust?"

There was a fraction of a moment delay before Rachael flipped.

"No." The answer was a mild apology.

Al had worked for the Mueller family for more years than he cared to remember. He started straight out of college in the legal department, and worked himself up to chief legal officer. As CLO at Mueller International, the late-night meeting did not ruffle him, nor was he unduly surprised by the task he had been given earlier that day.

Rachel was a consummate professional. She never let her guard down. She never allowed Al to cross the line or attribute more to their relationship than the business at hand.

Years before, Al had served as mediator when Rachel was abducted. The girl had disappeared for eighteen months. Yet, if anyone asked him what made her tick, he would have been at a loss for words.

God! What a mess, he thought. Rachel had fallen in with a group of ghetto thugs, and even though he did not know the whole of it, the upshot was that she was kidnapped and held for ransom by her black boyfriend. When Mercedes did not immediately respond to the demands of the hoodlums, negotiations fell apart, leaving Rachel in the hands of her kidnappers for months.

Mercedes had gotten Al involved two weeks after the kidnapping, but she had ignored Al's advice to bring in the police. Fearful of the scandal, Mercedes had retained a private detective agency to investigate the kidnapping. They had made a mess of the investigation, bungling the operation from the start. No one associated with Rachel's abductor had been willing to give the white private detectives any solid information, in spite of the thousands of dollars they had spent with informants. Al and Simon had argued that the police had an underground network of stool pigeons who could really help with the search.

Their arguments fell on deaf ears. Al had become frustrated. At one point, he suspected that Mercedes was deliberately slow-playing negotiations. And his suspicions were correct. Rachel could have been dead for all Mercedes cared...and secretly hoped. That was until she found out that even if Rachel died she and Simon would not be able to control or manage Mueller International.

Adam Mueller's Will stipulated that if Rachel died without an heir, the family estates, including their home in Pacific Palisades, were to be sold. All proceeds from the sales would be donated to the *Beatrice Mueller Health, Education, and Arts Foundation for Disadvantaged Families.* The privately held stock in the company would also go to the foundation.

That information had finally given rise to a reaction from Rachel's mother. Al smiled to himself at the memory. Mercedes had started to scream, screeching and shouting at the top of lungs. She hadn't acted like the cultured lady about town then, and even fourteen years later, Al could still hear Mercedes yelling at him to "Get her back, dammit, get her the fuck back. Now!"

But the line of communication had gone dead. There was no word from her kidnappers. There was complete, unadulterated silence.

Mercedes called in the police then, but so much time had elapsed, the trail was cold. The police suspected that her ex-boy-friend, Karl Usher had taken her out of the country into Mexico or Canada. There was no trace of him in the Bay Area, and a regional search had turned up empty.

The case was being treated like a runaway. The police concluded that the young couple had skipped town together. Karl's family and friends were questioned. But the twosome had vanished.

One year went by and Mercedes was frantic. Al was sure that she had vivid visions of homelessness and there was an air of desperation prevalent in the family, which included Mercedes' brother, Bob Stanhope, and his wife, Karen, their two adopted sons, and Simon. Not one of them was independently wealthy; all depended on Rachel's estate for their livelihood, especially Mercedes. At least, she reasoned, the others have youth and skills to get them by. *What do I have?*

Then after months of absence, a rail-thin, hollow-eyed Rachel showed up at Al's office, mum to all of his inquiries. She bounced back miraculously, and it was as if she had never been gone. Within weeks, the girl had resumed her education, transferring to the University of Southern California, and graduated in record time, receiving a MBA in finance.

Gone was the bubbly inquisitive, trusting teen. Al took note of the new Rachel, shaking his head sadly at the reserved, soft-spoken, astute businesswoman obsessively dedicated to her work and Mueller International. The difference was obvious and very telling. Where she used to be open, she was now aloof. Rachel allowed few people close, keeping most of the staff and colleagues at arm's length. She rarely if ever went out socially, and only then with Angela Ryan. Nanny Peters appeared to be her sole confidant.

Whatever had happened to Rachel during her captivity took her from girl-child to a woman who was incapable of trusting anyone. Privately, the family speculated that she might have been tortured and raped by her captors, but Rachel neither confirmed nor denied their suspicions. Instead, she built an invisible wall around her feelings, insulating and protecting herself from all except Nanny Peters. She relied on no one, and her emotions were husbanded fiercely.

Rachel's distrust was translated in a variety of ways; most revealing was her inability to form an intimate relationship with a man...or woman. As far as Al could determine, Rachel returned from her captivity asexual.

Her only passion appeared to be Mueller International. She had put in long arduous hours, first as an apprentice, and then as a junior manager. In the end, her hard work paid off. Five years after her return, Rachel wrestled the reins of power from her half brother in a brilliantly executed coup that put her in the lead position of Mueller International; she became the official chief executive officer and chairman of the board. These days her brother was her trusted second-in-command, and though he rarely revealed it, Al knew Simon was not happy about the change.

The late-night meeting with Rachel went smoothly. Smiling to himself, Al thought he would give a million dollars to see Mercedes' face when Rachel gave her the news.

The meeting with her mother had been no better and no worse than Rachel expected. "What do you mean you have a child?" The question, which was at first spoken in a monotone that Mercedes thought made her sound like British aristocracy, but in reality only made her sound pretentious, rose an octave as she repeated the question.

Rachel would have laughed if the situation had not been so deadly serious.

"I meant exactly what I said. During my eighteen months of captivity, I had a baby, a little girl. Her father is African American."

"Is African American? Black? Are you telling me that you had a child by a black man? Are you crazy?" By this time, Mercedes was screeching. She had dropped her fork on the table sometime between African American and black man and was staring at Rachel in stunned disbelief.

Rachel felt it was almost worth the current trauma to see a crack in Mercedes' face, which normally appeared frozen and stiff with a smug self-satisfied expression. Her mother had been under the knife so many times that her skin looked like alabaster. Her features were stretched beyond recognition. There were no character lines, no human traces of joy or pain, and while her face was smooth, there was no hiding the deterioration of her neck, hands, and too-thin body. No, the years had not been kind to Mercedes, and at this moment, she looked every bit of her seventy years. In the end, Rachel could almost, but not really, feel any sympathy for her mother.

"You know the terms of my father's Will," Rachel continued, holding her hand in the air to forestall her mother's next question. "Everything goes to the Beatrice Mueller Foundation if I die without a natural heir. Mercedes' eyes, which had begun to protrude, searched Rachel's face incredulously. She could not have spoken if her life depended on it.

"There is more that I need to tell you, Mother." Rachel hesitated, unsure as to how to proceed, and with a flash of insight decided that blunt honesty would be best.

"I am dying." If it was possible, Mercedes' face became even more translucent, while a litany of emotions flashed in her eyes.

Now Mercedes' voice was barely audible. "What do you mean?"

Rachel was moved in spite of herself. "I've seen several specialists. There is no hope really." There was a finite quality to Rachel's disclosure and Mercedes recognized it immediately. Her body deflated like a balloon. The air was sucked from her cheeks and she looked lifeless. It was inconceivable, she thought. Rachel would die and she would be left to fend for herself. Self-preservation, not grief was foremost in Mercedes' mind and transparent in her eyes.

Rachel understood her mother. It would have been nice to think that Mercedes was saddened, even concerned about her well-being. The fact was that Mercedes did not care about Rachel at all. It was not personal. It was just who Mercedes was.

Even before Adam Mueller's death, Mercedes showed little interest in her daughter. A consummate hedonist, her life was built around personal pleasure, self-indulgence, and conspicuous consumption. Mercedes was fascinated with "Mercedes." Like Narcissus, who had fallen in love with his own image, she found little of interest outside of herself, and could spend hours gazing in a mirror admiring and examining her reflection.

To this purpose, when she began her trysts with Adam she had a large ceiling-to-floor, wall-to-wall mirror installed in her bedroom which she duplicated in her Palisades suite when she married him. Her favorite pastime was watching, as she squatted, legs akimbo in self-love. So close to the mirror, that her panting would fog the glass, she ritually massaged and pinched her nipple with one hand coaxing the small bud into a nugget, while she slowly fingered the hidden spot at her core.

Fingers damp with her own juices, the room permeated with her pungent scent, Mercedes would love herself in self-adulation. Swaying, she would perform this private dance several times daily, her practiced steps, honed and choreographed over years, would spark rippling, multiple organisms again and again, until spent she would fling herself across the bed shouting a final release. She never worried about the cries emanating from her room, never cared who overheard her passionate outbursts.

She was an addict. She loved the dance. She craved it. Whenever she could perform it, she did so, for the pure and simple rapture of the sexual high. Her fetish was self-stemming. Mercedes did not need anyone, had never needed another for the private dance, except Adam.

There had been a time when Adam had joined the dance, talking dirty to her, calling her sluttish filthy names while she gyrated in front of him, lost in her private play. Then when she finished and lay panting on her bed, he had thrown himself on her, thrusting his thick tool into her until he had yelled his release.

She had loved the way he had cleaned her afterward. Placing his head between her legs, where she dripped with their combined juices, the air filled with the scent of semen, Adam lapped at her, making soft purring, passionate sounds, until she was completely dry.

They did not know which of them was more surprised when after six months of their bed play Mercedes was pregnant.

At sixty-six, Adam had vowed never to remarry. Nevertheless, the moment he confirmed his paternity, Adam married Mercedes and established an eight million dollar trust fund for her and a two million dollar endowment for her nineteen-year-old son,

Simon Seymour. The trust and endowment went into effect the moment Rachel was thrust from Mercedes' womb and placed into his eager hands.

Adam adored the child. From the start, he kept the baby as close as possible. His instincts told him that Mercedes resented their child. The couple's relationship had always been precarious and based upon an equal enjoyment of their partiality to bizarre sex. But with the arrival of Rachel, Adam's desire for Mercedes underwent a sharp decline. He was less enamored of their sexual antics, and more fascinated by his daughter.

He found Rachel enchanting, but noticed that Mercedes was distant and detached from the baby from the beginning. She seldom held the child, not even to calm Rachel when she cried. He knew Mercedes was self-centered, but he thought she would be different with a girl child. Not so. He found her to be even more self-indulgent than he ever imagined.

Even before Rachel came home from the hospital, Adam had recruited Christine Peters as a live-in nanny. Their first meeting was in the visiting room at Beverly Hills Hospital three days after Mercedes delivered Rachel.

"I am grateful to you, Christine. I really appreciate you meeting me here on such short notice."

Adam Mueller sat comfortably across from Christine Peters, his elegantly clad legs crossed, and smiled sincerely into her chocolate eyes. He had asked her to meet him in the maternity ward so that if she agreed to his plan, she would take charge of his daughter's care immediately.

"This means a great deal to me, and I want you to know that I would not put my child into anyone else's hands. You will not be sorry if you decide to join my household. You and those you love will never have another financial worry."

Adam dropped his head for a fraction of a moment to gather his thoughts. "I am sorry to learn of your recent loss. Losing your husband and child so soon after your delivery...I am truly sorry, Christine."

Christine Peters watched the well-dressed man as he carefully rearranged his legs. At sixty-six, he had not lost any of his sex appeal. He was tall, stunningly handsome, and could give any Hollywood movie star a run for his money.

Adam's hair remained thick waves of ebony with no noticeable grey, and his full lips were a lustful beacon in his tanned, masculine, chiseled face. Surprising, especially to most of his business associates, was that his looks were vastly surpassed by his intelligence. He was an exceptional businessman, exuding a charm that was disarming and utterly overwhelming.

Adam Mueller was a master communicator. He had used his powers of persuasion to build one of the largest cosmetics conglomerates in the world; and at the moment, he was directing his energy toward the woman seated across from him.

No one observing the two individuals would have guessed the life-altering negotiations in process. Nor would they have believed that the stylishly dressed *Dapper Dan* was orchestrating the meeting with the same finesse and expertise he used to negotiate multimillion dollar acquisitions.

"Little Rachel needs care. I know my daughter will never replace the lives lost to you, but maybe in some way, she will fill the empty space in your heart." Uncharacteristically, Adam's voice cracked and he cleared his throat.

"Mercedes refuses to breast-feed Rachel even though her little body rejects cow's milk." Adam's eyes dropped to Christine's swollen breasts. Christine squirmed self-consciously under his scrutiny. The heaviness of her breasts, which leaked milk nonstop, was a constant reminder of the baby girl she had buried a week before.

Adam raised his head and looked squarely at the handsome brown woman conveying his acceptance of her as his equal. With laser beam precision, his eyes bore into her.

"We need you, Christine. Our lives, our destinies, are intertwined. I believe there are no coincidences in life."

Adam gazed at Christine steadily and pulled his trump card. Speaking softly, he reminded her of their link. "Ve Tuk ya ve mein-gutool ya Zankli, toli ya ethvenu, yiftul ya ve vul ti gull e yulto cee utivi. Tuk tultoo vii m tultoo tuki peke."

Christine stiffened, and her eyes blinked as she bobbed her head in acknowledgement of the ancient words and affirmed them silently. Then she gave the words back to Adam in the ancient way—mind to mind. *The God of the great-grandfathers of Zankli, giver of life, creator of the heavens and earth, is forever with us. God always was and always will be.*

There had never been a chance that she would refuse Adam's request. There was too much on the table, too much at stake for her people, and too much for her to gain personally as caretaker of the newborn child. So in the end, Christine accepted Adam Mueller's proposal. She gave a two-week notice at her job, retired from Los Angeles Unified School District as a middle school nurse, and joined the Mueller household as a private nanny to Miss Rachel Seymour Mueller.

On her first night home, the infant slept cradled on Adam's chest. The next day, Rachel's crib was placed next to her father's bed. Mercedes showed little interest in where Rachel slept, as long as she was not disturbed.

Adam swore that some insects were more protective of their young than Mercedes, and when Rachel was old enough to sleep in her own room, he placed the nursery next to his bedroom.

He was a very attentive father. Rachel was a pampered and spoiled child. Nothing was too good for her. She was coddled and nurtured as a toddler. She was cherished and respected as a youth, but above it all, she was loved and adored by her father. Unfortunately, all that changed with Adam's death. Weeks would pass without Mercedes requesting to see her daughter.

Once, when Rachel was eleven, Mercedes did not see her for almost three months, even though they lived in the same house. When Nanny Peters went in search of Mercedes to discuss the oversight, she interrupted Mercedes in the middle of one of her private dances. Scrambling, Mercedes just managed to cover herself as Nanny Peters, after knocking softly, walked into the room.

Unembarrassed, but furious at the interruption, Mercedes eyed the tall, brown-skinned woman scornfully and hissed with cold contempt, "I can't keep such incompetence around me. I'll never understand why Adam hired you in the first place. Who ever heard of Spellman College?" With an icy glare, Mercedes demanded, "Where did you say it was located? Arkansas. No, Georgia. Well, who cares? I'll look up and Rachel will be speaking just like you, with your yes'em and no'em.

"I won't have it." Mercedes' voice reached a hysterical fevered pitch.

"Pack your bags, and get out! I said get out of my house," she cried. "I want you gone by the end of the day."

Christine Peters watched the woman in amazement, her mouth opened and shut speechlessly. She could not believe what she was hearing. *The woman was mad*, she thought, shaking her head grimly. Then with the regal dignity of some long dead African ancestor, she turned gracefully and walked out of the room.

In the end, Nanny Peters stayed. In reality, there was never any doubt that she would not do so, since Adam Mueller's Will stipulated that she was to remain with Rachel until his daughter entered college. At that time, Christine Peters could choose to retire or continue with Rachel in a personal capacity. He had set aside a huge trust for legal contestation to ensure that his wishes were met. Mercedes despised Christine all the more for it, resenting her lack of authority in the matter of Rachel's upbringing, and hated Adam for usurping her power even from the grave.

Thus, the pattern was set. It was Nanny Peters, not Mercedes, who combed Rachel's hair, bathed her, and sponged her scrapes. It was Nanny who held and rocked the child at her father's funeral, muttering soft comforting words as Adam Mueller's casket was lowered into the ground.

"It will be all right. You'll see. He's not really gone, as long as you have him in your heart."

But he was gone; no one knew that better than Rachel. To the child who was tightly clutching her nanny's hand, the words of comfort were empty. She was inconsolable. She knew her father would not be returning. After all, he had told her so himself. Rachel knew that her life would never be the same again. He had told her that too!

There would be no more visits to his office, and no more private tutoring lessons on the manufacturing and merchandizing of cosmetics. But as much as Rachel would miss their chats, she would miss his love and approval more.

There was a huge hole in her heart; even though her father had told her what to expect the day he had sat across from her at the large conference table, holding her hand, speaking hesitantly about his illness.

He told her that he had seen the best doctors, and that they had all agreed that he had cancer. The cancer was bad, he had explained, and it was eating away at him.

"Nothing can be done," he said softly.

"I've had a good life, Rae, better than most. I had two wives before your mother, but I've never cared for anyone like I have you. You are the love of my life."

He bent forward and kissed Rachel's small hand, "I am leaving everything to you. Oh, I am taking care of your mother and your brother, so that they will not go after what is yours, but the bulk of my wealth will go to you in the form of a trust. That way, even if they try anything, your wealth is protected."

Adam's face was solemn, and Rachel placed her small hand on his wet cheek. He was crying, not for himself, but for the times he would not be there for her.

"I want you to promise me something, Rae. Promise me that you will study and learn everything you can about Mueller International. Promise me that you will one day run this company."

"It is yours by right as my heir," Adam stated firmly.

"Promise me that your children will inherent what I pass to you," he went on hoarsely. "No one else should have what is ours.

Blood to blood," he said as he captured and held her gaze with his own, "My blood to your blood."

Rachel had never seen her normally calm father so upset. She watched him with solemn, clear eyes that mirrored his own, and nodded her head somberly.

"I will, Papa. I promise. Just don't be unhappy," she said, taking a deep breath so that the tears hovering in her eyes would not overflow and cause her father more distress.

Clearing his throat, Adam spoke just above a whisper and captured her bluish-purple eyes. "I must give you something that you are never to share with anyone except your heir. He walked over to the heavily built credenza at the opposite side of the room, and removed an ornate, rectangular carved wooden box from a top drawer. The richly decorated chest had delicate figurines circling the base and was an antique strongbox from the seventeenth century.

Handing the antique chest to his daughter, Adam cautioned Rachel gravely, "The information in here is for your eyes alone. It is my legacy to you. It will be your decision who you share it with. But promise, blood to blood, Rae. Do you understand what I am saying?" To emphasize, Adam continued gravely, while Rachel watched him with round saucer eyes.

"I know you are young, and I know that I am repeating myself, but your brother is not of our blood. He is your mother's son. Remember always, my blood to your blood, otherwise everything will crumble." There can be no other way. With a smothering hug, Adam held Rachel close to his heart burying his face in the curve of her neck.

I am going to teach you a prayer, and when you are frightened, or alone you must recite these words. They are ancient and powerful.

"*Tuk tultoo vii m tultoo tuki peke.*"

The words rumbled from Adam's chest, deep and different from any language Rachel had ever heard. Rachel repeated the prayer dutifully until she had memorized the passage and mimicked the clicking sounds to her father's satisfaction. Adam smiled approvingly, stroked Rachel's hair lovingly, and patted her cheek.

"That's very good, Rae; you speak the language almost perfectly. I have asked Nanny to teach you the rest of the prayer. It is your talisman. Do you know what a talisman is?"

Rachel shook her head. "No, Daddy."

"It is like a good luck charm, but this talisman comes from a higher power. It comes from the God of your great-grandfathers, and it affirms that *God always was and always will be...Tuk tultoo vii m tultoo tuki peke.*"

Rachel nodded and repeated the prayer, and asked, "But how does Nanny Peters know our family talisman?"

Adam was silent for a moment, thinking privately about the best way to answer his daughter. "Nanny is like family, Rachel. Never forget it. Long ago, her people and ours were connected, and that connection is eternal," he continued carefully, telling Rachel all that she needed to know.

It was the last private conversation Rachel had with her father. Three weeks later Adam Mueller was dead. Telegrams and flowers arrived from all over the world, and Mueller company managers flew in from Europe and Asia.

Adam Mueller had been liked and admired by most of his colleagues. He had many friends and fans, and the funeral was packed. It was a social gathering of the elite, and while some people came to mourn, most came to be seen and admired.

Rachel sat huddled in the front pew, surrounded by family members, yet completely alone. Clutching Christine's hand, Rachel held back tears and thought how useless it all was: the singing, the sermon, the testimonies. Even at nine, the desolate child saw through the superficiality of the gathering.

All she could think about was how useless these people were when it came to what really mattered. Looking around her, Rachel felt a deep sadness. Not one of her father's friends had the power to return him to her.

Nor had God, thought Rachel, *elected to intervene.* She had prayed and prayed, promising to give needy children her toys and prized possessions. She had spent hours on her knees, repeating over and over the sacred prayer her father had taught her. *Tuk tultoo vii m tultoo tuki peke,* she had prayed as she vowed to do good deeds in His name. But either God did not hear, or chose not to listen. Either way her prayers went unanswered, and at that moment, Rachel determined that God was a cruel jester.

That night after the funeral, when it was time to go to bed, Rachel declared, "I'll never pray again, Nanny. So don't ask me to."

Prayers had been a nightly ritual ever since Rachel had learned to talk. In order, the Lord's Prayer and then the Sacred Prayer of Zankli. Christine Peters had made sure that it was her first act in the morning, and the last thing she did at night.

Deeply troubled, she stared at the stubborn child and shook her head. "You'll regret those words one day, and I pray to God I am not here to see it when you do. I love you too much to see you suffer."

Looking back over her shoulder as she walked out of the room, Nanny Peters assured, "There is a higher power, child, and you will call his name before it is all over with. This I know as surely as I know my own name."

With a puckered mouth the child, mimicking Nanny Peters' sound of distaste, blew and hissed with her lips, then toed off her pink satin ballerina slippers and placed a dainty foot on the bed stool. Climbing into bed, she swore that she would never allow anything to hurt her so badly again.

Over the next ten years, Rachel dedicated herself to fulfilling the promise she made to Adam Mueller, the cosmetics mogul—but she longed for her father, whom she did not want to disappoint. She learned as much as she could about Mueller International. She often fantasized that Adam was watching her, applauding her accomplishments, and cheering her successes.

Rachel was gifted with a photographic memory and exceptional intelligence, and by the age of fifteen, she knew as much about the financial holdings of Mueller as John Davies, the company's long time chief financial office. Unknown to several of the Board members, she had orchestrated a number of important executive transactions, including the establishment of several off-shore corporations.

As a mandatory stipulation in Adam Mueller's Will, Rachel began attending Mueller executive board meetings when she was sixteen. The intellectually gifted teenager had sat quietly in the meetings, and her presence was largely forgotten by the thirteen men overseeing the business and financial portfolio of the company.

The monthly gathering was small, consisting of nine board members that were chaired by Rachel's half brother Simon, who was CEO of Mueller International.

Rachel's mind functioned like a sponge and, despite what her elders thought, the taciturn teen understood even the most intricate business transactions. Naturally endowed with an economic aptitude, Rachel had the early coaching from her father to thank for her understanding of business in general and the cosmetics industry in particular.

She could process information as rapidly as she thought, and it was a gift that her father had recognized early on. She was a master chess player, and, as early as eight years old, could anticipate her father's moves—beating him as many times as she lost.

In 1964, at the time of Adam's death, the privately held cosmetics manufacturer had an estimated worth of six hundred million dollars. By the time Rachel attended her first board meeting, the company had grown to over one billion dollars in holdings and assets. The growth was largely due to the stewardship of Rachel's half brother Simon Seymour.

Simon was not the visionary that Adam Mueller had been, nor did he have his charm, but he was a meticulous businessman. His success was due largely to his ability to focus on the details and to his unwavering persistence.

When Adam Mueller was diagnosed with terminal cancer, he invited Simon to a private lunch. Over an excellently prepared *steak tartar*, Adam informed Simon that he wanted him to join the executive board of Mueller International.

"I want you to watch my back, and when I am not around I want you to take care of your sister's interests." Adam cut into the seasoned raw beef, placed it in his mouth with a practiced flair and then scrutinized Simon over the rim of his wine goblet.

Shrewdly, he wondered how accurate his reports were. If the briefs were correct, and Adam had no reason to doubt them, Simon preferred men in his bed and kept an Asian lover in a quiet section of West Hollywood.

According to the dossier, Simon lived somewhat extravagantly, but had no known drug or criminal perversions. Few knew or even guessed at his sexual preference, and what Adam respected most was that Simon managed to keep his private life private. Nothing in the report shocked Adam. Remembering his own sexual antics with Mercedes, Adam felt he was in no position to cast stones.

"You are family, son." Adam flashed the toothy smile that had charmed shrewd businessmen the world over.

Simon thought, *he's a handsome devil.* He wondered if Adam had ever tried a man. The picture of him pounding into the older man flashed in his mind and his tool stiffened.

Wow, I would like to fuck the bastard.

His stepfather's eyes became hard, steel shooting from their depths, and for a moment, Simon feared he had spoken aloud. He felt a cold chill go down his spine, and the word – *No* – exploded in his mind as disgust twisted the older man's lips. Simon blinked several times to remove the image, and flushed with guilt. Adam was still talking.

"I want you to begin to learn the business while I am still in a position to guide you." Then he winked at Simon and placed his wine goblet on the table. Standing, he signaled the lunch was over. As simple as that, a new page turned in Simon's heretofore, uneventful life.

Seven years later, Simon sat at the head of the Mueller International's massive polished mahogany conference table and surreptitiously scrutinized his younger sister.

No one at the table would have suspected that the handsome, suave man resented his sister's presence. Nor, for that matter, would they have believed that Rachael sent her older brother critiques of their meetings with directives outlining how she felt the company's interests would best be served.

It is infuriating, thought Simon. *Not even twenty years old, and she is already a bona fide bitch. Do they have a bitch school*, he wondered, *one his mother directed, and where his sister was an honor student?*

He studied Rachel with masterfully concealed resentment. How dare she send him a punch list of items that she wanted him to cover with the board members? It was beyond infuriating, it was downright demeaning, a child sixteen years old drafting the board's agendas and orchestrating international decisions.

With a mental shudder, Simon quieted his fuming, reminding himself of the need for patience. It would not do to reveal his disapproval of his sister's attendance at board meetings, he thought, with a mental reprimand. *I'll work it off with Chang tonight.* Simon moved restlessly in his chair, the vision of him and Chang face-to-face, the young man's legs spread and lifted onto his shoulders as Simon drilled into his ass, was a sweet vision. It softened his bitterness, calmed him and allowed him to return to the discussion with unruffled cool.

At the opposite end of the table, Rachel observed the proceedings with a far greater insight into the complexities of the real estate deal than her fellow board members suspected. Her father had handpicked the men and women, and each one had his or her own level of expertise. The issue at hand was the acquisition of a large tract of land in the British Honduras. The Central American country was off the coast of Florida, and her brother was doing his best to stall the partnership.

"I'm not saying the deal isn't attractive..." Simon's pause was perfectly timed to plant doubt, "but I believe we need to go slow, make sure that we have thoroughly investigated the government's wherewithal to perform."

Rachel watched amused. No one questioned Simon. The board members' heads bobbed in unison, acquiescing to his rationale.

What a bunch of bull. She wanted to laugh at the absurdity of Simon's remark.

The Honduran government was offering an attractive opportunity. It combined land with cheap raw materials and even cheaper labor. Simon's opposition to the deal was puzzling— or not—when one considered his personal agenda. Watching from lowered eyelids, her lush lashes shielding her eyes, Rachel studied her brother.

She suspected that the hiccup in today's proceedings had to do with Simon's interests, and not the feasibility of the deal. His sweetheart arrangements with their suppliers, which included a sizeable financial reward for contract approval, were well known to Rachel. The company CFO, John Davies, had exposed Simon's underhanded dealings months earlier, and as long as it did not interfere or jeopardize sound business, Rachel had resigned herself to turning a blind eye to her brother's pilfering.

Today was different. In Rachel's mind, there was no real reason not to accept the Honduran offer. Their government was underwriting the project, putting up $1 million and acting as a temporary partner in both the developmental and construction phases.

Mueller's financial risk was limited. The project was excellent, and Rachel intended to make her decision known to Simon after the board adjourned. Any side deal that he had made would have to take a backseat to the interests of the company. With astuteness far beyond her years, Rachel decided to call Al Rosenthal after the meeting and make him aware of her decision.

Later that evening Christine Peters watched Rachel with pride. Oh, she could be stubborn, pigheaded, and even impatient with those less intelligent, but Rachel was fair, and she was always willing to listen to the other side, even if she had an opposing view. She was not self-centered or mean spirited like that cow that called herself a mother, the loyal woman thought.

Adam Mueller had always been an exceptional chess player, and it was remarkable how forward thinking he had been regarding Rachel. *Yes,* thought Christine, *Adam could take pride in the way his daughter turned out.*

As she straightened the sweater over Rachel's shoulder, Christine reminded her, "Robert is waiting for you, and he will drive you to Chasen's. That's where your mother will meet you."

Anticipating the girl's request to drive herself, Christine rolled her eyes toward the ceiling and said, "No, you can't drive the Volkswagen. Your mother specifically requested that Robert bring you in the Bentley."

Rachel hated the monthly dinners with her mother. She had never understood the why of it, but for some reason several months after her father's death, her mother suddenly remembered she existed, and began inviting her to the ridiculous dinners. Rachel suspected the outings were just as painful for Mercedes.

What she did not know was that Nanny had orchestrated the interactions. Christine had gone to Al Rosenthal and apprised him of the situation. In a no-nonsense manner, Al had outlined Adam's Will and the accompanying conditions and penalties to Mercedes and Simon. The following week mother and daughter began their monthly interludes.

Rachel and her mother had little in common. As far as Rachel was concerned Mercedes was a narrow-minded, dogmatic, elitist who never failed to find fault with Christine Peters, the one person in the entire world Rachel truly loved and was certain loved her back. Unfortunately, the teen did little to hide her feelings from her mother. To a woman like Mercedes, who found everything about herself fascinating, Rachel's thinly veiled contempt was paramount to sacrilege.

Seated across from her mother, gazing at her plate as she mechanically speared artfully prepared snow peas, Rachel was unaware of her mother's malicious stare.

She has everything, Mercedes seethed, observing her daughter from a lowered gaze.

It is not fair. It has never been fair, she thought and lamented sourly. *The little shit. She has the money and control of the company, and if that wasn't enough, she has ownership of the houses.* Mercedes glanced at her daughter thinking, *to add insult to injury, she could almost be a nigger with those full lips and swarthy Mueller looks.*

While Mercedes stewed, Rachel was preoccupied with her upcoming move. She smiled automatically at her mother, nodded her head when Mercedes criticized the waiter, and wondered how long before she could excuse herself. She was always amazed at how little she resembled her mother in temperament or looks. Mercedes had Grace Kelley's regal golden locks and pale skin that differed enormously from her own Mediterranean image. No doubt about it. She was her father's child.

Observing her mother's obvious contempt for the waiter, Rachel mentally shook her head, and thought Nanny would be appalled by her mother's rudeness toward the servant.

Such behavior was unacceptable to the loyal retainer, who Rachel believed had more class in her pinky finger than her mother had in her entire body.

Nanny frequently told her about her father and how gracious he was to everyone, no matter there station in life. She told Rachel that her father measured people by their deeds.

"Treat people the way you want to be treated, was the credo your father lived by," Nanny reminded often. And as time passed, this sense of respect for others was internalized into Rachel's psyche, and she grew to abhor her mother's pretentious and nasty behavior toward individuals she considered lesser beings.

Rachel smiled, knowing next week it would all change. *I'll be a resident at Stanford University.* Unfortunately, the smile was misinterpreted by Mercedes as contemptuous of her and a snide dismissal of the meal.

The little bitch, seethed Mercedes silently.

In actuality, Rachel's thoughts were light-years away. She was focused on her acceptance into Stanford and life beyond Pacific Palisades. And she was relieved as the uncomfortable interlude came to a close. Slowly, she raised her eyes from her plate and met the baleful gaze of her mother, bidding Mercedes a silent good-bye.

Angela Ryan was everything Rachel was not. The brass, cheeky, chain-smoking Angie did everything at high speed, and she talked and lived as if she were in a race with time.

"Hello, I'm Angela. Are you the supper-rich snob everyone is talking about?"

The inquiry came out in a rush, and without pausing for breath, the fresh-faced girl gushed, "Guess you are, or you wouldn't be standing there with your mouth wide open. What's the matter? Did you leave your tongue in the hallway?"

For the first time in her life, Rachel was dumb struck. Never had she been treated with such ill-mannered cheekiness, and she actually sputtered, paused in amazement at the girl's sheer audacity, blinked, and broke out in giggles. She found the impudence of her roommate audacious.

Adam Mueller had insisted that his daughter be home-schooled and tutored by a professional governess on the Mueller Estates. Rachel's interaction with children her own age had been limited to eleven handpicked girls and boys who were the off-spring of Mueller's West Coast executives.

Since Rachel was heir to the vast Mueller holdings, the other children as well as the teachers treated her with deference. No one could fault her education. The instruction was exceptional; the learning environment outstanding, but the social interaction was artificial. Rachel was never allowed to forget she was the daughter of the boss.

To Rachel, Angela's audaciousness was invigorating. She was intrigued by Angie's energy and her brazen honesty, and the girls became instant friends. It was a perfect match. They complemented each other in looks and intelligence.

Angie's family had been a part of the Southern California cultural backdrop since the mid-1800s. Although not nearly as rich as the Muellers—few were—the Ryans were safely immersed in old money, and their lineage could be traced back to the early Spanish land grants. According to Angie, she was an American garden salad. On her father's side were Irish Catholic immigrants, and her mother's family, according to Angie, were American mutts, combining Spanish, English, and German ancestry.

"I am a mixture of everything," she proudly announced to a shocked Rachel on their first night together, "including Apache Indian."

With that, the redheaded, freckled-faced girl jumped on the bed, hopping up and down, dancing like an Indian on the warpath. Loud whooping yelps rang in the room as Angie slapped her mouth and eyed Rachel swirling her arm with fierce jerks.

Then, with a sudden spring, Angie jumped on Rachel, wielding a pillow she had grabbed from the bed. And when the raven-headed beauty reacted by snatching up her own fluffy weapon, they both collapsed on the bed in hysterical laughter.

The girls were soon seen everywhere on campus. Their natural exuberance and high spirits were magnetic, attracting fellow students in the dorms. Their room was a central gathering place for classmates and friends. Angie and Rachel were a beautiful study of contrasts, a picture of glowing fire against moonlit night.

Rachel was truly gorgeous with ebony hair, Elizabeth Taylor violet eyes, and a *please-come-fuck-me* body. Angela's looks were more subtle, but nonetheless striking. She had gold-red hair, a wide mouth, rose petal lips, and a laugh that charmed and seduced at the same time. They were a package of splendor, irresistible in their youth and vigor.

The first year went by rapidly. The girls mixed hard study with episodes of fun and games. When the holidays came, instead of going home, Rachel visited Angela's family in San Francisco. Her only regret was that Nanny Peters had declined to join them. On Christmas Eve, the beloved companion, bundled in a winter coat and scarf, showed up on the Ryans' door steps.

The family was in the den, a huge two-story playroom, complete with a theater-size entertainment center, pool table, and game boards. The room, in spite of its size, was lived-in cozy, and it was ringing with laughter when Christine Peters was announced. Angela, her mother, father, five siblings, and Rachel were seated on a horseshoe sofa that framed the fireplace. They were all razzing each other when Millhouse, the family butler, interrupted the cozy gathering and announced, "Ms. Christine Peters."

When Nanny walked into the room, Rachel flew into the woman's arms, her eyes shiny with unshed tears, and whispered into her neck. "I am so happy you're here. Christmas wouldn't be the same without you." With pride, she turned to the Ryans and introduced Christine Peters as her "guardian angel."

Angela was the first to step forward. Refusing Nanny Peters' extended hands; she walked into the older woman's arms and gave her a tight hug. Releasing her, she smiled, stepped back and took Nanny's hands in her palms, then said gravely, "I'm glad to meet someone from Rachel's family." That holiday, the Ryan gathering was the best that Rachel had had since her father's death.

It was midway through the second year that everything changed for Rachel. It had begun so innocently. Both Rachel and Angie were pledging Phi Alpha Beta Sorority, and two of their sorority sisters pressed the girls into attending a frat party.

The fraternity was honoring Johnny Weir who was a star quarter-back on the Stanford University football team.

That is where Rachel first met Karl, and her life was forever altered. Karl was not the type of guy one overlooked. He had an earthy allure that permeated a room, magnetically drawing attention to his perfectly honed, six foot two inch athletic frame, and his smile was *to die for*. It displayed a dazzling white matinee of even teeth.

Karl's lips were perpetually at a practiced angle, pitched to display his masculine chiseled jaw and cleft chin. He was aware of his draw and sexual appeal to both women and men, and like a hunting animal, he used his charms to seduce and manipulate prey.

Rachel was captivated the moment she laid eyes on him. With dark silky skin, Karl was a primate in peak form. He was African American. He was mysterious. He was off limits. He was taboo, and Rachel wanted him. Taking a deep breath, she imagined she could smell his arousing scent from across the room. It was intoxicating. Observing him from lowered lids, Rachel actually could feel herself get wet, her panties were suddenly soaked, and her body hummed, literally sang in heat.

It had never happened to Rachel before, this feeling of mesmerizing attraction, and it would not be repeated again in her lifetime. When Karl headed toward her, she could not believe it. Years later, she marveled at her own naiveté, but years later, she also understood the instinctive need of her kind to answer the hum of a soul mate.

Karl had a weak come-on. But to the twenty-year-old virgin, who had spent most of her life in a sheltered environment, he seemed hip and raw. His voice was low and sexy, husky with barely contained lust. He bent down. His lips almost touched her earlobe, and she could feel his fiery breath.

"Baby, you look like you need something," Karl whispered in Rachel's ear. His voice sent a shiver of secret delight through her body, and she felt a new flood of liquid heat in her panties.

He handed her a drink, his large masculine hands covering hers as he gently pushed the glass to her mouth tilting it until she swallowed some of the amber liquid. It could have been anything, and she would not have cared. His voice was hypnotic and she had an unquestioning desire to please him.

Rachel was amazed at her reaction to this man. Karl had not touched her, and yet she felt like she was on fire inside. She was frightened and attracted at the same time. She wanted to be alone with him, and she wanted to run away.

Years later she wished she had run, sprinted like Flo-Jo. But that night she ignored the danger signals, and he was dangerous. She felt it intuitively, but like the moth that is drawn to candle-light, Rachel was enthralled, captivated. What she did not know was that their meeting was prearranged.

Karl had been a star running back with the Stanford football team. He was cut from the team in his third year when, under the influence of drugs, he had crashed into a car driven by a young mother with her four-year-old son, killing both instantly.

As a first offender, his sentence was comparatively light, five years' probation. But he was stripped of his athletic scholarship, and with no defined or specific academic skills, Karl became the campus drug dealer. You name it, he had it. Speed. Steroids. Cocaine. Acid. Pot. He was a one-man pharmacy.

Karl learned of Rachel when he overheard two of her sorority sisters discussing how filthy rich she was. He almost pissed his pants in excitement. He had no doubt he could get to the girl, and if he could get to her, he would get to her money. His mind was leaping with entrapment ideas and plans. He promised himself he would orchestrate her demise, and his ascent.

The plan was to meet Rachel and introduce her to cocaine. Karl's goal was to get her hooked on a million dollar habit. He figured he could retire on that. His fantasy included getting off drugs, buying his mother a home, and getting into a rehab program that would break his freebasing habit. As a drug dealer he was a flop. He was an addict. Every dime he earned went into his glass whore.

"Why don't we get out of here? I want to have you to myself."

Karl held Rachel's gaze with a sexy stare that roved down her body, paused heatedly on her breasts, and returned to her mouth with a promise.

Rachel watched as his tongue slipped from his mouth and rolled to his top lip, suggestively licking the small sinuous bud in the middle of his mouth. She was hypnotized by the act. She might be a virgin, but she had seen enough and heard enough to envision his tongue on her own button.

The foolish girl had not a clue that she had become Karl's new mark. He played women the way he played ball, earning the nickname "Kingfish."

Karl was a predator—a shark. And like most practiced predators, he was an expert at controlling his prey. Removing the glass from her hand, setting the half-finished drink on a nearby table, Karl turned to Rachel and ordered, "Get your coat."

Rachel eagerly obeyed Karl's command. She rushed over to Angie, who had watched her friend talking to Karl from across the room. In an excited whisper, Rachel told Angie she was leaving. Hiding her shock, Angela with wide questioning eyes, asked who the guy was, and if she would be coming back to the party. But Rachel waved her hand dismissively.

"I'll call you later," Rachel remarked with a backward glance over her shoulder.

She never remembered the ride from the party to Karl's house. Did not remember getting into bed, or removing her clothes. It was all a blur. But she would always remember what came after. He took her gently, sliding between her legs with practiced gentleness. There was no pain. A little blood. But no pain. He had prepared her well, slipping his fingers and then his mouth to the jewel hidden behind her ebony curls.

He tongued her, sucking and nibbling greedily. The smacking feeding was loud, drowning out everything in the room. Rachel twisted with mewling cries under Karl's ministrations. The more she wriggled the more pressure he applied as he nursed at the slippery button. Rachel was insane with lust. She had no idea she could feel so good.

She grabbed his head digging her nails into his scalp. At one point, Karl stopped licking and Rachel lifted her hips off the bed begging.

"Lick me. Oh, God, please don't stop."

He had her. She was his and he knew it. Karl loved the power he wielded when he gave pleasure. Not as much as he loved the surges of energy he felt when a woman squirmed under him in pain. But that was a particular pleasure he saved for the whores, the *ladies of the night* who did his bidding for a suck on his glass dick.

The picture of Maria with her large red lips circling the pipe, sucking in the sticky sweet vapors, her nipples pinched with iron clamps, sent Karl over the edge. Grabbing Rachel's legs he flung them over his shoulder, spread her wide with his fingers, and dipped his mouth to the hidden mother's milk.

Rachel screamed. Her body exploded in shivering tremors that rocked both of them to their cores, and time faded. Silence resided in the room for several minutes. Rachel blacked out. Karl rested his head on her spread thighs, exhausted.

When Rachel regained consciousness, Karl was easing gently into her welcoming body. The thrusting rhythm was beyond wonderful, and her senses spiraled to another level as she screamed her second climax. The rest of the night blurred into a merry-go-round of sensuous delight. At some point, Rachel vaguely remembered Karl handing her a bottle with a bulb on the end. He told her to inhale, and she did. It was the best feeling she had ever had. But within moments she was violently ill, spilling her guts on Karl, his bed and the floor before rushing to the bathroom and spewing the remaining bile into the toilet.

"Mutherfuck! Shi-it! You nasty bitch!"

Hugging the floor of the toilet, Rachel heard Karl's insults, and assumed she would never see him again. Sure that he would kick her out of his house as soon as she finished in the bathroom, she stood up. Bracing herself on the edge of the sink, with slow deliberate motions, Rachel turned on the faucets and watched as the jets of water splashed over her hands. Cupping them, she lowered her face, rinsing the sour taste from her mouth. She felt like a wet mop. She looked like one too, she thought, opening her mouth. With a wide slant, she gritted her teeth and then stared at her reflection in the mirror. *Awful,* she thought, turning away in self-disgust.

Returning to the bedroom, Karl asked if she was felling better. He had cleaned up the mess, and with a conciliatory wave of his wrist motioned for Rachel to return to bed. Surprised and delighted, Rachel scurried into the bed lifting the clean sheet high as she maneuvered her long legs under the blankets. She was disoriented. The room revolved crazily, and Rachel's stomach was in an uproar.

Karl started to hum. He rubbed her back. His voice was soothing.

"Don't worry, baby. I'll take care of you. I am going to make you feel real good." She was drowsy and dozed off feeling safe and secure. During the night, Rachel opened her mouth to a gentle pressure. Karl's voice was in her ear, telling her to suck.

"You'll see. This will make you feel better." Obediently, Rachel opened her mouth and felt the glass bottle slipped between her lips. She sucked. But it didn't make her feel better. It had just the opposite effect, and when Rachel was ill again, Karl's temper spiraled. Through a haze, she heard Karl cursing. He was angry. He began yelling at her, trying to shove the pipe into her mouth, but whatever was in it was making her sick, deathly ill. Rachel swatted at the pipe. She didn't want it, pushed it away again and again, twisting her head back and forth, struggling to keep it out of her mouth.

Karl's frustration grew with each moment. He could see that the cocaine was making Rachel ill, and he was bewildered. He had never seen anyone react to cocaine this way before. Refusing to give up, he raised Rachel's head off the pillow, and rubbed the pipe against her lip.

"Come on, baby. Try it for daddy. That's it. Just inhale deeply." Rachel started to gag. Coughing, almost strangling, her body rocked spasmodically. Karl pounded her on her back, sick to his stomach.

Fuck! This is fucking unreal, he thought flinging himself from the bed. Pacing to the window, he removed a Kool cigarette from the pack on the table, took a drag, and looked out into the night.

"Son of a bitch!"

Rachel was having an allergic reaction to cocaine. Each time Karl tried to get her to try the pipe she became sick. Finally, near dawn, he gave up. If he did not know better, Karl would have thought Rachel had a *guardian angel* blocking his devious plans.

To Karl, it was a hard blow. The plans that he had so painstakingly made were evaporating, crumbling like a stack of cards. Returning to bed, he eyed Rachel, glaring at her tousled hair, wanting to shake her from her rejuvenating slumber. With a disgusted hiss, he shoved her away from him, thrusting Rachel on the opposite side of the bed, causing an abrupt halt in her soft snore.

He had to think. He needed the money desperately. He was in heavy debt to his supplier, and the bastard would not wait forever. Lars had a nasty streak in him. One of his dealers had mysteriously disappeared last year when he would not, or could not pay his tab, and he had not been seen since. Karl believed the erstwhile dealer was *resting with the fishes*, so to speak, and he wondered if it was a preview to his own fate. Karl laid his head in his hands, which hung low between his legs.

"What the fuck am I going to do?"

Rubbing his forehead, looking at the girl again, as if the answer to his question would miraculously come from the silent sleeper, Karl slowly began to formulate a new plan.

The next morning Rachel felt horrible. Her stomach was still queasy, she had cottonmouth, and her head throbbed in rhythm with her pulse. Bending over the dazed girl, Karl looked at her with an actor's kindness as he placed a cool washcloth on her forehead. He turned the cloth over automatically, continuing to parrot concern, while he contemplated his next move.

"How do you feel, baby? Want something to eat?"

Rachel looked at Karl through quivering eyelids, struggling to sit up, and murmured, "I feel like hell."

And it was true. She did feel awful. But it was also true that she felt satiated, and more at peace than she had felt in a long, long time. Not since her father's death had she felt so connected to another human being. Not even Nanny Peters.

The emotionally starved girl ignored the warning signs. Any street-smart kid would have recognized Karl's insincerity, his game. But Rachel, with little to go on, with few references for genuine affection, and no dating experience was oblivious to Karl's artifice.

She was ripe pickings. And over the next few weeks, Rachel was totally seduced by Karl's winning ways and flattery. In short order, she fell under his spell. And she was not alone. All those who witnessed his performance were fooled by Karl's acts of devotion. None suspected his sinister plan. His act was flawless. The couple was seen everywhere together. At the library, coffee shop, art galleries, campus stores, and movie theaters, they were the new twosome. They were a couple at frat parties and at football games.

He appeared to be the doting boyfriend at her beck and call, a constant companion and confidant. For three months, Karl portrayed a perfect picture of an infatuated, loving boyfriend. Finally, Angela, who had been the most suspicious, succumbed to his charm. He won her over by including her in many of their excursions, appearing to respect and value her opinions and friendship.

No one would have suspected that Karl was carefully weaving a web of deceit. He combined street cunning, with the instincts of a ruthless marauder. And he enjoyed hurting his prey, causing physical pain by biting, twisting, and pinching the tender parts of their bodies. But most of all he loved to inflict mental anguish by subjecting his victims to cruel designs that broke their will.

After three months, he was ready. All the arrangements had been made, and Karl felt confident that little could go wrong. His boys were in place. His alibi established on the overcast morning. It had rained during the night, and a fine mist fluttered in the air blanketing everything it touched. Cars swished by on the wet, slick streets. The swooshing sounds invaded the bedroom, disturbing the quiet.

Rachel woke to a hazy contentment. Placing her arms over her head, curling up like an infant, she stretched, displaying a catlike smile as she mentally replayed the night's delicious bed play. Her bottom was sore, and she squirmed in guilty pleasure.

The evening had begun in what had become a familiar prelude to lovemaking. Karl had undressed, reaching first for his jean button then sliding his zipper over the hard bulge in his pants. Like a stripper, he used his large hands to push the tight jeans over his hips, and let them fall to the floor, pooling at his feet. Not bothering to step out of the jeans, he pushed his hips forward and motioned Rachel to him, and then pushed her to her knees. He wore white, Calvin Klein briefs. The cotton stretched tightly over the tent bulging close to Rachel's eyes.

Her mouth watered in anticipation. She rubbed her face, one cheek and then the other, against him adoringly. She loved how he smelled. He had begun to leak with desire, and she opened her mouth in anticipation.

He reached into his briefs, caressed himself, and looked at the woman groveling at his feet. "You want this, don't you?" Fisting himself, he stroked his nine-inch hard-on with a slow sensuous motion. "You want daddy's cream, don't you? Beg daddy to give it to you."

Rachel looked up at the man she had come to love. She wanted him in her mouth, wanted to nurse on him, love him, and swallow his prize. "Please give Rachie her bottle. Rachie will be a good girl. She wants daddy's cream."

The baby talk had evolved over the weeks, and Rachel had perfected what she knew Karl wanted to hear her say. She really was pleading. Tears hovered in her eyes. She craved this form of lovemaking almost as much as what came after.

Finally, he brought his thick member to her mouth. Rachel's mouth opened wide. She hummed her sigh of contentment, and for the next few minutes, her smacking ministration rang noisily in the room. Karl flung his head back and roared his release seconds later. He liked this part of their lovemaking to go quickly. "It is the appetizer to the main meal," he would say.

Later he'd lifted her legs over his shoulders, his knees tucked under her back while he drove deeply into her moist body. One hand held her hips high. The other worked furiously at her backdoor. Weeks before Karl had begun using a dildo in her bottom, while he plowed his thick tool in her tunnel of love. That is what he called her vagina. He had a name for everything, for her body parts, and for their acts of love.

"Open your tunnel to me," he had ordered. "That's it. Take your fingers and spread that pussy." He would have her spread her legs wide, and then spread her hairless mound even wider until she wanted to scream with frustrated lust. Every now and then, he would finger her boy, his name for her clit.

That first time, when she was so wet she could have put out a forest fire, she begged him to come to her, but he would not. That is when he introduced her to the dildo for her backdoor.

She had been kept in a constant state of arousal for over an hour. Her voice was hoarse with begging, and her fingers were slippery with her own juices. "Are you ready, baby, daddy has something new for you."

"Yes. Oh, yes."

Karl got into the bed, and positioned Rachel's legs over his shoulders. But unlike the times before, he did not ease into her. Instead, Rachel felt him probing at her rear. At first, she thought he had missed his mark, and then she realized he wanted to enter her bottom.

"No. Not that." Rachel was frightened, he was huge and she feared he would tear her apart. Rachel began to wiggle in protest, trying to move out of his path. Suddenly, with a ruthlessness he had never showed before, Karl lowered his head and began to feed at Rachel's mound, his wicked tongue flicking mercilessly at the hard nub.

Rachel swung her head from side to side, lost in the pleasure of his mouth and tongue. In this state, she was only vaguely aware that Karl had resumed his attack on her bottom. His tongue began to move wildly, tickling the rosebud entrance. It was delicious. It was wicked. And when his tongue returned to her center, she felt pressure at her bottom. She allowed it, wanted it. Moments later the dildo was being plied, while Karl nibbled at her center, then raised his head triumphantly and looked into her eyes. Slowly he positioned himself. His staff rubbed her moist center, dripping in anticipation. He slid home. His mouth opened in a silent cry of ecstasy. Clutching the dildo, his fist labored wildly. His hips moved with a primitive rhythm. Rachel saw stars as her entire body trembled to climax.

Heaven, she thought. *This is pure Heaven.*

The sun peeked through the shades. Rachel ran her hands over the sheets in satiated bliss. Karl was gone, but she expected Karl to return at any minute. He frequently left her sleeping, while he went out to get coffee and croissants. But the morning passed, and he did not return. Growing restless, Rachel showered and prepared to leave.

Hidden, Karl surveyed his apartment building. Adrenalin flashed in his body, his heart skipped a beat as he watched from the rooftop. It was an agonizing wait, but finally, around three o'clock, Rachel exited the building tugging on her trench coat and headed toward her Volkswagen.

Karl stood up, brushed off his pants, and headed back to his apartment. Picking up a walkie-talkie pushing down on the button, he spoke one word with ominous quiet.

"Go."

He returned to the apartment immediately. Sitting on the large king-sized bed, he reached into his pocket. There was a solitary cigarette in the Kool soft pack, and he crumbled the package as he slowly placed it in his mouth. The match hissed and flared orange-red. Karl took a deep contemplative draw on the cigarette.

He leaned back against the headboard, carelessly putting his booted feet on the comforter. *By the end of the week, I'll be able to buy a hundred of these things if I want to,* he thought gloatingly. The wheels were in motion. There was nothing for him to do but wait. Karl felt he had been waiting all of his life for a break. This was it, and he was not going to let it pass him by.

Angie pushed the apartment door open with the toe of her shoe. The grocery packages were balanced precariously in one arm as she shouldered the door closed.

She was not supposed to be back until Sunday afternoon, but the conference ended early. *Thank God,* Angie mused. *It was the most boring business seminar she had ever attended. Jeez, she had never listened to a nerdier bunch of misfits. She could not wait to imitate the group, aping them for Rae and Karl.*

Angela had always had an uncanny ability to see the comical in most situations, reenacting it with witty precision. Hoping that Rachel was home, she called out to her as she laid the groceries on the kitchen table, but was greeted with silence.

An hour later, Angela stepped from the shower toweling her hair dry when the phone rang. It was Karl. He was looking for

Rachel, telling Angela that they had missed each other, and that she had left when he returned to the apartment. He sounded frustrated.

"I got some business I need to attend to. Tell Rachel I will call her later."

Five minutes later, Rachel walked through the door. The girls rarely had time alone. Karl and Rachel had become as inseparable as Siamese twins. And Rachel was in a festive mood, enjoying the girlie intimacy that had been absent for the past few months.

Munching on an apple, Rachel sat on the kitchen countertop while Angela cooked pasta regaling her with comic renditions of her classmates' bizarre antics as they tried unsuccessfully to impress Dr. Jerry Houser and the seminar speakers.

The room rang with laughter. The girls moved to the dining table, and continued their witty repartee, joking and poking fun at the late night show hosts and their guests. Angela could mimic a perfect David Letterman. At eleven forty-five, Karl called. He had a job interview in the morning, he said. This is big stuff baby. I need a good night's sleep, and he chuckled lightly, saying, "I definitely won't get any rest with you here. You know I can't resist you." Rachel put the telephone down with disappointment showing on her face.

"Is everything OK?"

Rachel looked at Angela and shook her head. "Yeah, I guess. Karl has an early interview and he thinks it will be better if I stay here tonight." Angela placed her arm around Rachel's shoulder and grinned, pulling at imaginary whiskers, and said, "The better for us, my dear." The two girls looked at one another conspiratorially and burst out laughing.

Sleeping alone was a novel experience for Rachel. She had slept with Karl almost every night for weeks, and it took Rachel some time to doze off. It could have been minutes, or it could have been hours later, when Rachel was abruptly awakened with a hand over her mouth.

Another hand was twisted roughly in the tender wisps of hair at the nape of her neck. Her neck was bent at an awkward angle, causing Rachel to stare up at the ceiling. The curtains of the sliding glass doors to the patio blew inward, and Nanny's warning about living on the ground level of the apartment building came back to her. With a sickening sinking in the pit of her stomach, Rachel wished she had listened.

"If you move, bitch, I'll kill you! Don't make a sound." A vicious tug on the twisted hair punctuated the man's raspy voice. His mouth was so close to Rachel's ear, she could smell sour beer and cigarettes on his breath. She was terrified. Her breathing was shallow, and she could not get a sound past her swollen, dry throat. She froze in fear. His demand for silence was unnecessary.

"Show her the knife, Max."

A gloved hand held a large hunting knife above Rachel's face. Rachel's eyes bulged, and in her terror, she lost control of her bladder as urine seeped slowly onto the mattress.

"I'm going to remove my hand from your mouth real slow. Max will stick you like a pig, if you make a peep."

"Are you pissing, bitch? Do I smell piss? If you mess yourself anymore, I'll use your hair to dry it up."

Rachel began to gag, making choking sounds deep in the back of her throat. The man's fingers dug into her cheek, causing Rachel to open as he jammed a cloth napkin into her mouth. A wide swath of duct tape was slapped over her lips, holding the napkin snuggly in place.

Rolling Rachel onto her stomach, he taped her arms behind her back, then, grabbing her by the hair, he pulled her into a standing position. He was intentionally rough. The plan was to inflict as much fear and pain on her as possible so that she would be docile.

It was working. Rachel was cowed. The front of the oversized T-shirt was soaked from her waist down. No one cared. She was given boots to put on. A large raincoat was placed over her T-shirt, and she was shoved toward her bedroom door.

To Rachel it felt like a lifetime had passed since the two people had woken her from her sleep. In reality, it had only been moments. The abduction was being executed with the sleuth of a SWAT team and was performed with military precision. As well, it should. Maxine and Brian had been practicing the maneuvers for months.

Everything had been planned to cover he smallest detail. There was only one hitch. Rachel's roommate was at home.

Angela's arrival hours earlier had delayed their plans, and they had considered canceling the operation, but the boss said no, "Go ahead with the plan. Subdue her roommate if you must. It could work to our advantage."

Angela was awake studying, when she overheard scuffling sounds coming from Rachel's room. At first dismissing it as a late night visit from Karl; she realized that she had not heard the doorbell ring, signaling his arrival. The sounds were different, muffled as if Rachel was struggling with someone. Deciding to investigate, Angela opened her door as a hooded man shoved Rachel from her bedroom into the living room.

Angela sized up the situation immediately. Screaming she rushed the man with her nails clawed, posed as weapons. But before she could reach him, Angela felt an ice cold sensation in the back of her head. She went down hard. Hitting the floor with a loud crash, partially conscious, she glimpsed Rachel as she disappeared through the living room door. The last thing Angela saw before everything went black was the terror in Rachel's eyes as she was dragged from the apartment.

"This is some shit, man. I did what you told me to do! You told me that her roommate would be out of town. What a fuck up! You have always been a fuck up! I don't know what made me think you had finally gotten it together."

Karl watched his brother. He was furious, and he would have cold cocked his sibling, but he did not want to waste the energy. He never understood why his mother had taken in Brian. His father was long gone by the time his half brother had showed up at their door asking for the loser. But, the skinny preteen, looked so much like Karl that they could have passed for twins, and Karl's mother had taken to Brian immediately. Both boys had inherited Roscoe Brown's build, hair, and coloring. Even today, twelve years after their first meeting, they looked amazingly alike. But that is where the likeness ended.

They had vastly different personalities. Karl was a thinker, slow and methodical with his decisions, and extremely confident about his ability to design and execute a plan of action. Until the car accident, he had been on a personally orchestrated road toward fame and fortune.

On the other hand, Brian was impulsive, emotional, and very insecure. Not much had gone right for him in his twenty-seven years. In spite of Karl's mother's support, Brian dropped out of high school. He had gone from low-paying job, to seasonal job, to no job. He was a small-time hustler.

After Karl had been kicked out of school, Brian introduced him to his dealer. He also introduced Karl to Maxine. She was their father's sister's youngest girl, their first cousin, and their willing whore. Maxine did whatever Karl and Brian told her to do, from petty thievery to a personal blow job. Although Brian was the older by three years, Karl had always been the leader. He was the leader today. Brian's bravado was just that—hot air.

"Are you finished?"

Karl looked at his brother with disgust. He was not much, but he was all that Karl had. And in spite of it all, the brothers were fiercely loyal to one another. They had two things in common, their father's blood and their sexual perversions.

"Did her roommate see anything?" Karl asked.

"Definitely not! I had my mask on, just like we planned, and Max hit her in the back of her head. She never even saw Max. And nobody was in the hallway or in the garage when we left."

"Then, no harm done."

"We proceed as planned. Is the house ready?" Karl watched Brian closely as his brother moved his head affirmatively.

"I want you and Maxine to leave tonight. I'll be right behind you. I want to make sure the bitch does not call the police. Besides, I've got to hang around and show my concern and play the part. I need to put in time with Angie...and that house nigger 'Mammy Peters.' Karl snickered. "Those two bitches are my alibi."

Rachel opened her eyes. She was in a tiny storage room. There were no windows. It was dark and damp, with a musty, unused smell. The only furniture in the room was a narrow cot, which was pushed up against a corner where the plaster peeled from the wall. A ladder-back wooden chair was on the opposite side of the room.

A woolen army blanket covered the cot, and Rachel lay on top of it. She still wore the urine-soiled T-shirt she had been captured in and it reeked. Her trench coat and shoes were nowhere to be seen. The threesome had driven for hours, and Rachel had no idea where she was.

Looking up at the rain-marked ceiling, Rachel felt terror for the second time in her life. A single light bulb hung from a roped electrical cord strung in the middle of the room. Rachel stared in disbelief as a cockroach scurried across the dirty floor.

Uncontrollable shivers racked her body. Teeth chattering, lips blue with fear, she displayed classic signs of shock. Who were these people? What did they want? Rachel's mind flew from one scenario to another in rapid succession, and landed on the only logical conclusion. Ransom—they had taken her for money.

Her thoughts were interrupted when she heard a key turn in the door. It swung open, and a man walked into the room with a tray. His head was hooded. Rachel watched as the man crossed to the bed, then motioned for her to sit up. Sitting up, she scooted to the head of the bed, looking at the ski-masked man with pleading eyes.

"Who are you? What do you want?"

The man did not answer. Instead, he placed the tray on the end of the cot where Rachel's feet had recently rested. With no forewarning, no threat or sound, the man raised his hand and slapped Rachel a stunning blow, knocking the girl back against the wall. A vivid handprint, white against her rose flushed cheek, appeared on her face.

"Don't speak unless you're spoken to." Rachel recognized the voice immediately. It was the vicious voice of the kidnapper from the night before. He was ominously calm. Rachel cowered against the wall and flinched as if she had been struck again. Her raised hand covered her cheek, and she bobbed her head in a jerky motion, signaling her submission.

Tears slowly seeped from the corner of her eyes.

"When you speak to me, you are to address me as sir. Do you understand?"

Rachel bobbed her head again, and was promptly delivered another vicious blow.

"I said you are to answer, 'Yes, sir.' Do you understand?"

"Yes, sir," she sobbed, clutching her cheek petrified. Her heart raced in terror. Behind the narrow slits in the ski mask, Brian's eyes glittered in triumph, and his pants tented obscenely. He watched Rachel, horrified, stare at his arousal and he laughed. The cackling sound was both a promise and a threat.

Nanny Peters' Princess telephone chimed insistently. It was four o'clock in the morning. Startled from sleep, she had a foreboding premonition. Who would call her at this hour? Nervously reaching for the phone, she was startled to hear loud sobs, rendering the caller unrecognizable. Finally, she made out Angela's voice.

"What? What are you saying? Who got took? Girl, slow down. I can't understand you. Take a deep breath. Speak slowly."

Nanny Peters' heart fluttered. She balled her nightgown in the center of her chest, listening to Angela's sobbing story of the break-in, of being hit from behind, and of seeing Rachel dragged from the apartment by a hooded man. The woman's heart continued to flutter. Rachel was like her own flesh, her daughter. After all, she had nursed her since her birth.

Angela's voice trembled. "I have a note. They left a note. It says if we go to the police, they will kill her."

Nanny Peters felt a sharp pain in her chest.

"Angela, I need to make a call. Stay by the phone, I'll call you right back."

Angela's response was subdued. "Do you think I should call Karl?"

"I'll call him. You just stay by the phone."

Christine Peters clutched the phone to her chest for a moment then quickly dialed Karl. He answered, his voice deceptively groggy, until he heard the panic in the older woman's voice as she told of Rachel's kidnapping. The practiced actor exclaimed a four-letter word loudly. "My God; God, no!"

"Exactly," she responded humorlessly. "Stay by the phone." It was an order, not a request. Karl swallowed his resentment like a bitter pill. Smirking silently, he reminded himself, *I have the trump card.*

Nanny Peters hung up and immediately dialed Mercedes Mueller's phone number. On the twentieth ring, Mercedes' sleepy voice croaked into the receiver. In short order, Nanny Peters relayed the crisis.

"I'll call Simon and get back to you. Tell that Ryan girl not to do anything. Uh, and Peters, tell the girl, under no circumstance is she to call the police."

Mercedes sat up in the bed, looking around her gilded room, and wanted to shout with glee. Ten minutes later, she called her son. Making light of the situation, she told Simon she believed the whole thing was a hoax.

"I don't think we should contact the police, not because I think her supposed kidnappers will actually harm her, but because of the scandal a ruse would make. Then, of course, there is the fact that she has been dating that colored boy. What could she be thinking? But then, blood always runs true. It's her Jewish blood. Everybody knows that it is flawed." Simon interrupted his mother's tirade.

"I agree, Mother, I think we should wait before we contact the police. This may be serious, and the threat could be real. I'll call Al Rosenthal to let him know what is going on."

"No!" Mercedes' voice raised an octave. Modulating her voice to simulate normalcy, Mercedes warned Simon softly. "Darling, we don't want anyone to learn of this except family, at least at this early stage. I am not happy that that Negro and Rachel's roommate are aware of this travesty. Unfortunately, it can't be helped. Al should only be called in when, and if we discover that there's been a real kidnapping."

Simon listened to his mother, silently questioning her rationale. But out of habit, he deferred to her counsel, agreeing to take a red-eye to San Francisco and talk with Angela in person.

"Oh, Simon, will you call that Negro and tell her that you will be handling everything. You know how difficult it is for me to understand her. She really does speak dreadful English." Simon hung up the phone thinking that Nanny Peters spoke perfect English, albeit with a soft Southern drawl.

Simon's interview with Angela was disturbing. At the close of their talk, he had no doubt that the abduction was no hoax. When he read the note, which was composed of print clipped from magazines and newspapers, he realized how serious the kidnappers were. They had planned well, and it did not appear that the abductors were amateurs.

He was shocked to learn that Rachel had been spending most nights with her black lover, and that their affair had been going on for months. She had practically moved in with him. The boy was still around, so Simon doubted that he was involved in the kidnapping.

It was obvious to Simon that Angela's injury was serious, and at his insistence, she went to the emergency room to have her head wound examined by a physician.

During his return flight to Los Angeles, Simon examined the facts, and he became convinced that they should meet the kidnapper's demands. He debriefed his mother immediately. But she scoffed at his conclusions, making light of the entire incident. Christine was enraged at Mercedes' lighthearted treatment of Rachel's abduction, doubting Mercedes' motives.

Simon too remained unconvinced by Mercedes' reasoning, and agreed to the ransom demands. But Mercedes managed to foil every attempt Simon made to settle with Rachel's abductors. At one point, she ordered a bag of dirty laundry delivered to a drop-off spot instead of money. Christine was furious, and did not waste words telling Rachel's mother what she thought.

"You are a pitiful excuse for a mother. Look at you, without a care in the world, while your own child is in the hands of murdering kidnappers." Christine's scorn dripped like acid from her down turned lips.

Mercedes sputtered her indignation at the nanny's impudence, and strolled from the room with impotent rage, well aware that she could not fire the woman.

Karl's response to the dirty laundry was to send Rachel's ear in a white cloth napkin. That was the last straw for Simon. He called in Al Rosenthal and the police. Mercedes was livid.

The strain was too much for Nanny Peters. Seated beside Mercedes when the messenger delivered the UPS box, she crumbled to the floor when it was opened, and the bloody ear rolled near her feet. She woke up in the hospital with a mild myocardial infarction—a heart attack.

Excruciating pain invaded Rachel's sleep, flooding her consciousness with throbbing agony. She tossed on the cot. She was being forced awake, dragged into wakefulness by nagging pain. Her mind resisted, but she could not ignore the burning ache and the right side of her face was on fire. She felt hot and feverish. Her head was swimming. Something was wrong. Horribly wrong.

Groggily, Rachel raised her hands to her face and encountered bandages over her right ear. Tentatively, her hand inspected the left side of her head. Her fingers fumbled inquisitively over the bulky padding, and she moaned in agony as stabbing pain exploded in her jaw and ear.

The door opened, and Maxine walked in. "I see you're finally awake."

"What's the matter ...me?" Rachel's speech was slurred. She struggled to look at Maxine. Her vision was hazy, her hearing seemed muffled, and it was impossible to focus her eyes on her jailer.

"Your mother sent us a bag of dirty laundry last night, and we sent her your ear. Guess that'll teach the bitch not to fuck with us."

Shock ran through Rachel. A cry of denial rang in the room.

"Here. Take this." Maxine shoved Rachel a glass of water and dropped an antibiotic capsule in her hand. "We don't want you dying on us, now do we?" Maxine's voice was callous and she was dispassionate as she helped Rachel sit up. But she was not unnecessarily cruel. Later, when it became apparent that her family was not going to pay the ransom, her captors became more vindictive and vicious. Each day that passed without payment, her two guards became more coldhearted.

By the second month of captivity, the neglect had become dire. Her meals had diminished to one a day, and sometimes they forgot to feed her for several days in a row. She had been left alone for two days, when she heard the lock on the door click. Dehydrated and starved, Rachel looked toward the door hopefully. It was the middle of the night, but without windows she had become disoriented, sleeping fitfully in three- and four-hour stretches.

Karl slammed into the room, and Rachel thought she was being rescued. But the cry of joy died on her lips when Maxine and Brian walked into the room and stood beside him. The three people stared at Rachel, and she looked back recognizing the family resemblance. Maxine leered hatefully, and Brian looked smug, but it was Karl's stony eyes that made Rachel tremble in dread. Cold. His eyes were freezing, and they flashed fury.

In a moment, everything became crystal clear. Karl was the orchestrator, and his participation in her kidnapping confirmed what she had known emphatically since her father's death. God had abandoned her.

"It's your fault, bitch, all of it." He snatched Rachel by the hair and twisted as hard as he could, wrath propelling him to drag her across the bed. "But, I'll get my money one way or the other. I didn't spend the last three months catering to your stupid white ass for nothing." He shoved his face into hers, and she could feel the heat of his breath against her cheeks.

Karl was desperate. He owed $150,000 to his supplier and time had run out. He was deeply in debt to the wrong person. The kidnap scheme was supposed to take care of that problem, but nothing was working out as he had planned.

Rachel's family had not paid the ransom. They were stalling and playing games that could get him killed. Lars had already made a visit to his mother's house sending a clear message to Karl that his family was not off limits.

He looked a Maxine. "Take her clothes off," he ordered. "A bitch like her doesn't need clothes."

Rachel backed up on the cot. But it was hopeless. The narrow makeshift bed provided little scrambling room. Brian grabbed Rachel's legs and dragged her onto the floor. Maxine helped Brian rip off Rachel's nightdress. She was naked in seconds.

Karl looked a Rachel with disgust as she huddled on the floor, legs crossed, and attempting to cover her breasts with her hands.

"Damn, baby, you need to exercise. You're getting fat. I ain't ever been into chubby white girls. Shit, your ass is flabby, and damn if your tits haven't grown two sizes. But my dick is hard, and that's all that matters."

Rachel looked from one capturer to the other. Her eyes bulged with fear as she watched Brian strip slowly.

Karl, Brian, and Max took turns with Rachel. They used her like a pair of male canines responding to a female dog in heat. Karl was first, Brian second, and then both of them together. The inside of her legs were splattered with semen and blood when Karl flipped her on her stomach, grabbing her from behind, and slamming Rachel against his cock, lunged and drove into her unprepared body.

"Damn your ass feels good," Karl whispered under his breath as he sodomized her viciously. He grunted as Rachel screamed a gut-wrenching cry of anguish. Brian, taking advantage of the opening before him, shoved into her mouth. "If you bite me bitch, I'll kill you."

Rachel prayed for the nightmare to end. It went on forever.

"We're going to break you in, baby, real good." Karl spat.

When both men finished, they ordered Maxine to clean her up. Rachel was shocked to feel Maxine's tongue swirled on her pubic mound, and then lower. "God help me." Nanny had said she would call on God one day...and she screamed his name again. Karl laughed mockingly, "That's right baby...I'm your God."

Silently, she screamed as Maxine found her clit. "No. No," she moaned, but she found herself responding, lifting her pelvis off the floor, welcoming the soothing tongue. The two men watched excitedly, servicing each other as they knelt, spilling their seed as Rachel climaxed. They left her crumbled on the floor like a broken doll.

A week later, Rachel had her first paying customer. That's when the nightmare spiraled into hell. They brought her customers day and night. Karl, Brian, and Max made their visits between johns. It was unending.

In Rachel's fourth month of captivity, it became evident to her captors she was pregnant, something she had suspected even before the kidnapping. Although she was five months gone, she was barely showing. The initial spurt of weight gain had quickly reversed, and she was scary thin. Her face was gaunt and her body looked wasted except for a slight budge in her middle.

But there was no letup with the stream of customers. Brian and Karl were hard-core addicts. Rachel wondered why she had never noticed his drug use before. They freebased every waking moment, staying up for days at a time. Rachel and Max became the breadwinners. They would turn tricks during the day in the house, and in the evening, Max would drive them to the Sunset Strip. She would park the van on a side street near Gower and Hollywood Boulevard, and they would take their customers on a mattress in the rear of the gutted cab.

Rachel lost count of how many men she serviced. She felt dirty and unredeemable. Fear and shame were constant companions. She felt nothing for the baby, choosing to ignore the changes in her body. Sometimes she thought of escape, but thinking past the immediacy of the moment was a monumental task.

Where could she go? Who could she turn to? The shame was overwhelming. Most of the time, Rachel sought oblivion. When she wasn't on her back or knees, she slept. Her feelings were not a consideration. No one cared about the girl anymore. Karl hid behind the pipe. Unreasonably, he blamed Rachel for his downfall. He knew that Lars and his Long Beach hit men were looking for him, and in his drug-clouded mind, he felt Rachel was responsible.

His hatred toward Rachel grew more intense with each day. By the time Rachel was seven months pregnant, Karl and Brian had sunk into a foggy stupor of drugs and sex. The lovers seldom left their bedroom. Rachel had learned of the brother's incestuous relationship the day the three raped her. She found it revolting. She despised herself for ever having anything to do with Karl, and wondered how she could have been so blind.

The idea of Karl's baby inside her body sickened her, and she felt that her pregnancy was an aberration, an evil that was begot in sin. She prayed nightly that the fetus would die, and as her time drew closer, that the baby would not survive delivery.

Meanwhile, Maxine became Rachel's sole jailer, and the girls formed an acerbic truce. She wondered why Maxine did not see herself as a prisoner also. *After all*, Rachel thought, *the two of them made the money. They were both pimped and whored equally.*

When they worked the streets, they had to depend on one another for safety. On more than one occasion, a customer had been rough with one of the girls or decided he had not gotten his money's worth. So when Max looked at Rachel one evening and told her that she wanted her to go to the drug store to get something for menstrual pain, she didn't hesitate. She grabbed her jacket and purse.

"Thanks, Rae. I can't go out tonight. I'm cramping so bad, I think I'm gonna die." As crazy as it seemed, the two abused women had bonded, and Rachel felt real empathy for Maxine's suffering.

Max was balled up on the sofa in the living room. The group had been hiding out in the small three-bedroom house since the kidnapping. "I got my period." Looking meaningfully at Rachel's distended stomach, Max moaned. "That's something you don't have to worry about."

Sweat dotted Max's forehead. "Damn, it hurts!" She punctuated her words with a fisted blow to the sofa pillow, emitting another smothered groan.

Reaching for the van keys Max held out to her, Rachel never thought twice as she headed for the door, flinging over her shoulder, "I'll be right back."

It did not occur to her that she could have driven straight to the police station. She rarely thought of escape anymore. Rachel had become a mental prisoner, and it was more effective than steel bars or electronic gates.

The trip to the drug store took longer than Rachel anticipated. A power outage had shut down a section of the store, and the cash registers were locked. The drawers would not open. Rachel debated going to another store, but reasoned it would only take longer if she left. So, she stood in the line behind several other impatient customers staring at the hapless cashier who alternated between remorseful glances and frustrated sighs.

Forty minutes later Rachel gunned the van as she sped back to the small three-bedroom house. Nestled behind several large eucalyptus trees on a cul-de-sac in North Hollywood, the house was a perfect hideout.

The first thing that Rachel noticed when she drove into the driveway was that the house was dark. Parking the van in front of one tree, she wondered why Max would turn off the living room lights. Observing the house, her head tilted to one side questioningly, Rachel's pace accelerated. The eerie feeling increased as she unlocked the door, pushing it with her shoulder. It opened.

The room was black. *The Richard Pryor Special* was on television, and the laughter on the bedroom television blared loudly in the otherwise quiet house.

"Max. I'm back." Rachel felt her way past the sofa, using the back of the divan to guide her to the hall light. The living room switch had not worked in weeks, and the table lamp was too difficult to find in the dark, so Rachel headed to the hall light and flipped the switch. She closed her eyes as the blinding beam flashed in the room.

The living room was empty and unusually silent. Rachel moved down the hall slowly. Karl and Brian's door was closed, but a beam under the doorjamb cast a bluish tint on the hallway floor.

An adrenalin surge rushed through Rachel's body as she approached the door. The hair at the back of her neck rose. It felt eerie and odd, like she was being watched by hidden eyes. She could not shake the uneasiness.

Slowly, hesitantly, she pushed the bedroom door open. The hinges made a crying squeak, little by little revealing an unforgettable horror. Sprawled in the lounge chair naked, his head at an awkward angle, sat Karl with his throat slit. A scream stuck in Rachel's throat. No sound passed her lips. Brian lay at Karl's feet with his hands duct taped behind his back, blood seeping from the side of his head, which lay on Karl's thigh. His nude body and open mouth grotesquely suggested his last act.

Maxine hung from the ceiling fan. Both of her hands were bound together, as she swung suspended, a surprised expression on her face, and a small spot in the middle of her chest. Blood streamed from the hole between her breasts, oozed over her stomach, and seeped steadily onto the beige shag carpet, staining it scarlet.

Rachel backed out of the room, stumbling in her haste, turned and fled the house. She raced across the lawn clutching her stomach with one hand and the van keys with the other.

Rachel Mueller's battered suitcase contrasted sharply with the cut and style of her donated designer suit. Few observing the striking woman would have surmised her story, or guessed at the eighteen-month odyssey that had transformed an innocent, naïve girl into a jaundiced, cynical mutilated woman incapable of trusting or exposing her emotions to anyone.

The suitcase was weightless as she passed through the glass double doors, and Rachel walked with a resilience that belied the turmoil of the past months. She had spent a good nine months at Saint Ann's Women's Shelter, but she had accumulated little. Arriving with only the clothes on her back, scarred by more than the missing ear, she had delivered her child, and submitted to months of therapy for the psychological and physical abuses she had suffered at the hands of Karl and his family. There was no closure for the emotional loss of her baby daughter; she refused to allow the experience to be a part of her consciousness, any more than she allowed St. Ann's to be more than an bad dream.

Today, she was leaving the godforsaken place, and she vowed she would never look back.

CHAPTER ONE

Tyler

LOS ANGELES ~ 1984

"What I want to know is how the hell the child got misdiagnosed." Spoken softy, the question had the impact of a two-ton truck smashing into a brick wall. You could hear a pin drop in the silence that followed. No one at the table moved. Not the Los Angeles County Foster Children district supervisor, not the LA County Health Care practitioner, or any of the other half dozen people sitting around the oval conference table.

John Myer, the chief executive of the Foster Care Review Board, was livid. His face was as red as a lobster. The thick file opened in front of him was one of the worst examples of case negligence he had ever seen. After years of mismanagement, it had been discovered that Tyler Miller had been misdiagnosed with HIV, and as a result, she had spent four years in the Pediatric AIDS Ward at Olive View Hospital.

The good news was that she had not been given experimental treatment for HIV. The bad news was a *Los Angeles Times* reporter had gotten wind of the mix-up and had contacted his office to verify the story. John had been able to squash the scandal only by swapping information about another high-profile case that was already in the news.

With molten eyes, the chief executive drilled his managers, crucifying each one individually as he eyeballed the table.

"I want this business taken care of today, or believe you me, heads will roll."

Two weeks later, Tyler Miller sat on Sophie Tyler's lap as the nurse explained that she was going to go to a new home. The years had passed quickly. *Jet propelled*, thought Sophie Tyler, who had come to love and care for the child as her own. What a loving child she had turned out to be. She was helpful in every way, especially with the chronically and terminally ill children. She was simply delightful.

Tyler had always been advanced for her age, gifted even, when one considered how quickly she had walked and talked. Sophie shook her head fondly and smiled. The infant had never crawled, just climbed out of her meshed playpen and walked at eight months.

In her first year, she was talking and using words that her two- and three-year-old peers could not pronounce. It was clear that she was intellectually superior when, at age two and a half, she could identify all of the chess pieces and by three was playing the game with the nursing staff.

Everyone was dumbfounded. Not just with Tyler's demonstrated superior intelligence, but with the miraculous disappearance of her illness. The HIV virus just vanished. One day she had the disease, and the next she did not. It was a puzzle that none of the doctors or researchers could explain, but more, all refused to believe. Skeptical, they continued to list Tyler as a HIV patient. Thus, the toddler remained a resident of the chronic ill children's ward.

Sophie smiled again remembering the first time Tyler had read to a young cancer patient. Brian Brogan had had half his jaw removed, and he was not a pretty picture, but Tyler insisted she wanted to read the little train story to the hostile boy who had been lying in his bed with flat dull eyes for weeks. When his bandages had been removed, all of the other children avoided him because he looked "scary" and unfriendly.

"Let me read, I can read," the three-year-old had stated adamantly. Then she climbed onto the boy's bed nimbly, not missing a step, and scooted down beside the eight-year-old, unfazed by the empty space in his face where his chin should have been. Brian had looked at Tyler fiercely; when that did not work, he ignored her.

"Look at this," she said, pointing to a picture. "I'm going to tell you a story about a train that everyone doubted, but the train knew he was special, because he said over and over, *Yes, I can.*"

Brian stoically looked at the ceiling, his eyes unwaveringly focused on a water spot next to the florescent light. But Tyler refused to be ignored, and her high-pitched voice was sweet in its innocence and faith. Even at three, she understood that Brian needed to hear a story of hope. She wanted to see him smile, and unafraid, she took his hand. Brian jumped when Rachel touched him, but for some reason, he was unable to remove his hand from hers. He stared at Tyler again, this time without hostility. The child transmitted an undercurrent of peace, and Brian was unable to reject the spiritual call.

The three-year-old knew the moment Brian's soul calmed. Tyler smiled up at him, and his mouth, which hung into open space, twisted back in a semblance of a grin. His large brown eyes sparkled, revealing his pleasure in the moment, and Tyler settled herself more comfortably into Brian's side.

Soon Brian was glancing over at the pictures and looking at the printed words. His cancer had prevented him from attending school regularly; although he hid it well, his reading level was pre-primer.

Sophie had walked out of the room satisfied that Tyler was welcome. When she poked her head in a half an hour later, Brian was pointing at the book and unashamedly asking the younger child, "What is that word?" And he was reading, actually reading the book to Tyler. It was a miracle because none of the staff had been able to get the boy to respond to their overtures.

As Sophie watched, both of the children began to giggle, and she thought what a remarkable gift Tyler was, wondering once again about the woman who had abandoned the amazing child. In the silence of her mind, the rhetorical question went unanswered.

What a joy the woman had missed.' With a mental shake, Sophie returned to the moment and her own challenges.

She was heartbroken. If only life was like a cassette tape, and she could rewind it with a remote control. *But no*, she reflected sadly, *life was full of twists and turns*. Looking down at the top of

Tyler's head, she lovingly caressed the fat curls as the past flashed before her eyes. Sadness overcame Sophie and she slumped.

Her attempts to adopt Tyler as a single parent had been rejected twice. The first time, her adoption application was turned down because she was applying as a single parent. The second time she was refused because her homosexuality had been exposed. Sophie's hand froze over Tyler's curls as she recalled looking into the knowing stare of the child services' arbitrator.

"Ms. Tyler, I see here you are single." Sophie remembered the cold look on the man's face as he asked the question. "Do you have plans to marry?" Sophie could not hide the brief distaste that distorted her features in disgust. "No. Definitely not!" Sophie had known immediately that she had given herself away, and her heart skipped a beat.

"You are aware, Ms. Tyler, that the agency conducts a thorough background investigation of all adoption applicants. We are very circumspect about the families—" pausing, the arbitrator cleared his throat and looked meaningfully at his female counterpart, "—we place our children with."

It was 1981. Single parent adoptions were in the dark ages, and gay or lesbian parent approvals were a dozen years into the future. So, Tyler had been stuck in limbo, labeled HIV positive… and difficult, if not impossible to place for adoption. She had remained at the hospital for over four years.

In spite of it all, Tyler was a happy, loving, precocious child. She was the delight of the Pediatric AIDS Ward. The nurses at Olive View loved spoiling and pampering her. Ever since Sophie had taken the child in her arms, declaring her the most beautiful baby she'd ever seen, Tyler had received an abundance of love and attention from the nurses and doctors. Charge Nurse Tyler made sure of it.

Early on, Sophie suspected Tyler had been misdiagnosed. The baby had never displayed any HIV symptoms. But Sophie kept her own counsel. She had believed the longer Tyler stayed misdiagnosed, charted "HIV Positive", the better her chances became to adopt her. Time ran out when someone leaked the information to a *Times* reporter, and the clinic doctors accepted what Sophie had suspected all along. Tyler was not HIV positive.

It was a departmental scandal. Everyone was scurrying to cover their tracks and to put things in order. Bodies were everywhere. But, the two real causalities were Tyler and Sophie. The agency decided to send Tyler to a foster home, and Nurse Sophie was fired. She was dismissed, not because of incompetence, but because of her participation in a blatant cover-up.

Sophie suspected Ethel Mae Matthews had leaked the information. The private duty nurse had always resented Sophie's attachment to the child, and resented even more not being hired as permanent on the nursing staff at the hospital. She blamed Sophie for the slight, and conversely did everything she could to undermine the charge nurse.

Ethel Mae's duplicity was confirmed on Sophie's last day at Olive View Hospital. She had packed her personal items late to avoid embarrassment and the shame attached to her departure. She did not want to be pitied by the nurses or other hospital administrators, so she planned her exit for after midnight. The corridor was empty, and Sophie was walking down the hall, her steps slow and measured, when she was hailed loudly by a familiar voice.

"Hello, Ms. Lady. So I see you're sneaking off without any good-byes."

Sophie stopped and turned to look at her nemesis.

"Hello, Ethel-Mae. And good-bye." Sophie's terse reply resounded in the hallway, and she turned dismissively.

"Oh, hell no! Hell, mothafucking no, Ms. uppity white gal! You don't turn your skinny ass on me. You ain't my boss no mo. And one other thing, Ms. Dike, if you wondering who dropped the dime on yah, don't wonder no mo! Yeah, that's right. I did it." Ethel Mae's smile was big and wide and her hands were on her hips.

"How does it feel to lose something you really, really want?" She did not expect Sophie to answer and kept talking without taking a breath. "Doesn't feel good, does it? So, now you know how I felt all those times I applied to be permanent here, and you blocked it."

As surprise filled Sophie's face, Ethel Mae's smile widened even more—if possible. "Didn't know I knew, did yah?" The large woman laughed outright and continued down the hall slinging over her shoulder. "Payback's a bitch, ain't it? See ya."

From the moment Ethel Mae had cursed and called her white gal, Sophie's mouth had hung open in disbelief. She suspected Ethel Mae was the culprit behind the leak, but the foulness falling from the woman's mouth was staggering and the hurt she had fostered was devastating. Her heart wrenched when she thought about the conversation she had with Tyler earlier. The child's voice rang in her ears.

"I don't wanna go away. I wanna be with you." The child looked at the woman, her small face beginning to crinkle into a seldom-seen frown.

"I know, honey. But you will love your new family. You will. I promise. You will have brothers and sisters…and a mommy and daddy." Tears spilled from behind the child's tightly shut eyelids, cascading down her cheeks.

Tyler placed her head on her favorite spot, right under Sophie's cheek, in the space between her neck and collarbone. "I don't want a mommy and daddy; I just want you."

Tyler sounded so forlorn that Sophie found it almost impossible to hold back her own tears. Sophie's heart was breaking. Holding the child close, placing her cheek on the top of her head, Sophie vowed, "I'll always be there for you Ty. Always."

Unfortunately, it was a promise that Sophie Tyler was unable to keep. Two weeks later, she died in a Southern California fog-laden, fifty-car freeway pileup. Her last thoughts were of Tyler and the one hundred thousand dollar insurance policy she had planned to leave in the child's name.

South Central
Los Angeles ~ April 1980

Mother Price was a community icon. She had lived in South Central Los Angeles all of her life. Born not far from her rambling, two-story wood-framed home, Mother Price was dedicated to bringing joy to the lives of abused children.

She was the daughter of a minister who had migrated with his second wife and eight of his fourteen children to Bakersfield, California, in the late '50s. A farm worker, he stayed in the rural community for almost two years before moving his ever-increasing family to Los Angeles. Joe Johnson wanted better for his children than back-breaking field labor.

Emma was the last child born to the Johnson breed. She grew up surrounded by love, and when her father was called to the ministry and started his small church she became the light of everyone's eye. The church started small, but before long had a large congregation in the heart of Watts. The ministry was from the beginning philanthropic, and Pastor Johnson made sure that all of his members had a real sense of community. The church provided housing, food, and clothing for families down on their luck. They had a rehab program for alcoholics and ex-offenders, and a youth ministry that helped seniors with their housecleaning and shopping on Saturdays. Emma was a stalwart member of the church. She was a youth leader, member of the choir, and totally committed to community betterment.

Her husband, Pastor Ivory Price, was equally committed. A product of a broken family and the foster care system, he was aware of the pitfalls of an agency-supervised childhood. If not for the U.S. Army, he knew he would have been emancipated from foster care into homelessness.

Ivory grew up in the trenches of Vietnam, and swore that when he returned home he would make a difference in his community. On a veteran scholarship, he attended theology school in California.

Emma and Ivory met at a summer revival of Baptist Churches, and the rest was history. The couple was well matched. They were married six months to the day of their meeting, and Bud, their first child, followed a year later. Shortly thereafter, Ivory became a junior pastor in Emma's father's church and a few years later founded his own ministry.

It was late one evening right after the young couple had put their children to bed. Emma was washing dishes and Ivory was reading the Thursday edition of the *Los Angeles Sentinel* when he called to his wife.

"Emma. Baby, come here. Look at this."

Emma dropped what she was doing, wiped her hands on her apron, and rushed into the living room. Her husband rarely raised his voice. Her pretty, oval face was puckered into a frown, and she looked at her husband inquisitively. In answer, he handed her the paper and pointed to the headlines.

The Los Angeles County Department of Adoption is unable to place African American children...Many have become institutional residents. According to Children Services statistics, more than two hundred and fifty children of color are housed in County facilities and go unplaced in foster homes or with adoptive parents annually...

The article went on to reveal that many of the children were never placed with families, and they spent their entire childhood in the sterile environment where he had been raised. Ivory's gut twisted into knots, and he could feel the pain he had felt as a child when he had watched child after child leave the orphanage while he remained behind.

Emma pulled her husband's head into her waist wanting to remove the pain she saw reflected in his eyes. She knew he was reliving his past and it hurt her almost as much as it did him. "What do you want to do, Daddy?" Her voice was charged with love.

"We've got to do something." Ivory looked up, an unspoken plea on his face, and Emma nodded her head. "Well, then. We'll go see those people tomorrow." Just like that, the young couple decided to become foster parents.

By the time Tyler was transferred to Price foster care, the family was bursting at the seams. In addition to their two natural children, Patty and Bud, the household contained three foster children. Tyler rounded the racially diverse group of six children, all living under the same roof, and ranging in age from fourteen to two.

For the most part, it was a happy family. The elder Prices were organized disciplinarians. Their motto was GOD first, family second, and personal gratification, a distant third.

Tyler would never forget the ride to the Price home. She had been transfixed by the speed of the cars flying past their minivan and clutched her doll Susie, a treasured gift from Sophie, to her chest for security. The ride on the freeway was an adventure for Tyler, and the drive from the San Fernando Valley to South Central Los Angeles was a real leap.

The four-year-old was excited and scared at the same time. Ms. Robeson, the social worker, had told her that she would be going to a new family. When they arrived at the seven-bedroom house on the double lot, Tyler's eyes rounded in awe. A picket fence enclosed an area that was attached to the house, and it was filled with colorful swings, a slide that dipped into a sandbox, and a tetherball. The Price home had its own private playground.

To Tyler, whose exercise had been confined to an inside playroom, the play yard was paradise. She trailed behind Ms. Robeson staring in wonder, and the child service counselor tugged Tyler's hand gently as she ascended the porch and pressed the doorbell. The chimed summons tinkled musically, and the door swung open immediately.

Tyler hugged Susie tightly, and looked up at the tall woman standing in the doorway. Her kind welcoming face spoke volumes, and the child's fears lessened.

"Tyler, this will be your new home. Say hello to Mrs. Price," the plump woman urged. "She is a little shy," Alice Robeson said, smiling at Mother Price. Tyler clutched Ms. Robeson's hand, glancing from lowered lids at the friendly lady.

"Come over here, sweetie. I've got something I've been saving just for you. It's a surprise that will welcome you to the family," Mother Price said, smiling again into the child's eyes.

"Come on, baby," the tall woman said to Tyler taking her small hand and leading her into the family room.

Tyler held on to Susie as tightly as she could. It was her link with the hospital as well as Sophie, and she was afraid if she let the doll go something bad would happen. As long as she had Susie, everything would be OK. So, Tyler held on to Susie and looked around her new home.

At one end of the front room, against a colorful orange wall, was an ancient upright piano. At the opposite end was a large screen television. And in the middle of the room were four sofas, forming a boxlike theatre with a solid mahogany coffee table in the middle. It was a warm and comfy room, one that gave testimony to frequent use.

On one of the sofas was a small, bright yellow, opened box. A pretty red ribbon circled the sides, and a huge red bow with silver glitter was placed in the middle of the box.

"Well, look at what we have here," Mother Price cooed as she lifted a fluffy golden kitten from the box.

Tyler's eyes swelled and her mouth formed a perfect circle.

"Kitty. Kitty. Pretty kitty," the child cried out as she opened her arms to the furry gift. Sitting Susie down carefully, Tyler walked over to the kitten. She had never had her own pet. She had read about them, seen animals in the zoo, and even petted them when they were brought to the children's ward, but she had never had a pet she could call her own.

Tyler was spellbound, totally entranced, and watched with wonderment as the kitten's small pink tongue licked her tiny hand. Captivated, she tentatively stroked the fluffy coat and whispered loudly enough for both ladies to hear, "I'm going to call you Sophie 'cause you are the same color as my Aunt Sophie's hair."

Placing the kitten on the floor, the little girl stooped down, lay prone on the floor, and pressed her face against the animal. Staring directly into the cat's eyes, she whispered behind a cupped dainty palm, "I'm going to love you so much; you'll never want to go away, and Susie will love you too." Tyler looked at the doll with her face glowing. "Won't you, Susie?"

Mother Price met the social worker's eyes over the child's head. Things would work out, and both women breathed a sigh of relief. Then she reached for Tyler's hand extending her own and said, "Call me Mother Price, baby, this is your home now."

Tyler's introduction to the other Price children went well, until Mother Price asked Lonnie Jackson to greet his new sister. The children were standing in a line, oldest at the head, and youngest at the end. Still clutching the kitten, Tyler was led down the line as Mother Price presented each child individually. When they reached Lonnie, he stared at Tyler with cold malevolence, but it did not faze Tyler. She greeted his menace with a tentative smile.

The boy was immediately suspicious. Lonnie's physical appearance was anything but pleasant. When he was four, his father in a fit of rage unloaded a 357 Magnum meant for his mother. Unfortunately, when Lonnie's father pointed the gun, Monique grabbed her terrified son and held him in front of her as a human shield. Lonnie's father fired anyway. One bullet fatally wounded Monique and the other tore through Lonnie's left cheek, permanently damaging the muscles on that side of his face.

Lonnie's reconstructed cheek was frozen, and his mouth was twisted upward. It was impossible for him to smile without sneering. And while most adults were moved to sympathy, children would cower in fear or shy away.

Tyler had grown up in a hospital ward. Disfigured and injured children were no novelty. So, in the friendly manner that had captivated the nursing and support staff at Olive View, Tyler gave Lonnie a tender smile that would melt the heart of a Jihad terrorist.

"Hello. I have a kitty. Her name is Sophie. Wanna see?" Tyler's naive offer of friendship was met with a frosty gaze.

It was not just that Tyler was pretty, though Lonnie had a violent abhorrence to beauty. What Lonnie loathed most about Tyler was that she so effortlessly gained what he so desperately craved, but rejected. He especially despised her, because he sensed in her an unselfish, nonjudgmental capacity for love—something that he did not trust or believe. How could he, when his own mother had betrayed him while hugging him to her chest?

Lonnie had come to the family five years earlier. And in all those years, he had never opened up to his foster parents. He was a loner, seemingly needing no one and nothing. Yet, there were times when Mother Price sensed a deep loneliness in the child.

Her instincts were correct. Lonnie was aching and hurting inside. The merciless abuse at the hands of his crack-addicted parents had twisted his thinking. The absence of love and affection in his infancy and as a toddler left him in a state of constant yearning, and he despised this *wanting* as a weakness. Even at ten, he was determined to stomp out what he perceived to be his character flaw.

Tyler hugged Sophie and pulled Susie into her arms, and her head dropped to nuzzle the cat. She looked up at Mother Price with a tentative grin, her small arms crowded with her two prize possessions. Her heart was in her eyes and some of the fear she had had about her new home disappeared. Tyler's mouth widened and her eyes sparkled. She lowered her head again and whispered into the doll's ear. "I think I like this house, Susie." Looking back up to the adults hovering above her, Tyler smiled.

Lonnie watched the tiny beauty captivate the Prices with her charm, and he burned with envy. His deepest desire was to gain the affection and respect of his foster family. With Tyler's arrival his dream dissolved. For Lonnie it was the last straw and the beginning of a life obsession filled with hatred directed toward Tyler.

TYLER AGE 6
FRIDAY

Tyler sat on her cotton-candy-pink bed and held Sophie in her arms, stroking the silky coat as the cat purred. In the two years since she had arrived at the Price home, they had become constant companions.

"Now, Sophie, I want you to watch Susie while I go to school. Don't let her get into trouble, and don't let her go outside without you." Tyler pointed her finger at Sophie seriously, and the cat curled her whiskered face into her hand. Tyler giggled and hugged the cat who was now a large tabby. "You and Susie are my best friends."

Tyler genuinely loved Sophie and Susie. She knew that her conversations with the cat and doll were make-believe, but she liked having them regardless. For one thing, she could tell Susie all of her secrets and never worry about her giving them away, and for another, Sophie liked to cuddle no matter what.

Tyler would bury her face in the cat's fluffy fur for hours, and Sophie would not budge; so unlike her foster sister Jan who would wiggle and squirm until Tyler was forced to let her go. Sophie was a willing playmate whose loyalty was unquestionable, and she rarely left Tyler's side.

Unsuspecting of another presence in the hallway, Tyler backed out of her room and bumped into Lonnie who was still in his pajamas.

"You'll be late if you don't get dressed, Lonnie." Tyler rushed her words together. She never felt at ease when she was alone with this foster brother. "And you will make us all tardy for school. Papa Price won't like that." Lonnie just stared at Tyler, blocking her path. She tried to push past him, but he was jamming the narrow hallway. When she leaned to one side, so did he. And, when she ducked to the other side, Lonnie stepped in front of her.

"I'm gonna tell Momma if you don't move." Tyler was indignant, and although only six, her voice reflected fearlessness. Lonnie's eyes squinted. He wanted her to fear him, to understand without him saying so his need to hurt her and make her squeal like the mouse he had roasted over a fire last week.

Tyler was afraid, but she would die before she would let Lonnie know. Inside she was trembling in alarm. All of her senses were on alert. She understood on an intrinsic level Lonnie's malevolence toward her. However, she also knew that revealing fear to Lonnie would be the worst thing she could do. It was a standoff, and one the six-year-old was not willing to lose.

Without blinking, or giving herself away, Tyler stomped on Lonnie's big toe. Her saddle oxfords were a great weapon, and when Lonnie howled, grabbed his toe, and hopped on one foot, she ducked and skirted under his arm. She ran like the wind.

When she looked back, Lonnie's glare of hate made her blood freeze, but he was not looking at her. He was staring into her bedroom where Susie and Sophie remained.

SUNDAY

"Stay still, Tyler." Patty Price had gathered Tyler's tumbling curls in her hand and held them high as she twisted an elastic band around her foster sister's hair forming a thick ponytail.

"Please hurry, Patty. I wanna walk with Juan and Bud." Patty fluffed the six-year-old's hair, turned her around, and continued to groom her sister. She fussed under her breath, as she pulled and straightened Tyler's dress. "They won't leave you, baby girl. It's first Sunday. The children and adult choirs are going to sing together this morning." Giving her little sister's dress a tug, she retied the bow at her waist. "Momma says there is no one that can sing *This Little Light of Mine* like you.

"Now, there!" Patty gave Tyler a final pat. "You can go. But don't you go letting those silly boys muss your dress. If I know Bud, he's going to flip you around like a rag doll the moment he sees you." Patty pushed Tyler affectionately toward the door. "And tell 'em Dad said to sweep the front steps the moment they get to church."

Tyler was out the door before Patty had completed the sentence. Running down the hall as fast as her little legs could carry her; she turned the corner to the living room and ran right into Lonnie.

Lonnie was a year younger than Bud and Juan, but he never treated her the way they did. Lonnie didn't like her, and Tyler knew it. It wasn't so much what he said. It was the way he watched her, like he wanted to hurt her, but didn't because he couldn't without everyone knowing. In front of the others, her foster mother and father especially, Lonnie treated her no differently from the rest of the kids. But whenever they were alone, his eyes said something else.

"Hey, watch where you're going!" Lonnie spoke in a dry, calm voice. Anyone overhearing him would see no harm in his words for he had learned to eliminate emotion from his voice. He always spoke in a monotone. But one glance at his face would give even the most charitable adult pause. His eyes revealed the menace behind them. He hadn't forgotten their last confrontation. His toe still hurt, and his smirk was evil. This time he had his shoes on.

The two children were alone in the hall, and Lonnie did not bother to hide his feelings. He held her in a paralyzing stare for a heartbeat, savoring the fear she was unable to hide. Tyler's heart lifted when she heard Bud.

"There you are," he mumbled as he crammed one of Mother Price's fluffy buttermilk biscuits into his mouth. Juan was at his heels. Startled, Tyler jumped and dashed past Lonnie, who had braced himself against the wall.

Bud and Juan were Tyler's adoring big brothers, and unbeknownst to them had just rescued Tyler from Lonnie's hateful glare.

"I saved one for you. That's all you can eat if you wanna go with us." Bud offered Tyler a biscuit wrapped in a paper napkin, the butter left a clear sheen on his palm.

"Hey, where'd you get that?" Juan asked trying to rustle the biscuit from Bud, who held the tasty morsel over his head then tossed the prize to Tyler. Her smile was his reward, and he watched her with big brother tenderness as she swallowed her first bite.

The three siblings left the house. Their noisy argument over the biscuit rang with friendly comradely. "If you keep eating Momma's biscuits at every opportunity, your stomach is going to blow up. It'll be so big you'll have to lift it off the ground with both of your hands," Juan joked.

"No, I won't. I won't, will I, Bud?" Tyler cried, already picturing Pinky Martin and her swollen eight-month-pregnant stomach. "Am I going to look like Pinky?" Only a year before, Pinky had been a star performer in the youth choir. Now, the unwed, fourteen-year-old was in her third trimester of pregnancy, and

Tyler, who knew nothing about childbirth, found Juan's story believable.

"Of course not, button. Juan, stop teasing her!" Bud reached over and slapped at Juan's head, intentionally fanning air, as the threesome strolled from the house. Their cheerful banter floated into the hallway.

Lonnie was furious. The sound of the back door banging left an acid taste in his mouth. He had observed the trio in silent loathing, already planning how he would make Tyler suffer for the other boys' kindness.

The next morning, Lonnie went into the bathroom and stuck his finger down his throat. Dry heaving loudly, he told Mother Price that he had an upset stomach, and did not feel like going to school.

Since Monday was Mother Price's day to go grocery shopping and Papa Price was out visiting the sick and shut-in, Lonnie knew he would have the house to himself. Fluffing the pillow, Mother Price placed her hand on her foster son's forehead, concern wrinkling her brow. "I'll be back in an hour. Are you sure you'll be OK?" The worried woman was reluctant to leave the sick boy alone.

"Don't worry, Mom. I'll be all right." Lonnie grimaced painfully, watching Mother Price fuss with the glass of water at his bedside. He smiled to himself at his successful ploy. Step one of his plan was completed.

As soon as Lonnie heard the car pull out of the driveway, he was out of the bed. He went straight to Tyler and Jan's room. The cotton-candy-pink concoction of bed spreads, curtains, and ruffled pillows made Lonnie noxious. He spun around in the room, disgusted, searching for his target. Spying the doll, he snatched her up and hurried out of the room. In the corner, Sophie arched her back and hissed.

"Next time, bitch." Lonnie's voice was low and laced with spite. Sophie charged, but he slammed the door before she could reach him. On the other side of the door, Lonnie let the air out of his lungs slowly and walked away from the cat's impotent wails with single-minded purpose.

Clutching the doll in one hand, he almost skipped down the hall. The thrill of taking what Tyler cherished most exhilarated the preteen. He ran through the living room and sprinted through the kitchen to the trash bin. For several seconds, Lonnie stood motionless, savoring the sensation of omnipotent power as it surged through his body. He lowered his head onto his chest reverently.

In one hand he held the doll's legs, and in the other her head. He took a slow, deep, lung-filling breath and pulled them simultaneously, decapitating the toy, and then tossed the body into the dumpster. Flinging Susie's head to the ground, he stomped and jumped on it until it was unrecognizable, except for the doll's gold curls. Spitting his ire, he watched the spittle splash on the crushed plastic, and imagined it was Tyler lying at his feet.

Finished, Lonnie tiptoed back to the house and returned to his bedroom. He lay down on the bed, cupped his head with his hands and savored the thrill of destroying one of Tyler's prize possessions. His body stiffened as he recalled the pleasure he had tearing and shredding the doll. He was hard, and he had a lovely tingle in his private area.

He removed one hand from under his head, and placed it on the small member tenting in his pajamas. He pushed the elastic band of his pants low on his hips and rubbed, at first slowly, and then as the pleasure increased, more vigorously.

At eleven, Lonnie had not experienced an orgasm, and so when the fluids erupted from his manhood he thought he had pissed on himself. His entire body trembled with ecstasy. The feeling was wonderful, intoxicating. It was his first sexual high, and he would search for the feeling throughout his life, again, and again, reenacting the joyous pleasure of destruction.

Lonnie closed his eyes, and drifted off to sleep envisioning Tyler's discovery of the mutilated doll. He had a peaceful nap, and later when the entire household was in an uproar looking for Susie, he watched, silently smiling as Tyler cried copious tears.

What Lonnie did not know was that Pastor Price had returned to the house early. Although he did not see Lonnie go into Tyler's room, or see him dump the doll, he had seen the boy creeping through the house from the backyard, and it had struck him as odd, sneaky, and devious. Later, when the doll came up missing, he recalled Lonnie's stealthy movements when he was supposed to be sick in bed.

That night he shared his misgivings with his wife. "Baby, I have a bad feeling about Lonnie." Ivory Price's loving gaze settled on his wife as she prepared for bed. Her sheer nightdress accentuated her slender hips and gently swaying breasts as she moved toward their bed. It was amazing, he reflected with a mental smile. Even after eighteen years of marriage and two children, the sight of his wife's nightgown-clad body still delighted him.

Twisting her hair under a silk nightcap, Emma Price looked at her husband questioningly.

"What do you mean by that, Daddy?" At forty-eight, Mother Price was a willowy woman who had not lost her youthful energy or earthy beauty. She turned, giving her husband her full attention as she walked toward the bed.

"It is not just that Lonnie is quiet, it's that he never seems to connect with anyone. He has been with us for seven years, and in all that time he has never started a conversation with me without my prompting. Has he ever confided in you? No. I know he hasn't. All of the children avoid him, and it is not just because of his face."

Emma Price sat down on the bed thinking, and then slowly shook her head as she looked again at her husband. She had always felt uneasy about Lonnie.

"There is definitely something wrong." Ivory Price punctuated his words by shaking his head thoughtfully. "And, there's another thing. Have you ever seen him cry?"

"Baby, what are you trying to say? Just come out with it."

"I am saying that there is something odd about that boy. He never cries. He rarely laughs. And I am saying that I do not trust him. Early today, I saw Lonnie sneaking around downstairs, even though he was supposed to be in bed sick. I know he had been out back near the trash bin. I'm certain of it."

Emma Price took the information in, mulling it over slowly, and then slid into the bed, reaching for her husband's hand.

"What should we do?" Emma Price trusted her husband implicitly. She respected his judgment, often telling him that he had been gifted with a second sight.

"We need to keep an eye on Lonnie. I found Tyler's doll in the trash bin this afternoon. It was destroyed. The head was separated from the body, and the face had been smashed, deliberately mutilated. Whoever did that to the doll has some real rage in 'em."

"I didn't want to mention it to you until now, and I don't want the children to know." Pastor Price looked at his wife and shook his head.

"Baby, I believe Lonnie did it. If my feelings are true, we need to watch him very carefully, especially around the younger kids. I believe he has a mean, vindictive streak that is dangerous to all of us."

The couple whispered late into the night, discussing Lonnie, and whether or not they should share their suspicions with his social worker.

Finally, after much soul-searching, they decided to keep their own counsel until they had gathered more proof.

The doll's disappearance left a huge hole in Tyler's heart. She was devastated. Susie was her baby, as real to Tyler as any of her siblings. She had spent countless hours feeding the doll and changing her wet diapers. Mother Price's replacement of Susie with an exact replica did not go over well.

"Don't you like her?" Encouragingly, her mother confided, "She's Susie's little sister Sally." The child was not impressed. She took the doll, gave her mother a sad smile, and put it aside. Unlike most children her age, Tyler felt loss deeply. Her early life had been a study in abandonment and loss, from her mother to Nurse Sophie and now her adored Susie.

But three days after Susie disappeared; the family received a new member. His name was Bobby Pike. Coincidence or divine intervention, the senior Prices could never figure it out, but Bobby's arrival was the perfect remedy for the child's malady. Soon, the two-year-old toddler had replaced the doll in Tyler's heart. He became Tyler's constant playmate.

Bobby was a bundle of energy with a silky mop of white-blond hair and huge cornflower-blue eyes. He adored Tyler, and from the beginning, he followed her around like a little puppy. When he was not following her, he was sitting in her lap listening to Tyler read stories from *Dr. Seuss Beginner Books*. It was a perfect match. His mother had abandoned Bobby several months earlier, and the two children needed each other.

The next several years were uneventful. Not that Lonnie stopped harassing Tyler and playing his dirty tricks. He did not. Most of what he plotted involved the disappearance of her hair ribbons, school papers, and other petty incidentals. But no matter how hard they tried, the Prices could never catch Lonnie in his mischief. So, they could never tie him to the deeds, or identify him as the culprit. Over time, they began to ignore the incidents, labeling them as childish pranks. Tyler, who was the butt of his mischief, relied on her inner strength to defend herself against Lonnie's thinly veiled malice.

But on Tyler's tenth birthday, life, as it were, took a sharp turn for the worse. It had been an unusually active week. The family celebrated Tyler's birthday at Chuck E. Cheese. The children were ecstatic, and their infectious play and cheerful teasing lifted the spirits of the entire restaurant. The servers sang "Happy Birthday" before Tyler opened her gifts and then surprised everyone at the table by giving them a party favor she had made for them.

One by one, she passed out the gifts. A flowered handkerchief to Mother Price, a satin book marker with a Bible scripture embroidered on it to Pastor Price, a decorated ribbon to Patty, a flower hair barrette to little Jan, a treasure box made of popsicle sticks for Juan, a picture of Muhammad Ali in a beaded frame for Bud, and a James Brown cassette tape for Lonnie. But she saved her most prized gift for last.

"Bobby, I have something special for you. You will never have to worry about misplacing your pencil box again." With a shy smile, Tyler pushed a hand-sewn pouch hanging from a nylon-beaded rope that spelled out Bobby's name across the table to the little boy. Inside were two pens and a yellow highlighter.

Bobby looked at his gift and beamed at Tyler. His expressive face glowing with pride, he put the beaded sack around his neck, smiling widely. Lonnie watched the small boy from lowered eyelids and fumed. The six-year-old was Tyler's favorite brother, and it was evident Bobby loved her back. Lonnie burned with envy... but, managed as usual to conceal it from the others.

The children were animated as they poured out of the restaurant. Their good will with one another a testimony to the foster parenting of the Prices as well as Patty and Bud. Miniature replicas of their parents, the two teens had rejected the drug and gang culture rampant in South Central. They chose instead to concentrate on school, Christian outreach, and their foster brothers and sisters, but they were too popular to be labeled geeks. Bud was a star athlete, an all city quarterback, and Patty was head of the high school's glee club. Both kids served on the student council, and Bud was King of the Manual Arts High School Homecoming Dance.

It was after nine o'clock when the family reached home. Patty and Bud helped the younger children dress for bed. Bobby was the only naysayer. Bud chased the energized boy down, flipped him over his shoulder, and plopped him on his bed. "Say your prayers, you little heathen." Bud emphasized the order with a playful slap at Bobby's rump and followed with a rough hug.

Shortly after ten o'clock, everything had quieted. The children were asleep and Pastor and Mother Price had settled into a spoon position, nestling snugly in the center of their large California king bed.

They had just begun to doze off when piercing screams rocked the house. A few seconds later rapidly pounding steps resonated in the hallway seconds before Patty burst into the room.

Pastor Price flung off the bed coverings, leaped from the bed and met his panic-stricken daughter in the center of the room.

"What's the matter with you?" He asked, fear lacing his question, as he enfolded the young girl in his arms.

Patty's response was a rush of words that sounded like gibberish. "It. They. Why? Oh, my God. Oh Lord Jesus, Mom, Daddy.

It." Patty's words ran together, and it was evident that the girl could not organize her thoughts. Tears streamed from her eyes. She was in shock.

"Baby, what is it?" Mother Price had gotten out of bed, nightgown floating at her feet as she crossed the floor and joined her husband and Patty in the middle of the room. "What is it? Ivory, get the child some water." She urged her husband with frightened eyes.

All the children were crowed in the doorway, and Pastor Price elbowed himself out of the door as he ran to the kitchen for water.

Patty placed her head on her mother's shoulder. Her body quivered and shook. She was unable to utter a coherent word.

Patty was a sheltered, naive sixteen-year-old. In her entire life, she had not harmed a living creature, finding it very difficult to squash even an ant. Tonight she had encountered the devil's work. And she recognized it for what it was.

After she and Bud had put the younger children to bed, Patty had gone into the backyard to empty the trash and clean the barbeque pit. Every Sunday the family hosted two homeless families at dinner. This Sunday, because of a three-digit temperature forecast, the elder Prices decided dinner would be served outdoors. Thinking she would get a head start on clearing out the ash waste and stacking new coals in the pit, Patty walked over to the pit and raised the large drum barrel hood.

A stench of burnt flesh and hair wafted out of the barrel, freezing Patty on the spot. The smell was overwhelming, and in that moment, the odor was indelibly imprinted on her mind.

Adrenalin rushed through her veins, and Patty felt a cold ominous breeze shoot toward her, then come to a silent halt that hovered. The air around her was glacially cold, and she felt an invisible force drawing her into the pit. In spite of the cold, she felt the heat. Sweat ran down her face, as mesmerized, she was drawn closer to the smoking lump.

The heat was intense, and the stench was suffocating. She gagged as the airborne filth filled her lungs and seared her eyes. She thought of *Dante's Inferno*, but Patty knew that she was drawn toward evil, not a *religious quest to find God.*

This is bad, really bad, she thought, and jerked her head back.

Patty's hand flew to her mouth, while her finger and thumb pinched her nose, and her eyes became round saucers. Steam rose from the pit. A lumpy object smoldered on the grill in a smoky heap. She could tell it had been burning for some time.

Most of the barbeque pit was in the dark, and it was difficult for Patty to recognize the object. But her curiosity overcame revulsion. Slowly, she inched closer to the grill, thinking one of the neighbors might have put a chicken on the grill without plucking it.

What a dumb thing to do, especially as it stank so badly, Patty thought, condemning both the person and the act. She looked around quickly, fearing she had spoken out loud, and automatically begged God for forgiveness for her uncharitable thoughts.

Using a long sharp grill fork, Patty poked at the lump turning it toward the back door where a bright light illuminated the porch. The sharp, three-pronged fork sank into the lump, and blood red fluid oozed from its hind part. Patty jumped, realizing it was as she suspected a cooked piece of flesh.

It has to be a chicken, she repeated to herself. Stabbing again with the fork, the teen tried to turn the flesh over, but it would not budge.

The yard was dark, and she had never felt so alone. Unseen eyes seemed to peer at her from beyond the trees and she could swear she heard a rustling sound in the bushes. She looked over her shoulder, staring into the shadowy hedges trying to see beyond the thick florae. Unsuccessful and frustrated, she turned back to the pit. A chill washed over her body and she trembled. She turned her head and stared into the gloomy yard, tempted to go back into the house to get Bud, but scoffing chided herself for childish fear.

"This is stupid," Patty muttered aloud defiantly, refusing to be frightened of imagined ghosts. She looked blindly into the bush and raised her voice, "Is there anyone out there?" No one answered, but something felt terribly wrong. The chilly breeze had returned, in spite of the warm night.

Patty shivered. It felt like someone had just walked over her grave as another cold blast of air stung her cheeks. She shivered again. Her teeth chattered with loud machine gun taps in the quite yard.

Patty mentally shrugged her shoulders, and shook her head. Her imagination was running rampant, and she giggled, trying to boost her confidence, but fear was getting the best of her. Her eyes were wide as she looked over her shoulder and laughed nervously. The sound was eerie in the dark, silent night. She wanted to walk away, but an unknown force kept her glued to the spot.

Stubbornly determined, squeezing her nose against the stench, Patty renewed her efforts to move the lump closer into the light. It was difficult, because the meat was heavy and not at all easy to maneuver on the grill. She struggled for a few minutes, and perspiration began to form on her brow. But she was going to see what had been placed on the grill.

Again, she felt it, unseen eyes staring at her. She heard a slight movement in the bush. Quick as a lizard, Patty twirled around, her head whipping from left to right, but she could find nothing in the shadows. She turned back to the grill, muttering under her breath.

"I should have gone and gotten Bud. I ain't no Wonder Woman."

Finally, Patty moved the meat into to the light. She backed up, shaking her head, refusing to believe what she saw on the grill. Her hand flew up and covered a soundless scream. Patty felt that it went on forever, although only a few seconds had passed. A hyena cackle burst into the night. It was horrifying, evil, and Patty had no doubt that the malevolent laughter celebrated wickedness.

The cry tore from her throat and blended with the evil cackle with chilling promise. Patty's fleshed crawled. Backing up, almost tripping over the picnic table, she continued to scream until the blood-curdling anguish obscured the immoral titter. Her stomach churned.

Sophie the family pet, the cat that Mother Price had given to Tyler the day she came to live with the family, lay on the grill roasted like a chicken. The small golden bell, which had given off a cheerful tinkle every time Sophie moved, was charred black. The chain that held the bell was imprinted obscenely into the baked skin of the still smoldering cat.

Patty bent over and hid her mouth in nauseous revulsion. Her eyes stretched in disbelief and she lost her dinner. Bile spewed out from between her fingers and splashed on her dress. Tears of anguish streamed from her eyes.

Sobbing, hugging her stomach, she ran into the house with the sound of the vile cackle still ringing in her ears. On winged feet, her heels pounded against the floor, automatically carrying her to the safe haven of her mother and father's arms. Patty's terror-filled shrieks filled the bedroom.

When Mother Price finally calmed her down, the teenager said one intelligible word. "Outside..." Asking Bud to watch the younger children, husband and wife rushed out of the back door onto the porch. They looked around confused, and then in unison stared at the opened barbeque pit. Hand in hand, they walked toward the pit, focused on the smoking object on the grill. Then they saw it.

Mother Price slammed her hands over her mouth. Pastor Price walked closer to examine the remains of the family pet. His eyes gleamed with unshed tears. Abruptly, almost falling, he sat in the wooden chair next to the pit and motioned to his wife to join him.

Taking Mother Price's hand, he bowed his head and began to pray. "God, we ask for guidance in this moment of need. I pray for this poor animal. I pray for my house and the children who reside under the roof you have provided us. There is evil here, lord, and I fear that my home is under siege. We pray for deliverance, Father God, and ask for your protection in the name of Jesus our Savior. Halleluiah! Halleluiah! Amen."

Pastor Price's voice had risen in tempo with every verse. A loving, gentle man, who had never raised his hand to his wife or children, Pastor Price began to cry. The sight that greeted his eyes was an act of unconscionable savagery, and he was emotionally unprepared for the violence done to Sophie.

Mother Price drew her husband's head to her breasts, tears streaming down her face, her heart beating loudly in his ear. Without any concrete evidence, she believed Lonnie Jackson was behind Sophie's death. Her tears were for both the boy and the cat. And her tears reflected fear. For she rationalized, anyone capable of inflicting torture and pain on a helpless animal, would do the same thing to a defenseless child.

On Monday, Mother Price contacted Lonnie's social worker and told her about her suspicions. She demanded a conference and asked that a psychiatrist be present. By Thursday, Pastor and Mother Price sat in a room with Lonnie, his social worker, and Dr. Richard Jensen.

When Lonnie walked into the room, he was surprised to see the doctor. The man had been a pain in Lonnie's ass for years; his diagnosis had placed Lonnie in special education classes for the "Seriously Emotionally Disturbed," as well as prescribed daily doses of Ritalin. Lonnie smiled to himself, thinking he had fooled the Prices and the doctor by pretending to swallow the drug, but he had spit it out as soon as he could.

Lonnie's heart raced with apprehension, and his hands began to sweat. He feared his deeds had been uncovered, and he would be sent to juvenile hall where he would be given Ritalin again. Outwardly he was calm, none of the adults in the room would have guessed that the meeting gave Lonnie a moment's pause.

He had known when he placed Sophie on the grill, watched pitilessly as she screeched and howled, that this might tip his hand. But the urge was uncontrollable, in spite of the possibility that he might be discovered with the loud shrieking of the cat, his anger overruled precaution. The attention Tyler was given on her birthday was a consuming inferno, blinding him to self-preservation. The icing on the cake was the cat's agony. It had given him the orgasmic pleasure he could garner only when he destroyed another's treasure.

When they entered the social worker's office, the sixteen-year-old was coldly silent. There had been no conversation in the car during the drive to the social worker's office. Mother and Pastor Price had told him only that they would be making an unscheduled visit to his social worker.

Lonnie listened to Dr. Jensen and Ms. Patterson discuss his case with his foster parents as if he were not in the room. The Prices wanted him to go. Ms. Patterson and Dr. Jensen wanted him to begin regular counseling. It appeared as if they were going nowhere, and then Lonnie took a deep breath. In an academy-award-winning performance, he pleaded.

"Please don't send me away. You're the only family I've ever had. Momma Price, I want to stay with you and Papa Price." The sixteen-year-old's voice cracked on an Oscar-winning sob as large crocodile tears spilled down his cheeks and pooled on the collar of his prized Jimi Hendrix T-shirt.

Emma Price's mouth fell open in surprise. Lonnie had just spoken the longest, unsolicited sentence of her memory and shed his first tears, and her heart broke. "Why, Lonnie, I didn't know you felt that way. Of course we won't send you away." She looked at her husband for confirmation. "Will we, Daddy?"

Pastor Price rolled his eyes disbelievingly, but nodded his head in reluctant agreement, "If you say so, Mother."

And that was the end of that. If Lonnie could have laughed, he would have thrown himself on the floor in hysterics. *What dumb fucks*, he thought.

CHAPTER TWO

Andre

ANNAPOLIS ~ 1989

Andre Dunn looked at the sea of white-capped midshipmen in their pristine uniforms, cleared his throat, and began the valedictorian speech for the United States Naval Academy Class of 1989.

"Fellow graduates...

The applause was deafening. The white caps sailing in the air signaled the end of the commencement ceremony, and with it, the close of four years of an exhaustingly rigorous schedule of academics, athletics, and pressure from the upperclassmen.

Andre maneuvered through the crowd to his parents and siblings. His six-foot four-inch frame towered over most of the other celebrants at the Naval Academy commencement.

Claude and Françoise Dunn held hands as they watched their son make his way toward them with a grace rarely exhibited in men his size. Andre did not walk; rather, he prowled with a slow alpha-male tread, his muscles rippling sleekly with each rhythmic step.

Women's eyes followed him, drawn irresistibly to his masculinity. Men too were called to his alluring beauty as sexuality seeped from his pores in an irresistible magnetic pull. He was extraordinarily handsome, and his skin was bronze silk. His chiseled features could only be depicted as "Hollywood-ish," and without his manly frame, Andre could easily be described as pretty. But there was nothing effeminate about the aura that clung to Andre. It was primeval. He could be incredibly fierce, and he could focus with inflexible purpose on any object, living or inanimate.

As he closed in on his parents, several of his classmates stopped him so that they could introduce Andre to their families. He was polite, but brief as he shouldered his way toward his parents. Soon he stood in front of them, his broad smile filled with love and respect. His brother Paul stood to the side, his lips twisted in a proud grin, while his little sister Mimi jumped up and down with youthful exuberance. Momentarily distracted, Andre fluffed Mimi's hair, and gave Paul a high five, all the time intently focused on his parents.

Claude Dunn stared at his son. Pride illuminated his handsome, chocolate face. At fifty-four, Claude was a strikingly fit and long-legged, handsome man with a solid physique. Placing both hands on his son's shoulders, he held Andre at arm's length. Then the two large men embraced, only breaking the masculine clinch when the petite woman observing them asked, "Well, do I get some of that?"

Françoise Dunn observed her husband and son lovingly. She felt lucky and extremely blessed to have such beautiful men in her life. Born in France, in the late1940s, Françoise was the daughter of a Togolese mother and French father. Pierre Du Ponce, was the oldest son of a wealthy banker. Although the couple never married, her father and grandparents cherished François.

Françoise had a sacred bond with Africa. From the time of her birth, she and her mother vacationed at the family's compound in Togo. Nadu wanted her child to understand and take pride in her heritage, and so every summer mother and daughter traveled to the Zankli villages in West Africa.

Françoise met Claude Dunn when he served as a military attaché at the American embassy in 1965. His first night in Paris the homesick officer had gone to a popular club where American jazz was played.

Five minutes after arriving at the club, Claude met Françoise, and he was enchanted with her beauty and intelligence. The rest was history. They were married before Claude returned to America. Françoise joined him six months later against her

French relatives' protests, and Andre was born nine months later. The next year Paul joined the family, and the youngest and only girl, Mimi arrived eleven years after Andre.

Claude began his civilian career working in the Chicago Police Department, and by the time he was in his midforties, he had worked himself into a deputy chief post. The Dunns were a happy family. Claude and Françoise were loving parents, who made time for their children's academic and athletic activities. They filled their lives with culture, making visits back to France and traveled throughout Europe and Africa annually.

Andre was a beautiful, bright baby. He was a precious toddler and an outgoing, exceptionally smart preteen. By the time he was in high school he had lettered in basketball and football and was recruited by most of the Ivy League schools. When the honor student decided on Annapolis, his parents were delighted.

In Andre's second year at Annapolis, he was summonsed to the office of the dean of students. If he lived to be a hundred, he would never forget that day.

He sat in the reception office, nervously fingering his cap, and wondered why he received the summons. He had racked his brain for more than twenty minutes when the dean's secretary turned to him and said, "You can go in now."

Andre looked at the attractive, thirty-something secretary and exercised a gift he rarely used. Focusing, he entered her mind and looked into her memories, but found nothing that would enlighten him about the meeting. He placed his cap under his left arm, stood and crossed the room.

Candy Wilson's eyes followed Andre, unknowingly telegraphing her raging hunger for his youthful body. She had been studying the twenty-year-old as he waited in his pristine whites to be called into the dean's office. He was hot, devastatingly so, and she found herself fantasizing about the young African-American ensign. She had never been into black men like some of her friends, but Andre Dunn was truly special.

She sensed that the young ensign was exercising control over his emotions, restraining himself under a thin veneer of civility, hiding impulses that could—when unleashed—ravage a woman and inspire her to acrobatic feats between the sheets. Candy's panties grew damp as she imagined herself riding Andre hard while she performed squats over his engorged cock. The fantasy flashed vividly in her mind, and she unconsciously swiped her tongue over her lower lip.

Andre's eyes dashed to hers with a knowing twinkle before he opened the door. Candy Wilson flushed beet red, looked down, and shuffled the papers on her desk. He knew her thoughts. She did not know how, but she was certain that he knew what she had been thinking.

Andre was surprised to see that Dean Harrington was not alone. The two men stood. Dean Harrington came out from behind his desk, extended his arm, and grasped Andre's hand with a firm grip.

"Andre, I would like to introduce you to Mike Foster."

He promptly learned that Foster was a special operations recruiter for a branch of the United States government that conducted covert operations in hot spots around the world. In short order, Foster shared that the agency wanted to enroll Andre in an elite branch of the military.

"Every year we look at the Annapolis sophomore class, and identify candidates for our agency. We recruit those we feel to be the best of the best, and we've had our eyes on you for some time."

Mike Foster looked at Andre, then across at Dean Harrington. He launched into an overview of his agency and its importance to the U.S. government and survival of worldwide democracy. He was soft spoken, but he was eloquent and convincing in his delivery.

"You are a prime candidate for the agency, and I am here to extend a personal invitation to you to join us at an orientation about the Special Ops Division. We will explain what a career with us will mean to you. I can assure you there are lots of perks you'll enjoy if you join us." Foster looked at Andre meaningfully. "World travel, for one, and a great deal of money, for another."

Mike Foster went on to explain that Andre's gift for languages, and the fact that he was fluent in French, German, and Arabic was of special interest to the people in special operations. "The department wants to diversify. We especially want to include blacks, Asians, and Middle Easterners in our new strategies." Looking at Andre tellingly, Foster concluded, "The world is shrinking and America needs to stay ahead of the game."

Andre searched the man's mind and found nothing but sincere patriotism.

He was stunned. Never had he imagined an offer from the Navy that would take him outside of the mainstream services. He looked at the two men, his eyes moving from one to the other catching small pieces of thought. There was a short pregnant pause. You could hear a pin drop.

Andre's smooth voice splintered the silence. "I'd like to think about this. Can I give you an answer tomorrow?"

Mike Foster looked at Andre with a steely glaze. The room was very quiet.

"Sure." He handed Andre his card. It was expensive, white linen card stock. Foster's name was printed in bold letters. Under his name were two telephone numbers, an office number, and a cell phone number.

Mike dipped his chin and nodded his head at Andre. "I look forward to hearing from you."

Dean Harrington and Foster stood, signaling the meeting was over. The dean walked Andre to the door in a comrade fashion, placed his arm on the younger man's shoulder, and took Andre's extended hand in his. The handshake was firm, and his eye contact steely. His lips thinned.

"Of course, we expect our conversation to be kept in the strictest of confidence."

The next day Andre called Mike Foster and agreed to attend the orientation. One month later, he joined a clandestine and very elite division of the Navy SEALs.

South Central

Los Angeles ~ April 1992

Tyler Miller was a striking twelve-year-old, already showing signs of the beauty she would become later in life. Her unusual coloring, mahogany hair with blue-purple eyes and dusk-kissed, golden skin was car stopping even at twelve. One of the tallest girls in her seventh-grade class, at five feet six inches, she was also one of the most popular.

She was liked, not so much for her looks, as for the way she treated people. It did not matter to Tyler if you were the smartest in class, the hippest in the neighborhood, or the fastest on the track team. She treated everyone with the same care, which had garnered her confidences she never revealed and friendships she never betrayed.

People liked doing nice things for Tyler, mostly because she made them feel so good about themselves. She was her teachers' favorite, because she earned top grades in all subjects, and she always found time to help her classmates.

She attended King Drew Preparatory School, and two of her seventh-grade classes were taught at the University of Southern California. Although still in elementary school, Bobby and Jan were placed in the same program, which delighted Tyler, because she could keep an eye on them. One of her greatest fears was that she would wake up one day and they would be gone, just like Susie and Sophie.

Physically, the children were opposites. Bobby was a towhead with sky blue eyes, a lean wiry body, and large uneven teeth. Tyler's biological parents were Jewish and African American, Bobby's mother was from El Salvador, and his father was a Scandinavian merchant marine. His coloring was a striking contrast of white and gold.

On the other hand, Jan was as highbred African American as one could be. She had incredibly smooth, root beer brown skin, with petite features that were placed arrestingly in a heart-shaped face. Her hair was thick and coarse with tight curls, and both Mother Price and Patty complained when they had to straighten it. So, mostly Jan wore her hair in French braids pulled back in a long ponytail. Full of energy, she and Bobby were an explosive package when put together. As Mother Price often reflected, "They could be a handful."

The three children had two things in common: they were all exceptionally bright, and they had all been abandoned by their parents; Tyler at birth, Bobby when his mother returned to El Salvador, and Jan when her mother died in a drive-by shooting. But it was Bobby who was Tyler's favorite foster sibling. A Macaulay Culkin look-alike, Bobby was a precocious, mischievous nine-year-old. His playfulness energized everyone around him, especially Tyler who was the target of most of his pranks.

Bobby and Tyler were fiercely loyal to one another. Their bond had a lot to do with their quick wits and adventurous natures. They could spend hours together studying, playing Monopoly, or just listening to Whitney Houston as she sang her latest hit. Laughter would often ring from the back porch when the foster siblings huddled together mulling over a science project or a music magazine.

There was only one glitch in this picture-perfect life. Things that Tyler loved or cherished frequently disappeared; she began to feel haunted, and others wondered at her losses.

Lonnie Jackson was the first to call attention to the fact that before a ribbon or toy of Tyler's went missing; one of the other Price children had received special attention. If Jan received praise for earning a good grade in school, a day or so later a favorite toy of Tyler's would come up missing. If Juan excelled in a track meet, a treasured pair of Tyler's earrings would vanish. If Patty's birthday was celebrated, a school project of Tyler's would disappear.

With time, the other children began to follow Lonnie's lead and question whether the loss of so many of Tyler's valued possessions was not an attempt on her part to gain sympathy and attention.

In December 1991, things came to a head. It was New Year's Eve. It was also Lonnie Jackson's eighteenth birthday. Everyone in the house was excited. Mother Price had been cooking since early morning, and the smells from the kitchen were an inspiration to the senses. Tyler's mouth watered just thinking about the smothered chicken, stuffed shrimp, rice, yams, collard greens, corn bread, black-eyed peas, and peach cobbler simmering in the double ovens.

"Baby doll, if I tell you one more time to go and play, I'm gonna lock you in the closet while the rest of us eat." Mother Price's smile belied her quip as Bobby dashed past her on his way to the back yard. Turning, she playfully snapped the dish towel, just missing the back of Bobby's pants as he scooted out the kitchen door.

"Tell Tyler I want her to slice the bananas for the banana pudding," Mother Price yelled as she turned to check the large pot on the stove. Reducing the heat under the fluffy rice, she sang softly, the hymn echoing in the room.

"Why should I feel discouraged? Why should the shadows come? Why should my heart be lonely, and long for heaven when home? When Jesus is my portion, a constant friend is he. His eye is on the sparrow, and I know he watches over me. His eye is on the sparrow, and I know he watches me. I sing because I'm happy. I sing because I'm free. His eye is on the sparrow, and I know he watches me. I know he watches me. His eye is on the sparrow. I know he watches; I know he watches me."

Her beautiful voice filled the kitchen, floated out the window and blanketed the two children sitting under the large jacaranda tree, filling them with a comforting sense of security. Their heads close together, their contrasting strains of blond-white and deep mahogany hair intertwined. Neither Tyler nor Bobby realized how fragile their world was.

Tyler would never forget her last day at the Price home. It was the Sunday morning after Lonnie's birthday party. Since the family had celebrated late into the evening, the children were slow getting out of bed. With Bud and Patty away at college, and Juan enlisted in the armed services, Lonnie was the eldest of the

Price children still at home and most of the care for the smaller children fell on him. The rule was that all of the children attended eight o'clock Sunday school. Usually, Lonnie would round up Bobby, Jan, and Tyler and walk them the half block to the church.

"Let's go everybody." The girls gathered around Lonnie, and when he noticed Bobby missing, he knocked on Bobby's door, but there was no answer. After a few minutes, Lonnie opened the door. Bobby was laying unconscious, facedown on his bedroom floor. His head was covered with blood.

Turning, Lonnie ran down the hall to the Prices' bedroom and banged on their door. Excited, he pushed the door, but it was locked.

"Bobby fell out of his bed. His head is bleeding," Lonnie shouted beginning to bang on the door, fists flying in rapid secession.

Within seconds, Mother Price flung open her door, and one of Lonnie's fists narrowly missed her face. The trembling teen grabbed Mother Price's hand and dragged her down the hallway. When they reached Bobby's room, Mother Price saw Bobby slumped on the floor.

Blood was pooled on the floor under his head. Mother Price flew into the room, dropped to her knees and gently nudged Bobby calling his name. There was no movement. Bobby's eyes were open, staring unseeing at the ceiling.

With fear lacing her voice, Mother Price turned to Lonnie. "Go downstairs and dial 911. Tell the operator that we have an unconscious child, with a head wound, and he's not breathing. Tell her to send the paramedics now! Go!" she cried.

Placing her hands in the middle of his chest above his stomach, she searched with her fingers for his breastbone and began to depress, count, and then breathe air into Bobby's mouth.

"One, two, three, four."

Bending over, Mother Price placed her mouth over Bobby's and blew air into his lungs. Pastor Price stood in the doorway, silently praying, wondering if tragedy would visit them again. He felt helpless, and for the first time he questioned his faith.

Minutes later, the siren of the ambulance screamed to a halt in front of the house. The paramedics raced past the children into Bobby's room.

Five minutes later, as Jan and Tyler huddled together, the paramedics rolled Bobby's deathly pale body out of the house. His head was bandaged, and an oxygen mask covered his nose and mouth. A tube of fluids dripped slowly into an intravenous needle that fed into Bobby's arm.

Tyler stood to the side terrified that her greatest fear had become a reality. Twisting her hands together, knuckles white, Tyler watched devastated as the ambulance sped away with Bobby. Grief and guilt overwhelmed her.

She loved Bobby with all of her heart, and Tyler would have gladly taken his place on the ambulance gurney. Yet, Lonnie's evil seeds had taken root, and she wondered if she unwittingly cursed the ones she loved. He said that there was something wrong with her. Just last week she had heard him talking to a neighbor.

"Bad luck follows her, especially when someone in the family has received praise or favor. We have a party, and her cat dies. Things are always disappearing around her, and people are always getting hurt. She is either sick in the head, hurting other people intentionally, or she is a walking curse. Either way, I am sick and tired of her bad luck."

Tyler shuddered. Maybe Lonnie was right. They had celebrated Lonnie's birthday the night before, and Bobby was hurt. Tyler was consumed with doubt; everything she loved she lost, and she wondered if her love did carry a curse! But she knew she would not hurt Bobby, and no matter what Lonnie said she knew she would never hurt anyone or anything she loved.

Jan was only eight, but sensing Tyler's distress, took her sister's hand in her own. "Bobby will be ok. I know it." Tyler squeezed Jan's hand affectionately, but the living room was thick with fear when Pastor Price left for church. Sunday school was cancelled, and Tyler and Jan remained at home with Lonnie. Mother Price followed the ambulance to the hospital, and as soon as the service was over, Pastor Price joined her. When the twosome returned home later that afternoon, a solemn air clung to them. The news was bleak. Bobby was in a coma. His head injury was critical.

Lunch was uncharacteristically quiet. Afterward, Lonnie took Jan for a walk. Tyler went to her room. She was lying on her bed, consumed with fear when the doorbell chimed loudly. Tyler wondered if someone had come with news of Bobby; she sat up swallowing her fear. The moments ticked slowly, and Tyler was consumed with worry. Feeling like a coward, she had just put on her shoes to join the others when Mother Price knocked softly and slid into the room.

Emma Price was tired and for the first time in her life overwhelmed by life's challenges. The men she had just spoken with were as ruthless as they were inflexible. They wanted Tyler, and they would not take no for an answer. She felt like she was butting her head against a brick wall, especially when the men presented court documents that gave them custody of Tyler. The Children Services' officer was quite implicit when Mother Price protested.

"Mrs. Price, I am here to enforce the court order and ensure a smooth transition of Tyler Miller into the hands of the Mueller attorney and her uncle. She is, after all, a foster child, not your adopted daughter. You must have known this could happen to any one of your foster children." The officer had been apologetic, but firm.

Of course, Emma knew the possibility existed, but it had never occurred to her that a child abandoned at birth by its mother would later be sought after by the same mother years later. She turned to the officer, stalling.

"Yes, but can't we wait until my husband returns? He'll be home in an hour or so." Her efforts to delay Tyler leaving were evident to the three men, and she could see clearly that the ploy would not work.

Simon Seymour observed Tyler as if she was a speck of bacterium on a microscopic slide. Mother Price flinched. She felt his scorn as clearly, as if he had spoken it aloud.

Simon sniffed. "No, I am sorry, but that is not possible." He looked around the homey room dismissively, and continued. "We really must get back before nightfall."

Mother Price's body deflated. She felt as if the air had been sucked from her lungs. It was shattering, that after twelve years, the woman who had given birth to Tyler had sought and gained custody of the child; and it was mind blowing to learn that one of the richest women in the world—Rachel Mueller—was Tyler's mother.

How would she tell the child?

Mother Price inhaled deeply, and then she sat down on the bed and took Tyler's hand in hers.

To the child, Mother Price looked worried and afraid. This was something Tyler could not remember ever seeing. Her foster mother hesitated; then spoke as she blew out an exhausted breath.

"There are people here to see you." Tyler's heart skipped a beat. She knew what everyone thought.

"Momma, I didn't do anything. I swear. I love Bobby." Tyler's grief was overwhelming. The pain in her voice was heart wrenching.

"Hush, child. I know." Gathering Tyler in her arms and gently rocking her back and forth, Mother Price whispered, "The people come from your mother. She is very ill. She wants to see you."

Tyler stared at Mother Price as if she were speaking a foreign language. Seconds, that felt like hours ticked by. When Tyler finally made sense of the words, she thought her foster mother was kidding.

"I don't have a mother...I mean, you're my mother." The preteen was confused. One moment she was looking at the horror of Bobby's accident, and the next she was being told that she would be going to see a woman she had not known existed, who had given birth and then abandoned her—a woman she knew nothing about.

Pushing away from Mother Price, Tyler looked in disbelief at the distressed woman. "What do you mean? What are you talking about?"

"Listen, child, we don't have a lot of time. I want you to know, if you ever need me, I'll be there for you. Papa Price and I will always love you."

"No. No. Not again. Please don't send me away. I love you. Bobby needs me. I didn't hurt Bobby. I didn't. I won't go. I won't!"

Tears streaming down the young girl's face, she shouted. "You're sending me away because you think I hurt Bobby. You all do. But, I didn't. I swear!" Tyler began to sob.

Mother Price hugged Tyler tightly. She loved all of her children. But this child was special. She meant as much to her as her natural children. "I don't think that, and I am not sending you away. You are my daughter. You know that. And I don't want you to, but the law says I have to let you go with them."

Tyler's pitiful weeping was breaking her foster mother's heart, but she knew if Tyler were going to survive what was ahead, she would have to draw from an inner strength. So Mother Price posed her foster daughter in an upright position and gently framed the girl's cheeks with her palms. She spoke low and confidentially.

"Your birth mother is a powerful lady. I don't know why she has taken so long to come for you, but I do know that she wants you badly. You listen to me. No one can ever take away who or what you are. That's in here." Mother Price pointed to her heart.

"Papa Price and I have given you all that you need. God will never abandon you. Do you hear me? God is your source. Not me. Not Papa. Not Bobby. Not Jan."

Shaking the girl gently to get her attention, the woman willed everything she had into her words to reach Tyler.

"Baby do you hear me? You have everything you need, and you take it with you wherever you go. I want you to make us proud."

Tyler's sobs quieted. Mother Price was reaching her and an innate survival streak, a characteristic handed down from one Mueller to another was taking root. It was the same stubborn trait that had saved her mother when she had been taken hostage. It was the same streak of stubbornness that had strengthened her great-grandmother when she was told that women should stay at home and raise families not run businesses. It was the same determination that sustained a long-ago African ancestor who had been stolen and sold into slavery.

Looking into Mother Price's loving face, Tyler quieted. Her back straightened and her shoulders squared. Slowly, the twelve-year-old nodded her understanding and smothered a sob.

Together they started packing Tyler's things. Jan tapped softly at the door. She had come to help. The younger girl's eyes were filled with tears as she looked at Tyler. She threw her arms around her sister and said, "I know it wasn't you. I don't care what Lonnie says. You wouldn't hurt Bobby."

Jan's heartfelt declaration meant everything to Tyler, and she was unable to speak past the lump in her throat. Her heart was in her eyes. She nodded her appreciation and forced a trembling smile.

Only one suitcase was needed, because her mother's people had indicated they would buy Tyler a new wardrobe. Her uncle had been explicit. "Pack only those things that have a sentimental value to the child."

Tyler walked beside Mother Price, her head held high. She was afraid, but no one would have known. She was leaving everything she knew and loved, but she promised herself with each step that she would come back. She would see Bobby again. She would never forget the Prices. Nor would she forget Mother Price's parting words, whispered into her ear with a hug.

"We love you."

Tyler sat quietly watching the two men seated across from her from lowered eyelids. She had on her best dress. Mother Price had insisted she wear it instead of jeans.

"You want to make a good impression. You don't want your mother thinking you're backward." Mother Price's voice was still fresh in her head.

Tyler had looked at her foster mother. Her eyes were bright with unshed tears, and she said solemnly, "If that woman thinks that just because of my clothes, then she'd be just like when Papa Price says, *more interested in the cover than the book.*"

Mother Price mentally shook her head. She was not surprised by Tyler's wisdom. She was going to miss this child who'd always brought sunshine with her into every room. It was a spirit that she had even as a small child. Older people referred to that type of perception as knowledge gained from "being here before." It was what they said about children with intuitive intelligence, and Mother Price often felt it was an apt description of Tyler.

The child had an abundance of common sense, but she could not help worrying about her foster daughter's future. As she watched the young girl walk away with the two men, she prayed Tyler would find love and acceptance in her new home.

The classic Bentley zipped through the traffic and entered the freeway, leaving behind everything Tyler loved and trusted. She watched forlornly as the landscape began to change. She was devastated, but was determined not to let the two men know. Outwardly, Tyler appeared calm and not by so much as a twitch did she reveal the turmoil tearing at her insides. She wanted to cry. She wanted to die.

Every few minutes the preteen peeked furtively at the two men. Her thick eyelashes fanned flawless cheeks, cloaking her tear-glossed violet eyes. The white men were as strange to her as Amazon tribesmen. Everything about them was different, from their button-down dark suits, a sharp contrast to the brightly color coordinated outfits Papa Price and his deacons wore to church every Sunday, to their reserved demeanor. The Old Spice scent, which accompanied Papa Price or his deacons when they walked into a room, was replaced with a foreign fragrance. The scent was not offensive, just different.

No one spoke. Tyler was fearful, yet fascinated. In the eight years she had been with the Prices, the United States of America was reduced to areas and recreational venues within South Central. The family had visited Disneyland a couple of times and Magic Mountain once, but the activities with the outside world had been limited to excursions no farther than Hollywood.

The men seated across from Tyler were white folks, and in her short memory white folks meant authority that was not always kind or sympathetic. White folks were police officers, social workers, psychiatrists, judges, and principals. They were rarely friends. So, in Tyler's mind, the men across from her were alien and not to be trusted.

Al Rosenthal watched the girl seated across from him and marveled at her poise. She was exotic, naturally tanned, and very different from the blonde, blue-eyed beauties of the country club communities of his peers. Tyler Miller was no ugly duckling waiting to blossom into a swan. At twelve, the woman-child was a stunning, long-legged siren, with beautiful eyes like Rachel. But they looked different on the child.

Tyler's African-American heritage mixed dramatically with her Jewish-Gentile genes, gifting the girl with a sultry, irresistible allure that was impossible to ignore. She was going to wreak havoc wherever she went, and Al silently thanked God for his advanced years.

Her uncle was also thinking about Tyler's heritage. But unlike Al, he despaired at his niece's biracial ethnicity. Sure the girl was striking, especially those eyes, if one went for the darker types. But how in God's name, thought Simon, would they explain a black heir to their friends and business associates?

It was really too much, he lamented. If Rachel's plan went into effect, there would be hell to pay when the girl took up the reins of power as the head of Mueller International. The prospect was years away, but inevitable.

For the first time in a very long while, Simon felt defeat. He had spent more than half his life in the service of Mueller International, and now he feared the future. They did not even know if the girl could handle the challenges ahead of her. She would have to be home schooled for a while, perhaps a year or two of lessons focused on social etiquette.

After that, Simon speculated, they would enroll her in Scarborough. Her academics were not a problem. Tyler's grades were excellent. But how, dammit, was he supposed to get past the fact that she was a Negro? With the clear-headed efficiency he was renowned for; Simon explored his options, and concluded, *they would lie.*

Thank God, he thought, *her deep tan could be attributed to Israeli blood.* And with time, he supposed she would lose the ghetto twang, so they hired a speech specialist to correct her ethnic tones and enunciation.

He was amazed. *How could Rachel have kept her child's birth secret for so many years?* Simon's head was swimming, and he began to sweat. Reaching into his chest pocket, he took out a monogrammed handkerchief and patted at his brow.

The girl was watching him, and Simon sent a thin-lipped automatic smile in her direction. He was not aware that his smile had not reached his eyes, but the intuitive girl facing him sensed the ice behind his gaze. A shiver racked her body. "Are you cold?" The question came from the older man. Tyler swung her eyes in Al's direction.

"No, sir." Her response was a purr.

Stunning. Simply, stunning, Al thought.

Tyler was preoccupied. She rehearsed several speeches for Ms. Mueller. She refused to think of anyone other than Mother Price as her mother. She had to convince the lady she belonged with her foster family.

Thirty-five minutes later, the Bentley exited Sunset. At first, Tyler was oblivious to the elegant houses lining the boulevard, but she slowly began to take notice as the car passed row after row of apartment-size mansions. It was a different world. Years later, she truly understood the extreme wealth it took to maintain these grand homes. But even at twelve, the astute girl realized that the forty minutes that separated South Central Los Angeles from the Bel Air Estates was as vast as the Indian Ocean.

The stately automobile pulled onto a cobblestoned private street. In the distance, Tyler watched as an armed guard exited a security kiosk, housed on a raised grassy island in the middle of the street.

The kiosk stood about three feet in front of a massive twelve-foot monogrammed iron gate and was connected to an equally tall stucco wall. Tyler did not know it then, but the nine-foot stucco wall enclosed the six-acre estate, effectively sealing the grounds and ensuring privacy.

The car rolled to a stop, and the armed guard nodded to the driver as he pressed the remote key at his waist. Instantly, the massive gate parted and swung open. The car lurched gently, and the Bentley rolled smoothly onto a cobbled stone driveway. Tyler noticed that neither of her companions acknowledged the guard and wondered if it bothered the man.

If she lived to be a hundred, Tyler would never forget her first sight of Mueller Landing. It was a vision of graciousness and wealth. On a hill, overlooking the grounds was a stately white house. Hundreds of exquisite French windows covered the first and second floors, and a halo of sun reflected off the roof. Staring in wonder, it seemed a fairy tale confection to the awed youth.

On both sides of the pathway, perfectly manicured hedges flowed into lush velvet lawns. Tyler felt like Dorothy on the yellow brick road as the car ascended the stone driveway. It still had not registered that this would be her permanent home, and she viewed her surroundings like a visitor. But nothing in her life experience prepared her for the house at the top of the hill. It was magnificent with two huge Roman column pillars framing the double oak doors; the house reminded her of paintings she had seen of antebellum mansions in the old South.

The car rolled to a stop, and the driver rushed to open the doors. Simon got out first, and offered Tyler his hand, assisting her as she placed her foot on the raised step under the passenger door. It was a surreal moment. The roof of the palatial house loomed high above their heads, and Tyler felt dwarfed by its size. Intimidated, but unwilling to show it, she squared her small shoulders and bravely climbed the steps.

Magically, the massive oak doors opened. There had been no need to use the heavy gold knocker. An automatic sensor had sprung the doors, and an Asian in a white jacket stood just inside the marble foyer. The room was huge, towering two stories high. In the center, a beautiful Swarovski chandelier hung regally with thousands of crystal teardrops dangling overhead.

Ornately framed family portraits hung on cream and white walls, and several Ming Dynasty vases were arranged throughout the luxurious entrance hall. In the middle of the room, a grand staircase soared majestically to a balcony leading off into twin-sided suites. Lining the second-story walls were priceless Van Gogh, Monet, Picasso, and Basquiat paintings. The room was tastefully ostentatious, and Tyler's mouth opened slightly in awe.

"Good afternoon, Lee. Will you let Ms. Mueller know we've arrived?" Simon's cultured voice sounded hushed in the huge room.

"Yes, sir. I will. May I take those for you?" The butler reached for their briefcases.

"Ms. Mueller asked me to show you into the blue room. May I get you gentlemen and the young lady some refreshments?"

"Would you like something, Tyler?" Al Rosenthal asked politely.

Tyler found it difficult to answer. "No. Thank you." She had not eaten her dinner, but she had lost her appetite after Bobby's accident. Hunger was the last thing on her mind.

"Just water, please. *Pellegrino*, Lee," Al said dismissively placing his hand on Tyler's shoulder, and directing her toward a large room on the west side of the foyer. The three seated themselves comfortably in the airy room.

Several minutes later, a frail-looking woman in a motorized wheel chair swung into the room. Tyler's first thought was that their eyes matched. Although not as bright, Rachel's pale blue-purple eyes mirrored her daughter's, as did the shape of their faces. There was no doubt they were closely related.

Rachel carefully studied her daughter and recognized the part of Tyler that belonged to Karl. She had his athletic frame, square shoulders, long neck, and, although femininely curved, his long limbs. Like Karl, Tyler had an intrinsic sexuality that was utterly captivating. She was gorgeous, but seemingly unaware of her own beauty and appeal. Rachel's lips parted in a soft smile, and she thanked God that her daughter had been conceived before her abduction—before she knew what a monster Karl was.

In wonderment, she realized she did not hate her daughter in spite of Karl's treachery, and with that recognition, a heavy weight was lifted from Rachel's shoulders. She could do this.

She blinked back unshed tears, realizing she could love her daughter. It was a thought she had never entertained until that moment. Tolerate. Yes. Instruct. Definitely! Love, that was an entirely new concept that she had not believed possible.

Looking across the sofa table, she felt a bond with the slender child she found to be strikingly beautiful, who was perched on the edge of the sofa. Rachel coughed, clearing her throat.

Tyler observed the woman who was her mother with a watchful eye. She was curious about Rachel—and dispassionately scrutinized the woman who had abandoned her. She desperately wanted to know the why of it, but was too polite to ask the question. So it lingered in the air between them—unanswered.

"Please come here." Rachel's voice was cultured and laced with a charm that thwarted refusal. A hint of steel resonated in the request, an undeniable tenor that said, *I have the right to command.*

Tyler felt her mother's comfort with authority, but if there was one quality she had in abundance, it was courage. Straightening her shoulders, her mind's ear heard Mother Price's encouragement, "Go on, honey. Go see what the lady wants. Stand tall now."

Tyler pushed off the sofa and walked toward the stranger who was her mother. She stopped two feet in front of the chair. Her arms were straight at her side. Her wet palms were the only sign of her nervousness, and she concealed them in the curve of her dress. She had not planned on making the speech in front of an audience, but as Pastor Price always said, "When facing an unwanted chore or difficult situation, step up to the plate no matter how fast the hardball is thrown."

Rachel forestalled her, speaking first.

"I understand your name is Tyler." Rachel spoke breathlessly and watched Tyler nod yes. These days it was hard to breathe air into her ravaged lungs, and she was sorry that the first meeting with her daughter put her at such a disadvantage. Not since her days with Karl had she felt so helpless; Rachel hated the debilitating illness more than anything.

She's afraid, but hides it well, Rachel thought.

Mother and child were silent, awkward in this their first meeting. Rachel was desperate to gain, if not Tyler's love, her respect. All Tyler wanted was to go back home.

Holding the child's eyes in a soul-searching gaze, Rachel extended her hand, and Tyler hesitated only a second before taking it. It was a beginning, and Rachel's wistful smile acknowledged the moment. *I have so much to share, and so little time to do it in,* she thought.

Tyler found Rachel's hand icy cold in spite of the warmth of the afternoon. Then her mother's hand trembled slightly, and Tyler swallowed her speech, instantly aware of the frailty of the chalky woman who stared up at her with replica eyes.

Compassion, not pity, flowed from the child. Tyler's early years spent in the hospital ward with critically ill children had prepared her well for this moment. The room was electric with undercurrents of unanswered questions as the woman and girl observed each other, unsure as to how to proceed.

Neither Al nor Simon had spoken since the had entered the room, but now both men rushed to say their good-byes. "If there is nothing else you want, I'll be going," Simon said formally.

Al chimed in before Simon had completed the sentence. "Yes. Well, I guess I will see you both tomorrow."

Rachel sent the men a silent thank-you.

French windows ran the length of the room. Rachel turned her chair toward the windows, pressed a remote button on her arm, and the doors swung opened. "Would you like to go into the garden with me? It is very pleasant outside." It was a statement, not a question.

The garden was beautiful, an enclosed patio of lush tropical plants with a stone cascading-water fountain and a four-foot musical chime nestled high above in the middle of a twelve-foot eucalyptus tree. As they moved through the doors, a melodic tinkle of chimes floated on the breeze and mingled with the sounds of flowing water that was delightful in the late afternoon quiet. Tyler's mouth opened in wonder at the flora splendor. It was like nothing she had ever seen before, and as long as she lived, she would associate garden splendor with her mother.

The first meeting was awkward, but with time, Tyler came to respect her mother and her Mueller heritage. Rachel gradually introduced the family history. She spoke about Great-Grandmother Beatrice and the challenge she had starting the family business. She talked about Tyler's grandfather and how he had grown the business into one of the largest cosmetics companies in the world.

Over the months, Rachel shared everything she thought vital to Tyler's survival in the business world and the family. One evening she even talked about the estranged relationship she had with Mercedes. Tyler was lying on Rachel's bed, her head close to her mother's face, listening as Rachel spoke just above a whisper.

"You want to be careful of your grandmother," Rachel's breath expelled from her clogged lungs. She paused, her face grimacing in pain as she struggled to drag the oxygen-rich air through the thin tubes lodged in her nose.

"She does not look at life the way we do. She is not of the blood. Never trust her. Never confide in her, and above all, never, ever consult her about business."

Rachel was quiet for a moment, lost in thought, reliving the past. "There was a time, long ago, when I needed your grandmother's help desperately. She failed me." Tyler's mother coughed, her face contorted in pain. "Ask Nanny about it if you feel the need for details."

Rachel swallowed and continued in visible agony. "Your Uncle Simon is an ally in the boardroom." Shaking her head slowly, she warned. "Do not let him handle your finances. I have put safeguards in place to protect you from any pilfering of your inheritance—while you are a minor." Rachel's voice faded.

In the months that Tyler had been with her mother, the bed had become Rachel's world, and she rarely left it. She was speaking to her daughter clandestinely, and had become agitated and breathless. The crippling pain—a nagging companion—had returned with renewed vigor, and it was difficult for her to focus. She had to tell Tyler the things only she knew; things only she could reveal.

Rachel knew that her end was near, and she felt a critical urgency to safeguard her daughter's survival. She recalled her father's last months. He must have felt the same sense of urgency, but at least his desire to protect her had not been compounded by the remorse and regret she felt for not sharing in Tyler's childhood.

Rachel acknowledged that in spite of her absence from Tyler's life, she really was a wonderful human being. Rachel wanted to thank God for that—because she could have turned out to be like Karl. *What a nightmare that would have been. Yes, by the God of my Zankli ancestors*, she thought, *I am grateful. But how do I thank a God I don't believe in?* Realizing she had little time for regrets, she resumed speaking.

"There is a five-man team who will manage your business finances, and to keep them honest, I have asked Al Rosenthal to review their decisions quarterly. For every proven infraction one of the team members identifies, he will be awarded $100,000. For every year he stays on the team, he will be awarded $1,000,000. That will keep them honest and motivated to disclose any wrongdoing."

Rachel gave her daughter a weak smile before continuing softly, "Al will report to the three banking institutions where your personal trust and business accounts are held. Nanny will provide all the information you need. You can trust her with your life. Never forget that. She is family, the only mother I've ever known."

Tyler smiled. She knew all about substitute mothers. She thought of Sophie Tyler and Mother Price.

Nanny Peters, who had been standing quietly on the opposite side of the bed, leaned forward releasing the IV clip, starting the morphine drops. Rachel continued to talk, but with each drip, her speech became a whispered slur.

"There are two offshore accounts." Rachel reached under her pillow, and slid a thick legal packet toward Tyler. The emaciated woman struggled to remain conscious, her eyes fluttering as she licked her dry lips. If only she had more time, but the humming against the walls of her mind were persistent, unrelenting drumbeats that called to her. Rachel struggled and concentrated—a momentary triumph over the vibrating sounds.

"Nanny will review...papers...with you...later." Each word was spoken separately, as if it was a sentence by itself, and Rachel's voice was soft, so soft that Tyler could barely hear her.

Nanny Peters placed a cool palm on her charge's cheek, and crooned, "Go to sleep, darling, don't worry, Nanny will take care of everything."

Her eyes glued lovingly on Rachel's pain-ravaged face, the loyal nurse spoke to Tyler in a hushed voice. "Please pass me the moisturizer. I want to put it on her lips."

Unchecked, tears rolled down the surprisingly smooth and youthful cheeks of the sixty-eight-year-old nanny. She had never remarried, nor had another child to replace her daughter. Yet, one could not doubt that she was losing yet another beloved child, if not of her body, then of her soul. It was breaking her heart and, if not for Tyler, she doubted she would survive the pain.

During the next week, they turned the blue salon into a hospital ward. Doctors and nurses came and went in a hushed fashion, and Rachel spent most of the time in a drugged sleep. When she was awake she was lucid, but close to the end, she became delirious.

It had become Tyler's habit to keep vigil in the alcove of the seven-foot window, where she sat on thick pillows, her knees bent and her feet tucked close into her body. She was dozing, with her head resting lightly on her thighs, her arms wrapped snuggly around her calves.

Her mother began to mumble and thrash about. Most of what she said, Tyler could not understand. But she knew that in Rachel's delirium someone was making her do things against her will. "No, I can't. It hurts." Rachel whispered in a horror-filled voice, whimpering her pain and humiliation.

The scenario had played out many times, and Tyler assumed that in her mother's nightmare it was Karl and his people causing her pain. Often, Rachel would scream and curse Tyler's father, and at other times, she would profess her love to him heartbreakingly.

"I love you, Karl, you are my other half. We are one, I know we are...the hum, can't you hear it?" Rachel lifted her head and tilted it to the side. "My love, listen. *Tuk tultoo vii m tultoo tuki peke.*" The foreign words rolled off Rachel's tongue as easily as her given name, musically, and her face would flush with an iridescent glow.

Then there were times Rachel would gag, as if she was being strangled. She would make choking sounds, begging hoarsely, "Not again, Karl. Please, not again."

At these times, Tyler would go to her mother and place a cool towel on her head and talk soothingly, telling her it was ok. She had seen Nanny Peters do the same thing, and it was effective when her mother was restless.

One evening near the end, Rachel grunted and flinched, her entire body shifting as if she had been hit. Then her eyes popped open. She looked around the room, and when she found Tyler, she motioned her to her side.

As if she was continuing a conversation that they had been having together, Rachel squeezed her daughter's hand. "Rely on Nanny Peters. If you ever have a problem, go to her. Trust no one else. She will know what to do."

Rachel supported herself on her elbow, struggling, trying to sit up. "Look in the bottom drawer of my dresser. Over there." Pointing to a large dresser on the opposite side of the room, Rachel waved her hands anxiously, when Tyler pulled the drawer open. "Bring the jeweled box to me."

At first, Tyler did not know what her mother wanted. The drawer was stuffed full of beautifully colored, exotic silk scarves in four individual stacks. She did not see a jewelry box.

She carefully lifted one stack out of the drawer, and placed it on the floor. She still did not see the box and continued removing the piles from the dresser. When she lifted the third pile, she saw a small antique wooden chest. It was beautiful with exquisite inlayed carvings of flying angels circling the base. Tiny pearls formed the angel halos, and other precious stones—rubies, emeralds, and diamonds—glittered like jeweled Christmas lights on an exotic face carved in the center of the lid.

Rachel became animated as Tyler removed the chest from the drawer. She smiled when Tyler placed it on the pillow next to her head. "Your grandfather gave me this box when I was about your age. His mother gave it to him. It has been in our family for a very long time, passed from one Mueller heir to another for over two hundred and fifty years."

Cradling the box lovingly, Rachel held it close for several seconds and then passed the treasured antique to Tyler. "It's yours now. This is your history, your heritage. In time, all will be revealed. You are a *Chosen*, ...the descendent of Zankli."

"What do you mean...chosen?"

Rachel shook her head. "Your father...like... me... Not enough time...sorry, so sorry...ask Nanny."

Sinking back into a reclining position, her head flattened against the pillow. Rachel looked at Tyler, raised her paper-thin hand and touched her cheek. "I love you. I always have. I was just so hurt, confused, and angry. Life seemed unfair at the time. Forgive me, my love..!"

The words hung in the room. Tyler stared at her mother thinking, *there is nothing to forgive.* Sadness overwhelmed her. Her mother was suffering so.

Taking Rachel's hand with a maturity beyond her years, Tyler looked at her and repeated something that Pastor Price had said in a long ago sermon, "Forgiving starts within." Uttered in a strangled tone, Tyler laid her head on the pillow beside her mother and gazed into her eyes, "I forgive you, Mother. Honest. Please, please forgive yourself."

Rachel raised her head and tilted it to the side, her eyes sparked with excitement. "Listen. Can you hear the song? It's music from your father. He has come for me..."

Tyler watched her mother, confused. She had never heard her speak of Karl fondly, just the opposite. He had been unkind to her, even cruel by all accounts, so Tyler was baffled why Rachel would be joyful that Karl had come for her in death.

It was mind-boggling, and the twelve-year-old was mystified by the music—for she heard it too. The strange hum resonated in the room, vibrating throughout Tyler's body as her mother floated inches above the bed. Tyler shivered, and knew she was witnessing the mysterious power of the Zankli.

There was a huge turnout for the funeral. Some of the old-timers believed it was even larger than Adam Mueller's services. All the corporate princes of Europe attended as well as financial giants from Asia, Africa, and the Middle East.

Pacific Palisades

1992

The following two years, Tyler was homeschooled. Her courses were designed for one purpose, and one purpose alone, to prepare her for entry into "proper society." As Mercedes adamantly told her son, "The girl is a heathen, what do you expect? But we must make do—a pickaninny and a Jew, who would have thought it. Well, she can't be allowed to disgrace us. She must not expose the family by revealing who and what she really is. My, God, we'd never live down the scandal."

Mercedes gave a languishing sigh and ended with a loud sniff as if she smelled something odious. "Simon, my boy, I know you will take care of it."

Thus, Tyler's metamorphosis began. Her classes were rigorous. She would begin at seven, have lunch, and continue with her lessons until five in the evening, then have her evening meal. After dinner, Tyler had tennis, followed by three hours of academic review. Exhausted, she would fall into bed around midnight, and begin the entire routine all over again the next morning.

The one bright spot in her weekly regimen was the weekends. Tyler and Nanny Peters would roam like gypsies, as far south as Tijuana, and as far north as San Francisco. They toured and visited California's Historic Missions, the San Diego Zoo, and Yosemite. To get to their destinations, they would fly *the friendly skies,* ride the railways, or drive in Nanny's sturdy Volvo.

Often, they included the two youngest Price children—Bobby and Jan—as well as her adopted Seymour cousins. Nanny Peters said they looked like a nomadic tribe, but the robust senior loved it. Tyler treasured it because it was her only interaction with other children.

Every Sunday Tyler attended the eleven o'clock service at Mt. Sinai Baptist Church with Nanny. After church, they joined the Price family for supper, with the unspoken agreement that they would keep their weekend outings a secret from Tyler's uncle.

The only discord to their Sunday visits was Lonnie. Tyler knew that he resented their presence. His contempt for Tyler was thinly veiled, and one Sunday as the family sat around the table enjoying dinner, Lonnie found it impossible to hide his resentment.

She's such a fake, a little lying snake. I could squash her like a roach under the heel of my shoe. He looked up and caught Tyler's eye.

Tyler froze. She felt an evil chill as Lonnie devoured her with his eyes.

She wondered what she had ever done to earn his deep hatred, for there was no way she could deny the black rage reflected in his eyes. She returned his stare, wanting him to turn away first. He won. Tyler dropped her eyes to her plate, hating her cowardice, not because she was afraid of Lonnie, but because she hated to see the malice in his eyes. No matter how hateful he was to her, she still loved him, and she did not want to face the reality of his revulsion.

Bud laughed at something Juan said, and Tyler's eyes flew to his face desperately needing a distraction from Lonnie's glare. Her oldest brother had completed his tour of service in the U.S. Marines and had been accepted into a seminary for Baptist preachers. It was a great honor, and the table rang with laughter as the siblings teased Bud.

"Are you sure those guys know what they were doing? Maybe I should give them a call and confirm your admission. We don't want you to be turned away at the gate. What do you think, Papa Price?" Juan asked tongue in cheek, and everyone laughed at his silliness.

Lonnie devoured Tyler with bile-glazed eyes. She was animated, giggling in concert with the others as Patty quizzed Bud about his girlfriend April, asking him what they did on their long drives. Bud began to sputter, and the entire table hooted.

Tyler encountered Lonnie's venomous glare once again, and the joy drained from her body. The small square of candied yam on the end of her fork was arrested midair, her hand trembled, and the flatware fell to the floor with a noisy clatter.

Nanny Peters looked at Tyler inquiringly, noting her distress and took her charge's hand in her own. She sensed something was deathly wrong, and her eyes circled the table and when they landed on Lonnie, her mouth tightened. The boy was eyeing Tyler with thinly veiled hatred...his glare fearsome, and she felt a jolt of recognition.

Anomaly. Anomaly. The age old chant echoed in her mind. *Tibooqee ve ti booqee. The Anomaly, and the deliverer of death.*

Nanny felt Tyler's hand tremble and she exploded with fury.

"What are you looking at?" The question hung in the air. The entire table turned and looked in unison at Nanny Peters then followed her steely gaze to Lonnie. He was exposed. Taken by surprise, the hatred directed at Tyler was transparent—clearly written on his face, and everyone at the table was shocked by the depth of his rage, when he lashed back.

"I'm looking at the bitch sitting beside you. But I won't have to look at her lying face another Sunday. I'm leaving too! Why don't you celebrate that?" Lonnie's voice was low and sinister.

"Boy, what's gotten into you? You don't talk like that in this house, especially at the Lord's table and in the presence of your mother and sisters. I won't have it," Pastor Price said quietly, but there was steel in his voice. "Sit down."

"Fuck you." Everyone at the table gasped at the insult to the revered head of the family. Bud rose from his chair, but his father waved him back down. Mother Price was speechless as Lonnie's eyes lingered on her, then made a slow meaningful tour of the table taking everyone in and forcedly announced.

"If I never see any of you again, it will be too soon." He pushed back from the table. His chair fell and hit the floor with an ominous bang. He strolled from the room purposefully, his back rod straight—as if he had just shed a huge burden.

Everyone at the table watched, their mouths agape. Nanny muttered under her breath, "That boy's got serious problems."

Juan whispered, "Amen to that!" Jan and Bobby snickered.

Pastor Price bowed his head, motioning for the others to follow.

"Let us pray."

Every three months Tyler would take a vacation outside the United States. The first journey was to Israel, where Tyler had a month long stay with an affluent businessman and his family. Moshe Hoffman was Tyler's concocted uncle, a relative of an invented and deceased father that explained her exotic looks.

Nanny Peters was Tyler's trusted companion on all of the trips, and along the way, the orphaned teen came to think of the older woman as a treasured grandmother. They were kindred spirits—gypsies—that loved exotic food, people, and places. They were in heaven whether in Kenya, France, Istanbul, Brazil, or Jamaica. The excursions introduced Tyler to the world at large, not through books and videos, but through actual experience. She learned Yiddish and Hebrew, and added them to her satchel of other languages.

When Tyler joined the Mueller family, she was already fluent in French and Spanish—and during the two years of home schooling, she learned Japanese. She also received instruction in ballroom dancing, classical music, and history of some of the leading families in America. In time, Tyler knew as much about the family background of her fellow students as they did themselves.

Hancock Park

Los Angeles ~ 1994

Scarborough Academy was an all girl's boarding school located in Hancock Park—an *old money* section of Los Angeles—and had a pedigree that went back to the 1890s. Its traditions were as entrenched as the United States Constitution, and the girls who attended the Academy came from some of the oldest, most respected families in the nation. Names like Vanderbilt, Ford, Doheny, Hearst, Rockefeller, Kennedy, Hilton, DuPont, and Bush dotted the registration. The lineage was impressive, and school graduates went on to attend prestigious colleges like Wellesley, Vassar, and Rutgers.

The girls of Scarborough were entitled and aware that their bloodlines guaranteed them a privileged place in society. They were clannish, spoiled, pampered, and the overindulged daughters of the ultrarich. Courted by the elite couture houses of Europe, they were frequently stalked by the paparazzi for their *over-the-top* and shocking escapades. But for the most part, they flew under the public radar.

After two years of homeschooling, Tyler was dying to interact with girls her own age, and she was starved for academic stimulation. However, her first day at the academy provided a totally different and unforgettable lesson—not in academics or socialization—but in the power of money.

The tutorial session was taught by Scarborough's headmistress, Katherine Burns. The woman groveled, and at one point Tyler feared that Ms. Burns would *genuflect* before kissing her uncle's hand in homage. It was embarrassing, and Tyler found herself staring at the polished asphalt tile floors to avoid Ms. Burns' undignified simpering.

She knew the Muellers were important benefactors of the school, having built an entire wing and a library in 1913 and 1958, respectively, named in honor of mother and son, Beatrice and Adam Mueller. Rachel Mueller's Will sweeten the pot even more. She bequeathed a $25,000,000 endowment to Scarborough for *full academic scholarships to be awarded annually to four disadvantaged girls* –of African, African-American, Hispanic, Native American, or Asian descent.

An additional $5,000,000 was allocated annually to fund the Mueller Cultural Studies Program in Racial Tolerance. As *the* Mueller heir, Tyler would one day preside over the endowment. Headmistress Burns never forgot Tyler's importance to the school and she never let anyone else at the academy forget either.

The four years at Scarborough passed quickly. True to form, Tyler won friends to her side—early on winning the respect of her instructors and the admiration of fellow students. Tyler was a social magnet, kind by nature, with an uncanny ability to make everyone around her feel good about themselves. She was supportive, did not gossip, and could be counted on to take the high road in disputes.

Kelly Mallory was the only detractor, a critic, she was the bane of Tyler's existence her first year at Scarborough. Blonde and blue eyed, she personified Westside sophistication and chic. She was always dressed in the latest fashion, and was always...always pursued by the most popular Westside hunks. Before Tyler's arrival, Kelly had been the uncontested campus *femme fatale*. She was a smart, hard-working, overachiever who didn't take seconds—or second place—well.

Kelly resented Tyler from the very beginning, recognizing in the raven-haired beauty a rival in looks and intelligence. As time went on, and Kelly watched the ascension of Tyler's popularity, she jealously looked for ways to undermine the new comer, often resorting to snide remarks and lies. At one point, Kelly spread a rumor that she had seen Tyler using a cheat sheet during a biology test. The lie was squashed, when Tyler requested and *aced* a second oral exam administered by her biology instructor.

For the most part, Tyler ignored Kelly, labeling her pettiness harmless in comparison to the venom of Lonnie, but everything erupted when Jan joined Tyler at Scarborough.

Jan was one of the recipients of the 1995 Rachel Mueller Scholarship for Cultural Diversity. There were three other scholarship winners: Isabel Martinez, Hazel Bantu, and Brandy Big-Horn. Tyler was friendly with all of the girls, but her preference for Jan was evident from the beginning. No one at Scarborough knew that there friendship reflected a deeper bond.

Tyler was protective of Jan, making sure that she was not slighted or ostracized by fellow students and she spent as much time in Jan's company as possible. They often studied together, and Kelly, observing them, was puzzled by their closeness. For the life of her, she could not figure out what the two girls had in common.

Physically, they were as different as night and day. Literally—one a deep chocolate and the other smooth cream—and, as far as Kelly was concerned, they were cultural mismatches. She thought their friendship was like mixing oil with water and wondered what Tyler, heir to over sixty billion dollars, saw in Jan.

Kelly even considered they were lesbians. This was an open secret for several girls, and there had even been a scandal the previous year when the hockey coach had been caught in bed with a student. But in no way did Tyler and Jan act like lovers—more like close friends or even sisters. So she dismissed the idea.

It was a mystery, and Kelly hated unsolved mysteries. By nature curious, she was dying to unravel the puzzle. Several months after Jan was admitted to Scarborough, Kelly got her chance. As a volunteer in the admissions office, she had access to the student files. Normally, there were two admissions clerks in the office, Ms. Weekly and Mrs. Dugan. But this day, Ms. Weekly had gone home early. As soon as Ms. Dugan had taken her break, Kelly darted over to the file cabinet, opened the drawer, located Jan's file, and peeked inside.

Her mouth fell open. Jan was a foster child, her mother was deceased, and her father was a convicted sex offender. Kelly's hand rose and covered the center of her chest in shock. She read on in amazement. He had sexually abused his stepdaughter—Jan's older half-sister. According to the file, he had been released two years earlier and was currently residing in Los Angeles. She read on, and the more she learned, the more shocked she became. She paused and focused on one sentence that warned Scarborough administrators.

Barrows is dangerous, and on no account be allowed contact with his daughter.

"Jan's father is a child molester!"

The tips of Kelly's tapered fingers covered her rounded mouth. The statement has slipped from her mouth, and Kelly furtively looked over her shoulder to make sure no one overheard her. Returning to the file, her eyes ran down the page, scanning the information quickly before she returned the document to the cabinet.

When Ms. Dugan returned, Kelly was sitting behind the volunteer desk dutifully tallying the student attendance log for Ms. Avery's English class. But her mind was racing. She knew if she exposed Jan, she would discredit Tyler and hurt her personally.

"Got yah!" Kelly was ecstatic and could not contain her glee.

"Pardon me?" Mrs. Dugan's inquired turning toward Kelly.

"Oh, I'm sorry, Mrs. Dugan, I just removed a hangnail from my finger. It was really bothersome." Kelly smiled to herself… yeah…I'll soon be rid of a real vexing problem.

Kelly Mallory was not malicious by nature. She was simply unaccustomed to coming in second. She did not really want to hurt Jan or Tyler. She only wanted to diminish some of Tyler's influence—bring her down a notch. Her plan was simple. She would contact Jan's father and let him know his daughter was attending Scarborough.

It was not hard for Kelly to locate Harry Barrows. He was listed on the Internet with other sex offenders residing in the State of California. It was even easier to send him an anonymous letter with Jan's address, and then sit back and await the outcome.

But nothing went as planned. It was more than a year later when Jan's father showed up at the school. By that time, Kelly and Tyler had mended their fences in a most unusual way.

Although Kelly had taken swimming lessons since she was a toddler, she could not swim. For some unknown reason swimming eluded her, and she envied Tyler's swimming skills. The afternoon of the accident Kelly had watched the Mueller heir execute a perfect dive, once again, to the oohs and ahhas of fellow classmates.

Kelly stood thinking, *anything she can do, I can do better. What the heck?*

With a determined stride, the blonde beauty marched to the diving board, scrambled up the ladder, walked out to the edge and froze.

Fear—heart-stopping terror—immobilized her brain and then her body. She could not move...she could not think, and stubborn pride would carry her no further. Mouth agape, trembling, Kelly began to retrace her steps on wobbly legs when her feet became tangled and she tripped. She teetered like a gymnast on the diving board, arms flailing frantically.

Kelly reached into empty air, one leg extended in an attempt to gain balance. It was hopeless. She felt the air at her back as she plummeted into the water. It felt like she had hit a brick wall. That was the last conscious thought she had until she looked up into a familiar set of violet eyes.

Tyler looked down into her schoolmate's face. She had never been so afraid in her life. When she had fished Kelly out of the pool, and felt for her pulse, there was none. Kelly's chest was motionless.

Tyler yelled for someone to call 911, and began applying CPR. Praying that she did not screw up the techniques she had learned in the first aid class, Tyler tilted Kelly's chin back, and began by counting and blowing into the unconscious girl's mouth. Four minutes later, when Tyler felt she could not possibly go on, Kelly coughed and spit water from her mouth.

Later that evening, Kelly knocked on Tyler's door. All of Scarborough's dorm suites were private, but Kelly was not surprised when Jan opened the door. The girls were obviously studying. Tyler was seated in the middle of the room, on the floor with her knees crossed Indian style, surrounded by books and papers. She had a pencil in her mouth, and she was biting on the eraser deep in thought. Tyler and Jan were dissecting a math equation.

"Oh, I'm sorry." Kelly murmured under her breath reeking with humility. "I can come back later."

"No. Please, come in." Tyler blinked, cleared her vision and focused on Kelly.

"How are you feeling?" Tyler's sincere concern was transparent, and Kelly felt deep shame.

"I just wanted to thank you. The paramedics told me that I might have died if I hadn't received immediate CPR."

Tears sparkled in Kelly's eyes. You are the only one who tried to help, even Ms. Reilly..." Kelly choked up as tears spilled from the corners of her eyes and rolled down her cheeks. "Ms. Reilly..." Kelly smiled through her tears thinking of *wily Ms. Reilly*, the student's affectionate name for their swim coach... "was dumbstruck. The girls told me how quick you were...how you didn't hesitate to help."

"No problemo," said Tyler, using Juan's favorite one-liner.

More tears rolled down Kelly's cheek unchecked. "I'm so ashamed of the way I've treated you both." Kelly looked down at Tyler and back up at Jan. Her eyes fell to the floor. "I just wanted you to know."

Tyler's soft heart contracted, and she stood up and closed the distance between them. She took Kelly in her arms, and she began to cry. Soon all three girls were sobbing, until Jan, who had gotten up and wrapped her arms around Kelly and Tyler, drew back.

"If we keep this up, we won't need a pool for swimming lessons." Jan's wisecrack lightened the moment giving them a sense of camaraderie. They looked at each other sheepishly, smiling through their tears then burst out laughing.

"I've been taking swimming lessons since I was five, with no luck. I guess I am just inept when it comes to water sports." Kelly said cheekily.

"No, you are not! I refuse to believe someone as graceful as you can't swim, and I plan to prove it to you starting tomorrow." True to her word, Tyler helped Kelly learn to swim.

And that, so to speak, was that. Tyler, Jan, and Kelly became a threesome—the best of friends. Kelly even forgot her letter to Harry Bellows, that is, until the day he showed up at Scarborough demanding to see his daughter and was unceremoniously carted off to jail.

Sudan East Africa

November 23, 2001—4:30 a.m.

It was dark, pitch black, and misty. The predawn fog clung to the ground, providing a thick grey protective blanket, effectively cloaking the night creatures scurrying in the underbrush.

The twenty-man squad silently inched down the encampment. Their night goggles allowed them to observe the movement below with the precision of daylight. The camp was well guarded. There were a dozen men posted in a spiraled pattern on the grounds, and two sentinel guards stood in front of a small wire, chicken-coop shed. The back of the coop butted up against a solid rock wall, which ascended fifty feet high to a killer cliff. The steep embankment was a natural barrier to unwelcome intruders. On the overhanging stoop, another guard scanned the thick brush below.

Andre caught the eye of the man on his right flank and motioned for him to fan out to the left. He began to inch on his belly toward the hut, with two of his men following at his heels. Pausing, Andre dipped his head, flipping a small scope forward. The antenna picked up the body heat of three people in the hut, although Andre had no need for the electronic device. Like radar, he had connected with the prisoners telepathically several miles out from the encampment. The high level of pain that the prisoners were emitting was a navigational magnet to Andre's empathic perceptions, and he was locked in on their location with precise accuracy.

"Now!"

Andre's forceful whisper into his headphone blended in with the night sounds. He waved his men forward, and gave the signal for one to remain behind. Pointing to his eyes, Andre motioned for the two men at his heels to look up toward the cliff. The guard was no longer at his post on the overhang.

Andre's finger hugged the trigger of his repeat riffle. Looking back over his shoulder, he held his other hand aloft, his mouth counting silently as his index and middle fingers flashed one at a time against the moon lit sky. When his ring finger pointed toward the sky, the encampment burst into rapid gunfire. Bright, explosive lights flashed repeatedly and the camp erupted into terrified screams that echoed with the ricocheting bullets.

November 23, 2001

8 p.m.

The two men smoked in silence. The hiss of the flames, at the end of the hand rolled cigarette, was the only sound in the sparsely furnished room. The ceiling fan creaked as the blades stroked the air above the table. The cool breeze spread a pungent aroma of marijuana in the small quarters.

Andre inhaled deeply, releasing the soothing herb through his teeth with practiced finesse. His muscular long limbs were extended under the table. He leaned back and balanced the chair on it legs at a comfortable angle. He felt good. Another mission completed successfully without injury to one of his men or the captives. He took another long drag and exhaled a long hiss between his teeth of pure satisfaction. The client had expressed delight with a six-figure bonus. Life was good.

He inhaled again, held his breath, and looked at the man seated across the table from him. Juan Lara was one of his best men. Almost eight years younger than Andre, he was the kind of man you wanted at your side in a tight situation.

Juan was calm in the most dangerous circumstances, causing some to remark that he had ice water in his veins. But Andre knew that Juan was just a born warrior. He had the stuff of a Spartan solider of old. Andre's mouth tilted in a philosophical smile, he shook his head with regret.

"I'm sorry you're leaving." There was no doubt about Andre's sincerity. Juan looked at the older man with quiet respect. He had joined Dunn & Burkett after one tour with the Marines because of the lack of military action.

What the Marines lacked, Dunn and Burkett had. Juan had traveled the world with the security company and knew joining them was one of the best decisions he had ever made.

Andre Dunn and John Burkett were seasoned veterans, real pros in their line of work. They never asked a man to do something they were not willing to do themselves, and never ever put their men in *no-win* situations. Especially Andre; the man was made of steel and iron, no fancy heroics, and was an indestructible fighting machine. So Juan had a genuine liking for his boss.

He owed his life to Andre. Several weeks after he had joined Dunn & Burkett, the squad was deployed to East Africa on a reconnaissance mission. A European oil executive had been abducted while on a hunting safari in Kenya. The exec's caravan was attacked, the guides killed, and he had been taken to a rebel camp in neighboring Sudan.

Their squad tracked the terrorist group and caught up with them. During the fierce battle, Juan was cut off from the squad and surrounded by the enemy. With a gunshot wound to his leg, he was cornered. Low on ammunition, he was slowly rewinding his life. Pictures of his brothers and sisters flashed in front of his face, and he could almost smell Mother Price's biscuits.

Shit. He was out of options and wondered how the family would take the news of his death.

"Hey, kid." The whisper was a welcome interruption in Juan's litany of gloom. The younger man's wide grin spoke volumes as he nodded a greeting. Andre placed a finger to his lips signaling silence. Placing his arm around the younger man, he began to drag him toward the squad's secured trench. Suddenly, Andre flung them down an embankment, rolling quickly as bullets exploded over their heads.

Andre's reflexes had been remarkable. Instantaneous! To this day, Juan wondered at his boss's ability to anticipate danger. It was something that all his men speculated about but were nonetheless extremely grateful for. There was no doubt Andre had an uncanny gift—some of the men called it *second sight*, others said it was plain old "platinum luck." Juan didn't care what they called it; he only knew that Andre's instinct had brought them through deadly encounters time after time. It was one of the reasons he never hesitated to back the man.

Juan took a long drag and passed the joint back to Andre. He wanted to say something, tell his mentor how much he had appreciated the years with the squad, how much he had learned, and how much he regretted not being able to stay. But it was Andre who spoke. Holding up his hand, like he knew what Juan was thinking and could look clear inside the younger man's soul, he assured with a half smile, "You know, if you ever need me, I'm only a phone call away."

Andre looked up when he heard the scratching on the door. He had felt Imani's presence from the time she walked into the lower lobby, heard her thoughts as she ascended the stairs leading to his room. She had special plans tonight.

Ahh…. This night I might, just might, let her have her way with me, he reflected humorlessly. *What do I have to lose? It would be a novelty, after all.*

He lifted the beer bottle to his lips and drank deeply. Many times he had wondered at his gift, this uncanny ability see into the future, to feel and hear another's private thoughts. His mother had told him that his supernatural abilities were foretold— prophesized and bequeathed by his Zankli ancestors.

"Enter," he commanded. He was bored and stared out over the city from the balcony, unaware that his voice betrayed world-weariness so deep, so disparaging that it launched most women on a hapless quest of rescue. His rescue!

He turned and stepped back into the room. His lean frame was a sexy silhouette against the gray-blue moonlit sky. He tilted his head back and filled his lungs. He could smell her readiness from where he stood. His senses were like that of a huge jungle cat on the prowl. The woman was ready, her scent forecasting a willingness to mate.

Air burst from his lungs in a long dragged-out sigh. He had need, an urge to thrust his body into Imani's soft *passion fruit*— John Burkett's erotic description of a woman's core, but there was no denying it, he was bored with Imani. He had tasted of her *fruit*, and while undeniably sweet, it was time to move on.

Imani stepped into the room, and her eyes wandered joyously over the man lounging causally in the wide French windows. Andre Dunn was breathtaking. His clean, freshly showered body was very different from the potbellied, fish-colored clients she usually serviced. This was a man in his prime, stunningly masculine.

She toured his body, marking each asset. His wide chest was the perfect spot for a woman's head. His flat stomach was a wonderful ridged pathway to his manhood, and his butt, those twin globes, was flawlessly molded to fill a woman's hands. Each time she saw him her soul danced with excitement.

He was a generous lover. She had never been with a man so giving of himself, so interested in satisfying his partner— not even Asubikai—her first love. Tonight she would surprise this gorgeous, giving man. She would look to his needs first, and if their lovemaking ended there, *so be it*, she vowed.

He was lonely, full of pain and despair. She knew it as well as she knew her own name. And she wanted desperately to replace his loneliness with joy and happiness, if only for the night. How sad, she lamented. Even when they were at their most intimate, he kept himself apart, unable to open to her and lose himself in the joy of lovemaking.

During those times, she knew that his spirit was far away, and that he was unable to reap the rewards of joining. He gave pleasure, but took none. Oh, his body would shudder, and his life force would pour freely. But it was only a physical release, his soul was not present, and she wept for the man.

Imani's desire to bring Andre relief and joy was unselfish, and Andre sensed it. He watched her approach through lowered lids. She was lovely. He had to give her that. She was dressed in native garb; a colorful serape made of the softest of cotton and tied in an artful knot in the center of her breasts.

Her hands floated to the knot, dancing over its ridges enticingly. Slowly, with the finesse of a flamingo guitarist, her fingers wove themselves under and around the knot, untying it artfully. Magically, the multicolored cloth slid to her feet in a frothy pool.

A gorgeous specimen of African beauty, Imani radiated primitive sexuality that promised erotic delight. Andre felt a welcomed hardening as she stepped over the fabric and moved toward him.

Her eyes leveled below his belt. Her lips lifted in a woman's smile. She noted the bulge in his pants giving evidence to his arousal. When her eyes met his, they were feverish, openly lustful and speaking volumes. Her body glistened with a healthy sheen that was in itself alluring. Her natural scent blended well with the oil made by the local women and gave off an aphrodisiac fragrance, which permeated the room with each of her steps.

His body responded with heated need.

Imani closed the distance between them, lifted his hand and placed his index finger in her mouth. Eyes smoky with promise, her tongue flirted between his fingers, traveled to his wrist, where she sucked and laved his pulse, then traveled sensuously with slow wet licks to the center of his palm.

Imani took her time, and it was the most erotic sensation Andre had ever experienced. Her mastery was riveting; he leaned back and decided to enjoy the moment.

She turned and walked backward to the bed, his thumb now lodged in her mouth, her tongue concentrated on the webbed flesh connecting his finger and thumb. The sensation was like warm lava moving under his skin, and his nerve endings were alive and tingling. Mesmerized, Andre followed, fervently anticipating her next move. She started to undress him, and when his unengaged hand lifted to assist her, Imani brushed it aside. This was her night, her right, she said with her eyes.

She removed his shirt and pants, becoming an instrument of pleasure. Her lips moved along Andre's forearm, and once again found an erogenous zone in the bend between his forearm and bicep where a large vein throbbed in concert with each tug of her mouth. Shamelessly, her lips and tongue gave the vein full attention as she knelt over him.

Andre was on fire. He was beyond thought, and for once in a very long time, he was oblivious to the empty aloneness that had become a constant companion. She loved every part of his body, his hands, his arms, the back of his legs, and his feet—he'd never known how erogenous his big toe was, but when her lips reached his underarm, he closed his eyes and let go a volcanic flow of milky lava as he roared his release.

Imani slept soundly. Andre gazed at her and sighed silently. It had been a remarkable evening—a heady distraction. But the emptiness had returned, slamming into him with gloomy persistence. He wanted to shout his misery and feelings of bone chilling isolation as if a part of him was missing. It was overwhelming.

Andre sat up and stepped away from the bed silently. Where was she, his other half? His mother had told him that he would know his mate upon sight, and that she would sing to his soul with a mating hum that would vibrate throughout his body.

Andre wanted to believe, but he felt he had been waiting an eternity for his elusive mate. Empty, and forlorn, Andre looked out over the silent city and wondered if the Zankli prophesy would be fulfilled.

"Where are you?" The question drifted unanswered in the wind. He had scanned the sky, searched with his mind for a connection, a speck of light, a ray of hope.

"I need you." It was a cry from the depth of his soul.

He turned and retraced his steps to the bed, to the magic of Imani. Resigned, he lifted her into his arms. For now, this would have to do.

On the other side of the world, Tyler turned fitfully in her sleep, disturbed by an inexplicable howl in the silent night. The wail was so forlorn, and filled with such despair that a silent tear slid down her cheek.

CHAPTER THREE

Tyler Mueller

BEVERLY HILLS ~ JANUARY 2008

In 2008, Mueller International was the largest cosmetics distributor in the world. A dominant force in the beauty and perfume industry for over one hundred years, the new millennium saw Mueller International annual sales top one hundred and fifty billion dollars. Only the retail giant Wal-Mart had a greater gross income.

Mueller had cosmetics manufacturing plants in France, Japan, the United States, Brazil, and South Africa. Over one million independent sales associates distributed their products in every corner of the world. The company had come a long way from the days of its founder, Beatrice Mueller.

The magic of Mueller products was its exquisite packaging, artfully designed to promote feminine allure. The product charm, whether lipstick, eye shadow, or scent, was the ability of the brand to project the illusion of beauty.

Women the world over were convinced that Mueller enshrouded them in an aura of mystery, ensuring an irresistible appeal to the object of their desire. The tremendous success of the Mueller brand was due in large part to one simple, but highly effective theme—*Mueller will make you irresistible.*"

At the helm of the cosmetics giant was the exotically beautiful Tyler Mueller, who personified Mueller elegance and irresistibility. All women desired secretly to be as beautiful as Tyler, and the idea that Mueller cosmetic products just might make them so was worth it. No matter the price, they flocked to the stores to purchase the illusion of Mueller beauty. "Good morning, Ms. Tyler."

The towering bellman, in his perfectly tailored gold-buttoned uniform, respectfully tipped his capped head at Tyler. The formal greeting was accompanied by a fond twinkle in the doorman's eye, revealing an affection that had little to do with the fact that Tyler was his employer.

"Good morning, Thomas. How is your family?"

Pausing, as Thomas opened the massive oak door, Tyler looked up, and met the man's fond smile with one of her own. "Just fine, Ms. Mueller. My youngest, Mathew, will be graduating from high school in June."

Tyler's smile broadened with sincerity. "That's wonderful news. I know Mattie is proud."

"You bet she is. The wife's tickled pink that the boy's been accepted at Howard University. He's a prelaw major."

"That's great, Thomas. Don't forget to send me a graduation announcement. I want to personally congratulate Mathew."

Swinging the large door wide, Thomas gave Tyler an appreciative nod as she turned and entered the marbled lobby of the corporate headquarters of Mueller International. Her three-inch pumps glided on the polished marble as she gracefully crossed the regal lobby, and entered the mirrored, stainless steel elevator. Her perfect French tipped lacquered nail pressed the penthouse button.

Thomas' eyes followed the lovely young woman until the elevator doors closed, marveling at her natural warmth. He had started working at Mueller's when he was sixteen, and in the almost half century he had worked at the headquarter offices there had never been anyone like her. Not even the old man. *Sure,* Thomas mused, *Adam Mueller had plenty of charm, but you always knew that there was a distinct line between you and him, and you knew to never cross that line, or him, for that matter.*

Tyler's mother had been courteous, but there was always a self-imposed barrier erected. Rachel Mueller allowed no one to get too close. Thomas doubted that the woman would have been fazed if he had dropped dead at her feet.

Tyler was different. She knew all of her staff by name. And she always found time to address them personally, never seemed too busy to offer a pleasantry or inquire after their family.

Her uncle was outraged by her friendliness to the staff, and never missed an opportunity to tell her so. The fact that she allowed a servant to address her by her first name was—for Simon—socially unacceptable.

Thomas had overheard his frequent criticism when her uncle had taken Tyler to task, and had secretly thought him an asshole, though he would never dare make his feelings clear. That would have been a major mistake—one he would likely not recover from, at least not with a job.

Simon gave the impression of tolerant kindness and rarely dressed an employee down publicly, but like a cobra, he would retaliate with lightning speed to perceived insubordination. He would chop an offender's head off without a second thought—or backward glance.

Thomas shook his head thinking, *most people don't realize it, but that man is one mean S-O-B.* He knew. He had been at the corporate offices long enough to know where the Seymour bodies were buried.

He smiled silently. Her uncle could never wear his girl down. Tyler would listen to Simon respectfully, nod her head thoughtfully, tell her uncle she appreciated his opinion, and continue to address Thomas and other employees personally.

Yes, he thought, *that's what made Tyler so special and so well liked by her staff. She takes an extra step to make the other person feel valued. Nope,* thought the veteran employee, *I can't think of any place I'd rather work.*

At twenty-seven, Tyler Seymour-Mueller was not only genuinely nice, but also one of the wealthiest women in the world with an estimated personal portfolio of twenty-seven billion dollars. As the majority stockholder of Mueller International, she was chairman of the board, and one of the youngest to head up a multibillion dollar global corporate giant. According to *Vanity Fair Magazine,* "Miss Mueller is younger by seven years than Sergey Brin and Larry Page, the founders of Google."

At first glance, Tyler appeared to be a college intern. Her exuberant friendly manner, her exotic beauty, gave the impression of naivety. When it was disclosed Tyler was the chairman and chief executive officer of Mueller International, most assumed she was just a figurehead.

But unlike the children of other billionaire czars, Tyler had been groomed for leadership from the time she had entered her mother's house. Not even the Trump heirs could come close to her business coaching and hands-on instruction.

Her grandfather's Will was specific. His heir was to attend board meetings, review Mueller financials with the CFO, and participate in management decisions from the time he or she was a junior in high school.

Like her mother before her, Tyler had a photographic memory and could read at an astonishing pace. She consumed and mastered technical books in a few hours; the same text would take learned economist weeks to grasp. By the time she was twenty, she was a talented business strategist, with uncanny negotiating skills.

In short, Tyler was shrewd, tactically brilliant, mathematically gifted, but in no way intimidating. Colleagues and peers truly liked Tyler. Competitors respected her. They marveled at her charm. Like her grandfather before her, she had the ability to make you like her even when she was breaking your back, or bank.

Few knew of Tyler's years in the foster care system or that her father had been a *smalltime* drug dealer with a *big-time* drug habit. Nor would they ever guest that he had whored out her mother. Likewise, her mother's eighteen months of captivity went undisclosed. The entire incident remained hidden. Even astute, muckraking scandal magazines, had not uncovered the truth. No one was alive to tell; although, Rachel had been terrified that some past john would recognize her. But no one had ever done so, and she took the secret to her grave.

Great wealth like the Mueller's could perform miracles and rewrite history to manufacture truth. Money could cloak what one did not want to disclose, so the family had spent millions of dollars concealing Rachel's abduction. The family had known nothing of the daughter Rachel had given birth to during captivity, nor had they suspected that Rachel had spent much of her eighteen-month captivity as a prostitute. Only Nanny Peters knew the deprivation of Rachel's captivity, but even she had not known about the child.

Tyler sat in her office listening to her uncle as he discussed the upcoming advertising campaign to launch Revlon's antiaging line of products. Members of Mueller's chief executive management team were seated around the large conference table.

Simon finished his overview, closed the PowerPoint presentation and turned to Tyler. "Is there anything you'd like to add?"

"No. I think that pretty much sums it up. Our job is to keep the consumer's mind on Mueller cosmetics, and I think you all are doing great in that area, thanks to Bobby," Tyler fanned her hand elegantly toward the handsome man on her left.

"Halle Berry signed on for another two years as the face of Mueller, and Lance Armstrong is confirmed for the holiday campaign."

"Al," Tyler said, turning to her chief legal advisor. "Did you get the contracts to Demi's and Lindsey's people? We need to secure them for the spring campaign, before the *ReVive* press conference."

"Yes," Al Rosenthal responded, proud of Tyler. He had served three generations of Muellers in his seventy-three years, and none had held his loyalty like the woman who sat at the head of the table.

Little remained of the frightened girl he had delivered to Rachel. The twelve-year-old beauty had been a surprise to all. It was obvious that the child was frightened, but her small shoulders were held straight and though her mouth trembled, she had bravely held back her tears as she stepped into the black Bentley.

Blinking, Al focused on the people at the table. "June is handling the project personally. She made contact with their attorneys last week, and we should receive the contracts by the end of the week."

"Great, Al. That's great." Tyler's smile was genuine. There was not a person at the table that she did not like personally or respect professionally, and she was more than happy to see Al's daughter June begin to take over her father's responsibilities.

The two young women respected each other. Both understood the significance of family and their unique connection. Tyler knew the attorney wanted to retire, but was reluctant to do so until he ensured her interests at Mueller was secured. His daughter June, and her commitment to Mueller, was his way of protecting Tyler's back.

"I believe the next twelve months will be exciting for Mueller. I project a season of growth and expansion. While it is true our competitors are increasing their market share, Mueller still dominates the market and has had another great quarter financially."

"Angela."

Every head turned toward the elegant red head at Tyler's right.

"The Marketing Department's strategic plan for *ReVive* is brilliant, and if executed as forecasted, Mueller will position itself as an industry leader for years to come. Few will be able to rival us. Are we ready to launch?" asked Tyler.

Angela Ryan's emerald green eyes sparkled, "We are good to go! The only possible glitch would be a leak before next month's press conference." The forty-eight-year-old woman was stunning. Age had yet to catch up with her, and Angela's youthful outlook on life kept her at the top of her game. The closest thing Tyler had to an aunt, she loved Angela and welcomed the times they spent together reminiscing about Rachel.

"I don't think we have to worry about that," David Seymour, Tyler's adopted cousin, interjected confidently. "Josh and I have made sure our researchers operated in nuclear groups. No one knew what the other was doing, or how his research was connected to the overall project."

Josh, David's twin, nodded his head in agreement, adding, "On Juan's advice, we've retained Dunn & Burkett and they are handling industry espionage. So far our team is clean."

Tyler's cousins were gifted dermatologists; together they had discovered and computerized *ReVive*. The product was the most revolutionary topical cream the cosmetics industry had ever produced. The patents placed Mueller leap years ahead of their competitors.

She had no doubt that *ReVive* would do for the beauty industry what airplanes had done for travel, positioning Mueller International at the forefront of cell rejuvenating research and product development. The tests over the last five years were remarkable. Reversing, and then effectively halting cell deterioration and aging. So far, *ReVive* could remove ten years off age spots and wrinkles from the face and hands.

Smiling to herself, Tyler blessed the day she had rescued David and Josh from her grandmother's tirade as she belittled the boys, telling them they were little bastards. Even today, she could hear her grandmother's acid remarks to her cousins.

"Heaven knows who your real parents are. You're adopted, for goodness sake," Mercedes' voice had dripped with sarcasms.

Tyler was infuriated at her declaration. At the Price home, it was instilled in the children to be sensitive to the feelings of the less fortunate. The downtrodden and underprivileged were given extra helpings at meals, were talked to as if their opinions were valued, and most importantly, were never, ever, verbally abused.

Mercedes had been shocked speechless when her newly arrived granddaughter defended her adopted cousins, saying in a fiery speech, "I'd receive them into my family a lot sooner than I would you!" The child had spat at her grandmother.

She looked right at Mercedes with transparent scorn. Tall for her age, she was the same height as her grandmother. Tyler did not budged an inch. And for a moment, Mercedes saw Adam Mueller come to life in the girl.

Later, Mercedes cupped her hand over her mouth, squinted as she looked at Simon and confided in a hushed tone, "I tell you I was scared the little savage would hit me, the beast! I mean, how dare her. She is little more than a gutter rat."

Tyler made a bitter enemy of her grandmother that day, but earned her cousins' undying devotion. From that day forward, they became her personal champions. It was no stretch of the imagination to say that either one would gladly lay down his life for her.

The sun had begun to sink when Tyler looked at her watch and called the meeting to a close. Everyone had begun to file out of the room, she reminded Al Rosenthal, "Stay on top of this, I want to know the moment that Demi's and Lindsey's attorneys return their contracts to us."

Simon was the last in line to leave the room, when his niece softly requested, "Simon, would you please stay. I have something I want to discuss with you."

Tyler was always polite and respectful of her uncle. She had grown to care for this man more than any other Mueller relative. He had made her life so easy, when she knew it could have been just the opposite. She was aware that he might resent the fact that he was excluded from top position at Mueller International, not because of a lack of talent, but because of the circumstances of his birth. He was not a Mueller, and Tyler believed that it must have riled him.

Her uncle was a very handsome man. In his late fifties, Simon Seymour had picture perfect silver streaked hair and old world elegance. Trim and fit, with a perpetual tan, he spent an hour every "weekday" in the gym and another half hour in the sauna. Weekends he spent pursuing his private passion.

Chang, his Asian lover of thirty years adored him for the very reason that Tyler had learned to treasure him. Her uncle always managed to make everyone around him feel appreciated, and he rarely criticized a colleague in public. These were the two characteristics that Tyler respected most, and she tried to emulate him in all her business dealings. Even when there was great fault or stupidity on the part of one of her staff members, she had learned to hold her tongue.

Once, shortly after Tyler joined the family she asked her uncle about his ability to take a negative and turn it into a positive. Simon told her, "I learned the skill from a master, your grandfather."

Looking away from her, focusing on an invisible point off in the distance, Simon spoke fondly. "He taught me that the art in human relations was in making lemons into lemonade." She had not understood what he meant when he first shared that concept, but as their relationship matured, and she observed him over the years, Tyler came to understand the difference between sour lemons and sweet lemonade. She had learned a chastised and resentful employee was never as effective as a happy one.

Tyler considered the lesson invaluable, and turned toward her uncle still reflecting on his patient mentoring. "I have something I want to run by you," Tyler spoke to Simon, with the two worry lines between her eyebrows prominent.

"Please sit," Tyler motioned to the chair in front of her desk, took the seat across from her uncle and reached into the desk drawer. She removed an envelope and placing it on top of the desk pushed it toward her Uncle.

"This is the second letter I received this week with the same message." Watching her uncle open the letter, Tyler resisted biting the edge of her lip, a habit she developed whenever she was worried.

The room was quiet as her uncle read the brief message. Then slowly, he reread it. Finished, he looked up, locking Tyler in a steady gaze.

A part of the message reverberated in Simon's head. *"...the next time, bitch, it won't be your car, it will be your face."*

"Well, what do you think?" Tyler questioned with a slight tremor. Fear and anger shone in her eyes. "I have to admit, I laughed at first. I'm not laughing now. I received a call from Jim Wheeler informing me that last night the tires on my Volkswagen were slashed, sugar placed in the tank, and lye poured on the hood."

The Volkswagen was Tyler's prize possession, a classic thirty-seven-year-old talisman left to her by her mother. Rachel drove the car when she was a student at Stanford.

Simon's gaze did not waver. He delivered a low whistle, "Hell yes. You should be worried." With rapid fire he quizzed, "Where was security when this happened? Don't answer. It doesn't matter. Whoever tampered with your car obviously eluded security."

"OK, the son-of-a-bitch wants to play...we'll schedule a hardball game with him." Tyler was shocked. Her uncle rarely used profanity.

"I'm going to have Juan assign an around-the-clock body-guard to you, and I'm calling in Dunn & Burkett. They're already working with us on the corporate espionage details, but they also specialize in abductions and the sort of threats that involve stalking and kidnappings. According to Juan, the company has a team of crack shot militia, ex-Green Beret, special ops men, and mercenaries who work all over the globe combating rogue governments and terrorist groups. Juan says they're the best, and we need the best right now. We don't know what we are up against, and I won't take chances with your life."

Tyler wanted to tell her uncle that he was being silly, that he was overreacting. But the words would not come. Her gut told her that the entire incident was something she would be foolish to disregard.

"I'll tell Jan to clear my schedule. I don't want to, but I agree it would be foolhardy for me to ignore the letters and the vandalism."

The next morning, Tyler, Simon, and Juan met to discuss corporate security. A half hour into the meeting Jan Bellows knocked on the door and showed Andre Dunn and John Burkett into the room.

Tyler was impressed that the owners of the security company had responded to the meeting request on one day's notice. She thought their attendance said a lot about them and the commitment to their clients. What she did not know was it was a personal call from Juan that had the two men on their private jet and in Los Angeles within twenty-four hours.

The two Mueller executives stood. Simon extended his hand in a firm hand shake, and as soon as Juan finished greeting Andre and John, he turned toward Tyler. "I want to thank you for responding to our call so quickly. Let me introduce the chairman of the board, Tyler Mueller.

Her pictures don't do her justice, John Burkett thought as he took Tyler's hand, grasping it lightly, reluctantly letting it go.

Then it was Andre's turn to take the extended hand. *Human silk*, he thought as his large palm engulfed the elegant fingers and an electric current passed between them. Andre dropped

Tyler's hand immediately, but he was on full alert, rocked by an instant connection.

John was still staring at Tyler. She was the type of woman one could not overlook. She was simply breathtaking. He supposed it would be impossible to duplicate the creamy perfection of her skin, even in a glossy layout in *Vogue* magazine. *Damn*, he thought, *she's drop-dead gorgeous, not the painted, artificial look of a Hollywood glam, but naturally gorgeous. Hair, curves, lips to die for. Shit*, John thought, *Angelina Jolie's got nothing on you, sweetheart.*

Down boy, John silently warned himself. *Keep it business, remember you've got a wife and baby at home.* Next to him, Andre Dunn felt as if he had been hit by a two-ton truck. Tyler Mueller was the most stunningly beautiful woman he had ever seen, and he had seen plenty lovely women around the world, but everything about her was incredible. *Holy shit, who'd put her together?* Her skin looked milky soft and begged for attention. He wanted to give her a slow, sensuous lick, *and what was that fucking hum*...his body was actually vibrating.

Andre's mind raced. He pictured himself intertwined with this woman, imagined the way he would stroke, pet, and caress her. He stepped back in shock. His body became still, motionless like a huge predator cat before mating. He had never responded to a woman this way before. He was on fire, and he opened his senses and took her scent in, forever imprinting it on his mind.

Tyler Mueller was captivating, a haunting beauty, and Andre wanted nothing and everything to do with her. His eyes dilated. The pupils expanded to the size of the iris and shrank in rapid secession. The humming was insistent, drowning out all other stimuli. With tremendous effort, he held himself in check—when all the while he was flooded with tsunami desire. He felt as if he were sinking in monstrous tidal waves, and there was no lifejacket to keep him afloat.

Watching Andre's and John's responses to Tyler, Simon would have laughed, if their meeting were not so serious. It never failed. Men had an instant reaction to Tyler, purely sexual. It did not matter if they were eight or eighty. Within seconds, without fail, they behaved as if they were meeting a siren of their innermost fantasy. Her effect was across-the-board. Even men who had a different sexual preference felt a pull and were irresistibly drawn to her.

Motioning the men to be seated, Simon and Juan sat down on the sofa opposite them. Tyler came out from behind her desk and strolled to a chair at the head of the sofas. Andre had a perfect view of her mile-long legs.

"Let's get right to the point." Simon reached across the low sofa table, handing each man a letter. "Ms. Mueller received these last week."

The only sound in the room was the crackling of the paper as each man opened and read a letter. Andre took his time reading the message, then closed the letter and handed it to John. He finished the second letter. He looked at Tyler and asked with a poker face, "Before last week, Ms. Mueller, had you ever received a threatening message?"

Privately Andre Dunn thought Tyler Mueller had gotten someone very angry. Killing mad. Both messages revealed the kind of smoldering hatred Osama bin Laden harbored toward the United States—deep, dark, and ugly. Insane. Whoever wrote the letters was insanely committed to destroying Tyler and everything she loved or cherished.

The letters reflected the extreme hatred usually displayed by an enraged lover, a deceived partner, or a thwarted competitor who had lost everything, and had nothing else to lose.

You're a fake. I know who you are miss goody two shoes...you've taken everything from me...and I'm going to pay you back in kind.

Maybe the lady wasn't a lady after all, Andre privately mused. *Maybe her appearance was a foil, a well-orchestrated façade that seduced with the false promise of sensual delight, but like the black widow, offered fatal consequences.* It was an interesting thought and one that Andre considered seriously.

Simon Seymour wore a smug look on his face, but noting John Burkett had intercepted his look, he quickly resumed an aloof, professional posture.

Hello, John made a mental note of the revealing glimpse into the man's thoughts. The transparent and unrehearsed expression on Simon's face probably meant nothing, but it was interesting, and John tucked it away in his detective box of inquiries.

Tyler's answer to Andre's question was low, spoken under her breath. "No." Her eyelashes, which layered over expressive violet eyes, fluttered down, then up. She looked at him and he could swear she was peering into his inner most thoughts, an occurrence that was unusual for him. Typically, he was the one that gained privy to another's mind. He felt naked.

"I do not remember ever receiving threats." Tyler's voice gained volume and confidence. "No. Definitely. No threats before now."

Mentally, feeling like a man drowning, Andre shook his head in irony. *Wouldn't you just know it? She had a voice like heaven. I can't take this! Am I the only one affected by this woman? No, John was reacting, and he is a very married man with two rug rats at home.*

Forcing himself to concentrate on the discussion, Andre turned to Juan, pinning his old comrade with a set of vivid brown eyes.

"What security measures have you put in place?"

Juan had joined Mueller International after leaving Dunn & Burkett. He grew up in the Price home as Tyler's older brother, and in the years following her departure, Juan was amazed by Tyler's loyalty. She never forgot the family, and never, ever missed an opportunity—birthday or holiday celebration—to express her love.

She made sure that she visited them on a regular basis, like a guardian angel. Later, as the necessity arose, she explained her relationship with the Price family as a philanthropic project of the Mueller Foundation.

When Juan wrote and told Tyler he would not be re-enlisting in the army, she had offered him a job in the Loss Prevention Department at the corporate headquarters of Mueller International, but before he received her offer, Dunn & Burkett came calling.

Juan had never regretted the detour. In fact, he knew that the time with the company had sharpened his security skills and prepared him for his job with his sister's company.

Juan cleared his throat. His confident answer was not brava-do. It was the result of hard-won experience gained during mili-tary campaigns in the Persian Gulf and Somalia, and honed to perfection in the numerous reconnaissance missions with Andre and John. The two men were a part of the military elite that had gone private.

"We added eight surveillance cameras at corporate, doubled our security force from twelve to twenty-four, and assigned two personal bodyguards to Ms. Mueller." Juan looked between both men, his steady gaze communicating the camaraderie of combat survivors.

Tyler observed the men and exchanged a knowing look with her Uncle. It was obvious that John and Andre had passed a test, some subtle exam that only Juan understood. She trusted her brother implicitly. If he was satisfied, so was she.

"Gentlemen, I want to thank you for joining us at such short notice. I am satisfied that between you...," Tyler looked at each man, communicating absolute confidence, "...we will get to the bottom of this. Please excuse me, I am expected at a meeting downtown."

All of them stood in unison as Tyler gracefully rose from the sofa. She was exquisitely dressed in a pale lavender Armani suit that accentuated her eyes and drew attention to her ten-mile-long legs. Smiling, her full lips accented by a provocative dimple at the edge of her mouth, she spoke directly to John and Andre.

Her husky voice sent another wave of sensual tremors through Andre. He was responding to her like no other, and the hum buzzed loudly in his ear and continued to resonate throughout his body. Above the internal clamor, his mother's words came back to him. "When you meet your mate, your body will sing to you and you will answer the call." Suddenly, he knew, and froze.

Tyler was speaking. "Simon and Juan have full authority to work with you and provide any information or assistance you need."

Andre Dunn watched Tyler float like a dream come to life; there was no other description for the way she walked toward the door, and his response was primal. Mine. His pupils expanded, his nostrils fanned, and his eyelids lowered knowingly.

He breathed her woman's scent in again, cataloging the lusty perfume so that we would be able to track her anywhere. His eyes locked on her as she glided from the room. There was no doubt. Tyler Mueller was the stuff of hot, steamy nights and flapping sheets. His eyes marked her possessively, and his soul began to sing. The Zankli prophesy was true...He had met and recognized his mate.

The two men were quiet during the drive back to the airport. They had finished the meeting with Simon and Juan an half hour after Tyler's departure.

At the close, Andre turned to Juan and Simon and explained, "We're going to have the letters dusted for finger prints and DNA. My hunch is the spots on the right corner are semen.

"We don't hold out much hope that we'll get a lead from the fingerprints. All the handling has contaminated the letters. Any evidence that might have existed is most likely compromised. But it won't hurt to check. We might get lucky," Andre remarked.

Juan agreed, liking his thoroughness, "What about the stationary?"

"It can be purchased at any office supply store. It's pretty generic. No lead there. Our best hope is these spots." Andre used his pinky finger to point at the irregular spots on the letter.

"I'll contact you tonight with an update. Hope you don't mind if it's a late call." Andre gave an ironic smile, which spoke volumes...

"Not, at all." Juan's rapid response was not unfriendly, but terse, appropriate for the seriousness of the moment.

Andre blinked, jarred from his reminiscing when John quizzed. "So, what do you think? His question had hidden meaning.

"What do you mean, what do I think?"

Andre's response was met with a wide grin from John. "What the hell do you think I mean? I'm talking about the case. What do you think about the case?" John produced another tongue-in-cheek grin. A whistle and soft laugh followed.

"Hell, man. I'm talking about that walking Viagra. I ain't never seen anything like Ms. Tyler Mueller outside of a movie complex and a huge wide screen. I mean, she's unreal."

John dramatically drawled "Ms." out, emphasizing Tyler's name when his fingers touched his lips, and ending with a loud smacking kiss. Guessing, rightly, he had gotten to Andre. He watched his friend's reaction clandestinely, lids lowered over knowing eyes.

He knew Andre had been deeply affected by Tyler. It was not so much what he did, as what he didn't do. During the meeting, his partner had been deceptively quiet, very still. It was a ploy that Andre often used during a drill that preceded a fury of brilliantly executed combat moves ending in a killing blow.

It was Andre's way of commandeering complete control, and he was careful not to expose any emotion. It required great concentration, and sometimes John could swear he saw a visible glow surrounding his partner's body.

At those times, Andre became a destructive machine, and it was the very reason that John had paired with Andre during the Gulf War. Andre was very effective, unbeatable on reconnaissance missions. He was a master at subterfuge. You never even saw the attack coming. Before you knew it, he would pounce, and you were down or dead.

Over the years, John Burkett had become Andre's most trusted friend. They were more than combat buddies, brothers of the blood. They had been in some tough situations, tight spots that required quick thinking to survive the moment. John was a trustworthy comrade, someone you could bet your life on. Andre had been the best man when he married Chantal and was godfather to their eldest son. He could not think of anyone he would rather be with under fire.

But this situation was different. It was so different that Andre wanted to shove his fists into John's face for even mentioning Tyler's name. She belonged to him, and for the first time in his life, he understood what seeing red meant. He was furious at the thought that Tyler could belong to anyone else, even in conversation.

He had marked her as his, and he wanted to lay claim to her, as in times of old, plundering the spoils. He envisioned her in his lair, spread beneath him, welcoming his body in moist soft places. Her mouth! Her private lips! Standing up! Lying down! From the rear! He wanted her in every way a man could have a woman. But most of all, he wanted her wanting him.

Andre was obsessing over a woman he had just met, knew less than nothing about, and who might have the moral ethics of a sociopath. The letter was explicit. As far as the writer was concerned, Tyler was a heartless thief, a person who ruthlessly and callously hurt people.

He silently acknowledged the possibility that everything in the letter was true. It did not matter. She could be an ax murderer, and he would still want her. And that was what paralyzed him, stopped him in his tracks. If she could make him trash his concept of right and wrong, forget everything he had held sacred as truth, then she was more lethal than anything he had ever encountered, and he wanted no part of her. But she was irresistible, a never-ending flame that ignited his soul. *God help me*, he thought. He was trapped, captured by an irrepressible call from the Chosen.

Andre had spent most of his adult life defending the defenseless and protecting the weak. Just seven years prior, he turned his back on the U.S. Department of Specialists, an agency so secret and covert that only top government officials knew of its existence.

It turned his gut when the agency and its minions had thoughtlessly crushed entire Third World villages, or ruthlessly destroyed the dreams and aspirations of an individual without any regard for the rippling consequence of their actions.

Tyler might very well be as morally bankrupt as the agency managers he grew to despise, but she was the Chosen, his other half. There was no getting away from it; her survival was his survival.

Andre closed his eyes and tried to focus on the task at hand. It was impossible. Her image was tenacious, an unforgettable aura, and it was impossible to get her out of his mind. But the worst thing was, he knew John knew.

Andre would have been astonished to learn that at that very moment, Tyler was thinking about him. It had begun with her questioning his company's experience and ended with her admitting he was the most captivating man she had ever met.

There was something about Andre that made Tyler feel privileged. Not the privilege that accompanied wealth, but an unreasonable pleasure generated each time his eyes fell on her.

Everything he did, the quietness of his moves, spoke of danger. Yet Tyler did not feel personally threatened. She sensed that others might fear where she would be safe. She did not know why she felt this way. She just did. She felt calmed in his presence; and he wanted her. She knew that too.

She had plenty of men who had let her know that they were attracted to her and desired her physically. But Andre Dunn was different, and she wanted to know everything about him. It was obvious he was well bred, and he was incredibly handsome, the stuff of night sweats, with his smooth caramel skin and rootbeer eyes that could see into her soul.

His long eyelashes were the perfect foil to those eyes, and his wavy hair framed a face that resembled an ancient Ashanti mask. But it was his full masculine lips that caused visions of naughty delight.

Only God in his divine artistry could have created such masculine perfection, Tyler thought.

When she felt the electrical sparks as their fingers touched, her eyes had flown to his face. What she found sent tremors through her body. She knew him. His face was familiar, as if she had lived the moment before, and she experienced *déjà vu*, seeing them together in another time, entwined on twisted sheets, with sweat pooled on his muscled stomach. It was uncanny, and Tyler's face blushed rose when he gave her a knowing secret smile.

She found herself doing something she had not done sense she was a child. She shielded her thoughts, putting up a mental barrier as Nanny had taught her to do during their travels in Africa. Andre's eyes had actually dilated, his pupils growing huge. Tyler shuddered.

Had he felt the same connection?

Lost in thought, she wondered at his effect on her. And how her body responded to his touch. She was unaccustomedly moved, and fascinated. She watched Andre sit down and assumed a pose of suppressed energy. He reminded her of a huge carnivore: dangerous, exotic, mysterious.

He had held her spellbound in a steady gaze; his beautiful brown eyes radiated confidence. But it was his lips, so magnetically sensual, that captivated and begged to be kissed.

Stop it! She chided herself, and almost laughed aloud, thinking she was losing it. *Who has ever heard of a man's lips begging for a kiss? Ridiculous!*

Now she understood Jan when she said just looking at Juan made her wet. Looking at Andre Dunn's mouth made Tyler wet, gave her a tingling sensation that started in her stomach and moved down, centering in the private triangle of her damp curls.

It was not a feeling that Tyler was accustomed to. She had three serious relationships in twenty-eight years, and only one of them had reached the bedroom.

Tyler met Hara as a freshman at the University of Southern California. He was a Nigerian, whose Hausa family was soaked in oil and mineral money. His exotic background, cosmopolitan air and disdain for American wealth appealed to Tyler. She found him charming, he found her irresistible, but their relationship was a disaster from the start.

Hara was an arrogant, controlling, demanding chauvinist, who believed that women were inherently inferior. He believe that they were little more than property, designed for the pleasure and singular enjoyment of men. His idea of a good time began with Tyler sweating over a pot of ground nut stew, and ended with her flat on her back.

The first time he had taken her was tortuous. His sex was huge, hanging long and wide, so thick that it was good he had not insisted she use her mouth on him. He had plowed her body with little regard for the pain he inflicted. Her pleasure had not been a priority, and he mindlessly used her until he reached his own reward. He was not intentionally cruel, just selfish.

As for Tyler, she found the entire act disgusting, and hated every second that his sweating, puffing body sank into hers. Her body never secreted welcoming juices for lovemaking. Each encounter grew more and more painful, and it was not long before she shrank away from him when he reached for her. His verbal abuse began around the same time, perhaps because he sensed she detested his lovemaking.

Hara called her "stupid woman" so many times that she began to think it was her name. The affair was short lived, and the experience so soured Tyler on sex that she had avoided it ever sense.

Andre Dunn was different. He made her juices flow, something Hara had never accomplished. The attraction to Andre both intrigued and frightened Tyler because it was so physical, and she could not help but wonder what it would be like to tame him. She was fascinated...It was more than his looks, which were a threat to any woman's sanity, it was the way he moved and watched everything without appearing to watch anything.

He reminded her of a caged Siberian Tiger she once viewed at the San Diego Zoo. The white stripped cat had moved gracefully, his powerful muscles rippling as he paced slowly from one end of his steel prison to the other. Every few moments he would pause to stare at her, his yellow-green eyes unblinking.

Tyler had been saddened. On a primal level, she understood the confined cat's pain and wanted to lessen his loneliness. It was the same feeling she had for Andre, only it was more intense!

Andre called Juan at midnight. Whitney Houston's melodic voice announced the call...*And I will always love you, always love you*...Juan reached over Jan with one arm, hugging her close into him with the other and lifted the phone off the base. She stirred in his arms, and he placed a reassuring kiss at the back of her neck.

"Hello." His voice was groggy, but his mind was instantly alert, a trick he learned in the Army.

"Juan." A smooth masculine voice flowed through the receiver. "This is Andre. We've gotten the DNA results, and it's just as I suspected. It's definitely semen. I'm having a friend of mine run a check in their data bank against known terrorists, stalkers, and sex offenders. I should have some results back tomorrow afternoon."

It was three o'clock in the morning on the East Coast, and the man sounded like it was the middle of the day. Juan was impressed. He was also tired, snuggled next to his woman, and wanting very much to go back to sleep. There was a pregnant pause. Neither man spoke. Then the voice on the other side of the continent asked professionally. "Is Ms. Mueller secure?" Andre's heart skipped a beat waiting for Juan's response.

"She's fine. I checked with security at eleven. She turned in early, around nine. I have two guards patrolling outside the house and one inside staffing a video monitor. Tyler is safe," Juan assured.

Hoping he had not made a fool of himself, cursing his impulse, Andre signed off and placed the cordless back on its base.

It had been a long day, he was sleep drunk, though his voice had not betrayed fatigue. He leaned forward in the oversize leather chair sipping Chardonnay, his strong square fingers circling the short stemmed crystal as he swished the pale liquid around in the goblet.

Andre gazed through the glass, looking into his future. The stark reality of the emptiness of his past was transparent in the aseptic, ultramodern, thoroughly boring penthouse furniture. His mother's forecast was true.

He paced the room, energized. His body was alive with recognition. The humming that had begun when he had first laid eyes on Tyler permeated the walls of his mind, drowning out all other sounds. He had experienced an emotional jolt when his eyes met Tyler's, and he knew she was the only woman in the universe who could complete him.

Until that moment, he had never dreamed—in spite of *the Zankli Prophesy*—that he would find reprieve from the shattering loneliness. Oh, there had been plenty of women, hundreds of sexual encounters really, but all had left him empty and alone—unfulfilled. At times, he had ached with the sense of loss, aware that he was wretchedly incomplete and missing a vital link to his humanity.

"Tyler."

Her name was a song, and Andre wanted to shout his joy. He sat down in front of the fifty-inch plasma television screen, oblivious to the early morning news. He owned several houses in North America, including the Manhattan condominium, and a hunting lodge in Canada. He had taken women to both places. But he had never taken a woman to his cabin in Big Bear. He knew that was where he would take Tyler. She belonged there, tucked away in his California den.

Unbidden, a picture of Tyler spread on his bed with her naked legs partially covered, her full breasts outlined beneath the white sheets, flashed vividly in his mind. Andre grinned, his smile shameless, enjoying the fantasy.

He walked over to the window. Where was she? What was she doing?

Tyler was exhausted, bone tired. She stifled a wide yawn as her hand rubbed the back of her neck. Her schedule was grueling. She arrived at the office at seven in the morning, and rarely left before seven in the evening. She had a strong work ethic, and she never asked anyone on her staff to do something she was not willing to do herself.

The influence of the first twelve years of her life as a foster child was indelible. It had made enduring impressions on her character and personal preferences.

Tyler loved gospel music, preferred home-style cooking, and felt more comfortable in the company of her staff than many of her wealthy peers. Behind the sophisticated corporate polish and veneer was a simple girl who liked nothing better than to kick off her shoes, curl up on a sofa, and watch the Discovery Channel on Cable TV.

She yearned for moments where there were no questions to ask, no problems to solve, and no decisions to make. Although few would have guessed at her true desire when they observed her in board meetings.

Tyler craved the peace and quiet of her home. Her bedroom was her favorite place in the house. It opened out onto the seaside and provided a peaceful view of the Pacific Ocean.

She stood inside the sliding glass doors and watched the foamy waves as they washed on shore. Her body was in quiet repose. She listened to the water crash against the rocks. Dreamlike, Tyler reached up and gracefully removed the large knot twisted into an Asian bow at the base of her neck.

Thick ebony hair tumbled down to the middle of her back like fine silk. Tilting her head, she flung the luxurious hair to one side of her face, and turned and toed off her shoes as she unzipped her skirt and let it slide to the floor. With deft efficiency, she pulled the silk half-slip over her head and padded to the bathroom, removing her front clasped bra and lace panties as she stepped into the shower.

Refreshed, twenty minutes later Tyler turned back the comforter on her bed and slid between the sheets, easing her head against the pillows. Her treasured oversize Lakers T-shirt hugged the tips of her c-cup breasts. She loved to sleep in the knee-length top. It was a gift from Cookie Johnson after she had volunteered in a Pediatric AIDS Telethon. The T-shirt was autographed by the entire Lakers team. She knew that she should have framed the priceless shirt, but she wanted to be cloaked in their spirit and energy—their championship!

Tyler fell asleep thinking about the good works of the Magic Johnson Foundation, but her dreams were of Andre Dunn. He joined her in bed, his strong arms encircling her, pulling her toward his heat. She could feel him, the length of him sliding along her leg. His masculine smell was a perfume so erotically hypnotizing she raised her hips, an invitation to welcome his invasion. Shivering in ecstasy, she moaned, the sound breaking the quiet of the room.

In his bedroom three thousand miles away, Andre Dunn opened his mouth in a silent scream. He had used his physic abilities in the past, but never as he was using them tonight. It had come in handy on reconnaissance missions when his abilities had given his squad the edge in skirmishes and hostage recoveries. Few knew of his physic powers, and in the past, he had used them sparingly.

Tonight he was desperate to reach Tyler. He had to assure himself that she was safe. Andre reached out, harnessing all of his powers. He consciously projected himself through time and space, his mind seeking and reaching for her. He didn't know if it was possible, but he had to touch her, confirm she was safe. He could barely breathe with the need to establish a union.

Andre filled his lungs, searching for a path to Tyler. "Where are you?" he asked as he exercised his energies with ruthless purpose.

When he first became aware that he was in her room, Andre almost lost the connection, he was so amazed. Tyler was asleep. Her hair seductively fanning her cheek, soft puffs of air escaping her pouting lips. She was beautiful, so haunting that he had to stroke her. His strong fingers brushed her throat and slid around the slender column, marveling at the hunger that raged through him.

His formless body slid into bed, dragging Tyler next to his thick length. Her T-shirt rose, and he felt the damp moistness through her sheer lace panties. He grew. His tool was solid, painfully rigid. Positioning Tyler on her back, he invaded her mind, pushed hard and created a dream of their bodies merging and intertwining.

Her legs bent and lifted off the bed, with her toes pointed toward the ceiling. Then they embraced him in a siren dance as old as time, pulled him snuggly into her body, and locked her legs around his hips. It was like sinking into a tight glove filled with cream. She was incredibly wet, and the perfect fit. Half a continent away, Andre's hips bucked and pumped inside the warmth.

Tyler rubbed her legs along the length of his thighs and hip, moaning deep in her throat at the sensation. Andre knew he could lose himself in her forever. He looked down into her face and fastened his lips to hers tenderly. He felt triumphant, exalted. He moved, she moved, their union was magnificent. Her body followed him, pace for pace, in a perfectly orchestrated dance.

Tyler was smooth, silky, and so hot that the kiss of her nether lips was as real as anything Andre had ever experienced. Lifting her legs, Andre rocked in a timeless rhythm, the crescendo of motion building with each stroke. Her heels rode high on his back. Her breath came in short puffs on his neck urging him into a frenzy of motion.

She was molten lava, so hot and moist he was drowning in ecstasy. He nuzzled her breasts, his mouth finding the dusty rose nipple, and thanked God for this gift. He suckled, whimpering from deep within. He wanted to love her forever. Nothing was as good, nothing would be the same again.

Unable to stop, Andre swelled, and deepened his thrusts. He filled her, mentally expanding as he surged in and out. He wanted to possess her for all time. She was his, and he would kill anyone who tried to take her from him. His silent roar was primal.

Three thousand miles away, his heart pounded, his soul exploded. With a shudder, his life force splashed against her womb. His cry resounded in their minds. His seed spilled forth filling Tyler with a sea of emotions that had been buried, undisclosed until now.

Shaken to the core, Andre withdrew back into himself. The parting was like leaving pieces of his soul behind, and he knew that indeed he had. Sometime during the night a sound, so slight it was more like a vibration, awoke Tyler. Listening for a moment, the dream still vivid in her memories, she heard no more, and thinking that the noise was a part of the dream, she fell back asleep.

The sunrise was spectacular, spreading an orange and yellow rainbow of color over the water and sandy beach. The gray dawn peeked into Tyler's bedroom. She woke refreshed. She could not remember having a more peaceful sleep and sprang out of bed humming as she headed to the shower. For the first time in days, she had forgotten the threats and vandalism to her car.

The phone rang just as she stepped out of the bathroom still toweling her hair. Answering with her smoky voice muffled, she flung her damp ebony locks over her shoulder and used her chin to balance the phone.

"Hello." There was a smile in Tyler's voice. "Hello." At first, there was only static at the other end, and then a man spoke ominously.

"You can run, but you can't hide."

The hairs on the back of her neck stood up as she listened to the dial tone. She knew immediately that the call had come from the author of the letters. The phone fell to the floor, the thud muffled in the thick carpet. Suddenly, the day had gone gray. Her safe haven vaporized, her home invaded by the ominous phone call, and Tyler had a sense of evil brooding nearby. She pressed the button on the intercom. Jim Hayden responded immediately.

"Yes, Ms. Mueller." The familiar voice was reassuring.

Tyler's voice trembled. "Jim. I just received a strange call. I think it was him, the person who's been writing me letters. Could you call Juan, and ask him to meet me at the office in an hour. And Jim, please call my uncle and ask him to meet me there also."

She looked around the room. The phone remained on the floor, buried in the carpet. Tyler stared at it for several seconds before she scooped down and picked it up. Crossing the room to her purse, she reached in and pulled out Andre Dunn's card. She wanted to hear his voice. Somehow, she knew he was her only asylum in a world gone mad. Trembling, Tyler's fingers pecked out the eight hundred private number.

"The phone rang only once. Then Andre's voice came over the line, confident and incredibly sexy. "Dunn here."

Tyler held the phone with both hands. Her grip was so tight that her bloodless knuckles were chalk against her honeyed skin. "Mr. Dunn." Her voice was raspy as if she had been up all night. "Mr. Dunn, this is Tyler Mueller."

Andre would have recognized the melodic tones anywhere.

"I received a phone call this morning at my home, on my private line. I believe it was from the person who wrote the letters." She was shaken. Her fear was beating at him, and Andre could barely contain his rage. Fearing that he was telegraphing his anger, Andre was brief, terse, attempting to hide his emotional connection to her.

"Yes."

With a sinking heart, Tyler regretted the call. "I'm sorry. I hope I am not interrupting. I can call later..." Tyler hesitated and stumbled over her words, an act that was both unexpected, and unusual.

"No. I am sorry. How can I help you?" Andre had recovered. He listened at the other end of the phone. She was confused by his initial response. He sensed Tyler's need to gather her thoughts.

"My concern is that this person has my private phone number." Tyler had regained her composure and continued efficiently. "Only a very few people in my inner circle have that number, and to ensure my privacy, I change it frequently."

"I've called Juan and my uncle. They will be at my office later this afternoon. Will you be available for a phone conference?"

Again, Andre's response was sparse. "Yes."

Tyler relaxed. She didn't know why, but she suddenly felt very safe. "I'll call you around six-thirty Pacific standard time." Andre listened as she hung up. He touched the end button on his cell phone, and dialed his pilot. "Andrea. I need to return to the West Coast. I'm on my way over. Have the plane cleared for takeoff in twenty minutes. I want to leave as soon as I get to the airport."

His second call was to John Burkett. "I'll stay at the Château Marmont. Ask Kyle and Ron to meet me at JFK in an hour. I'm taking the Cessna, Andrea will pilot." The eight-seat, 2001 Citation Jet was one of three carrier planes and two helicopters, a Black Hawk and a Sea Hawk owned by the company. The planes and pilots were on standby twenty-four hours a day, seven days a week.

Corporations all over the world, especially those doing business in Third World countries, sought Dunn & Burkett's services. The security company also subcontracted with various federal agencies. The operation included two elite squads of commandos, and the company had access to over a hundred contract personnel around the globe. Dunn & Burkett were respected worldwide for their speed and accuracy. But more importantly, they were feared for their lethal efficiency and deadly precision.

The Mueller case was right up their alley, but Andre felt like a novice. He was too close to the job. Last night's excursion, a feat he had never accomplished before, was nothing less than miraculous. He was still reeling from the sensations and physical aftereffect that had been so real and wet that he had required a shower afterward.

Since childhood, Andre had been able to reach out and touch people mentally. Many times, he could hear another's thoughts, especially if the person was in an emotionally charged situation. But he had never linked with another human being the way he had linked with Tyler. He had known she was special the moment their hands touched, knew she was his when he had gazed into her violet eyes and heard the hum of Zankli. She had scorched his soul, and in doing so, had branded him hers.

When their fingers touched, he saw flashes of her life, read parts of her memories that went back to her early childhood. He saw her running through corridors, playing with children in wheelchairs. He saw her bending over a book with a towheaded youngster; saw her enfolded in the arms of a tall black woman.

He even saw her as she cringed in pain when a large man plowed into her body, his hips plunging and thrusting in a violent piston manner. It was a vision he did not want to see, and he placed his hands on his head squeezing tightly. The thought of another having her was bone chilling, and he squashed the thought.

As arranged, he called Tyler, participating in the meeting while in flight. He did not reveal that he was on his way back to Los Angeles, or that he had given the instruction that all of the Mueller phones—from top executive to mailroom clerk—be bugged. Andre believed whoever was terrorizing Tyler was close, perhaps even inside her organization.

The team arrived at Santa Monica Airport just as the sun was setting in the east. Andre had spent the flight time strategizing the security plans with Kyle and Ron, their instructions were clear. They were to be moles, hiding their role with the D&B security team.

Andre checked into the Chateau and called Tyler immediately. Dialing her phone number, he strolled purposely toward his cottage. Her phone rang several times with no answer. He redialed, impatient to hear her voice.

She was breathless, as if she had rushed to the phone. "Hello."

The woman was incredible, he thought. She had many layers, and if he lived to be a thousand, Andre did not think he would grow tired of her sexy, bedroom tones. She was the most desirable woman in the world to him, and he felt his body tighten and stand at attention. He felt like a pubescent teen.

"Ms. Mueller. This is Andre Dunn."

Tyler wondered how a man could sound so professional and alluring at the same time. His voice was pure sex, and her body responded to him with heat each time she heard him speak. Unsolicited, the steamy dream of Andre wild and untamed flashed before her eyes, and Tyler blushed into the phone. Andre felt her heat even though miles separated them.

"Yes, Mr. Dunn. How can I help you?"

Andre smiled into the phone, his body so hard it hurt. Man. Talk about a loaded question!

"I'm calling to see if I could come over tonight. I have a piece of technology, some equipment I would like to install on your phone. It will allow us to record and trace incoming calls, and..." She did not let him finish.

"I don't understand." Tyler spoke hesitantly. "What do you mean? I just spoke with you in New York."

"I returned to Los Angeles this evening." Andre's explanation was matter-of-fact, but to Tyler it sounded like an invitation. Fascinated by the speed in which he had crisscrossed the continent, Tyler agreed to the visit, giving Andre her address and directions to her seaside cottage.

Thirty minutes later, the doorbell rang. Tyler opened the door, and thought, *He is definitely better the second time around.* She had not noticed the way his eyes changed colors, or the way the little dark iris expanded catlike when he focused on her. Mostly, she noted how small she felt looking up at him. Her eyes trailed up his body. *The man is huge.*

He walked into the room. Tyler's eyes followed him. He was perfect. Wide shouldered, narrow hipped, with tight muscled buns that would rival any Miami Dolphin wide receiver. She turned and they almost collided, he was so close. Tyler inhaled deeply, her nostrils flaring slightly as she took in his clean scent.

Nice. No cologne or perfumed deodorant blocking his maleness.

She found him intriguing, different from the men she had associated with in the cosmetics industry that appeared in contrast weak and unprepared for life outside the corporate world. Tyler walked with Andre, almost two stepping to his long stride, unaware that her desire was transparent, revealed in a bouquet of femininity that flowed from her pores. It was a sexual call that was irresistible to men the world over, and it awakened in Andre primal instincts that were territorial, possessive, and wild.

"Have a seat. Would you like some water or juice?"

Andre stood in front of the sofa waiting for Tyler to join him. It was the kind of thing older men did naturally, and Tyler took note. The gesture was refreshingly courteous for someone Andre's age.

I bet he opens doors too, she thought, smiling silently.

Andre's intelligent eyes made her suspect he knew exactly what she was thinking.

"Yes. Water would be nice."

Tyler crossed the room to the wet bar, hips swaying invitingly. She bent down, giving Andre a clear view of her perfect bottom, and his heart leaped. "Sparkling or plain?" she tossed over her shoulder, conscious that he was watching her with a tilted smile as if he were enjoying a private joke. And he was. In his mind's eye, Andre envisioned a champagne cork pop and burst open with rivets of snowy foam that spilled over Tyler's dimpled hips.

His body clenched as he saw himself drinking from the sparkling oasis in the small of her back.

Man, does this lady have a way with words, he thought. If the situation hadn't been so serious…it was hopeless, he couldn't help it…he threw his head back and barked a laugh at the audacity of the vision.

"Excuse me." Tyler looked at Andre as if she thought he had lost his mind. She waited quietly for his response. Choking, Andre looked at Tyler, swallowed another laugh, and apologized, thinking, '*My mind needs to be disinfected*'.

"Sorry. What you just said reminded me of an incident earlier today."

He grew serious, his facial expression stoic, giving nothing away. Andre knew that Tyler was questioning his sanity. She handed him his water and sat down, her eyes still questioning. Hoping to regain lost ground, Andre pulled a small microchip from his jacket's inside breast pocket.

The silver chip was paper thin and no bigger than a dime. It had two hair-thin satellite wires attached to it, and Andre placed it in Tyler's palm. She looked at it, and then back to his face questioningly. "With this, we'll be able to listen and track any incoming call from the moment it connects with your line. You do not even have to answer the phone. It is not necessary for the monitor to work, and it doesn't matter if the call originates across the street or in China, we will be able to follow and identify its location of origin."

Tyler was impressed. Her slow smile was rousing, and his body hardened.

Focus! He reminded himself.

"How many phones do you have in the house?"

Tyler crossed the room and held up a cordless. She looked apologetic, "Only this one. And, of course, I have a dedicated cell phone for the company." She crossed to her purse, and took out a G-1 wireless phone with Internet and browser features.

It was Andre's turn to be impressed. His mother and sister had a phone in every room. He held out his hand. "Let me see your landline."

He removed the receiver head, and in a flash, he had the micro monitor hidden in the phone. His mission was accomplished.

He should go, but he knew he would not voluntarily. She would have to ask him to leave, but he anticipated her and asked.

"Have you had dinner?" The question was deceptively casual.

Tyler's tongue slipped out of her mouth, nervously wetting her top lip, eyes wide, she bit down and pulled the flesh between her teeth.

Jealous, Andre felt his body clench and harden again. He wanted to be the one biting down on Tyler's lip. In his mind's eye, he saw himself tenderly soothing and kissing the love sting away.

She shook her head, and Andre watched her hair swing from side to side. He was hypnotized. She was laying claim to his soul, and he welcomed the captivity. He had waited a lifetime for her call.

Tyler's response was thoughtful. "I haven't had time." She was indecisive, unsure about the consequence of her answer. She thought Andre Dunn desired more from her than a dinner, and she felt emotionally unprepared—overwhelmed by his physicality. He looked at her as if she had already succumbed to his demands, as if he had the right to her. She found the idea annoying.

I belong to myself. It was a defiant thought, and the refusal was on the tip of her tongue.

But before Tyler could mouth the rejection, Andre suggested, "We can eat here...I'll cook, or we can eat out."

Amazing. Incredible, really. This manly-man would cook for her.

Tyler hesitated. In a million years, she would never have predicted an evening with Andre so soon. She was attracted. But she did not have the time or energy for what she suspected he wanted.

Her eyes had never left his face, and once again, she noticed a knowing flicker, as if he knew her thoughts. Tyler's chin lifted and raised an inch. To those who knew her well, it was a sure clue that she was about to engage in an act of defiance.

So you think you know me, she silently mocked.

"I have two salmon steaks in the fridge. You cook the steaks, and I'll make the salad." An hour later, Andre pushed back from the table, offering Tyler an outstretched hand. Once again, she hesitated, and then she boldly placed her tapered fingers in his.

Andre slowly engulfed Tyler's hand, swallowing it in his larger one. He stared at her hungrily, famished in spite of the meal he had just consumed. With a slight tug, he helped her from her chair. She flowed up, gracefully, and was deposited less than an inch from his sleek body. The room was suddenly charged with tension. She wanted him. He wanted her. She opened her mouth to say what, she never knew, and he dipped down magnetically drawn to the sweetness of her lips.

His tongue slipped in, swirling and tasting remnants of wine and her natural flavors. *Honey*, he thought, *pure honey*. Tyler's body moved closer, nestling him with her woman's core. It was a perfect fit. She whimpered and felt him grow, and her thigh rubbed against his length.

Andre nibbled at the corner of her mouth, concentrated on the small dimple, then returned to the pillowed softness of her lips, urging her mouth to open wider. Their tongues fenced and intertwined as if old friends magically reunited. He buried himself in her mind, desperate to experience their mating as one.

The room filled with impassioned moans. Tyler could no more deny him than she could her next breath. A vision of them flashed in her mind; they had done this before, been here before. Andre saw the picture, but he did not want Tyler to remember their first union. He redoubled his efforts, seducing her with hot, blistering kisses, successfully blurring the memory of their telepathic union.

It was a dream, my love, only a dream.

He feasted on her lips as he walked her backward toward the sofa, his fingers removed the hair clasp at her nape and threaded through the thick waves as they tumbled over his hands past her shoulders.

Tyler felt like she was playing with fire, but could not turn away. She moaned her surrender. He picked her up in his arms, turned and headed for the bedroom.

The shrill ring of the phone shattered the moment, and Tyler wanted to scream her frustration. Andre closed his eyes, struggling to regain his composure, and let Tyler slide down his body, chest to breasts, the solid steel of his manhood pressing into her with raging need. He exhaled and signaled for her to let the phone ring.

Tyler did not know whether to laugh or cry. *The man must be a robot, or was this just a sadistic game he played with all women?* She had no sooner finished that thought before she felt his condemning gaze. *Jesus, Mary, and Joseph, what does the man want from me?*

She nearly jumped out of her skin when he replied. *I want all of you.* Amazed, she heard him, but his mouth did not move. He had not spoken aloud.

No way, she thought. *No, frigging way!*

Andre smiled and picked up the phone. A professional mask instantly replaced the smile. Tyler watched anxiously as Andre listened to the caller. His face was blank. Then he put the phone down and turned, imprisoning her with his eyes. She could sense concern.

"That was Juan. Jan has not come home from work. Did she mention to you that she was going to run an errand before going home?

Tyler felt as if she was in an emotional tailspin. One minute her senses were being bombarded with arousing heat, and the next she was being interrogated about Jan's movements. Her hand flicked her hair to the side, an unconscious feminine appeal not lost to Andre. Her hair fell seductively over her shoulder, and Andre had to concentrate on her answer.

"No," Tyler's face was questioning. She waited for more information, which did not come from Andre, then quizzed. "Is there something wrong?"

"Maybe." Andre wanted to protect Tyler from undue worry, but he knew she should be informed. "Juan received a call about five minutes ago. The caller wanted to know if he knew where his woman was. Until then, Juan thought Jan was at the office. He told me that he had spoken with her around three this afternoon, and she told him she had a full desk and might run late.

After the call, he tried reaching her at the office, but did not get a response. When he tried her cell phone, someone answered and after a few seconds hung up. But what really alarmed him was that the caller's voice was in a computerized monotone."

Andre's eyes never left Tyler's face. He took her hand. "He checked everywhere, called her cell phone several times since, with no response. He says it is not like her. He even called Bud, thinking that Jan had driven to South Central with treats for the kids."

Tyler's heart was beating a million beats a minute. Andre drew her close, enfolding her in his arms. His hand slid over her hair and rested at the base of her neck. Tyler placed her head on his chest, listening to its steady rhythm and felt as if she had come home.

She felt safe, incredibly peaceful, and he was so, so alluring. Even though they were in the middle of a crisis, she knew that Andre would handle everything.

I am here for you, will always be here.

Once again, Tyler heard the calm sexy voice, knew he was speaking to her telepathically, but had no fear. It felt so natural. She had begun to accept the impossible. Lifting her head she gazed into his eyes, wanting him to read her thoughts, and know how protected she felt.

A sensation of warmth invaded her mind and invisible fingers cupped her cheek tenderly. It was surreal, but surprisingly, Tyler was not frightened. She smiled and trust illuminated her face.

"I need to call my men."

Without releasing her, Andre flipped his cell phone open, and pressed a button. He spoke into the phone. His eyes still glued on her face.

"Ron? It's Andre. We have a problem. Jan Bellows did not come home tonight, and she cannot be reached. I need for you and Kyle to put a tracer on her. She has a LoJack on her Jag. And, Ron, have the tracking chip installed in all of the Mueller executives' phones—mobile and landlines. You can get the list of their phone numbers from Juan."

Andre closed the phone and placed it on the table. "I should stay here tonight." It was not a request. Andre was clear on his intent to protect Tyler. Nor was it a sexual overture.

"I'll sleep here."

Andre motioned to a set of oversized sofas facing each other. The sofa he selected was opposite Tyler's bedroom. He pushed the other sofa out of the way so that it would not obstruct his access to the door, then crossed the room, opened the door and walked into the bedroom. He glanced at the sliding glass doors, and checked the lock.

His trained eye missed nothing. He walked into the master bathroom, checking for vulnerable spots. The window was made of four-inch-thick glass wall tiles. Only a bulldozer would crack it. Satisfied, he walked back into the bedroom. There was no way he was going to let her sleep in this room alone. The sliding glass doors, which opened onto the beach, were a home invader's dream, and a security nightmare.

Tyler, I need you. He sent a mental message and summoned his woman. Yes, he silently affirmed, she was his woman. She was "his" the moment their fingers had touched. He had mated with her, and though she might think it only a dream, he knew it to be real in the supernatural world. There souls were mated. It was only a matter of time before he claimed her with his body.

God save the man who tried to take her away from me.

Andre's feelings were instinctive. He understood on a very basic level that Tyler was necessary to his survival, essential to the continuation of the Zankli.

Tyler rushed into the room. "What's the matter? Is something wrong?" His call had felt urgent, full of uncertainty. Andre crossed the short distance and, taking her arm respectfully, walked her to the sliding glass doors.

"Tyler, these windows are not safe." Silencing her protest by placing a gentle finger on her mouth, he went on, "It is not safe, sweetheart."

The endearment quashed Tyler's protest instantly. What was the matter with her? Was she going crazy? She was crazy. This was crazy...or was it? Without any sane reason, Tyler was connected to Andre. Her body and her soul responded to his.

She could not explain it; she only knew he was an essential extension of her. Indispensable to her wellbeing. Like a joining of two halves. It was an astounding puzzle. His voice interrupted her thoughts. Tyler shook her head focusing on Andre.

"What did you say?"

"I'm going to ask you to trust me. What I would like to do is sleep in here with you." Andre waved his hand indicating the bedroom. "I'll sleep on the sofa." He waved his hand at the ivory, three-pillowed sofa near the glass doors. Tyler was surprised, not as much by the proposed sleeping arrangements, as by the way Andre's words were rushed indicating how uncertain he was of her compliance.

A moment later, his smile told her he was sensing her approval. "Well now that that's settled," Andre started to move past Tyler, "I'll get my bed."

Tyler stopped him with her hand, tapered fingers spread on his chest. "How do you do that?" Tyler asked.

"Do what?" Andre knew she wanted to know about his gifts.

Tyler tilted her head with, "Hey, don't play me with that look," which did not require use of his special abilities. She was not going to let it go and he knew it. Andre inhaled deeply letting out his breath slowly. He turned and looked out the glass doors somberly watching the waves.

"The truth is I don't really know. I've always been able to sense strong emotions, but with you it is different. I can hear your thoughts; sense your feelings, as if you're speaking them to me. The impressions are very clear, not cloudy like when I touch my brother or sister.

"My brother, Paul, is the only other person I feel so acutely. Other people's emotions have to be strong, like anger, hate, fear, terror, happiness, passion...I feel these things, but not always in words, more like strong sensations and visual snapshots."

"I have an inexplicable connection with you, sweetheart...a link that I have never had with any other. You are like a server and I'm plugged in." The last was said low, as if he was making a very shameful confession.

"I need you, Tyler. I was empty without you. And that kind of emptiness eats away at you, consumes you until your soul is dark and nothing really matters."

Tyler came up behind him listening to his anguish; she wanted to end his suffering, erase the years of loneliness. She wrapped her arms around his waist, laid her head against his back, and whispered, "I don't know what all of this means. I just met you, and yet, I feel as if I've known you always," Her voice radiated conviction. "I'm glad you're here."

It was a rough night for both of them. Tyler tossed and turned aware that Andre was sleeping a scant three feet away, and Andre lay still, not by a finger movement did he reveal his wakefulness. It was torture. A fine sheen of sweat blanketed his body. What had John called her—"a walking Viagra." God, the man had never been more right.

Tyler was ambrosia to his senses. He was so hard and stiff he ached with unfulfilled passions. He considered visiting her in her sleep, but quenched the thought, realizing the proximity was too close. His desires were so strong he might not be able to control the dream. God forbid he violated her trust and joined her in bed.

When sleep finally arrived, Andre dreamed he was in a dark room. There was a man, hunched over a table, with his back to him. The vision was clear, but he could not make out the man's face. Andre looked over the man's shoulder. He was studying something. Pictures. The man was looking at photographs that were spread all over the narrow table.

On the wall, above his head, were several maps. One held the schematics of the Mueller Corporate Offices in Beverly Hills. The other showed the layout of Tyler's home, and still another held an organizational diagram of Dunn & Burkett—all of the officers and squads were identified pictorially. Andre's head snapped down to where the man was sitting, but the mysterious man had moved to the door. He was exiting the room.

Andre tried to follow but the door was stuck. He struggled with the knob, pulling so hard that he flew back, almost toppling on his unsteady heels. He awoke with a jolt. He had sensed an unidentified evil lurking in the room, a dark energy that belied the forces of nature and humankind.

It struck Andre as strange—the single-mindedness of the man pursuing Tyler, and his obsession with the destruction of all she held dear. But not so strange, after all. He remembered his mother telling him of a force that was bent on the destruction of Zankli, an Anomaly in human form.

Kicking at the blanket, which hugged his hips, he planted his feet firmly on the floor and sat up. With a soldier's precision, his eyes surveyed the room, found Tyler, and relaxed visibly. He did not question the why of his need to ensure her safety. He accepted it as he accepted his ability to join with her using pure thought. Nor did he question the existence of the Anomaly.

It was a little before dawn, and with a frustrated sigh, he pushed off the sofa. The vision disturbed Andre more than he would like to admit. There was real danger to Tyler and the people surrounding her. The man in his vision was a strategist. It was revealed in the maps and photographs, and his foe's focused concentration. The Anomaly paid close attention to detail.

Andre reached out for his brother. As a CIA field supervisor, Paul Dunn often consulted with Andre on matters of national security. They had been able to communicate telepathically since childhood, and it was information neither Andre nor Paul had ever revealed. Not even to their beloved, precocious sister Mimi.

Andre located Paul immediately. His brother was in a Border Patrol security meeting, and he could hear the conversation, although he could not visualize the meeting as he had in his recent telepathic merge with Tyler.

He connected, waited until he was sure he had his brother's attention, and flooded Paul with information, telling him about the terrorist letters to Tyler and her staff and about his vision of the man in the room with pictures and schematics of the Mueller's corporate offices. Andre's communication with his brother was like a computer downloading into a network hard drive. When he was finished, he asked his brother to run a criminal profile.

Paul, I know this is short notice, but I need you to turn this around on a dime. Time is crucial, she is the Chosen, my mate, and I fear an Anomaly is behind the attacks on her.

Andre could feel Paul's stillness as if he were in the next room. His bother sent a clear, crisp thought. *I am on it.*

Tyler had not stirred. Andre unlocked the glass doors, and stepped out onto the deck, phone in hand. He dialed Juan, who answered on the first ring. It was obvious that he had not slept. His voice was hoarse with fatigue.

After a brief exchange, Juan told Andre he had just received a call from the police department informing him that they had a young woman in the morgue that fit Jan's description. They asked him to come to the coroner's office to see if he could identify her.

"I'll get dressed and meet you there." Andre's voice was strained.

Andre walked out of the door fifteen minutes later. It was a gray overcast morning, appropriate for his mood. The seagulls flew low, but quietly as if they anticipated doom. Andre adjusted his thick black scarf at the collar of his jacket. He inhaled deeply, filled his lungs with air and sunk his neck into his hunched shoulders grateful that Tyler was still sleeping. If the body at the morgue was Jan, he wanted to be the one who told her.

For Tyler's protection, Andre had a man stationed outside, in front of the sliding glass doors, and another in the living room facing her bedroom. He was taking no chances with her safety.

Juan viewed the body stoically. His face was blank—emotionless—but his eyes spoke volumes; they were as dead as the beautiful young woman lying on the stainless steel table. She looked like she was sleeping, the only signs that she was not was the ring of blue-black bruises circling her neck.

Andre looked at the lifeless young woman on the table and deep sorrow flooding his senses. He had only met Jan the one time, when she had escorted him and John into Tyler's office. He remembered thinking then that she was lovely. He had noted her smooth ebony skin, and her beautiful smile, that revealed perfectly even, sparkling white teeth, but he remembered most of all her itty, bitty waist and amply endowed heart-shaped bottom that seemed perfectly shaped for a man's palms. Now she was dead, and it seemed such a waste.

Robot like, Juan turned to the attendant and murmured, "That's her." Clearing his throat, the sound startling in the silent room, he repeated, "That's Jan Barrows."

The police detective standing at the back of the room scribbled a note in a small black book that he shoved into his breast pocket. He pushed off the back wall and walked over to the table. He looked down at the female body dispassionately. He had seen dozens like her over the years, especially black ones. He looked up at both men, and then focused on Juan.

"I understand Jan Barrows was your girlfriend," he paused suggestively, "and you lived together."

You just don't like some people on sight. The detective was one such man to Juan. He detested everything about the man, from his disheveled frumpy suit, to his stubbly, unshaved face. Annoyed, Juan stared into the man's eyes, focused on the spiky growth of beard covering his puffy cheeks, hesitated, then asked, "And you are?"

"Detective Francis Gavin." The answer was defensive and unnecessarily gruff. He was surprised at Juan's professional response. Juan was obviously affected by the viewing, but at heart he was a security professional, and was not about to be intimidated by the detective.

"That's right." Juan looked squarely into the detective's face. "She's my girlfriend and we lived together." Detective Gavin opened his mouth signaling his desire to question Juan further, but Juan put a stop to the impromptu investigation.

"Right now, I've got some people to notify, people who loved Jan. I'm not going anywhere. If you have any questions you can reach me at this number." Juan handed Detective Gavin his card dismissingly, and he moved past the detective with Andre at his side.

The moment they were out of earshot, Andre turned to Juan and asked if he would come back to the beach house with him. "Look, I know you should be the one to tell Tyler." In reality, Andre did not want to leave the younger man alone. He felt intuitively that Juan was hanging on by a thin thread. He was a professional, true, but he had also just lost the woman he loved. Andre pushed invading the younger man's mind, seeing Juan's guilt and pain.

Juan looked at Andre the anguish clouding his face. "I can't. You do it. I just can't."

Juan knew he had not loved Jan the way she deserved, had not loved her the way a man loves his woman. Their living arrangement was a fluke, the result of a foolish dare.

One night, after a party at Bobby's, Juan had offered to drive a tipsy Jan home. No sooner had they gotten in the car than she dared him provocatively to take her to his place.

"Bet you won't take me home. I can always tell when a man can't handle me. It's in his eyes. I always know."

At first, Juan thought Jan was kidding. But when she put her hand on his crotch, ran her fingers along the inside of his thigh, found his manhood, and circled the tip, he knew she was serious.

Juan jumped as Jan's hand traced his hardness and circled him moving up and down. "Hey, baby sis, don't play with fire unless you want to be burned."

Jan's mouth slanted in a seductive smile. "I can handle the heat, and, big brother, I'm as serious as a heart attack. I'm so hot, I am about to burn up, and the only hose that can cool me off is right here." Jan slid his zipper down over the large budge in his pants with slow purpose.

Later, he blamed himself, because he was older by ten years, and he should have had more restraint. She was a kid, his foster sister, same as Tyler. But the full-grown woman sitting next to him, seductively rubbing his inner thigh, flicking his manhood, was no joke. And after a while, his little head took control of his big head and began to drip copious tears of joy in her hand. So, he took Jan, foster sister or not, home with him.

That had been a year ago. It had been a mistake from the beginning. Oh, he loved Jan all right, but he was not in love with her. To Juan she was his little sister, and he could not get past it. It still seemed incestuous to him, although they were not blood relatives, and it messed with his head. Jan knew. But she pleaded, said that she loved him enough for both of them. Now she was dead, and he couldn't help but blame himself.

Andre looked at Juan. He was being bombarded with Juan's guilt and shame. Gently, with deep compassion, he faced Juan. He placed his hand on his shoulder.

"It wasn't your fault, you know!"

Juan looked at the seasoned warrior, and wondered if he was that easy to read. A few seconds went by, and Andre thought Juan was going to ignore his attempt to console him. Juan took a deep, shuddering breath then exhaled; tears hovered in his eyes threatening to spill over his lids at any second.

"I wish I could believe that. But I know if I had made our home life more attractive Jan wouldn't have put in so much overtime at the office." Juan was silent for a few minutes, as if he wanted to keep his own council. But he had to talk, had to confess to someone.

"The only time I made her happy was in bed. I don't know how. I felt such guilt afterward. I couldn't get past the fact that she was my foster sister, and the things we did, the things I wanted her to do to me, seemed somehow wrong."

Andre felt Juan's pain. It was cutting the younger man up, debilitating him, and he knew what it was like to be sexually drawn to someone he did not love. He understood the emptiness in the aftermath of shallow sex, and searched for the right words to comfort Juan.

"Look. There is one thing I know for sure, and that is that none of us can undo the past. Besides, Jan loved you in spite of your inability to get past the foster sibling thing. She told you that she had enough love for the both of you. Man you are lucky to have been loved like that."

"Your guilt will do nothing for you or for Jan. But it will get in the way of us protecting the living, and right now, we need to make survival for Tyler and the others a priority."

Telling Tyler of Jan's death was one of the hardest things Andre had ever had to do. He stood by helpless as Tyler's mouth rounded in a silent scream. But he could hear her, and the cry of horror resounded in his head, vibrated throughout his body.

He reached for her seconds before she collapsed. Swinging Tyler up in his arms, he carried her limp body into the bedroom and laid her on the bed. Andre went into the bathroom, located a facecloth, turned the faucet and held the cloth under cold water. When he placed the cold compress on her forehead, she uttered a low moan of abject misery. She was devastated, and she had no words to convey the soul-shattering sense of loss.

Jan was not only Tyler's foster sister she was her best friend and closest confidant. A graduate of UCLA's School of Economics, she became Tyler's executive assistant straight out of college. Tears rolled down Tyler's cheek. The letter had threatened to destroy everything Tyler loved.

You think you can go on taking, stealing, killing...you think you are safe, and that those around you will protect you. You are mistaken. The hand of Allah will seek retribution...

You will be stripped of everything you hold dear, and in the end you will pay...I will not stop until you and those you love are wiped from the face of the earth."

Tyler sat up. She hated being afraid. She took a deep calming breath. "Would you pass me the phone? I need to make a call." Andre hesitated, thought about it, then reached over Tyler and took the cordless off the bedside table.

"Thank you." She was grateful for more than the phone. Andre's respect had come to mean a lot, and his giving her the phone expressed his trust in her judgment.

Her finger touched the auto dial. She waited while the electronic tone connected her with the number. The beloved voice wafted through the phone.

"Hello Bobby? It's Tyler." A fresh torrent of tears rolled down her cheeks.

"Hi, Tyler." The voice was full of affection.

Andre stiffened with jealousy. He felt Tyler's love for the man. She began to cry in earnest. At the other end of the phone,

Bobby sat down. He could not remember the last time he heard Tyler cry.

"Do you need me? I can be there in minutes. Tyler, honey, talk to me. What is wrong?"

Andre fought down amplified suspicion. Tyler needed all the support she could get, so he sent her a silent message, simple, but potently reassuring. *I am with you.*

On the other end of the phone, Bobby's heart raced with alarm. He knew something was terribly wrong.

"Tyler, baby, please talk to me." There was another sob, then a gush of air. "Jan's dead, Bobby. She's gone."

Bobby was stunned. The floor felt as if it had suddenly evaporated. His world had just turned upside down. "When? How?" The happiness in his voice evaporated, and Tyler answered in a stilted sentence.

"I'm not sure, but please come." She pressed the red end button on the cordless, and looked at Andre. He was solid ground in a sea of quicksand.

"I need all of my chiefs here." Automatically, Tyler thought. *Jan will take care of it.* Then with a horrifying jolt remembered that Jan's death was the reason she was calling her people together. Her eyes flew up, searching Andre's face. A silent moment of understanding passed between them.

Andre motioned Juan to his side. "Call the chiefs. Inform them about Jan and the executive meeting. Tell them that they will be escorted here by security, and that their families will be protected. Reinforce that they are not to come here unescorted."

He turned to Tyler. "Is there anyone else we should notify?" She paused. "Yes, Nanny Peters. Pastor and Mother Price. Patty and Bud. And, of course, my grandmother. They will all need security."

An hour later, the eight Mueller chief operating officers were huddled around Tyler's dining room table. Christine Peters had arrived with her bags in tow, and started a huge pot of coffee. The aroma of French vanilla coffee beans—Nanny's special blend— permeated the room, bringing with it a sense of normalcy. But the mood was somber. The Mueller International family of executives understood that they were all at risk, and they realized that they were facing a fanatic bent on killing them all. Not one of them was exempt.

It was a long meeting. They discussed corporate security, personal safety, and digital espionage. No leaf was left unturned. At two o'clock, Andre felt Tyler's fatigue. He stood up and took charge. He looked at Simon confidently, his tone laced with authority.

"I believe we should shut down for the night"

"Absolutely!"

Simon's response was respectful. He held his resentment close, silently cursing Andre as an upstart. Nodding to the others at the table, he gathered his notes and packed them in the five thousand dollar Louis Vuitton leather briefcase that accompanied him everywhere.

As the men silently filed out of the door, security guards in tow, Andre took Tyler by the hand and guided her into the bedroom. Closing the door softly, effectively closing the world out, he crossed to the bed, sat down and pulled her onto his lap. He cradled her in his arms and held her with possessive tenderness.

His only desire was to relieve her pain, if only for a moment. He shifted, fitting her more snuggly into his body. Tyler felt protected and cherished. She wiggled and cuddled into him, amazed that even in the midst of unimaginable sorrow her body quickened. Embarrassed, mentally scolding herself, she trembled with anticipation. *God*, she thought, *I am shameless.*

Andre's denial was immediate. *Be happy my love. Life is to be celebrated. We can do nothing to bring Jan back. We, you and I, will live in the moment.* Andre spoke to Tyler privately—his voice an intimate whisper—his concern soothing her worst fears. *Let me care for you. Rest, my love. You are safe.*

A week later, Bud Price fought back tears and looked out at his congregation. Thanks to Tyler, he was pastor of one of the most prosperous Baptist churches in South Los Angeles. Occupying almost a city block, the church hosted a ten-thousand-seat cathedral, K-12 school, doctorial college of ministry, community outreach and career training programs, intergenerational projects, youth ministry, numerous banquet and conference halls, a food bank, entrepreneurial resources, and a consortium of business owners for community and economic development. Mt. Sinai was one of the best-funded churches in Southern California, and Pastor Bud Price was held high among his peers as a clergy leader.

His cup truly did "runneth over." Yet, none of it mattered today. His heart was breaking. The youngest member of his family, his baby sister was gone, the first of his siblings to die. He looked at his two remaining sisters, one an acclaimed U.S. congressional representative, and the other a cosmetics czar, sitting in the front row flanked by his brothers. He loved them all dearly, but Jan had been his heart, the little sister who was like his own child.

He remembered the day they brought her home from the hospital. She did not have a name, and when Mama insisted that he name her, he had named her Janet, because he had a crush on Michael Jackson's little sister—Janet.

Clearing his throat, the spiritual leader, who had never questioned God, looked out at the assembly and began to speak. The booming voice that had moved his congregation to spiritual highs wavered.

"Brethren, we are gathered today to celebrate a life." Bud's voice trembled as he carefully enunciated each word. "Janet Bellows Price was an extraordinary woman, committed to this community and to improving the quality of opportunities for our youth. Her personal contribution, both in time and finance, is well documented. But, it was..."

Giving up the struggle, Bud's eyes overflowed, tears streamed down his face. He bowed his head and continued to preach one of the most difficult sermons of his life.

It was an uplifting ceremony, but there was not a dry eye in the church. Congresswoman Patricia "Patty" Price's rendition of *Amazing Grace* brought the entire congregation to its feet. The august woman had let down her congressional persona and revisited the days of youth when she sang in her father's youth choir.

Her voice rose to the rafters, and everyone heard her heartbreak in the gospel rifts that rivaled the Winans.

Afterward, the family exited the church together. A crowd of paparazzi shouting questions and taking pictures met them on the steps. Andre pulled Tyler to his side, shouldering his way to their limousine. Juan brought up the rear, trailing close behind them. Flashbulbs burst rapidly all around, and Tyler hid her face in Andre's chest. She had never felt so vulnerable, never felt so protected.

"Ms. Mueller." One of the more aggressive paparazzi rushed forward barking questions. "How well did you know Jan Barrows? What's your relationship to her?"Andre turned with an intimidating look, drilling the reporter with an intimidating glare. The man backed off immediately. But another voice rang out.

"Is it true that you were sisters?"

Tyler lifted her head, trying to see over the crowd of paparazzi. The voice was eerily familiar. It had a raspy timbre, like the one she heard on the phone the day Jan died. You could hear a pin drop in the sudden silence. Janet Barrows was African American. Until that day, none had questioned Tyler's heritage. Most assumed her dark wavy locks and exotic looks came from Jewish bloodlines.

The voice sent a chill down Tyler's spine. Andre sensed Tyler's distress. He looked over his shoulder into the crowd. *What is it, baby?* He spoke connecting with her mind. Her answering shudder telegraphed deadly alarm.

"I recognize the voice. It's the one that I heard on the phone the day Jan disappeared." Andre raised his hand and snapped his finger, pointing toward the photographers. Immediately, the paparazzi were surrounded. He turned to Tyler, his voice resonating against the walls of her mind. *Are you sure it is the voice you heard on the telephone?*

Until that moment, there had been no reason to question the prefabricated story the family had circulated about Rachel and her marriage to an Israeli. The spin was that Tyler remained with her father, but when Rachel became ill, she was sent to her mother.

No one had questioned the story. After all, who really cared? Rachel had not lived a tabloid life. Even before her illness, she was labeled an eccentric recluse, a brilliant business strategist, but a social enigma. She never attended the parties or galas, which did not matter to the organizers because she gave so much money to their charitable causes.

Tyler lowered her head, leaning on Andre for support. Her past was a family secret buried years before to protect her mother and the Mueller brand. The revelation was no more than a trivial nuance in light of the tragedy of Jan's death. But Tyler felt that the attempt at public exposure was meant to cast her and the family as shady and dishonest.

The limousines were lined up at the curb. Henry, Andre's private driver, opened the door and stepped back as she and Andre entered the cab. Once they were seated, Andre tugged and Tyler automatically fitted herself into his body. He placed his mouth close to her ear and spoke softly.

"Tell me."

How could she tell him? Where would she start?

Andre waited patiently for Tyler to organize her thoughts. He sensed her reluctance. Finally, after a few moments, she looked at him and answered in their private way.

It all began so long ago. My mother didn't study in Europe...she was abducted when she was a student at Stanford...her kidnapper was my father, a black drug dealer, who sold...pimped her to support his habit... she abandoned me when I was born, and I was raised in a foster home... Jan is my foster sibling, as are Bud, Patty, Juan, Bobby, and Lonnie."

The disjointed monologue ended with a sob. Tyler buried her head in his chest. Andre thought he would die from her pain. It was killing him. He tenderly wrapped her in his arms, pulling her close. She could hear the steady beat of his heart through the Armani coat.

"Why is it that I always lose what I love?" It was a rhetorical question. No answer was required and Andre remained silent.

Dejected, Tyler pushed against his chest, trying to pry herself out of Andre's arms. "She was my little sister, my best friend. They wanted to hurt me, and they killed her. Killed her!" Tyler sobbed. "Murdered—she was murdered to get to me."

He would not release her, silently accepting Tyler's disclosure as he had everything else since he met her. He lovingly bunched her curls in his fist; she was his soul mate, promised to him by the Zankli prophesy. His chin touched the top of her head, and his body hardened predictably.

God, he thought, *she will be the death of me.*

The black limousine pulled through the cemetery gates, winding up a narrow road caravanning behind the hearse and limos carrying other family members. Adjusting himself, almost laughing at his juvenile lack of control, he spoke softly, his lips once again close to Tyler's ear.

"You smell like honey. I want to taste you."

She responded with dampness, and flinched. She flushed with shame, praying Andre had not noticed. How could she forget Jan so quickly?

Taking Andre's hand, she slid out of the car and stepped onto the uneven turf. Looking up, Tyler thought that the overcast day matched the mood of the mourners. They were so sad, and so devastated. Bud looked as if he would collapse. It was apparent the only thing holding him up was his will. Juan was comatose, and poor Patty was a shell of herself.

Impulsively Tyler squeezed Andre's hand. It was amazing to her that she had known him for such a short time, yet felt closer to him than any of her siblings.

That is because we are meant to be. The voice was a caress in her mind. His answering squeeze was firm, comforting.

The group slowly picked their way around the flat headstones imbedded in the thick turf. There were seven folding chairs arranged in front of the casket. Tyler's body jerked in an automatic reflex when she saw Lonnie at one end of the chairs. She had not noticed him at the funeral. She took a seat at the opposite end of the row of chairs, as far away from Lonnie as she could get.

Andre felt Tyler's distress. His dark eyes found the source of her anguish and willed Lonnie to look his way. With a jolt, Andre saw pure evil. Lonnie oozed of immorality and hatred. Their eyes locked, fearlessly, neither wanting to be the first to look away. Finally, with an arrogant smirk, Lonnie looked down contemptuously and spat. It was a clear challenge.

Andre attempted a mind merge. He wanted to see behind the challenge, but was met by a mental wall, powerful and impossible to penetrate.

Andre heard his mother in his head, her warning as vivid as the day she had first cautioned him. "When you meet an Anomaly, you will know instantly, as you will sense pure evil. Know that the Anomaly is dangerous, illogically dedicated to the destruction of Zankli *Chosen*, and single-minded in their quest."

His mother had taken his face in her hands and confided seriously.

"They were once of our kind, but have forfeited their gifts, traded them for wickedness that is directed by a force of absolute malevolence—a monster—that owns their soul. They are known in the old language as *Tibooqee*, the giver of death."

He turned toward Lonnie, their eyes met once again, and Andre dipped his chin.

"I know you for who you are. Tibooqee."

The ceremony was short. The last good-bye was uneventful except for the prolonged removal of a flower from the funeral wreath by Lonnie. Looking at Tyler meaningfully, Lonnie's tight smile never reached his eyes, and she felt a chill go through her body that was numbing.

Later, during the ride back to Malibu, Tyler was silent. It had started to sprinkle and she felt the gloomy day mirrored her mood. She leaned back, grateful that Andre recognized her need for privacy. She was emotionally exhausted—spent—she felt life would never be same again. Going on seemed such an effort.

No. Not an effort, a joy. I promise. The voice was loud and clear, reverberating in her head. Suddenly, a feather touch slid across her cheek and down her neck. The sensual caress awakened a spark of desire she thought impossible in her grief. She glanced at Andre, his eyes were closed and he had not moved, yet he was inside of her, surrounding her with raw need.

She could not help it. She squirmed. The sensation was so intense. Featherlight fingers fluttered at her nether lips. Her eyes shot up, an unspoken plea transparent on her face. Andre was sweating, visibly taxed. But he was ruthlessly reminding her that she was alive with much to live for. It was impossible to hold out and she opened, enjoying the invisible fingers—naughty, nasty, wonderful fingers toying with her core. A small whimper escaped her lips. Her head rolled on the back of the seat, her hair tumbled from the knot at the base of her head, and she moaned in ecstasy.

She was lost. She was found. "Andre. Please."

It was unclear if she wanted him to cease or continue. *Tell me,* he answered. Tortured, her head rolled toward his. Andre had not moved. His eyes remained closed, and small beads of perspiration dotted the top of his lips. If possible, they looked more sensual, swollen as if bee stung. That is when Tyler realized what she felt was not fingers but lips—and, oh God, his wicked tongue. She could not talk.

Magically, he swirled and sucked on her woman's bud. It was too much. She flung her head back. Andre drew her to him and covered her lips with his own. *Come to me.* The command was whispered musically, and her scream was smothered in his mouth.

She was floating. Returning to earth, Tyler looked out of the window and saw that the sun had burst through the clouds. A huge rainbow was lodged high in the sky, its bright colors of yellow, blue, and green broadcasting a new beginning.

Andre. It was Andre. It had always been Andre. A tear slipped down her cheek. The loss was still there. She would never forget Jan. Now there was hope. Where just moments before, she had been miserable, filled with despair, she now felt alive, revitalized. Her despair came from her fear that she could never hold on to what she loved. Now there was Andre. It was a double-edged sword.

He had known what she needed and had given it to her. How stupid she had been. Where had she ever gotten the notion that she could live without love, live without passion? Her mother had chosen that path and died alone, suffering without her mate. Tyler understood better now. Zankli *Chosen* must be with a mate, or risk a living hell.

Don't get it twisted, baby. Andre's voice was silk, but there was no play in it. *Your passion is reserved for me! I am your mate. To no one else will you give yourself.*

Macho man! Ugh! Why he insisted on speaking mind to mind she did not know. No sooner had she had the disloyal thought than he answered.

We are one, you and I. I have been waiting for you all my life. And I never really believed that this feeling was possible. I used to laugh at my friends when they said they had found their one true love, the person that completed them. But today, I know it is so, and I know true love exists with you.

At that moment, Tyler believed it too. She had never felt so complete. The remaining ride was peaceful, both Tyler and Andre basked in the afterglow of fulfillment.

It was dusk when the limo pulled onto Tyler's street. Each beachfront house blended naturally with the shoreline. The eggshell and sand painted structures radiating wealth and elegance. Tyler's house was lodged in the cul-de-sac at the end of the private street. The good news was that visitors were required to loop around and retrace their drive down the long street to get to the main highway, but Andre thought that the entire scene gave residents a false sense of security.

When they stopped, Andre opened the door and placed one leg on the curb. Carefully surveying the area, he slid the rest of his body out of the car. Immediately, his radar was alerted. Something felt wrong and seriously out of sync. He looked up at the rooftops turning slowly around scanning the skyline of each house before reaching for Tyler's hand and assisted her from the car. His senses were working overtime, and the hairs on the back of his neck tingled.

Suddenly, he flung his body over Tyler's slamming her back into the car. Two bullets screamed past them and ricocheted off the open door. Lightning fast the driver started the car and sped backward down the street racing toward the main highway.

Bullets hit the street where the car had been seconds before. Then in rapid succession hit the trunk and bounced off the bulletproof window as the limo made a U-turn and hustled onto Pacific Coast Highway. Seconds later, the driver slowed and Andre straightened and closed the door. He franticly checked Tyler for injury.

"Are you hurt?" he asked.

Trembling, Tyler searched Andre's face for answers.

"No." Her voice was thin with fright.

With a growl, Andre took her in his arms and buried his face in her tumbling curls. He was in a killing rage, unable to concentrate or call upon his legendary cool. Neither of them noticed that the car had picked up speed and resumed along the highway.

"I love you." The tormented whisper was muffled in her hair. Terrified at the thought of losing her, he held her in a crushing embrace. How could he return to the loneliness that had characterized his life before Tyler? He swore he would send anyone who tried to harm her into the fires of hell. It was a sacred vow. One he intended to keep.

Encircled in Andre's arms, Tyler was lost in a sensation of warmth. But she could sense his anger and frustration at failing to shield her from the violence of the assault. She wanted to comfort him, defend him against the shadowy thing stalking her and those she held dear. Tyler realized she was falling in love with Andre. She studied the idea, mulling it over in her mind for several minutes.

Oh, she loved her siblings all right and adored the elder Prices. She loved Nanny. She had even loved her mother in the end. But until today, she had never been in love. And there was a vast difference between the two. The feelings she had for Andre put every other emotion she had in the past in the shade. Andre was light, blinding light. There was no comparison. He was her other half...the piece that had been missing to the puzzle of her soul.

As much as she loved Jan, Tyler knew she would recover from the loss, and life would go on without her treasured friend. But there would be no life without Andre, no reason for being.

Yes. I know. His whisper touched her and infused her with joy. *You are my other half—my life.*

Chill bumps rose on Tyler's arms. His voice was a tender caress, and to prove their union he mentally stroked her cheek. The weightless touch was a gentle warm breeze across her cheek and along her neck. Sensing her need, Andre's caress dipped lower and cupped her breasts, stroking each one in turn. He knew what she wanted. He had been in her mind many times and knew her sexual fantasies as well as his own.

Andre sucked the tip of one breast into his mouth. Tyler shuddered as she felt him suckle, his tongue swirling, laving her nipple as the supple nugget tightened into a hard peak. Heat once again flooded her body, and her head rolled from side to side on the back seat. He would be the death of her.

No. Not death. Life. My dearest, life.

His voice was a scalding stroke. She was on fire. Tyler felt him at her core, hands and mouth worshiping her body with masterful skill. Suddenly, there was a thrust. Andre filled her, a miraculous fit—perfect in every way. She turned her head and looked at him. He had not moved. No one observing them would know that he was wreaking havoc on her body. His head was lying back against the seat, his hand relaxed at his sides as if he was simply resting.

You are more beautiful than any woman has a right to be, and I have waited for you all my life. Andre renewed his effort, thrusting into her with a single-minded intent. *Come for me, love.*

It was a command she could not ignore. Tyler exploded with exquisite delight and wondered how she had ever survived without Andre. She felt his arms circle her invisibly, flooding her with his love, and glowed, *So this is what love feels like!* Tyler was basking in Andre's protective cocoon when the driver quizzed over the intercom.

"Where to, sir?" His inquiry separated the lovers' bond instantly. With a mental shake, Andre responded hoarsely, "My cabin. Take us to the Big Bear Cabin." Protectively, Andre tucked Tyler into his side, cupping her silky curls into his shoulder. His chin perched tenderly atop her head. Then he smiled ruefully. It was becoming a favorite resting spot for his chin.

Exhausted from Andre's assault on her senses, Tyler slept; her head nestled in Andre's lap she slumbered like a small child. Stroking her curls, looping them around his fingers, Andre called Juan and then John to review their strategy. Distracted, his eyes were frequently dawned to Tyler as she napped. It was irrational he knew, but he had to assure himself she was safe.

Three hours later the limousine pulled onto a hillside dirt road and climbed toward a majestic log cabin. It looked like a castle fortress of old, nestled against a rocky mountain backdrop of regal pine and evergreen trees. It was impossible for anyone to approach the hilltop home without his knowledge. He had built it right after he had left the Navy SEALs, understanding that the newly founded firm would dictate a clandestine residence that ensured privacy.

When the realtor showed him the remote lot tucked high on a Big Bear mountainside, he knew the secluded hilltop enclosure was the perfect hideaway for his home. A year later, the three-story log cabin was a security fortress. It overlooked a rugged quarry that dropped over a hundred feet into a narrow canyon. The view from the deck was breathtaking, and the hundred-foot ascension made the retreat virtually impenetrable from land. The cabin was his sanctuary. Tyler was the only woman he had taken to his mountainous lair.

The limo rolled to a gentle stop. Henry opened his door and jumped out of the driver's seat. In eight years, the only person he had driven to the retreat was his boss. There had been no prior visitors, and a feather could have knocked him over when he opened the cab door and found the two passengers sleeping on the rear seat.

While Henry watched, Andre stirred, opened his eyes and nodded at him. "Give us a minute, Henry." Andre's voice was smoky, sleep laden, but the driver recognized something else, a warning that the woman in his arms belonged to his boss. It was a male thing, primal and very possessive.

Nevertheless, Henry's eyes roamed over Tyler. He could not help himself. She was a hot one all right, made for secluded nights. The thought was brief and slightly disloyal, and Henry was ashamed the moment it appeared in his mind and ducked his head in penance.

Andre was watching Henry with a steely gaze. A thoughtful smile found his lips, and he leveled his eyes at the driver. For a brief moment, Henry believed his boss knew what he had been thinking, but dismissed the idea as crazy.

A picture of a large predatory cat flashed in the driver's mind, with the animal's huge canine teeth dagger sharp and gleaming ferociously. Henry jumped, grinned nervously, and snapped the door close, because the midnight black panther was so close he could feel its breath on his neck. His legs were almost too weak to hold him upright. He leaned against the limo door and drew a cross, using his finger to draw the invisible line from the top of his head to the middle of his chest, then lightly tapped each shoulder. "Jesus, Mary, and Joseph."

In the cab, Andre touched Tyler's mind. She was in a deep sleep. He covered her mouth with his lips, tasting her, the tangy sweetness stirring him again. He deepened the kiss. She was incredible, more addictive that any drug he could imagine. He would never get enough of her. Tyler stretched and purred in sensual delight, her eyes, slivers of amethyst that flickered, then widened in surprise.

"Oh." The muttered sound was unintentionally sexy.

Andre did not know if her sigh revealed shame or delight. It was a puzzle he wanted to explore. He raised his head, his mouth inches from hers, the unspoken question lingering between them when *In My Life,* the Beatle classic announced a mobile caller.

Andre reached above Tyler's head and pressed the intercom. "Yes." His eyes were glued on Tyler's mouth, mesmerized by the small dimple on the side of her lip. He wanted to bury his tongue in the irresistible depression.

"How's it going?" Juan's worried voice flooded the cab.

"Fine." Andre's answer was emphatic, laced with impatience, wanting to surrender to the siren call beckoning him from the curve under Tyler's lip.

"Henry said you ran into a little trouble." Juan continued persistently, his first priority their safety. He waited patiently, sensing Andre's reluctance, but unable to let it go. He had already lost one sister, and he would be damned if he would lose another.

"There was a small problem, nothing that can't be handled."

Tyler, fully awake, watched Andre, her forehead puckered. Andre was underplaying the ambush, concealing the magnitude of the attack from Juan. Why, she wondered.

Be still, my love. I will reveal all to you in due time.

"How do you do that?" she replied instantly, resisting the urge to punch him.

Why should I tell you my secrets?

His voice was a velvet caress, but she was irritated nonetheless. She was not sure that she wanted someone running around in her head twenty-four, seven—privy to her innermost private thoughts. She could feel his smile. Tyler's eyes flashed, her only signal before she gave into the urge and punched him on the shoulder.

He did laugh then; the baritone rumble resonated in the cab. He could not remember when he had been so happy. It was wonderful and frightening at the same time. He did not really want to care this much, not this soon. But she was like air to him, a necessity, critical to his well-being and essential to his life.

Juan's voice blared over the intercom. "Andre. Are you listening? There is nothing funny here."

Tyler's brother's tone rang of no nonsense. "Someone's trying to kill you, and they are going to try again. You were probably followed. This is not over. You need added security."

Juan's comment was sobering. Andre realized he was not thinking clearly. He was too close, and he admitted it to himself. There was silence at the other end of the phone, and then Andre snapped.

"You're right. I will expect you later tonight."

Andre wanted to kick himself. He could not remember being so careless while guarding a client, but Tyler was not just any client, she was his other half—addictive, a mind-altering stimulant that set his body afire.

He reached into the car, and helped Tyler slide across the seat onto the graveled driveway. She dimpled a smile, the fine pebbles grinding under the heels of her shoes and glided toward the double doors, her walk a magnetic summons. His body responded with a predictable hardness. Andre purred mentally, his voice a sexual rumble, and Tyler missed a step. She stumbled inelegantly through the door into Andre's mountain retreat.

Utterly amazed, her mouth dropped opened. His house was breathtaking; it was like being in a naturalist's fantasy. Tyler's eyes lifted to the ceiling in awe. In the center of the entranceway was a huge oak tree that had several smaller trunks carved into seats surrounding its base. It looked like something out of *Alice in Wonderland. How Rachel would have loved this place*, she thought.

Flowers were landscaped in patches around stump seats, and grass and other plants grew in tuffs at the tree's base. She was charmed, feeling as if she was at once, one with nature.

"This is amazing. I could stay here forever." She stated sincerely with childlike wonder in her voice then turned around in a circle with her arms stretched out and her head flung back. Her face was lifted toward the cabin's glass ceiling. The trunk of the tree angled through the ceiling, its branches spread out umbrella like, fanning and appearing to stretch miles above the roof. The ancient tree was as magnificent as the man standing before her.

Tyler wrapped her arms around her midsection hugging her delight close to her body. Her eyes found Andre, roamed his face with pride and then looked at the ceiling again in awe. It felt like she was outside surrounded by endless sky and majestic trees.

"I love your home, Andre," Tyler purred sweetly.

Andre was surprised at how much the simple statement moved him and even more amazed by how much her admiration meant to him. He had spent countless hours on the design of the cabin, overseeing every detail of its construction. In many ways, it mirrored his love of nature and respect for the environment. He was more than pleased that she found pleasure in his home.

He cleared his throat, resisting the urge to speak telepathically. "Would you like to freshen up first?"

Tyler spun around, her eyes aglow with unconcealed delight. "Yes. I would like that very much. I want to be out of this dress and into something more casual. Do you have something I can borrow?" she too spoke naturally, her voice sounding hushed in the grand room.

Andre turned and guided her down a long corridor toward the guest room, which was welcoming and surprisingly feminine. It was evident that he had furnished the room with a woman in mind. Tyler found herself a bit troubled by the thought.

With a jolt, she realized she was jealous! It was ridiculous, but true. She did not want to think Andre had another love...might have someone else even now. The thought was disturbing.

She felt it then, comforting arms surrounding her in love. His whisper held conviction. *Those who came before are already forgotten.*

She flushed. The pleasure irresistible, but she was peeved nonetheless. "How do you do that?" she asked the empty room in exasperation. "Am I never to have a private moment to myself?"

His answering laugh floated in her head. *Not if I have anything to do with it.*

Again, she felt his self-mocking pleasure. She rolled her eyes toward the snow-white ceiling, disgusted with herself as heat rippled through her body.

In twenty-seven years, Tyler had never felt so connected, so overwhelmed by lust, and she did not know whether to feel ashamed or proud. Deep down she knew that Andre was not shallow, that what he was sharing with her was his most precious possession—his soul. And it was breathtaking. But, it was also intimidating. What did he want from her? What did he expect? She had never revealed so much of herself before...Her life had required privacy—detachment from others—where they shared, and she kept unto herself, especially after she'd been removed from the Price home.

Over the years, she had created small rooms, separating the people in her life. One room was for her mother, another for her uncle, still another for the Price family and Nanny; one room was for her grandmother, another one for her business associates, and a special compartment, more like a suite of rooms where her classmates at Scarborough Academy were housed.

If she lived to be a million, she would never forget the self-centered, amoral, potpourri-blonde, spoiled girls who had set the social standards at the academy when she had first arrived. But that all changed, especially after Jan enrolled.

A cold chill ran down Tyler's spine. Her little sister, her best friend was now gone, and nothing would ever be the same. It was too painful to think about, and she turned away quickly—her thoughts returning to the loneliness she felt most of her life. She feared closeness one thousand times more than death, because she was terrified of losing what she loved. Loss was a recurring theme in her memory.

Where did Andre fit? Not in any compartment that was already constructed, that was for sure. A picture of their entwined bodies flashed in her head and Tyler's pulse quickened. Her imagination was ignited with snapshots of them loving each other in positions that were both naughty and nice.

That's right baby! You'll never lock me away and shut the door. I'm in your life for good.

Tyler felt Andre's smile, full of heat. With a frustrated sigh, she turned inward. *Will you please get out of my head? I mean it. I swear. I will leave this place if you do not leave me alone. I don't give a damn...I will fire you and find another security company.* It wasn't an empty threat.

She felt it immediately, Andre's withdrawal. She felt deflated, as if a part of her was torn away. The loss was tangible. She hugged her waist. He had done as she asked, but she was not happy. She was angry—not at him, but at herself. She had never been weak, and she was not going to start now. With a mental shake, Tyler straightened her shoulders.

Soldier like, she marched into the bathroom, removed her clothes and stepped into the shower. The warm water was refreshing, and Tyler loved the normalcy of rubbing the scented soap over her breasts and hips as the water rained over her face. Her wavy hair slid down her back as she stepped under the flowing beads. It was serene. She welcomed the cleansing water, as it drained away the emotional seesaw of the day.

On the other side of the house, Andre let his senses envelop Tyler. He had acquiesced to her request and he no longer listened to her thoughts, but his minds' eye watched her, unblinking and silent. He hardened; the steel of it painful as he observed the erotic soaping of the curly triangle. She was Eve incarnate, a temptation not to be ignored. His senses were filled with her, blocking out every other emotion.

Andre pulled his shirt out of his slacks, and slowly unbuttoned the fitted St. Laurent revealing plated pectorals and an athlete's body that reflected years of combat training. He slid the shirt off his shoulders as he walked, unbuckled his belt and hesitated, lost in thought. Committed, he mentally shrugged his surrender, and then with a flick of his wrist tugged his waistband apart.

His form-fitting slacks slipped over a muscularly rounded butt and fell with a swish to the floor. Corded thighs, a testament to countless hours of mountain climbing, carried him toward the guest room. He paused, kicked off his shoes and shed his socks with efficient calm. His lips parted smugly, and then he sauntered toward Tyler with resolute purpose.

He wanted to be patient, yet he boiled. The need to be deep inside her superseded every emotion; he wanted desperately to possess her. He turned the doorknob and grinned. Tyler had locked the door. He concentrated and invisible hands turned the lock. He breathed in deeply. Her scent lingered in the room, a combination of berries and woman. He would recognize her bouquet anywhere. His eyes roamed the room and landed on a pair of black lacy underwear. Her panties and bra lay haphazardly at the foot of the bed. He walked over, picked the lacy bits up, and brought them to nose. It was an erotic perfume, and his cock pulsated and jerked in his briefs.

Andre cracked the door and slid noiselessly into the bathroom. Tyler's silhouette was outlined clearly through the foggy shower doors. He adored her with his eyes.

Tyler turned, not surprised. She had felt him coming to her and knew that he yearned for her as much as she craved him. Andre slid the door open and stepped into the shower. She stared, unable to hide her hunger, licked her lips, unaware that the sight of the kitten flick of her tongue sent his emotions into a tailspin. He was on fire and for a brief moment he opened his mind and let her see him, his face buried between her legs, lapping at the honey that was hers alone.

Tyler trembled, overwhelmed by the raw transparency of Andre's need. He was electrifying. Inspiring. It was like nothing she had ever experienced before. He wanted to taste and drink from her; she saw the vision as vividly as if it were her own.

Tyler took a step backward with an unspoken invitation. Andre answered her irresistible call, and joined her under the cascading water. She circled his neck with one arm, brushing at the locks of tight curls framing his face before she slowly lowered her hands and threaded her fingers through the mat of silky short curly hairs blanketing his chest.

Andre reached and pulled Tyler against him, their bodies fitting together like matched pieces in a landscaped puzzled. He was immersed, lost in the heady sensation of the moment and oblivious to anything outside of the scent of Tyler as she slid against him in perfect synchronization.

He had never dreamed anyone could so completely fulfill his need. The feel of her was beyond anything he had experienced. She was his other half, and he could feel her pleasure, see her acceptance as their minds merged. The picture of spread legs, a moist center, and trusting hips eagerly meeting his tongue and delving kisses, flashed and lingered in his mind, but what he was experiencing was far greater than any fantasy.

The scene changed, Andre moaned as he saw the vision of Tyler loving him with her mouth. She had opened herself to him, and provided him with a vivid picture of moist lips encircling his manhood. He rocked forward giving her access to his body, his organ rampant against her stomach. Tyler buried her face in the space between his neck and shoulder, devouring the beads of water, luxuriating in the saline taste.

He whispered something soft and sexy in Togolese, the sound of it became muffled as he blazed a trail from her neck to the valley between her breasts. She gasped a sharp cry of need as she arched into his mouth. He lapped, giving serious attention to the sumptuous breasts.

Andre retraced his sensual trail to her lips. "You are my life," he whispered, covering her mouth. "I had lost faith in the Prophesy and doubted I would ever find you."

Andre's tongue explored the velvet of her lips, opened them and fenced expertly with deep purposeful thrusts into the moist caverns, his plunging motions mimicking in delicious detail a lover's thrusts. He flooded her mind with erotic pictures of his need and she turned the table, trailing a heated path across his chin to his neck, her tongue lapping and fueling his blazing desire. "*Tu etes parfait—you are perfect.*"

Her response was like lightning, sparks filling his head, "*Only to you my love, only for you.*"

Andre cupped Tyler's head, bunching her hair in his fist as her tongue gave heated attention to the corded vein at the base of his throat. His pulse jumped and leaped in response to her care. She was driving him mad with desire. He transmitted images of them entwined—joined as one—then grasped her bottom and lifted her, backing her against the shower wall. Beads of water hit his broad shoulders and cascaded over his muscled back in a sumptuous massage.

Tyler nipped Andre in passionate abandonment, lightly pulling his skin between her teeth, leaving rosy love bites on his neck and shoulder. He groaned and flooded her with sensations of his delight. The sharing was beyond anything she had ever imagined, her throaty response was low and primitive, and her heart thumped frantically against his chest.

Andre froze. Tyler opened her mind to him again. His heart skipped a beat. Amazed, he felt her longing. Carefully, he reached between their bodies, searched and tenderly fingered her slick opening, then fisted his tool, and slid a foot of love home. He closed his eyes for a moment, just savoring the feel of her, the satiny texture.

Tyler whimpered in delight. He was huge, but she was ready, slick and wet. Her slender body shuddered, stretched in welcome as he slid in, held on and locked around him like a satin glove, much to her surprise.

After Hara, she had no idea she could have joy in lovemaking. With Andre, it was smooth and not at all painful—rather, it was beautiful. The more he thrust, the more her honey flowed.

Andre moaned deep in his throat, realizing that their union was beyond exquisite. Motionless, buried deep within her body, he gathered himself. Instead of forcing the bond, Andre held her like the precious gift he thought her to be, his thumbs on her hips, his fingers stroking each smooth curvaceous cheek, soothing her, words of love tumbling from him in several languages. He remained still and watched her. His gaze so fixed and powerful that she felt he had merged their souls.

But his motionlessness was the calm before the storm, a momentary hiatus that confirmed her body's readiness, nature's flood—a creamy greeting—preparing the way for him. Andre captured her with a loving look that acknowledged the miracle that made them fit.

It was only a momentary respite, and an involuntary spasm tightened her inner walls, grasping his organ firmly. Andre sighed, aware of her pumping heart, her quick shallow breaths at his throat, and the intense heat that emanated from the living flesh that encompassed him. Then, as that contraction faded, he pressed in once more lifting her higher, pushing her down as he sank deeper into her moist cavern with exquisite finesse. He felt her tension fade and slowly abate as she trembled in ecstasy in his arms. She nursed on his neck, moaning in ripples of bliss. His scent was an incredible tonic, and Tyler was in a heated frenzy. Her inner muscles contracted in spasms of pleasure-pain.

Andre's hips began to move, eliciting a soft unintelligible whisper from Tyler. Encouragement? He did not know. He was beyond stopping. It was impossible. He lifted up, and slid into her deeper. He wanted to brand her irrevocably his. He mentally enhanced another inch, and Tyler screamed her delight. She loved him, adored him, and would never get enough of him. Her head rolled from side to side, she begged for release, her voice hoarse with sexual craving—"Please…..please, Andre."

She was full, so wonderfully full. Groaning, gasping, shaking, even imploring. Words of love. "More, more, more." Getting faster, harder. Hearing suction, wet, loose, becoming looser, wetter. One of Andre's hands was around her shoulder, pushing her down hard; the other grasped her buttocks, lifting her up high. He felt the joy of her love juice spreading between them. She was so tight, so perfect for him.

Tyler whimpered more words of love, which inspired Andre to give even more of himself. He moved faster—a primitive drumbeat—as he breathed in her unique scent of berries and cream. An unforgettable fragrance filled the room. He pumped in and out like a piston, his power measured by suction and stroke, each deep thrust bonding them closer. Tyler whimpered and stiffened, clinging to Andre, her hips bucking madly with the onset of orgasm. She was so alive and so beautiful in her fervor; it took his breath away to watch her and feel her enjoyment.

Aah, his voice was feather light in her head. *That's it; come to me, we are one.* Andre thrust and opened himself to Tyler, and she was in him, feeling his intense response to the friction of her slick walls as her body gripped and massaged him. It was incredible, this multiple pleasure. His. Hers. His. Hers. She screamed. The sound reverberated against the walls of their minds. Seconds later, she blacked out as they crest together in a soul shattering crescendo of delight.

Andre's damp forehead rested against Tyler's temple. Slowly, he lifted and eased her off his body. Her legs were wobbly and unsteady as she leaned against him for support. Short puffs of air fanned his muscled chest. He had seen to her need first, and Tyler recovered, aware of his rampant desire. She was inside him, and knew what he wanted. He held nothing back. The picture of her kneeling before him, loving him in the most intimate way flashed vividly in her mind infiltrating her consciousness.

"Do it. Please, Tyler," he pleaded, but Tyler continued to torment him, teasing his senses, her mouth and hands coming ever so close to his pecks. Almost, but not quite touching the distended buds. On the edge, at his wits end, Andre seized Tyler's mind ruthlessly and let her feel his agony. Straight away, her mouth landed and covered the hardened nipple.

Now it was Tyler who moaned and squirmed in heat as she drank from her man. She dripped with natural juices, her woman's core tingling yet again. On fire, she suckled loudly, pulling on the nipple, laving it with insatiable hunger.

It was not enough. She needed more. She needed his creamy essence. Her mouth released his distended nipple reluctantly and she slowly lowered herself. She knelt in front of Andre. Her eyes lifted to his face adoringly. Her hands slid over his ripped abs, fingertips finding and massaging the hard ridges.

Andre remained locked with Tyler allowing her to feel his pleasure. Her eyes, which had never left his, widened. She saw what he wanted. Her hands lifted, found his nipples, covering his pecks and taking them between her fingers tugged gently. Andre moaned deep in his throat and sent her another vision.

The picture was clear. Her mouth began to water longingly. Then Tyler rolled his pecks with her thumb and index finger, squeezing them. His member dripped, and Andre thrust his hips forward. He was shameless. The picture of her lips wrapped around him, pulling him into her moist mouth, drinking from him flashed across her mind. She smiled, her lips lifting with the wisdom given to women at the dawn of time.

Her lips drifted lower licking the silky curls surrounding his manhood. Her cheek rubbed his length. Water mixed with his weepy essence and she tasted his man salt. She breathed him in. She had waited all her life for this man, for this moment.

"Yes, baby. That's it. Take it. I have what you need."

His organ was beautiful, a life giving shaft of silky steel. Her mouth and hands memorized him. His globes hung low. They were gorgeous veined orbs of love. She opened herself and let Andre view himself through her eyes. She felt his joy, his love.

Andre looked down, opened his mind, palmed his tool expertly and fed it to his woman. She dinned. He served, dripping his soul in salty-sweet squirts as she suckled lovingly, mewling and whimpering her delight. She wanted his essence. Her head bobbed with purpose. She nursed, sensing his readincss.

Yes, love, yes! I'm yours. Andre whispered insidc of her head.

Her fingers dropped to her hidden lips, searched and found her core once again. Her bud was engorged in anticipation. She wanted them to arrive together. Her fingers worked frantically. Tyler feasted loudly, knowing it brought added pleasure to Andre. She could feel him building, his manhood swelling. She saw herself in his eyes. She rubbcd herself harder, her fingers dipping into her womanhood over and over, urged on by Andrc.

"Yes, baby. I'm almost there. Vous etes parfait, mon petite." His knees buckled. He blasted. His roar of release was loud, uninhibited, and full of love as he watched Tyler swallow, her throat bobbing up and down as she tenderly devoured him. It was the most riveting experience of his life. Every other woman paled in comparison.

He slid from her mouth as she continued to kiss and love him. His hand went to her face, and his thumb rubbed her bottom lip tenderly. He reached for her hands and drew her up to him. Their kiss was slow and gentle. His tongue swirled. He could taste himself in her mouth, and he was surprised when his shaft jumped in renewed desire.

Smiling he thought, John is wrong. She's better than Viagra. He kissed her again. His tongue loved her top lip. She opened and sucked his tongue into her moist opening. They fenced. He turned her toward the tiled wall, the earth colored Terrazzo tile outlined her body like a Fresco painting.

Andre kissed Tyler's neck while his lips feasted on her shoulders fervently. He was ready again. Silk steel. Amazing. His hand laced on top of her fingers, bracing them to the wall. The other arm circled her waist. Using his foot to gently spread her legs, he guided her, bending her at the waist, and with one smooth motion, buried himself in her warmth. Tyler groaned in pleasure when his finger found her again and rubbed tenderly.

He was in ecstasy. Tyler was exquisite, and her muscles squeezed his tool expertly. He placed both hands on her hips and cherished her. He loved her with abandonment—and to his shame—with less control than he had as a pubescent youth.

Later, he would believe their self-absorbance dulled his senses. He never heard the Anomaly's approach...

CHAPTER FOUR

Lonnie

THE ANOMALY

"You fucked up, and that is unacceptable." Z's voice was icy smooth, deadly in its coldness. Lonnie Jackson sat across from the man and knew that he was matched in evilness. He did not fear his partner. Not exactly. It was more like he recognized Z as a soul mate. The man was cunning and smooth. So clever that few suspected the depth of his partner's depravity! But Lonnie knew. He did not underestimate Z's wickedness.

Outwardly, Lonnie's partner was the picture of conformity and morality. Inside he was as corrupt and as empty as Lonnie. They were like two peas in a pod, partners in crime and co-producers of depravity...peddlers of flesh and ringleaders in the distribution of sexually perverted films.

No, Lonnie did not underestimate his partner's cunning or menace. They had made millions plying their trade. They loved the elicit business, both receiving as much satisfaction from the money as the film making.

"You're right. I did fuck up. I made a mistake. I should have taken care of the matter myself. It won't happen again." There was no subservience in Lonnie's response, just acknowledgment of responsibility to an equal, and it lightened the tension in the room. Lonnie watched his partner as he visibly relaxed.

Z's tight smile barely made it to his lips. "I just learned that Andre Dunn has taken Tyler Mueller to his cabin in Big Bear.

The place is a fortress. But I have a plan that should get you what you want. Do you still insist on capturing the slut alive?"

"Yes," he answered in a flash. It was one of the few times that Lonnie allowed his emotions to show on his face, a face that had been reconstructed with the best that money could buy.

"I want the bitch to suffer. I have a prince who will pay five million for her delivery in West Africa unscarred." Lonnie's face was twisted with hate.

"Can you assure me she will disappear permanently?" The question left no room for error.

"I promise she will never be heard from again. If she were to resurface, no one would recognize her. This particular prince likes to carve. His only request is that his meat be unscarred—unblemished." Lonnie smirked. "And if Tyler is nothing else she is that. His feminine cackle filled the room with sinister foreboding.

Juan Lara wanted to bury himself in the bottle of Scotch. He wanted to forget how he failed Jan, how he committed the ultimate betrayal and caused her death. He might as well have tightened the cord around her neck, and he was consumed with self-loathing. Oh yeah, he was the big man, the big brother who couldn't keep his shameless cock in his pants.

He heard the shrilled ring through a fog. He swatted at the sound, his hand fanning the empty air, then fumbled and slapped at the sound again, striking his half-empty glass and knocking it off the end table. The glass shattered on the hard wood floor, and brown liquid spread quickly toward Jan's favorite Persian rug.

The phone continued to ring, blaring in the room with ruthless disregard for Juan's desire to block out everything and everyone. It would not go away. Juan flung himself from the chair charging across the room. Deep in his throat, he growled, "Shut the fuck up! Shut up, I said!"

When he found the phone, he picked it up and snarled into the receiver, "Not home," then flung it across the room. Two seconds later, his cell phone chimed and would not stop. Juan dropped the phone in the toilet bowl, picked up the bottle of Scotch placed it to his mouth and drank deeply.

When the pounding on his door began, he was in an alcoholic stupor. The door crashed against the wall. Juan saw John Burkett stroll into the room and thought he was dreaming.

"Where...taking me...man?" Juan's words were barely intelligible.

John did not answer. Instead, he reached down and pulled Juan by his collar to his feet, then, half carried the younger man into the bathroom, turned on the shower and shoved him in fully clothed. Juan's sputtering curses could be heard a block away.

Twenty minutes later, Juan paced into the living room, swatted his face with the towel and flung it over his still damp hair. "Let me make sure I understand you, they're both missing?" Any trace of alcohol had been washed away with John Burkett's sobering news. Andre and Tyler had disappeared. No one had heard from them in twenty-four hours, and when John went to Andre's Big Bear cabin, it was empty.

"Right! There was no sign of a struggle, but it was obvious that the doors had been forced." The response was rapid fire, terse, professional. Juan's next question was interrupted by the jingle of John's cell phone.

LaToya Walker's voice trembled slightly. "We've found him. He was left for dead in a pile of rubble at the bottom of the cliff near the cabin. It looks like he was flung from the ledge."

One of only three women on the Dunn & Burkett reconnaissance team, LaToya had been rescued by Andre from the streets of Washington, D.C., ten years earlier. At thirteen, she had seen more than most people experience in an entire lifetime, and she always thought of the day they met as her birthday.

It was in the dead of winter, and it was a freezing night. LaToya had been huddled at the side of his building, and at first, he thought she was a bag lady. It was too cold for anyone to be out, and Andre walked over to give the woman money for a room for the night. He touched her shoulder. She turned, and it was a child.

Shocked, he looked down into ageless eyes, and lost his heart to the homeless adolescent. Andre never questioned the why of it, but he saw her as a kindred spirit, a surrogate daughter. He became the only father LaToya had ever known, and she would have given her life for him.

"His vitals are almost nonexistent." LaToya voice wavered again. "We're air lifting him to Vandenberg. Please come." It was a desperate plea. "I don't know if he can hold out."

"We're leaving now! He's a fighter. Don't you give up on him!" John commanded, more than asked, to remind himself of the power of faith and word.

John Burkett had experienced much in his travels and had been in tough, almost suicidal skirmishes, but looking at his friend, broken and battered, unconscious and helpless was one of the most sobering moments of his life. Andre's face was barely recognizable, and his head was swallowed in bandages. Tubes ran from an opening where his nose should have been, and an IV needle was taped to his left wrist. His right arm hung suspended from a ceiling frame, and he was encased in a body cast from his chest to his waist.

The doctors were grim faced when they joined the family in the waiting room. "The next twenty-four hours are critical," the lead surgeon said, looking at Andre's father. "We've seen this type of trauma before with RV bomb victims. His head injury is grave, and we have to wait to see how much brain damage has actually occurred." The military doctor cleared his throat, and self-consciously removed his glasses, wiping them with methodical thoroughness on a surgical mask that hung from his neck.

"We removed part of your son's skull and bone fragments from his left lobe. There is a great deal of swelling...and there is more extensive damage to his left side of his brain. I don't know if he will recover from the injuries, even if he lives."

Andre's mother involuntary gasped. "No," and her knees buckled. Claude Dunn, hugged his wife close. He supported her to a lounge chair. The doctor looked at her sympathetically. "I am sorry, but there is only so much that modern medicine can do." He paused. "Can we get you anything....perhaps some water?"

Her muffled sob, "Just save my son...save him, please..." echoed in the room.

The next day, Andre was still holding his own. The doctors were cautiously optimistic. With the permission of Andre's parents, John convinced the medical staff and military superiors to register Andre in the hospital under an alias.

"Whoever attacked Andre wants him dead. It is important that we hide the fact that they did not succeed, because he is our only witness," John argued convincingly. The next day he arranged for an obituary published in the local paper announcing Andre's death. A private memorial service was held for the following week. Only the family attended.

CHAPTER FIVE

Tyler

WEST AFRICA

Tyler woke to the loud sounds of seagulls, their cries a beacon of doom. She was at sea, on a cargo tanker that did not have the luxuries of a passenger liner. Her bed was a narrow, lumpy bunk without the support of a pillow to relieve her throbbing headache, and her mouth felt like a ball of cotton.

The door opened with a chilling creak. Tyler stared at Lonnie with abject sadness. She had known from childhood he disliked her, and felt intuitively that he had been responsible for much of the misfortunes she experienced, but she had never envisioned that he hated her so much as to plot her death.

She listened to him as he spewed venom, cursing her, blaming her for all of his woes. She wondered about his sanity. Then she thought, *I should have known when he called me a fake, and the letter said I was a fake, and the voice at Jan's services, the attack, it was all him.* Realization appeared on Tyler's face; she was overwhelmed with dread.

"Where is Andre?" She was hesitant as her eyes roamed the windowless cabin.

"Shut your fuckin' mouth. I'll do the talkin', and I'll ask the questions." Lonnie drew in his breath and visibly shook, unable to control his rage.

"You are a thief and a motha fuckin' snake. You whoring slut, just like that mother of yours...the lowlife cunt." Lonnie was foaming at the mouth. His anger had been held in for so many years that he felt as if he would explode.

"Where you're goin', there ain't no return! You hear that, bitch. No return!" Lonnie ended the last vow in a high pitched, elongated scream.

Tyler found her voice, and pushed the worlds out. "Why?" The question was more for herself than him. His fanatical laugh was chilling. "Why? Why? Because you stole everything from me. They loved me until you came along..." The brutal tirade reached a crescendo.

"Where you are goin', you'll never be able to steal again. Your pretty face and sneaky ways won't do you any good. Yeah, bitch, no good at all."

His smile was a sneer. "They told me to deliver you unharmed, believe me, or I'd fuck you up big time. I always wanted to, but never had the opportunity." He was deadly earnest, and Tyler had no trouble believing he meant every word.

"You're my brother," Tyler said seeking empathy and trying to connect with Lonnie and bring about fond memories of the Price foster home. Her tone was cool, showing no sign of fear. It was the wrong thing to do. Lonnie had no fond memories from their shared childhood. If possible, he looked more sinister. Insane anger glistened in his eyes and he teetered precariously at the edge of hysteria.

"You stupid bitch, do you really want to go there?" His face was only inches from hers, and she watched him calmly as his stale breath filled her nostrils. He raised his hand, crazed with the thought that she was taunting him with her fearlessness. He thought, *I'll kill her now. Fuck the profit.*

He stood frozen. In his mind's eye, he saw her dead. Not like Jan. He had killed Jan to torment and terrorize Tyler. So, he had been swift with Jan. He had drugged her and strangled her in her sleep. Jan never knew what happened.

No quick, merciful death for Tyler. She was special. He wanted her to scream, suffer, and beg. He saw it all like a motion picture, played out in glorious detail.

Lonnie trembled in ecstasy. *Wouldn't that be great, I could record it and use it as a snuff film? My partner would love that.* His face was so close that his breath caused her bangs to fan away from her fore-head. His anger was terrifying, and Tyler mentally flinched, but she was determined to show no fear. She would die, she vowed, before she would cower before Lonnie. She had not retreated years before as a child, and by the grace of God, she thought, *I won't now.*

Moments ticked by. Tyler could see the flecks of dried spittle congealed in the corners of his mouth. Their eyes clashed in an unspoken battle of wills. Surrendering, Lonnie backed up and slammed out of the room. He knew if he stayed a moment longer, he would have killed her, and then he would have to forego millions. He did not know which would be worse, losing the money, or losing the opportunity to place Tyler in a desert harem where she would suffer a living hell.

The moment Lonnie slammed out of the room, Tyler's body went limp. She had waited and prayed for Andre's touch. But there was no contact, just empty blank space and a macabre silence. She refused to believe he was dead and replayed their last moments together. Lonnie had forced her to watch as his men broke Andre's thumbs.

He had not made a sound, but small beads of perspiration dotted Andre's brow. Tyler tried to reach him mentally, but he would not allow it. She twisted and kicked at Lonnie playing right into his hands.

Her foster brother taunted Andre, watching him with snake cold eyes as his little finger obscenely toyed with her mound through Tyler's lace underwear. With lewd expertise, he found her clit, captured, and held Andre's glare. He smiled and sneered smugly at Andre's helplessness as a damp stain spread across the center of her panties. Tyler twisted and squirmed in embarrassment and shame.

Andre's mind had touched her then, reassuring, but quickly faded as blinding pain racking his body transmitted itself to her. She cried out, furious, kicking at Lonnie again, but was grabbed from behind and thrown to the floor. Lonnie lunged and dragged her to her feet by the hair, his fist painfully twisted in her curls. Enraged, Andre charged Lonnie, leading with his shoulders. But one of Lonnie's goons clubbed him with a baton across the temple. Andre folded like a rag doll, his head hitting the bedside table as he went down.

The loud cracking of the second blow echoed in the room, and a guard snorted, and kicked him twice. Andre's limp body rolled soundlessly on the floor. "How's that, pretty boy?"

The next thing Tyler knew was that she was being hustled out of the house and shoved into a helicopter. As soon as she was seated, Lonnie stuck a needle filled with a powerful sedative into her arm.

Three weeks later the ship docked off the coast of Africa. Tyler was ignored during much of the trip. Lonnie visited her rarely, which was the only good news. She was filthy, and she could smell herself. The only toiletry she had been given was a small bowl of tepid water. Not even a wash cloth or toothbrush. The food was sparse and consisted of coarse chunks of bread, a watery soup she did not recognize, and limes.

It was disgusting, and if she had not been so desolate she might have felt the loss. But she was oblivious to the subtle forms of abuse. Her last thoughts were of comfort. She was not sure she wanted to live...without Andre...panicking. She did not know when he had become so necessary to her. She only knew that it seemed impossible without him.

She could not feel Andre's touch. He had not spoken to her in his private way, not once during the ocean voyage, and she was terrified that he might be lost to her forever. Repeatedly, she had mentally called to him and begged him to answer. She had to know that he was safe and all right, but there was only silence.

The door banged against the wall, and Lonnie strolled into the room impeccably dressed.

"Damn! Did something die in here?" Lonnie's lips smiled, but his eyes were vacant, and Tyler knew he was enjoying her discomfort. She stared at him, knowing he did not expect an answer.

Lonnie hated that more than anything else; hated to be looked at, even though he had surgery to repair most of the damage done to his face years before. Automatically, his hand sought the left side of his cheek and traced the space where the disfiguring scar had been. It was a habit he had begun as a child, first to hide the puckered mark on the side of his lips, and later to remind himself that the scar had been removed.

"You stink, bitch. Didn't your mama teach you how to keep yourself clean?" Again, his face grimaced in the humorless smirk. It was the closest thing he had to a smile.

"By the way, I thought you'd like to read." Lonnie flipped part of a week-old newspaper on the bed, and Tyler looked at it for several seconds before glancing at the headlines.

MUELLER HEIRESS MISSING

Tyler Mueller, youthful heir and chairman of the board of directors of Mueller International, disappeared. Family and friends said the cosmetics heiress had been under a great deal of emotional stress with the death of her longtime companion and private secretary Jan Barrows...

Ms. Mueller has been at the helm...

Tyler dropped the paper refusing to read more. She met his glare with a blank stare infused with contempt. It infuriated Lonnie. He wanted a reaction, something that told him that he was breaking her down. "Oh, yeah, I forgot. Your boyfriend— what was his name, Andrew...Artie...? Well, I thought you would like to know how he's doing." With that, Lonnie flung the other half of the newspaper at Tyler's feet.

Tyler reached for the paper, scooping it up before he could change his mind and take it back. She did not care what he thought. As she opened and scanned the page, Lonnie burst out in a genuine laugh. The maddening cackle reverberated in the room making her skin crawl.

A picture of Andre stared back at her from the obituary page. The professional black and white photo was a pale shadow of the vibrancy she had known. Tyler's eyes began to leak tears, the glistening lines streamed down her cheeks as life drained from her face.

Lonnie watched gleefully. Tyler devoured the editorial. The room was eerily quiet. He smiled slowly. He had finally hit his mark. He had hurt the bitch. Happy for the first time in years, Lonnie turned and practically skipped from the room. Clutching the newspaper, Tyler crushed it to her heart.

….Andre Dunn, owner and senior partner of Dunn & Burkett, died from injuries sustained during a mountain climb near his home in Big Bear. The thirty-seven-year-old homeland security expert and Navy SEAL veteran was renowned for his daring and miraculous recoveries of hostages and kidnapped victims.

Mr. Dunn expired from massive head injuries on July 9. His family and partner, John Burkett, were at his bedside. Private memorial services will be held at Rose Hill Cemetery in Glendale, on Saturday, July 14, 2007, at 11a.m.

Tyler's muffled sobs echoed in the room. Outside, Lonnie Jackson pushed himself off the wall and strolled down the hall, comforted that her suffering had just begun.

"I delivered the package as we agreed. Unharmed; unscarred, and untouched by the crew or myself."

The man on the other side of the room looked at Lonnie through hooded eyes. This American was less than the pestering insect he thoughtlessly crushed under his heel. Sheik Zankli recognized the corruption of the man.

Yes, he thought, he knew him well, and despised him more. For he had encountered his type frequently in the deadly fierce battles he had fought with numerous tribal warlords throughout Africa. Those men had few morals, less conscience, and the instincts of a deadly python. Change the clothes, location, and language, and the man could easily be substituted for any one of the warlords.

Hands laced neatly under his chin, the sheik was dressed in traditional garb. The long white and black checkered scarf on his turban headdress covered the fine line of hair framing his face from sideburn to sideburn, the pristine bandana concealing his chiseled nose and sensuous mouth.

Six feet of honed muscle, Sheik Zankli, the cat, as he was referred to by the numerous women who sought him in their bed, was irresistibly handsome. His birthright and leadership wore well on his broad bronze shoulders, and he walked with a confidence that bespoke years of superior breeding and intellect.

"Yes. You are to be commended. The task is well done." The Sheik spoke in flawless English, with a slight British accent. Educated in a military boarding school outside of London, he had continued his secondary education at Duke University. He completed his college education at the University of Southern California, earning a Master of Science degree in electrical engineering by age twenty-three. But he distrusted NATO, and despised the westernization of African governments that left the people exploited and demoralized.

"I'd really enjoy a visit with you, but you see I have pressing business back home." Lonnie looked at the Sheik expectantly. "So, if we can finish our business, I will be on my way." The rudeness of Americans never ceased to amaze the Sheik. It astounded him, the depth of their greed and malicious distain for life.

"Yes. Of course," he said. Swiveling in his chair the Sheik turned to his laptop, opened the Swiss banking account Web site, keyed in a password then waved Lonnie to his side. Standing, he flicked his hand at an imaginary piece of lint.

"We need your password to transfer the money."

Sheik Zankli waved his hand toward the chair. Lonnie sat down gingerly. He had not survived the streets of South Los Angeles and gang violence, because he was dumb or naive. He had insisted on doing business electronically. There was no way that he was going to take anything but a bank transfer. No. He smugly mused. He was not stupid. He knew if he had received payment in cash, he would never reach the dock alive.

The transfer was completed with a few strokes on his BlackBerry. Hara returned to his desk, but ignored Lonnie's outstretched hand. "Henri will take you to your ship." It was a taut dismissal, insulting, but Lonnie was too satisfied with the outcome of the deal to take offense. Tyler would spend the rest of her days as a lowly harem slave, and he would return home five million dollars richer. He sauntered out of the room, unaware of the sheik's malevolent glare.

Tyler did not know how long she had been in the camp, weeks, probably. She had been oblivious to her surroundings ever since Lonnie had flung the newspaper on her bed. Most of what happened afterward was a blur. It was only in the last few days that she had begun to focus on her surroundings and the people who moved in and out of her consciousness.

There was an older African woman who brought food to her twice a day and insisted that she eat. When Tyler did not respond to the woman's guttural urgings, she rubbed her stomach with one hand and graphically fed herself with the other. The woman was not unkind, just insistent, and she would not leave Tyler alone until she had eaten at least half of the meal.

There was a reason for Kelmai's insistence; the sheik had made it clear that he wanted this woman alive and healthy. He would question Kelmai daily as to the woman's comforts, even going so far as to inquire after her woman's cycle.

Kelmai always answered in the negative. There had been no bleeding since her arrival, although by Kelmai's estimation there should have been two cycles at the very least. Other than that, the woman appeared healthy, though too skinny by half, by Kelmai's standards. No, as far as she could tell, it was the woman's head that was sick not her body.

"Where am I?"

Kelmai almost dropped the tray she was carrying. The cracked voice was hoarse with lack of use, and she did not understand what her charge said, but Kelmai was elated. In the eight weeks that Tyler had been in the camp, she had not spoken a single word.

She rushed to Tyler's side. She felt her forehead, which was cool, and nodded a smile. The servant cupped Tyler's cheek.

"So the young miss is awake. Good."

Tyler looked at the woman puzzled. "I don't understand. Please. Where am I? Who are you?"

"Do not fret. I will get my master."

Patting Tyler on the arm, Kelmai hurried from the room. Tyler watched her go, baffled, and then searched the quarters, her eyes slowly circling the room. The air was filled with herbal incense. The fragrance permeated the room with a calming balm and Tyler found herself relaxing in spite of the strange surroundings and closed her eyes.

Tyler had not understood a word that the old woman said, and she felt like she was in a dream. Lonnie filtered in and out of hazy visions that included a newspaper article and pain, not physical, but crippling mind-blowing grief. Tyler concentrated, trying to recall the cloudy memories through stabbing pain.

Andre, it was about Andre. What was in the article? An aching anguish gripped Tyler, and it all came back to her, flooding her senses with murky apparitions.

She wrapped her arms around her waist, hugging her stomach. It was too much to bear. She hurt. It was torturous. Andre was gone. She could not feel him. She would never feel him again. Hunched over she screamed. The shriek of horror filled the room and went on and on.

Someone was calling her name. Strong hands shook her. It felt like her body was going to break in half, and the blow to her face caused her head to snap back brutally. The screaming stopped abruptly. The room became oddly quiet. Then she was being crushed into something solid. Her hair brushed back from her face gently as soothing sounds comforted her. She was being rocked like a baby and she did not want it to stop.

Hara held Tyler gently. It had been more than seven years since he had seen her, and she was almost unrecognizable. She was so frail that he feared he might cause her an injury if he held her too tightly. He had visited her daily over the past seven weeks, but he had not realized how bone thin she had become.

"Be still, my love. No one will harm you."

The smooth baritone melodic rumble was eerily familiar. The voice was from her past. She remembered the accent. Cultured.

Foreign. British. Friendly. Where had she heard it before? Tyler pushed away from the human headrest. Her eyes focused on a pale gold sleeveless damask robe, which covered a sheer cotton shirt. The shirt, which was collarless, exposed a dark bronze chest of steel. Self-conscious, she inhaled deeply. He had a musky masculine scent that caused Tyler to fling her head back fully alert. She knew.

"Hara! Tyler's eyes widen in shock. "What? What are you doing here? What is this place?" Tyler's words were frantic and bunched together. When Hara did not answer immediately, she wiggled herself out of his arms and stared into his eyes.

"What am I doing here?" Fully alert, Tyler's question demanded answers. Hara stared at her for several seconds, indecisive how he should answer; finally deciding the truth was the best course.

"I bought you. You were being offered on the Internet at a ridiculously high price."

Hara followed this shocking information with an apologetic shrug and a smile that had charmed his way into many a woman's bed. Tyler sputtered, questions stumbling over each other in her mind. Before she could speak, Hara interrupted anticipating her question.

"No. He did not offer you by name, but with a description that I knew could only be you, or an identical twin. And since I didn't believe you had a twin, I gambled on it being you, and here you are. I figured if I was wrong, the worst scenario was that I would add another lovely to my harem."

Tyler whispered; "On the Internet? When?"

"Your offer was first posted nine weeks ago on an underground *Slave Site*. I have a cousin who disappeared several weeks ago, and my family believed a band known for trafficking in slavery had stolen her. I was surfing the net looking for her, when I came across your posting." Hara paused, tongue in cheek. "To your good fortune, I must add."

Hara produced another devastating smile. In spite of herself, Tyler found herself responding to the irony of the moment with a smile of her own. Hara had always seen humor even in the most distressing situations, and he had never failed to make her laugh even at her own pretensions.

"Who did you piss off? Because, whoever arranged your sale was someone who wanted you to really, r-e-a-l-l-y suffer." Hara raised his eyebrows and winked to emphasize the seriousness of his disclosure.

"The site he posted you on is frequented by the rich and truly shameless—people who have, shall I say, very refined tastes and sexual preferences. Hell, few survive their amorous attention."

Tyler had been listening avidly, her eyes widening with each disclosure.

"My foster brother orchestrated this. He's always hated me." She responded shamefully, as if she was somehow responsible for Lonnie's betrayal.

"Foster brother? I never knew you had a foster-brother. The Muellers didn't strike me as foster parent types."

Hara noted the slight flush, and sensitive to her embarrassment he attempted to lighten the mood even more.

"Well. The good news is that you are with me, and the bad news, as far as you're concerned, is that I have no intention of returning you…. at least not anytime soon." He wiggled his eyebrows comically.

When Tyler's mouth flew open in outrage, seeing no humor in the situation, and ready to do verbal battle, Hara held up his hands conciliatorily. "Be still, little one. It is for your safety."

The two men sat across from one another, with a thin veil of civility cloaking their mutual contempt.

"Was the package delivered?" The question was asked causally, as if the answer was of no account.

"Yes." Lonnie assessed the impeccably dressed man seated on the opposite side of the desk. He did not fool himself. This man might look as soft as putty, but he was a dangerous adversary and no one to mess with. Lonnie understood that the question was but a prelude to a permanent separation of their partnership. The game was over, and neither had use for the other anymore.

"I want my money," Lonnie said in a throaty demand; with no play in his fixed stare.

"Well now! Aren't we the greedy one! I thought you received a king's ransom when you sold your product over the Internet." The response was quick, said snidely to provoke. Lonnie noted that *the product* was not mentioned by name. No, thought Lonnie. This man was very careful.

"What I received for the...product...is not your concern. It has nothing to do with our deal. You know that! Am I making myself clear?"

"Oh, very clear...my dear man."

'How dare the son of a bitch question me?' Lonnie was furious, but held himself in check by silently reminding himself of the money to come. "It's late and I'm tired. I'd like my money... not talk! Do you, or don't you have it?"

"Well, you see, that's the problem." There was an expectant pause. "I don't have it...never did, and at any rate...Did you think I would give you money, you petty, small-time hustler? You are scum, privileged to work with me. You stupid bastard, as much as I like fucking niggers up the ass, I wouldn't fuck you with my butler's cock." Z laughed.

Lonnie rose from his chair, an inferno of fury, but sat back down as he watched his partner removed a revolver from inside his top coat. A silencer was attached to the barrel. The gun was pointed ominously at him, perfectly leveled with his head.

"I never intended to pay you."

Shocked, Lonnie had just an instant to register the danger before the gun flashed silently and a hole appeared at the top of his forehead. It was over in seconds. The man placed his gloved hands on the table and pushed out of his seat.

And to think the gutter rat thought he would get the best of me. Z flipped a card on the table next to Lonnie's head, and strolled from the warehouse unnoticed in the quiet of the night.

The cell phone vibrated and then chimed on the nightstand. It was almost midnight, and John was tempted to ignore the summons, but the seasoned veteran reached across his wife with an apologetic shrug and flipped open his BlackBerry.

"Yes. This is Mr. Burkett. No, problem, yes, we were awake. I see."

"Who is it?"

John held up one finger silencing his wife.

"That's great! I'm on the way." John shot out of the bed and grabbed for his pants, which were folded with a soldier's neatness across the trouser rack in the corner of the room.

Janis Burkett put her book down and studied her husband over the rim of her glasses. John glanced at his wife and answered her unspoken question with a tight smile.

"Andre's awake. They want me to come right away." He tugged on his plants, zipped his fly and pulled the form-fitting knit shirt over his head. At thirty-nine he had a perfect physique with an Usher-like six pack. He crossed the room, reached for his wife and gently framed her chin with the palm of his hand. His head dipped. His kiss was slow and promising, full of the love he had for her.

"That will keep you until I return."It was a confident statement of fact, and John winked at his wife to emphasize his point.

Janis pouted with feigned disappointment, batting her eyes as she reached over and gave John a suggestive pat on the butt, then blew her husband of twelve years a finger-tip kiss. "I'll keep!"

Five minutes later, John gunned his car, pulled the shiny black Mercedes out of the three-car garage and raced toward the secluded sanitarium in the Santa Monica Mountains. He had relocated his family and the corporate headquarters to the area after the attempt on his partner's life. He thanked God for a gorgeous, understanding wife and young children; otherwise, the move would have been contentious, if not impossible.

Andre had been in a coma for three months, but John had never doubted that his best friend and partner would recover in spite of the doctors' grim forecasts. The doctors were not encouraging, warning the family that Andre might never come out of the coma, and even if he did, they should not expect the same man.

"The type of head injury Mr. Dunn has sustained may leave him paralyzed with limited speech and auditory perception. We won't know how serious the damage is until he regains conscious-ness. And. I'm sorry. We can't guarantee if," the doctor paused and looked at Andre's parents hopelessly, "or when he will wake up."

Françoise Dunn turned into her husband with a sob, and he enfolded her in his arms, rocking her lovingly. He spoke softly. His comforting words were private for her ears alone.

Paul watched his parents, convinced that Andre would re-cover in spite of the doctor's dismal words. His close relation-ship with his brother began as a toddler when Paul heard his telepathic call. Lost and confused, the four-year-old had been wandering for more than twenty minutes when he heard Andre's voice in his head.

Andre had guided his younger brother back to the family us-ing his powers and from that day on, the two boys communicated privately. The night of the accident Paul spoke with quiet author-ity to his parents.

"I feel him mom. Every now and then, I feel him reaching out to me." Paul was confident, and his words rang true. "He is fight-ing to heal himself. Trust me. He will come back to us whole."

John looked at Andre's younger brother. Andre had often spoken of the special connection he had with Paul. Once, in a particularly tight situation, when their squad was under heavy attack, outnumbered, and out gunned, Andre had confided to John that he could communicate with his bother telepathically.

"It's weird, John. I can talk to him and he can hear me no matter where I am." At the time, John had looked at Andre dis-believingly, wondering if the pressure had gotten to his friend. But Andre had gone very still, closed his eyes and meditated. Several minutes passed, and when Andre opened his eyes again, he spoke with unshakable certainty. "Help is on the way." Three hours later a platoon of friendly troops parachuted into the area, and the rest was history.

They entered Andre's room together. Andre was sitting up in the bed. It was an emotional moment. The weeks had been kind to Andre; his arm and collarbone had healed, and the casts had been removed, but what amazed the doctors most was that in spite of the trauma present in the initial examinations, the latest CAT scans revealed no permanent damage to Andre's brain. The doctors were stumped.

"Don't ask me to explain it, Mr. Dunn. In all my years of practicing medicine, I have never witnessed such a miraculous recovery. If I had not personally examined your son when he entered the hospital, I would not believe he had ever been injured."

The family gathered around Andre's bed. Claude eyed his son, grateful to God that he was returned to them. Taking Andre's hand in his, he squeezed and spoke first.

"Hey, buddy."

Andre's eyes were completely clear, as if he had just awakened from a refreshing nap. He looked at his family members in turn, studying each face lovingly. A frown creased his brow, and his eyes went deadly serious, drilling his partner with a razor stare.

"Where is she?" Andre's voice was raspy from lack of use, but it was strong. Forceful.

'*Oh yeah! He's back.*' John smiled to himself. "She's in a safe place, with a friend who understands the need for armed security."

"I want her here with me. I can feel her confusion."

Andre's eyes wandered the room touching everyone. They all felt it, the piercing glance that was not opened to discussion or challenge.

"Done!" John response was immediate.

Andre exhaled deeply. It was as if a huge weight was from his shoulders. Visibly, he relaxed, turned toward his father and mother and smiled. Then his eyes fused with his brother, love shinning through.

"Paul. I felt you with me often." Silently for Paul's ears alone, Andre whispered telepathically. *I could not have made it without you.*

That same evening, Hara sat on plush pillows and studied Tyler over a steaming bowl of ground-nut soup. The soup smelled delicious, and Tyler's stomach grumbled appreciatively. Her eyes sprang up. "I'm sorry."

"No need to apologize, little one."

Hara inspected Tyler, his inquisitive gaze sensuous. He was sinfully handsome, a temping package of masculine allure. Six five in his stocking feet, his waist tapered triangularly into slim hips and a tight backside. Tyler would have had to be blind not to notice his sultry appeal. In truth, few women could resist his lusty beacon.

Hara had a magnetism all his own, crowned by an animal pulse, a jungle beat that he radiated. And his scent was something Tyler could not, would never forget. Years before, when she had asked him about it, he had laughed and said his mother had prayed and asked the gods of his great-grandfathers for a favor so that, "I would sweat honey from my pores. My mother wanted you women to find me irresistible so that I would make her lots of grandbabies. She asked that women swarm to me like a bee to a hive." He had chuckled then, smug in his male splendor, his full lips flashing perfect white teeth.

Even now, years later, after experiencing Hara's sexual selfishness, Tyler felt his raw appeal. She observed him clandestinely from beneath lower lids. Her thick lashes concealing her confusion. She found him sinfully attractive. Her eyes roamed his thick arms and corded biceps, secretly lingering on the curve of his long, muscled thighs. His body promised everything, but experience told her that he would deliver little.

Andre had taught her the real pleasure of muscled legs, especially his magnificently thick leg of manhood. Tyler's heart fluttered. A deep, searing pain invaded her heart. Andre. How could she forget him for even a minute? There was no comparison. Hara was just a pretty picture, and when you scratched the surface, there was little else.

Sick with herself and with her momentary disloyalty, Tyler reached out, mentally searching, attempting to make contact with Andre. But there was no response, yet she knew, in spite of what Lonnie had said, Andre was not dead. She felt his presence—faint, unresponsive, but alive nonetheless.

Hara reclined against the floor sofa, one leg casually bent at the knee accentuating his lean lines with an overt invitation. His thick manhood was outlined against the robe invitingly, and Tyler swallowed loudly, lowering her lids against the lusty call. She sat across from him, a hand-carved sunken dining table in between them.

Hara watched Tyler without seeming to do so, noting how little she had changed. He found her irresistible, stunning, and effortlessly beautiful. She was a tempting morsel. Yet there was something different about her. She had a new sensuality that beckoned. He found her more womanly and more sexually attractive than before. Her woman's scent was lush, a powerful stimulant invoking a lustful response from him. Sadly, the attraction appeared one sided.

Tyler had erected an impenetrable wall, and the barrier made her untouchable. She was present, and conversely not. With a sudden and unbidden urgency, Hara wanted to take her, pound into her body, make her respond to him, bring life to her eyes, and passion to her lips. He wanted her complete submission with a heady compulsion more potent than any he had before.

His tool stirred, and he reached across the table with fluid grace handing Tyler a plate of steamed rice. Motioning for her to hold the plate over the table, he spooned the savory stew over the rice. The delicious flavors permeated the room, and Tyler's stomach rumbled again. She laughed apologetically.

"I'm hungry." Hara chuckled, happy to see Tyler's vagueness lifting.

"My aunt will be pleased to learn of your appreciation. She has been at her wits end to concoct dishes that would tempt your palate."

"Was I unappreciative?"

"Let's put it this way." Hara's eyes twinkled with mischief. "You didn't eat."

Tyler seemed to take this in slowly.

"How long have I been here?" She waved her hand, encompassing the room and its intimate setting.

Hara searched her face, wondering if she was prepared for the truth. In many ways, Tyler resembled some of the battle-weary soldiers in his band. Their troubled souls were open wounds of sorrow, incapable of healing, and for some irreparably damaged.

Like those men, Tyler had arrived at his camp emaciated, filthy, and mute. He could only speculate about the trauma she had undergone at the hands of her captors. Whatever happened, he concluded, the experience had been so devastating, it had robbed her of her speech, and it appeared for a while, her desire to live.

"Not long enough." His answer was a not so subtle evasion of the question. His eyes gazed into hers. He brought a spoonful of the spicy soup to his mouth and chewed meaningfully. The slow methodical movement of his lips held a naughty invitation.

He was ridiculous, and Tyler started to giggle uncontrollably. Sliding to her side, bolstered by the divan pillows, she hugged her waist, and her infectious laughter eliciting a huge smile from Hara. He wanted to keep her with him forever. Watching her possessively, a plan began to unfold.

"Seriously, I am worried about your safety. We are moving the camp tomorrow. How would you like to vacation with me in my mother's village? You will be safe there, and I can communicate with your family and find out the state of affairs with your security team.

"My mother loves you. She used to refer to you as, *our wife*. Remember. She was determined that we marry."

Tyler sat up, wiping at the tears, which had sprung from her eyes joyously, and considered Hara's proposal. There was really no reason for her to refuse his offer. There was nothing but pain back home. Jan was gone, and Andre was missing. Her heart flipped in painful denial of Lonnie's taunt. She would not believe that he was dead. A small voice whispered to her that this was not so. But Andre was not speaking to her in their intimate way, and she felt confused and lost without his touch.

Instantly, sadness overwhelmed her. She was tired, exhausted, and weary of decisions and deadlines and, Lonnie. He was out there somewhere, ready to pounce and hurt the ones she loved. For the first time in her life, she honestly wanted to harm another human being. She wanted to punish him for the hurt he had done to Jan and Andre. She wanted to tear, kick, bite, scratch—even to kill him. But mostly she wanted to know that he was no longer a danger to those she loved.

She had to think and heal. Dear God, she wanted to feel Andre's touch again. And if she was going to accomplish that, she needed a place to go to meditate, a peaceful setting where she could hone her newfound gifts. What better spot than Hara's village? With her mind made up, she turned and spoke with conviction, "I'll go."

Andre lay in his bed, listening to the steady beep of the machine monitoring his vital signs. He had undergone a battery of tests, and the doctors were literally scratching their heads in amazement. He could hear them all questioning repeatedly

"But how can this be?" The medical exams and X-rays did not show signs of Andre's emergency room injuries. It was as if the images were of two entirely different people. There was nothing, in recent tests, to indicate he had ever sustained a deadly brain trauma, no scar tissue, no fracture, telling cracks, nothing. The scars and signs of his bodily injuries, broken thumbs, collarbone, and ribs had miraculously disappeared.

While the hospital staff buzzed with the phenomenon, Andre continued to concentrate on healing himself. It was an entirely new experience, this tapping into energy so powerful that it allowed him to seek and heal damaged tissues and fractured bones at will. Although unconscious throughout much of his initial examination, Andre had been aware of internal hemorrhaging and his failing life forces.

In the past, he had directed his energy toward warding off simple illnesses like colds and flu. He had even been able to speed up the healing process in minor abrasions and muscle strains, eliminating or accelerating his body's recuperation to mere minutes, or in severe cases, hours. But this was different—miraculous—for him.

Andre had been on the brink of death, his vital signs so low that doctors had given him over to forces out of their control. He had been aware of their frantic efforts and use of clamps and pins to obstruct the flood of blood pooling into his chest cavity, drowning him in his own fluids. He was in so much pain that the temptation to follow the light was overwhelming, and but for the fact that he would have left Tyler behind to face Lonnie alone, he would have done so. And there was something else, a voice, pure and absorbing that told him that the light was not for him.

"You are Zankli, of the Chosen, and your destiny is not yet fulfilled." The message reverberated in his mind, as he lay motionless, perhaps for hours. When the voice quieted, Andre felt his powers enhance—grow exponentially—and he became infused with healing energy beyond anything he had ever known.

The doctors had forecast irreparable damage to his nervous system, and prepared the family for the worst. The fact that he was alive, with no apparent damage to his brain or spine was a miracle in the eyes of the medical staff. The knowledge that Andre's fractures and other injuries were continuing to heal at a pace heretofore unrecorded in medical annals prompted the hospital administrators to report his case to the World Health Organization (WHO).

Twenty-four hours later, WHO researchers converged on the hospital, and were meeting with the hospital's chief operating officer. Andre listened, projecting himself into the chief of staff's office. The WHO representatives wanted to transfer him to their facilities immediately, without his family's authorization. The hospital administrator was reluctant, citing legal ramifications.

"Listen. I understand the need for urgency, and I acknowledge the need for secrecy. But what you're asking is outside of my jurisdiction. I need board approval for what you want, or a legal warrant from a federal judge."

Peter Lerner sat in the large executive chair, facing the three WHO representatives. They were a motley crew. *Real creeps*, he thought, and the most arrogant team he had ever met, more interested in their own agenda than the patient's well being.

"We'll have a court order by this evening," Dr. Jason Keller barked with confidence. Recruited from Cornell University, he had been with WHO for over twenty years. A research prodigy, he graduated with a PhD in physics at eighteen, and was considered one of the world's foremost authorities in quantum physics and the paranormal.

"Do that!" Peter Lerner replied calmly, thinking, *my dick is just as big as yours.* Lerner gave Keller a tight smile, and stood, signaling the meeting closed.

When the last of the three WHO representatives passed through the door, Dr. Lerner picked up the phone and punched in John Burkett's cell phone number.

"We have a problem." His firm tone punctuated the seriousness of his statement. "I just had a visit from representatives of the World Health Organization. Someone on my staff, probably Rick Dean, the prick, called WHO and told them about Andre."

The silence at the other end of the phone spoke volumes. "Can he be moved?"

"At the rate he is healing. Definitely!"

"I'll be there within the hour."

Satisfied with the outcome of the meeting and Lerner's call to his partner, Andre returned to his body. His out-of-body experience had been exhausting. He slept; secure that John would take care of the details.

True to his word, John and his team rolled Andre out of the hospital on a covered gurney and secured him in a private ambulance less than an hour later. Hospital release forms indicated his parents had taken responsibility for his post-accident therapy and the patient would be convalescing in the Bahamas. The WHO representatives were outraged when they learned that Andre had left the hospital.

"What do you mean he's been released to his family?" Jason Keller stood stiffly, his ire communicated in the curve of his mouth and tone of voice. He had been outmaneuvered, and he was furious.

Dr. Lerner wanted to laugh at Keller's impotency. The man could sneer as much as he wanted, postulate and shout, but the deed was done. Andre Dunn was no longer at the hospital. He was clearly outside of the World Health Organization's reach for the moment. Legally there was nothing they could do.

"I'm sorry, but it was not my call. His parents insisted on the transfer, and took full responsibility." Lerner placed his hands on the table and pushed himself out of the chair, rising. He was a little man, only five feet six inches in his custom elevated shoes. And while, his erect stance gave the illusion of tallness, he resented the taller man's height, and Keller's superior attitude.

"If I can be of further assistance, let me know. Meanwhile, I need to address an administrative issue." Lerner paused, looked at his nails casually, hesitated, and then looked into Keller's face tellingly.

"I know you understand." Moving with a business poise that was close to a swagger, Dr. Lerner ushered Keller to the door and out into the hallway. With obvious contempt for the other man, he turned and ambled away. The message was clear. Keller and his problems were insignificant, a trivial interruption in his busy day at most.

Andre's slumber was undisturbed by the flight to Togo, the landing, or inland trek to his family's compound. When he opened his eyes, he was in a spacious room, luxuriously furnished in teak, bamboo, and white linen. Sheer white mesh surrounded his bed and the overhead fan buzzed above. The repetitive swish was a backdrop to the soft hum of the air conditioner.

Across the room, Françoise Dunn dozed on a daybed. A large photo journal of early-twentieth-century West African tribes lay open beneath her breasts. The beautiful face of an adolescent girl with shaved head, colorful beads circling her neck, and huge hoops dangling from her ears stared regally from the book cover.

Andre's lids fluttered and slowly opened. Pain exploded in his head, and he squeezed his eyes shutting them against the piercing light; the white-silver glare was blinding. He raised his arm shielding his eyes. It felt unnaturally heavy, lethargic, and he was sluggish, but he recalled bits of the conversation between Lerner and Keller.

Puzzled, he wondered if he was in a WHO lab, and anxiously searched the room until his eyes fell on Françoise. Instantly, his body relaxed.

"Mother." Andre's voice was raspy and barely above a whisper. He cleared this throat and tried again.

"Mom." Françoise turned her head toward her son, feeling more than hearing his summons and moved so quickly the book slid from her stomach onto the floor. Rising, Françoise crossed to Andre and took his hand in hers.

"Hello, son. Welcome back." Her beautiful face radiated love. At sixty-two, she was lovely, a poster image for aging gracefully. Her unlined faced was framed by shoulder length, silver-white locks, a startling contrast to her youthful figure and appearance. At five feet four, she was accustomed to being dwarfed by the towering men in her family. Claude and his sons were robust, bigger than life, strong muscular men, who made her feel safe.

It was humbling to see one of them felled and near death. Her own sense of helplessness was not to be born. Oh, she understood how fragile and provisional life could be. She had lost her resilient robust father earlier in the year. But somehow, until Andre's accident she had felt that she and Claude would be gone long before their children; a fact, one of her mother's people, a native doctor, had prophesied years before.

She would never forget their post-marriage audience with the revered tribal sage. Claude and she had agreed to have a Catholic and traditional ceremony. After their grandiose wedding at Our Lady of Lourdes Cathedral near her father's estate in the South of France, Françoise and Claude had traveled to Togo for a traditional ceremony and celebration.

The ceremony was officiated by her grand-uncle who was the regional prince. The Zankli were a family of tribesmen who could trace their oral history to a time before the days of the sub-Saharan caravan trade.

The three-day celebration and banquet culminated in a trek into the bush. They had set out early in the morning, right after sunrise. Although Françoise had visited her mother's village annually from the time she was an infant, and had felt herself well versed in the terrain surrounding the township, she was unprepared for the arduous march into the wild untamed grasslands where few tourists had visited.

Two machete-chopping guides who kept a grueling pace led them. It was hot and humid, an inferno, blistering in its intensity. Claude slapped at a mosquito, and Françoise was glad they had taken their malaria shots. The bush was alive with insects and wild animals. Several miles outside of the village, chimps cried loudly in the trees announcing the foreign invaders, and huge cats sulked so near that Françoise wondered at the wisdom of their journey.

Finally, they reached a clearing where domesticated cows grazed in an open pen. Trees surrounded several earth colored structures that almost blended into the landscape. A dirt-brushed lane led to the compound of rounded shelters with thick burlap coverings for doors. In the center was an ancient mud and grass hut and the newly married couple was ushered inside. The room was dim, and the newlyweds stood motionless until their eyes adjusted to change in the dusty light.

A man scantily dressed in a loincloth, animal tooth necklaces, ivory wrist and armbands, grass anklets, and a beautifully carved jeweled face mask, sat in the middle of the hut on a colorful floor mat. He was surrounded by fragrant bottles of oil. Incense smoldered in the room clouding their vision.

The native doctor motioned for the couple to sit before him. The macabre mask stared sightless into their faces. The blood red ruby in the center of the mask glowed. It was surreal. Françoise felt a chill, and looked again at the hypnotic ruby mask. A light breeze stirred the incense in the room. Impossible, she thought. There were no windows and the air was humid and hot outside.

Nonetheless, Françoise felt a mystical energy. She wondered if Claude felt it too when he enfolded her hand in his protectively. She shivered, wanting to see past the mask. But the hollow sockets revealed nothing. The man began to speak in his native tongue, the language, a beautiful melody of clicking sounds.

Ve Tuk, ya ve mein-gutool ya Zankli, toli ya ethvenu, yiftul ya Etlvenu, yiftul ya ve kul ti gull e yilto cun utivi. Tuk tultoo vii m tultoo tuki peke.

Françoise understood some of the prayer, but many of the sage's words referenced things long gone. *Tuk tultoo vii m tultoo tuki peke...* "God always was and always will be."

She wondered if it was even important that they understood. The singsong humming of words invaded Françoise's body. The native doctor began to sway, each grouping of words bringing him closer to a trance state. The room remained cool. He was mesmerizing. His hypnotic lilt beckoned and seduced the young couple subtly.

Claude and Françoise had a sense of floating and levitating. They were in the hut, but not, and the experience, although unique, was alarming. Claude tightened his grip on Françoise's hand. He felt weightless. His soul was no longer under his personal control, and he feared for Françoise. There was a bright light, blinding in its intensity.

"Your marriage was foretold in the annals of our great-grandfathers. You will be with this woman for all time. Now! And in the hereafter." The sage spoke in his native tongue, and Claude, who had never spoken a word of the ancient language, understood him perfectly.

"There will be three children from this union. Your first, a boy, will be a gift to humankind. He is destined to marry and produce a world leader, a man called Zac who will usher in an age of peace and unity among all nations. Your second, also a male, will be unparalleled in the world of finance. Your third child will be named Mimi. She is destined for a Zankli of old, and she will live a long and luxurious life. Few will match her power."

"You will live to see their greatness, yet you will be blessed to go to *the-land-of-see-me-no-more* long before the demise of your children."

The sage placed long fingers over Françoise's and Claude's layered hands. The warmth of the sage's hand radiated. Energy flowed from him to the newly joined couple seeking with purpose the rapidly multiplying cells in the woman's body. The tiny life planted in Françoise' womb received the illuminating beam, flared brightly and absorbed the light.

"Go now with the well wishes of your ancestors."

The trip back to the family compound was surreal. In all the years since their audience with the native doctor, Françoise and Claude never questioned the wisdom of the sage. As she studied her eldest face, she thanked God and counted her blessings. She had not credited native medicine, nor had she valued the beliefs of her mother's people. But she could not discount the miracle that lay before her. And she knew the ways of the Zankli were at a level of spirituality that boggled the mind.

Mired in an unshakable belief in God, the Zankli religious lore told of a visit from a celestial messenger who had lived among them for three hundred years. During that time, he had taken twelve wives. The messenger promised to return, and said if his word was followed, the earthly Zankli would be gifted with great spiritual powers.

Françoise's eyes shimmered with unshed tears. Obviously, Andre was one of the messenger's chosen. He was the prophesized Zankli who possessed spiritual gifts of mystical proportions. She felt both pride and bone chilling dread.

Her hand smoothed the hair on her son's head, fingering the coarse waves, lost in a recollection from years past. Andre was six. It was at Paul's birthday party, and Andre was balancing a boiled egg on a serving spoon. It was a race to see which child could walk the fastest without dropping his egg. Andre's little legs were pumping fast and in his rush to win, he tripped and cut his thigh on a garden chair.

Françoise rushed to her son. Andre was stoic as he lay with the chair twisted above him. She picked him up and took him into the bathroom where she washed and bandaged his cut. It was not deep, but it bled profusely. Deciding the wound was not serious enough for an emergency room visit, she had patted him on the shoulder and they returned to the game.

Later that night when she went to change the bandage there was no evidence of the wound. Nothing! No scar, not even a scrape or bruise. Francois was amazed. She searched her son's leg frantically, and then asked.

"Andre. Where is your cut?" Francois' looked at her small son in wonderment.

"I made it go away, Mommy. I didn't like the hurt. So, I made it go away."

The little boy was casual in his revelation as if it was something that everyone could do. Francois was floored, and sat down heavily on her son's bed. Her mouth opened and shut several times, baffled.

"Have you done this before? Made the hurt go away?" The question was whispered as she stared intently into her son's eyes. Andre bobbed his head slowly, affirming her fear.

Francois gazed at the sturdy replica of her husband standing before her, tall for his six years. She enfolded him in her arms, hugging him closely and mentally shivered. His innocent disclosure was frightening. She did not want it to be true.

"Listen to me, son. I do not want you to ever discuss how you can make hurt go away. Not with anyone. This is very important. You must keep what you do a secret. I do not want you to talk about it ever, not with your brother, your sister, or your father." Françoise stared into her son's eyes willing his compre hension. "Not even with me. Do you understand?" Françoise took Andre's shoulders between her hands and shook him gently. Her stern tone and expression was a thin veil to her panic. And Andre was aware. He felt and read his mother's fright.

The child took heed. Although he applied his skill often over the years, he never discussed or demonstrated his healing abilities to another living soul. Nor, for that matter, did he speak telepathically to anyone other than Paul. His mother's scolding had left a permanent impression, and until Tyler, he had never communicated with another human being using his mental prowess from *out of his body*.

Francois watched her son lovingly. He was a grown man. Yet today, she felt a return of the dread she suffered years before when she discovered her son's healing powers. She had no doubt the scientific world would treat him as a lab animal. They would dissect and bleed him to uncover the wonders of his gifts. This possibility was not an option. It was unacceptable.

Andre felt his mother's turmoil. He read her fear and understood her need to guard him against harm. He touched her mind, transmitting calm. She would have to let him go soon, and he wanted to prepare her for his departure. But unbeknownst to Andre, his mother understood his feelings better than he did himself, for she had felt the same loss when Claude had returned to America years before, leaving her behind until she received a visa.

"I feel your pain. Do not try to hide it from me. I am your mother, a Zankli, and my need to be with your father is as great as your need to be with Tyler."

"I've got to find her, Mother. Tyler needs me."

Andre's eyes met his mother's. He felt empty, incomplete without Tyler, and for some reason, he was unable to reach her on a psychic path. It was as if there was a deep fog blocking their union, but he knew she was unharmed. Confused, but unharmed. It was as if she had placed a shield between them.

Françoise placed her palm on her son's face, and Andre closed his eyes.

He needed all of his energy directed at the complete healing of his body, so he sought solace in a deep rejuvenating sleep.

It was another week before Andre could leave his bed. His first steps were child like, unsteady and wobbly, with a Frankenstein lurch. Soon he was walking sure footed, then running and climbing. He exercised a grueling five hours a day. The punishing regimen paid off. One month after his arrival at the Zankli compound, three months after his accident, Andre was as fit as he had ever been. His first cellular call was to his partner.

"John, I want a small unit here by tomorrow. Select our most experienced men. Don't tell them who they will be working with. I don't want them to know that I am alive until they arrive here."

"Oh. Make sure LaToya is on the team. I know that this has been hard on her."

"You got that right." John's pleasure in hearing his friend's succinct orders radiated through the phone.

"The girl's been in the dumps, questioning me a thousand times about how you were doing, and when she could come to see you. I swear you'd think you were her biological dad. I know she calls you Pops, but I didn't know until your injury what you meant to her."

Outside of John, LaToya was the only member of the Dunn & Burkett firm that knew Andre was not dead. On the other end of the phone, Andre was silent, thinking to himself. *I knew. She has no other family other than me. She was Zankli.*

"I knew. I've always known…and John, I feel she is my daughter. It is real to me, as if my blood ran in her veins. Make sure LaToya knows that."

There was a significant pause, both men were aware of the silent question. "So where is she?"

There was no doubt in John's mind about who "she" was. On the other end of the line, he waffled, hesitating to reveal what he had known for weeks. "She's in Nigeria, with our old friend Hara. You remember, I told you she was with someone who understood security."

"And?" Andre's voice was razor thin.

John realized he was sinking fast. "They've gone missing. Several weeks ago, they just up and disappeared. I've called and text him over and over, with no response."

"I see." The frugality of his words spoke volumes. "I want you to locate them. Use every resource available. I'll contact my brother and find out what he knows about Hara's movements. He is a Zankli. John should be able to track him through our relatives in Nigeria. Is he still running rebel activities in the north?"

"Yes. Hara's men are attacking the oil refineries and have been confiscating or destroying their machinery and equipment for more than three years. Inexplicably, a few months ago all activity halted and there was a lull in insurgent hostilities."

Unspoken, was both men's certainty that Tyler had provided the impetus for Hara's hiatus. Andre was unwilling to pursue this line of thought. Abruptly, he ended the conversation.

"I will see you tomorrow." He closed off the BlackBerry and examined the ultra thin iPhone. It was a deceptive piece of technology, outwardly an ordinary cell phone, but in actuality capable of an untraceable reception anywhere in the world. His service provider was part of a satellite surveillance system available only to Interpol agents. The number automatically changed in six-hour intervals. There was no way to trace the cell number or its registered owner, and Andre was thankful for his brother's contacts.

For the thousandth time, he let his senses fan out searching for Tyler. Once again, he ran into an impenetrable brick wall. Frustrated, he paced the room with nervous energy, then realizing the futility of it, strolled to his mother's favorite oversized wicker chair, exhaled, and eased down into the seat deep in thought.

Hara watched Tyler over the brim of his glass. He wanted her. The ache was almost unbearable, and he was growing weary of the chase. It had been weeks. He had placed his entire campaign on hold while he wooed and courted this woman, to no avail. He was more than frustrated. He sat the glass down and walked with determined steps to her side. *Patience*, he reminded himself.

"What is it, my dove? What worries you so?"

Tyler turned and looked up at Hara. He was so close his breath stirred the loosely bunched curls at the top of her head. Her beautiful eyes were cloudy, a mirror of her tumultuous thoughts. When she hesitated, Hara spoke.

"I feel you are not in this room, not with me. Where have you wandered, my love?" Confusion flashed across her face, and Tyler turned back toward the window.

Hara wrapped his arms around Tyler, and she leaned into his body exhaling with a noisy sigh. The weeks had taken their toll, and she was unusually fatigued. Unaware that she had been given an herbal remedy that tranquilized and dulled the senses, Tyler attributed her mental haze to the calming rhythms of village life.

Nothing could have been further from the truth. The herb had been known to Hausa tribesmen for centuries and used in the slave trade to control captives as they were moved to the coast for sale. The ground powder was a tasteless drug that made the user malleable and open to suggestion. Hara had ordered his aunt to add the powder to Tyler's food daily. This evening he had personally sprinkled an extra dose of the tasteless drug over her lamb stew.

Hara was not accustomed to defeat in his amorous pursuits, and he was unwilling to be denied. Since childhood, he had been feted by the women of his family—told that he was one of the chosen—a Zankli prince. Women had flocked to him, and he had never had to work to gain their attention or their bodies. Tyler was proving to be a frustrating challenge.

Tentatively, he began to massage her midriff and stomach. Tyler did not resist, rather she sank even more into his welcoming body. Encouraged, his hand moved higher, circling the soft swell of her breasts, his long fingers teasing under their curves.

Unlike dozens of times before, when his hands had strayed, Tyler did not move away. He silently moaned, delighted to have this new privilege. He nestled her neck, breathing in her personal perfume. She turned in his arms. The juncture of her legs was a perfect nest for his length.

He was heavy with need, hanging low, his iron-hard thickness cupped expertly by her womanhood. He knew her response was mostly a reaction to the herbal stimulant—but he did not care. It was the end result that galvanized him.

They began to sway, as he led her in the ritual mating of Zankli. His hips lunged forcefully, her body rocked, and Hara placed his mouth on the beckoning pulse on Tyler's neck. He laved the throbbing life source, his tongue preparing it for his sting of love.

CHAPTER SIX

The Prophesy

Andre removed the bandana from his head and wiped his face. His team had been following Hara's trail for two weeks. The fifty-man troop had airlifted into the northern flatlands and reduced their travel time immensely. He was close to the rebel encampment and knew it. If they continued at their current pace, they would reach Hara's band by nightfall. But his men were tired. He had pushed them hard, taking few breaks and crossing the rugged terrain in record time. He did not want to encounter Hara's rebels with his own men exhausted and fatigued. Though his men were seasoned veterans, they would be outnumbered five to one, and Andre reasoned it would be foolish to place them at a further disadvantage.

"Tell the men we camp here for the night."

John Burkett lifted his chin in an automatic jerk that was an acknowledgement of the order and passed the command on to the troops.

At the crack of dawn, the refreshed men looked down on the rebel encampment. They had taken out Hara's sentinels, securing them with duct tape, leaving them unharmed under thick bush at the edge of the rebels' camp. Andre raised his field binoculars. Squinting, he studied the camp as it came to life slowly. Nothing escaped his scrutiny, not even the muscular rebel guarding the large, camouflaged tent in the center of the camp.

A young houseboy exited the tent. The servant crossed to a cooking pit, stirred the fires and proceeded to haul two buckets of water from a stream that bordered the camp. Andre watched as the youngster carried the buckets to a large purification vat and poured the water into the cylinder. Other than the sentinel and houseboy, no one else appeared to be stirring. It seemed his old comrade would be caught napping, Andre thought grimly, or it could be a sly trap?

Cautiously, with two fingers held high, Andre waved his men forward. They fanned out, entering the camp in a crescent loop. When the troops moved forward, Hara's men began to poor out of the tents. As Andre suspected, the rebels had been aware of their approach, and unruffled, he made his way toward the guarded center tent.

Andre radiated self-confidence and pride. He stopped several yards in front of the tent. The flap doorway was closed, but he could hear stirring within. Voices. Tyler. He would know her scent anywhere.

Seconds later, Hara exited. His bare chest clearly outlined in the dusty morning sunlight. He searched the assembled crowd, his regal head fanning the crowd until his gaze landed on Andre and came to a screeching halt.

Absent was the wide smile and extended hand the tall Nigerian generally offered. Instead, Hara watched, grim faced, as Andre approached. The two leaders silently assessed one another. They were beautiful specimens, one dark mahogany, and the other polished oak.

Of equal height, both men were muscular, handsome, and perfectly toned. Their eyes met in mutual respect. It was small wonder that they wanted the same woman. Zankli blood ran strong in both of them, yet only one could have the prize.

"It has been a long time, brother," Andre spoke, reminding Hara of their kinship. Before Hara could respond, a thunderous sputter broke the silence of the morning, and a Blackhawk helicopter appeared over the ridge and hovered overhead. It was a fully operational war machine, combat ready, with a score of troops visible in both side openings.

Hara glanced up casually. "I see you have brought company."

Andre smiled, his shoulders lifted with a philosophical shrug. "Sometimes there is a need for a speedy retreat."

Reluctantly, admiration sparkling in his eyes, Hara laughed. Andre's gaze held an answering glimmer. The camaraderie came easy to them. They had known each other since childhood, had met at Zankli celebrations, and as seasoned warriors had backed one another in countless skirmishes.

Sadness washed over Hara. He would never have believed a woman would come between them. And yet, as the sun peeked over the ridge, he stood with his old comrade ready to kill or be killed. This time they were not comrades at arms. This time they were foes. And a woman separated them. Tyler. Her name hung unspoken between them.

Andre had resolved to never give her up. He had come for his woman, and he would not leave without her. Hara was equally determined that he would not lose Tyler again. The situation was explosive, and neither man wanted it to escalate. Many could die.

Suddenly, Andre felt a feather touch, a light calming stroke and instantly he was connected with Tyler. He froze. It was mind blowing. He had not initiated the merge. Yet, the link was strong, stronger than ever.

Where are you? It was a demand.

She responded immediately. Her voice was tender, joyful. *Here.*

A disheveled Tyler, hair tousled in sexy disarray, thick curls tumbling down her back, exited the tent. Dainty bare feet peeked beneath an almost transparent robe, and her unbound breasts were outlined suggestively in the clinging bit of nothing. She moved and her hips swayed in a siren's call.

Andre's head jerked and swung accusingly from Hara to Tyler. His eyes were frosty golden-brown chips. Riveting, they pinned Tyler to the spot. He had a laser focus on her rosy, just kissed, swollen lip.

She knew what he was looking at, and resisted the urge to squirm. Ruthlessly he thrust, trying to enter her mind. With new-found finesse, she blocked him and the uninvited intrusion. The muscles in Andre's chin tightened and flexed, ticking noticeably. Irked, he flared his nostrils.

Her laugh, for him alone, was mocking. *Gentlemen, ask before entering a woman's bedroom.* Her silent message was a clear challenge. The irises of his eyes expanded like the lenses on a camera. With a dip of his chin, he acknowledged her newly honed telepathic powers, and his lips curled in reluctant respect. He suspected she had been blocking his mental searchers for weeks, and he fumed suspiciously.

Tyler read the fury and distrust on his face, and flushed with resentment. In a flash, she went from unparalleled joy to boiling indignation. How dare he doubt her, question her loyalty and love? After all, she had been searching for him. It was he, who had not responded to her. Tyler's chin lifted a notch, and if possible, she looked down her nose at him, turned and stomped back into the tent, her flimsy robe leaving little to the imagination. The flaps of the tent swished, effectively communicating her displeasure.

When Andre attempted to follow her, Hara stepped in front of him. "I would not continue on that path, my brother." Andre never moved, but an unseen hand landed in the middle of Hara's chest, and he flew against the tent. Twisting like a cat, Hara righted himself immediately.

Stop! I mean it. Stop it right now. The shout reverberated in Andre's head. The order was for his ears alone.

The flap moved, and Tyler stood in the opening. She placed a calming hand on Hara's arm, and stared at Andre for a long minute. He was simmering, his rage at a slow burn, awaiting only a small spark to ignite his fury into an uncontrolled explosion of destruction. With superhuman restraint, Andre beat back the jealousy he felt when she saw Tyler's small soothing hand caress Hara's forearm.

"Lower the testosterone, boys."

With a resigned sigh, Tyler looked up at Andre. "I will go with you." Her voice held finality. In her heart, she knew that there had never truly been a question of whether she would leave with Andre.

It was not what Hara wanted to hear, and he stepped in front of Tyler. "You do not have to do this, little one. He cannot take you by force." Hara gave Andre a meaningful glance, "in spite of his arrogance."

Andre's temperature went up another notch as he listened to their conversation, and resented their obvious intimacy. In his mind's eye, he saw Tyler's memory of their bodies intertwined, Hara pounding into Tyler's softness relentlessly. He could almost smell their heat. It was too painful to bear. With a silent cry, he squashed the vision ruthlessly, and returned to the private discussion in front of him.

There was pleading and sorrow in Tyler's eyes when she looked up at Hara. He was a good friend, in her own way she loved him dearly. But these emotions paled in comparison to the bond she had with Andre. He was her other half, and she acknowledge their connection in the only way she could. She spoke to him, her telepathic plead heartfelt.

Andre. Leave Hara his pride. He saved my life, and if not for him, I would be toiling away in some desert sheik's harem, or dead.

Oh, so now you're talking to me? Andre's response was a chilly blast against the walls of her mind. Aloud, Andre spoke with frigid calm.

"Please cover yourself." His voice was filled with accusation, and guiltily Tyler's hands flew to her chest. She fumbled awkwardly with the neckline of the robe. Andre wanted to strangle her, well at least metaphorically, he conceded. And he wanted to send Hara deep into the sub-Saharan desert, without water, camel, and, oh yeah, his manhood. He could chop that male appendage up into a hundred pieces and feed it to the dogs.

Tyler was his and his alone. But if the choice was between her screwing her way across Africa, and never seeing her again, he'd go for the screw every time.

Tyler could feel Andre's indignation, but she also sensed his concession.

"I will return your money to you and sweeten it with an extra million." Andre raised his hand, forestalling Hara's protest. "Not for any reason other than I want to thank you for your help in caring for my woman, and for her life, which I value above all things." There was no doubt that Andre was sincere, and that he was offering an olive branch of peace. It was a shrewd move. But the *coup de grace* was revealed next.

"For your troops who have so valiantly protected her, I have a gift of one thousand dollars for each man. This is a token of my esteem for you and given in your name." Andre's eyes never left Hara's face. He had spoken loudly, and everyone near had heard the declaration.

Well done, my love. Tyler's voice was a caress.

Checkmate, thought Hara. *Excellent! Even if I wanted to refuse his offer of peace, my men would not let me. They would consider it a blatant disregard for their personal well-being.*

Hara's smile was one of irony. Bowing his head regally, he stepped back and offered Andre his right hand. "So be it, brother. It was my honor to serve." He turned slowly, his heart in his eyes, and bid Tyler good-bye.

At midday, the Blackhawk landed on the heliport at the edge of the Zankli compound, which was located in Eastern Togo, approximately three hundred kilometers from the Nigerian border. The village was ancient and could trace its roots back more than ten thousand years. The villagers loved the Dunn family, their connection to Zankli royalty was well known, and the arrival of Andre and his men was always an occasion for celebration.

People poured out of the small surrounding buildings even before the propellers stopped. The heliport and airplane landing strip was a modern addition built by Andre's company in the mid-nineties. The buildings included a small traffic tower, cargo bungalows, produce and vegetable warehouses, an automotive distribution plant and repair center, and a huge gasoline storage and reserve station.

The Zankli Village served as a distribution supply center for dozens of smaller, more isolated villages in Togo and eastern Nigeria, and Zankli farmers dispatched daily convoys of produce and goods, which traveled to the outland villages. On Mondays, there was a cash-and-carry mart which was opened to a network of inland wholesalers and retailers.

Andre jumped down from the helicopter and reached up to assist Tyler. He lifted her off the platform and eased her down along his body. Time slowed for them as the fingers from his large hands met in the middle of her back and his thumbs nestled beneath her breasts. He inhaled. She smelled like fresh berries.

With a mind of its own, his manhood hardened. It was surreal, and he mentally chastised himself for lack of control as he stepped back, clutching her hand possessively. He was unwilling to release her, had not done so since Hara had placed his hand over hers in the camp.

Tyler felt Andre's response. How could she not? It was humbling to know the power she wielded over this magnificent man. In spite of his anger, regardless of his suspicions, he wanted her, but he had not spoken more than ten words to her during the flight, and she wondered when the storm would break. He believed the worst. She had read it in his eyes when she rushed from the tent.

The couple ducked under the propellers, and walked over to a caravan of GMC Jeeps. LaToya sat in the front of the lead vehicle, and Andre guided Tyler to the rear passenger seat and slid in beside her.

"Hi, Pops." LaToya smiled at Andre and looked over at Tyler.

"Hello. I'm LaToya. I'm part of your new family." She reached back and offered her hand. Tyler liked the girl immediately. Her openness and youth reminded her of Jan, and Tyler guessed she was about the same age as her beloved sister. She took LaToya's hand and squeezed it softly.

"Family is something I've always valued."

The trip to the Zankli compound took less than twenty minutes. The landscape was beautiful and lush with bushes lining the two-lane road that lead to the main street of the village.

In the center of the town was a commercial square with a large marketplace where vendors sold produce, dried and fresh meat, fish, and other retail commodities. The main street intersected with two dozen residential streets that forked out to the edge of town where the schools, churches, and community centers were located. But the landscape and rhythm of the town was lost to Tyler.

Andre had not spoken more than four words to her at the rebel camp, and his continued silence during their flight to the village made her feel more abandoned than she felt during the transatlantic voyage with Lonnie.

Tyler glanced at Andre. His body language said he was still seething, but she found it impossible to maintain her own resentment. She turned to him, her face earnest.

Andre. I am not in love with Hara. I have never loved him, as I love you. Believe me. He is not...was not my lover in the camp.

What a perfect liar, Andre thought. No wonder Lonnie Jackson wanted to kill her. Maybe he would save Lonnie the trouble and kill her himself, fuck her to death. It was a lustful idea, and pacifying to his raw senses.

I see. You love me, but you fucked him?

Andre had never been crude with her before. His harsh reply was a shock. Speechless, Tyler remained quiet for the remainder of the drive.

They entered the Zankli compound through a double gate that secured the property from unwelcome guests. When they drove up, Françoise, Mimi, and Akosua stood on the large veranda of the spacious guesthouse. The six-bedroom bungalow had been reserved for the Dunns ever since her honeymoon with Claude. At their side was Teddy, the houseboy who maintained the vacation home during their absence.

When the caravan rolled to a stop, Françoise rushed down the wide stairs, her youthful spring belying her age. She was lovely, a picture of health, which was the result of a healthy lifestyle. She and Claude were avid cyclists, and for over thirty years, their main source of protein had been fish. When people met them, they assumed the couple was Dunn siblings, not the parents.

Andre stepped from the cab. His muscles rippled under his shirt as he helped Tyler out of the Jeep and clasped her hand in his. Both mother and sister hurried to his side, laughing and talking at the same time.

Akosua watched her cousin from the veranda, her eyes gleaming with lust. Floating down the stairs purposefully, she pushed past Françoise and Mimi and threw herself into Andre's arms. He caught her with one arm refusing to break his hold on Tyler who watched the family reunion.

I'm an outsider; I don't belong here, she thought, saddened at the notion.

Andre responded as if she had spoken aloud. *You belong with me. Always. Forever.*

Françoise's head tilted, as if she was listening to another conversation, and then she turned with a huge smile and walked over to Tyler.

"So, you are the young woman who has captured my son's heart? Welcome to Zankli. I am Françoise."

Oh my God, is he in for it, Andre's mother chuckled privately. *She's a beauty. And if what John said is true, she is gifted with an abundance of intelligence as well as Zankli powers.*

Tyler's answering smile revealed perfect white teeth, and if possible, made her even more beautiful.

He'll have to fight to keep her, Françoise reflected. *The Anomaly will be drawn to them with deadly intent.* In her mind, Françoise lifted her head to the heavens in prayer. *May the God of our great-grandfathers protect them.*

"I'm Tyler. It is a pleasure to meet you." She offered her hand, but Françoise stepped past it, taking the younger woman in her arms, and hugged her warmly. Then she stood back, her hands holding Tyler at arm's length and spoke sincerely.

"We embrace as frequently as possible in this family. And I want to give you a heartfelt welcome. The entire family will arrive by this weekend. My husband and son will fly in on Thursday, and other Zankli will come from all over the globe; we have family throughout Africa as well as the Americas and Europe. The joining of a Chosen is celebrated by all, and the gathering will be huge." Françoise paused and looked at Tyler approvingly, noting her trim curves.

"You need a traditional wardrobe. The family has not had a joining celebration of this magnitude in forty years—since Claude and I came together."

Françoise sensed Tyler's bewilderment. "I'm sorry, my dear, I haven't given you time to catch your breath. Please come with me and I will show you to your room."

Tyler was overwhelmed. Try as she might, it was difficult for her to take it all in. *Andre! Tell me what is going on. Please. I am so confused. What does your mother mean by joining ceremony?*

Andre did not answer. Instead, he peeled Akosua off his body, gave the twenty-year-old a kiss on her forehead, and drew Tyler back to his side, wrapping his arm around her shoulder possessively. "Mother, I'll show Tyler to our room."

Our room? Our room? Now wait a minute. I can't believe your mother is putting us in the same room. I am not your mistress, and I will not be treated as your whore, you arrogant ass. What did you tell her? You had better answer me, or I'm going to create a scene you will not be able to explain. Tyler stubbornly stood her ground.

I did not have to tell her anything. She has known from the moment I found you, how I felt. At any rate, if you think I am going to let you out of my sight again, you had better rethink yourself. I don't trust you...

Françoise interrupted their verbal battle. She knew they were speaking privately. "Darling, please take Tyler to your room. There is so much to do. Really, we need to get started on her dress." Françoise turned to Tyler. "Go with Andre, dear, everything will be all right. You'll see."

Tyler tugged her upper lip between her teeth, indecision clearly written on her face. Andre's mother's persistence was wearing her down. But, it was Akosua's crafty offer that tipped the scales.

"Don't worry, Auntie. Tyler can have my room. I'll bunk with Mimi. I'm sure Tyler would rather have her privacy." Tyler's violet eyes shot to the young woman's face, changing from deep blue to purple sparks of fire. Akosua's upper lip tilted at a sly angle, mimicking a grin.

Oh, no you don't, you little witch. I've handled better than you at Scarborough. Some of my classmates were professional bitches, with years and years of practice.

Tyler had noted the way Akosua had wrapped herself around Andre, sinking into his body in a blatant, un-cousinly manner, and had let her hands linger on his chest just a tad too long. No.

The girl's seductive maneuvers had not been lost on Tyler, and she did not like it one bit. With a meaningful glance at Akosua, Tyler curled her hand around Andre's bicep and purred.

"Show me the way to our room."

Tyler turned to Andre the moment the door to their private suite closed. The bedroom was huge, with its own personal bath and sitting room. But the elegant privacy was lost to her in the heat of the moment.

"Will you tell me exactly what is going on?" Tyler stood, her back straightened by Mueller steel, and spoke in her "don't mess with me" CEO voice. Andre had never been subjected to "Tyler the executive," not even at their first security meeting. She did not waste time speaking telepathically, but reminded him with tone and form that she was an astute businesswoman who was accustomed to charting her own course.

Andre did not intimidate easily, although taken off stride for a second, he rebounded immediately, and replied to Tyler's inquiry in kind.

"What is going on is my need to protect you and keep you safe from harm," he said dismissively, flicking a nonexistent piece of lint from his pants.

"You will agree that you have a way of attracting trouble by disappearing, or instilling in others a violent desire for your demise." The comment, delivered by Andre as an afterthought, was delivered in a tone as dry as a martini. There was absolute silence in the room. It was apparent that he did not intend to reveal any more.

At that moment, Andre was overcome with resentment, which he masked in sarcasm. Tyler did not know the extent of his injuries or the energy he had to expend to be in one piece and standing before her. *She does not have a clue,* he thought. *And I will not tell the self-serving witch.* His mouth twisted scornfully.

Tyler steamed. He was archaic, chauvinistic, and clearly old-fashioned for blaming her for Lonnie and Hara. She wondered what Victorian ship he was sailing on, and murdered him with her eyes.

Andre smiled. He knew exactly what he was doing, and it felt good. Tyler hated to be ordered around, rebelled against masculine chauvinism, and the small victory of male dominance expanded Andre's chest a few inches.

"I suggest that you refresh yourself. My mother is a brutal taskmaster, and I am sure that she will be walking in here any moment with a battalion of seamstresses. As for me, I am tired and exhausted." Andre strolled over to the bathroom. "Do you want to shower first, or do we wash together?" He waited for her reply, and when none was forthcoming, he walked through the door and spoke from the other room. "Are you going to join me?" The smirk he felt was in his voice.

Tyler was floored. She could not believe his audacity. *I've escaped to a lunatic asylum.* It was too much, and she lowered her head into her hunched shoulders.

I want to go home. Her voice was choked with tears, and Andre could feel her despair. It was revealed to him, if in no other way, than when she spoke to him privately.

Home is with me.

Andre. Please. Listen to me. I have a business and a family that has to be worried about me.

You didn't seem to be bothered by that fact while you were with Hara.

Tyler could feel Andre's bitterness, but she was unprepared for his adamant, *No.* Nonetheless. It was the finality of the answer that propelled Tyler toward Andre with a sob. All of the pent-up emotions, his reported death, her abduction by Lonnie, and the sojourn with Hara converged and fell on Andre. Incensed, Tyler's fists rained pounding, ineffective, blows on Andre's back. He was like an immovable brick wall, and she lost it.

I want to go home, and I mean now! Do you hear me, you dysfunctional control freak! Let me go! First, Lonnie! Then, Hara! Now, you! What do you think I am? I am not a plaything. Do you hear me?

Tyler's rant reverberated inside his head, slicing at him with the precision of a surgeon's scalpel. Andre twisted and grabbed Tyler's flaying fists, securing them in one hand and backed her against the wall. He slammed his body into hers, penning her hands high above her head. He wanted her. He ached with need, a fact that was impossible to hide.

Tyler felt the thickness of him throbbing against her thigh. Her pulse leaped in answer to his heat. Furious, she squashed her body's traitorous response. Unbeknown to her, the love bite at her pulse flared a dusty rose, and adrenalin shot through Andre's body. The sight triggered a combustive possessiveness in him.

"I mean it. Let me go." She refused to speak privately. It was too intimate, and at the moment, closeness was the last thing she wanted to encourage. Head turned into the wall, she would not meet Andre's eyes. He watched her, inhaled, and his tool pulsated. Tyler's scent permeated his senses, and he weakened, but hid it well. He was angry with himself for losing control, furious that he had so little willpower when it came to her.

Filled with self-disgust, Andre's strong fingers lifted Tyler's chin and turned her head to him. "You are a lying, cheating, conscienceless witch, and I curse the day I met you. But in spite of myself, and I do mean against any sane logic, I want you." Andre added pressure to Tyler's chin.

"You are my other half, and I won't let you go. Do you hear me?" Andre's low rumble reverberated in the room with intensity and suppressed passion.

Tyler glared her defiance, her beautiful mouth stubbornly flattened into a straight line. He wanted to tame her, pound himself into her until she screamed his name in submission. Slowly, her chin captured between his fingers, Andre lowered his head and seized her lips in a sizzling kiss. He pressed her into the wall as he took possession of her mouth ruthlessly, forcing it open. His lips feasted, and his demanding tongue darted in and out of her honeyed cavern sensuously parroting the deep thrusts of love. He wanted to dominate, break her down and let her know emphatically she was his woman. His tongue fenced masterfully and his hips swayed torturing her sensitive mound with promises of delight.

Fleetingly, she questioned why men always felt sex would solve the problem. Still, she groaned her surrender and moved her hips in a perfectly synchronized symphony of motion matching his. He released her hands and her fingers found his curls at the nape of his neck. She ran them through the thick tuffs of hair, luxuriating in the texture and feel. Andre bent his knees and lifted Tyler. He cradled her bottom in his palms. She was lost in the moment, lifting and widening her legs so that his manhood could fit more snuggly at her woman's core.

It was the signal he had been waiting for. With a superhuman effort, Andre ended the kiss, removing his hands from her lushly rounded butt as Tyler's feet touched the polished wood floor. He had not planned for her to enjoy their interlude, had not expected his punishment to be a reward. But within seconds he succumbed to her magic. Disgusted with himself, he backed up. The look of contempt on his face was inner-directed. Tyler thought it wad directed at her.

He thinks I'm a whore. She wanted to cry. She wanted to die.

Andre watched as Tyler swiped her hand across her mouth, heedless of the smear of coral lip gloss that streaked her cheek. Rebellious tears hovered in her eyes.

"I had no idea that you wanted this so badly." Andre sneered, adjusting his pants outlining his aroused maleness. "Didn't Hara satisfy you this morning?"

"You're a dirty-minded pig. I could kill you. How could you; how could you?"

Andre's rejoinder was lightning fast. "The death you offer, I might enjoy." There was no doubt to his meaning as his lust-filled eyes roamed her body. Tyler screamed her frustration when Andre backed out of the door, closing it with a careless snap of his wrist. Her shoe hit the wall with a muffled thump. Andre laughed, satisfied that he had transferred some of his hurt to her. Whistling his victory like a teenage boy who had just scored a touchdown, he went in search of his mother.

Little had changed in the five months of Tyler's absence. Mueller International remained an industry leader. *ReVive* was the hottest item on the cosmetics shelf, impossible to keep in stock, and back ordered until the second quarter of the next year. It appeared her disappearance had actually boosted sales.

Angela Ryan McPherson had done an extraordinary job marketing the product. The twins were continuing to reinvent and improve the *ReVive* line, and her uncle had made sure that there had not been a hiccup in domestic or overseas operations. Tyler reviewed the company reports, and she had taken the weekend to catch up. She was more than satisfied with the company's financials.

Her return was a closely kept secret. Only Nanny Peters was privy to the information. By Monday morning, she was ready, fortified with four months of company data. John Burkett called a meeting, and the executive team assembled themselves in the Adam Mueller Board Room. Expecting to hear news about the stalker, they were bowled over when Andre Dunn walked into their assembly. Everyone in the room experienced some form of shock.

Tyler's uncle, Simon Seymour was the first to regain his voice. "My God, Andre is that you?"

Andre smiled thinking, *not the best question in the world*, but certainly under the circumstances understandable. He nodded his head, acknowledging the men and women seated to his right and left.

"Ladies. Gentlemen. I know that you all thought me dead and…" Andre paused. "My presence here must be disconcerting to you. I apologize. The need for secrecy was critical to everyone in this room, especially Tyler."

Andre stood and opened the solid mahogany door and held out his hand. Tyler floated into the room. Her Loretta Young twirl elicited a collective grasp from the executives assembled. If they were astonished before, they were completely floored now. Not even Simon could find his voice.

Finally Juan spoke. "Where the hell have you been?" His blistering words were softened by the flight to his foster sister's side. Unceremoniously, he hauled her into his arms, then closed his eyes and squeezed her close. Their embrace broke the ice, and everyone converged on the two siblings at once.

Angela was crying. The twins were laughing. Al Rosenthal stood up, crossed to Andre and shook his hand solemnly. When Juan freed Tyler, Simon took her in his arms. "Well, niece. Well,

well, well!" For the second time in as many minutes, Simon was struck dumb, literally, speechless. He released Tyler and held her at arm's length. "Welcome home." He spoke affectionately.

Tyler's executive family took turns touching and hugging her. It was as if they could not believe the miracle without physical contact. Questions came from all sides. She was bombarded.

Tyler could not help herself. She looked up at the ceiling and laughed. "I'll never be able to answer all of you at once." Tyler raised her hand for silence. "Please everyone, be seated."

She took the empty chair, at the end of the conference table opposite Simon, and began slowly, taking them through her five-month odyssey with raucous candor. Her voice was purposeful in the end.

"Andre rescued me ten days ago, and we were joined in a Togolese ceremony by a village elder this past Friday. As soon as we can arrange it, we will have a church wedding on the Mueller Pacific Palisades estate. Angela, I would like for you to handle it." Tyler reached up and took Andre's hand.

"I would like to formally introduce everyone to my husband, Andre Dunn."

You could have heard a pin drop. The room was so quiet. Angela pressed her chest, her hand placed over her heart as if she were about to say the *Pledge of Allegiance.*

"Darling, do you have any more surprises?" Angela's voice was thin with wonder.

"No."

"Good. Then I would like to congratulate you, and wish you wedded bliss." Tyler looked down, her cheeks rosy, and smiled her appreciation.

"Al, would you please remain behind. I would like to go over a prenuptial agreement as well as the estates' succession mandates." Turning to her uncle, Tyler asked respectfully. "Simon, may I see you in an hour? There are some documents I would like you to review with me."

Tyler stood signaling the meeting was over. "Please hold your other questions until I have had time to adjust." Her eyes traveled the table, touching on each of her executives individually. "I can never fully express my gratitude for your loyalty. Thank you for carrying on as if I were here." Her eyes landed on Simon. "I am especially grateful to you, Uncle Simon, for all that you have done."

Andre and Tyler walked from the board room with hands intertwined. There was no doubt they were a couple. The news had traveled fast, and by the time they had entered the ground floor lobby the staff was congratulating them. Andre tucked Tyler under his arm as they exited the building, but in the car, he dropped her hand and kept his distance. Their ploy had worked, but every moment with her was torment.

Tyler was in agony. She had not shared herself with Andre since their return from Togo. The ceremonial night had been a farce. From the moment she had arrived in the village, Andre's family had surrounded her.

Françoise was refreshingly organized. She arranged the accommodation for her family and other guests like the hospitality manager of a five star hotel. Meals were communal and served in a large banquet hall constructed during Andre's recuperation.

Tyler's ceremonial dresses were completed in record time, and any inquiry she made regarding the occasion for the family gathering was gently brushed aside and went unanswered. "Ask Andre, dear," was the serene rejoinder from Françoise, and it was all that Tyler could do to hide her annoyance. Andre was conveniently unavailable, and in the end, Tyler found herself succumbing to Françoise's charm. She was swept up into a windmill of activity.

Beginning the Sunday after her arrival, Tyler was given instruction on Zankli folklore, dances, and traditions. Between fittings, instructions, and introductions, Tyler was kept constantly busy. There were so many people to meet, so many customs to understand that her head was in a tailspin. She rarely saw Andre before bedtime and had no idea what he did with his time.

Most nights she went to bed without him, only to wake up at daybreak to the sound of the door clicking as he quietly exited the room. Only the impression in his pillow gave witness to his presence during the night.

Finally, on Thursday evening Andre made a surprise visit and joined Tyler in their bedroom following dinner. She looked up from a colorful, artfully sketched ledger of Zankli folklore, and Andre was in the room.

"I'd like to discuss tomorrow's ceremony with you."

He pulled a ladder-backed chair from under a small circular glass table, and straddled it. The tall wooden backing was pressed against his chest, and Andre's hands dangled over the top. His long muscular legs were spread wide, framing the chair provocatively. For Andre it was an unconsciously sensual posture. Tyler shifted, feeling her body respond to his unintentional overture. She watched him expectantly.

Andre looked down and their gazes locked. "The people trying to kill you are still out there, Tyler, and if we do not flush them out, they will continue until they succeed. The ploy I propose is a little unconventional. But, I believe if you are to remain safe, it is the only course of action."

Andre's facial expression was intense, his eyes glued to hers as if he could see clear to her very soul. "You and I will be bonded tomorrow in a traditional ceremony."

Andre held up his hand in anticipation of her questions. "Don't worry. It is not a legal marriage. More importantly, it is not recognized by any government in the world other than Zankli. The goal and only purpose of this ceremony is to flush out Lonnie."

Andre appeared sincere. But Tyler had a nagging fear that there was more to the ceremony than he was divulging. "I don't understand why we need to participate in the ceremony. Can't we just say we did?"

"No." If possible, Andre's face became even more intense. "Listen. I do not know how far reaching this plot is, and who exactly is involved. I cannot believe that Lonnie Jackson, no matter how disturbingly evil he may be, is the sole culprit."

Tyler thought for a moment then nodded her head. "I agree. He was always vicious and malicious. But, he was never quite this strategically cunning...and I do not believe he had the resources to orchestrate the attack at your home."

Her acceptance of Andre's rationale led to a floodgate of shared insights. They were both keen strategists, master chess players in the game of intelligence and business, and the two lost themselves in diagramming a plan of action. Underneath, they welcomed the opportunity to cease their silent hostilities. It was dawn before they were satisfied.

The ceremony was scheduled for noon the next day, and it went off without a hitch. Like Andre's parents, the newlyweds made a solitary trek through the bush to the native doctor's hut. No one had ever seen the doctor greet a bonding couple at the entrance of his dwelling and escort them inside like honored guests. Nor had the august man ever bowed his head signaling subservience to another's power.

Like Claude before them, Andre and Tyler found they understood the ancient dialect perfectly. The native doctor motioned the pair to opposite sides of the room, facing each other, and began to speak in a sing-song manner as soon as they were seated.

"Sit, honored guests." Tyler and Andre sat and crossed their legs Indian style. The native doctor looked at the couple in wonder. "We have waited for your arrival for more than ten thousand years. Your bonding will mark a new beginning for Zankli, a new beginning for mankind." Andre and Tyler felt energy passing from one to the other—forging them together as one. The room crackled and a beam of light emerged from the center of Andre's chest and found the exact spot between Tyler's breasts. The string of light connected the two.

The ancient's voice rang in the room, his intonation a blending of notes so enthralling that it was mesmerizing. The couple swayed circularly like seasoned dancers. A breeze swirled around and between them, drawing them together as one. A ruby red circle appeared in the center of their foreheads matching the crimson jewel on the native doctor's mask.

The jewels glowed in the hut, and the jars and clay dishes began to rattle and hum with a crackling force. The native doctor stood, backing away, awed by the force of energy radiating from the couple. His lips never stopped moving. He was praying in a tongue long forgotten, but clearly understood by the three people in the room. Tyler recognized the prayer. It was the one that Rachel had shared with her years before, and she realized that Andre was her destiny.

"You will live long as one, and you will prosper beyond your wildest dreams. In years to come, you will return to this land. Along the way, you will birth sons and daughters who will ensure the survival of humankind. As foretold, by His son and messengers, he will return for his righteous children and until that day, the Zankli will hold his trust."

Back in the village, they danced until midnight. The choreographed movements learned by Tyler earlier in the week were well matched by Andre. The drumbeats beckoned a primitive dance known to lovers before Tut, before Ramses, and before Lucy. That night they fulfilled the prophecy of the messenger and came together as one. The next day, neither Tyler nor Andre recalled what transpired in the hut or the fertility dance. Their only recollection was of their passionate union, which fused them body and soul.

At the close of the meeting, it was agreed that Angela would issue a press release announcing Tyler's return and reinstatement to the helm of Mueller. Everyone was elated with the turn of events. Tyler was back, and the managers and executives moved with revived energy, but there was one detractor.

Z was livid. He adjusted his tie as he strolled toward his car. He wanted to kill, draw blood, better yet—he wanted to put another bullet through Lonnie's brain. He cursed the day he had met the sorry son of a bitch. He could not believe it. *Fuck. Fuck. Fuck. The bitch had nine lives. How could this be? Who would have thought she would survive the sale?* Lonnie had assured him that she would never be heard from again, and here she was fucking with his life once more.

Z pulled out of the subterranean garage and pressed the gas pedal to the floor. The cream-colored Ferrari roared onto the street. He was late. The video shoot had begun hours before and his scenes were scheduled for nine o'clock. He glanced at the dashboard; it was nine, forty-five. He was not worried that they would begin without him—after all, he was the producer. No. The crew knew better than to cross him in any way, but he hated to be late. It was a courtesy drummed into him early on. It was one of his mother's pet peeves.

Jeez, what a God-awful childhood he had. Mentally shuddering, he quashed the memories of his father and mother as the car purred onto the Ventura Freeway. Celine Dion's soft tones of *My Heart Will Go On*, the love theme from *Titanic*, resonated throughout the car. It was soothing and he found his mind drifting, reenacting his latest bank transaction that transferred a large sum of money into the Von Meter account. He smiled and congratulated himself, marveling at his own cunning.

Who would have thought smut could be so rewarding financially and the fringe benefits so fantastic. A picture of Robbie, his latest boy toy, flashed in his mind. Adrenalin rushed through his body, and for a moment, he forgot Lonnie's ineptitude. Instead, he recalled how delighted he was when he learned that the adult movie distributor was fixated on destroying the Mueller heir. It was an unexpected perk, the icing on the cake.

After the revelation, he and Lonnie had bonded with each other, often envisioning Tyler as a defenseless playmate in one of their videos—preferably as a dog's bitch. In retrospect, Z missed Lonnie's camaraderie and their solidarity of purpose in eliminating the Mueller heir. He shrugged philosophically, thinking, *a necessary sacrifice for success*. The problem was they had not succeeded, which left him to take care of the job himself.

Z rolled to a stop in front of a tall security wall, pressed his remote and watched the ornate iron gates slide open. The Ferrari passed through the opening and climbed to the single-story house. He parked the car on the circular driveway, walked to the chalet door, slid his electron key card into the lock, waited and pulled it out when the green light flashed. He looked back over his shoulder to make sure that the automatic driveway gate was closed and stepped into the dimly lit entranceway.

A large playpen sofa dominated the living room, which was positioned in front of a marble fireplace and fifty-inch plasma television screen. No one stirred in the room. The action was in the soundproof studio at the rear of the house. The family room and four bedrooms had been gutted to create a video set that held a Jacuzzi and indoor deck, a voyeur's bathroom—enclosed in transparent tempered glass—beds, living room décor, a kitchen, and an interior garden. Off to the side were dressing rooms with modern and period costumes for men, women, and children.

It was a perfect front for a non-celebrated business. Hell! This was a surefire investment, the one industry keeping America afloat while the rest were struggling to survive. Banks were crashing all around, as the president denied any serious economic problems. Yeah. Right!

Z smirked humorlessly. *How the mighty do fall.* His chuckle was pure evil. *All those snotty Wall Street boys who held their noses up in the air at the smut industry were hypocrites. They were all closet perverts, secretly consorting with the likes of him in backroom parlors, or surreptitiously jacking-off into Web cams shamelessly to an eager voyeur audience.*

Z secured his silk ski mask over his eyes and nose, and strolled into the large open room. It was a full-fledged production set, with lights, sound equipment, and cinematographers. Two actors were in the kitchen. The woman sat on the kitchen sink in a slinky floor-length, skintight spandex dress slit almost to her waist. Her large melon-size boobs spilled over the top of the strapless gown. The tips of her fat elongated nipples were visible.

She had bright red fire engine lips and fingernails, and platinum Christina Aguilar hair flowing down her back, while her partner's hands danced over her exposed alabaster thighs with purpose. The scene was steamy. A small bald-headed man wearing thick bifocal glasses directed the couple. His voice was pitched low, but his hands were animated, moving like a symphony conductor.

"Kiss. That's it; let me see your tongues. That's right. Go for it. Make those suckers fight. Now, Joey, spread your legs so that Mike can inch his hand toward your crotch. You're a slut. You want it. Pant. That's it! That's it! Mike, move your hand slowly. Not too fast. Slowly. Now palm that crotch." The director's voice was husky.

"Mike. Stop kissing and lean back. You're surprised. Look at Joey in shock. Now smile smugly. Let your face show delight. Hand fuck that bitch. Now make a fist, circling something long and hard. Work it. Let me see that fist move beneath that dress. Stretch the fabric. Joey, open your mouth in ecstasy, let us know you like his hand action. That's right throw your head back and let's hear you sigh. Swirl your tongue and lick your lips."

Z had seen this scene play out a thousand times with changing scenarios, but the vignette was always the same, and it never failed to arouse him. His hand dropped below his waist, found his bulge and cupped it appreciatively, and unzipped his fly.

The action on the set heated up. Mike lifted Joey's dress, exposing more flesh and more of her thighs. His hand rolled it back, exposing the bare mound. His fisted hand began to jerk up and down sensually, his palm hiding, then revealing a bulbous cock head. In seconds, Joey's fully erect nine-inch thick cock emerged within the pumping fist.

The image of the beautiful woman sporting a huge piece of man meat was sinfully perverted. More obscene was the way Joey spread his legs giving Mike access to the large baby making bulbs beneath his thick stick. The rampant member hit his stomach with a noisy plop and his essence oozed from Mike's hand in copious jerks. Joey roared, and Z exploded. The white milk spilled over his fingers and shot down his thighs.

The ride to Malibu was uneventful. Tyler held herself apart from Andre, afraid that any discussion that did not center on Mueller security would break their fragile bond. It was all so inauthentic this assumed cordiality. Tyler found the entire situation frustrating, but she did not know how to tear down the barrier. Andre had drawn a symbolic line in the sand, and she had found it impossible to cross. Dejected, she gave a mental sigh and stared out of the sedan window.

That evening, Tyler paced the floor restlessly. Andre watched her over a glass of Chardonnay. His scrutiny was not lost to Tyler, and enviously, she watched his lips touch the goblet, folding over the brim seductively. His large masculine hands were a magnet and her eyes focused on his tapered fingers as they caressed the fragile stem of the goblet. The very same appendages that had stroked her breast, with such erogenous skill, now held a glass. He placed the crystal on the bar, and pushed himself off the stool.

"You know you will wear a hole in the carpet if you keep that up. Why don't we take a walk on the beach? It's healthier."

Caught staring at him, Tyler jumped, her eyes rounded with guilt. She was convinced he was going to drive her crazy with need. She wanted to shout. *I don't want to go for a walk. I want to feel you inside me so wide and deep that I think you are a part of my body.*

Instead, she murmured. "That's a wonderful idea."

Andre smiled to himself smugly. *I bet.*

"Great." He crossed to her and grabbed her hand possessively.

He'd found a way around her mental blocks several days before, and, although she did not know it, he was a shadow in her mind listening to all of her thoughts, private and not so private.

He understood that she had not betrayed him and that the vision he had seen was of a time long past when Tyler and Hara were college students, and Andre knew she had hated the intimacy. Her distaste was so potent that even now, years later, he could feel Tyler reversion to Hara's hardcore sex.

Andre cringed at the thought of another possessing her, but how could he hold Tyler at fault for a life before him. That would be like the pot calling the kettle black. He would not welcome an examination of his amorous life. Let bygones be bygone, and leave the past buried, Andre thought. Tonight he would reclaim her in a manner that would leave no doubt to whom she belonged.

Lonnie opened his eyes, looked around the room and blinked several times. It took him a minute or two to remember where he was. Then the peace that had greeted him each morning for the past several months washed over him. He inhaled deeply and let his eyes travel the room.

The décor had not changed in twenty-five years. A set of double-deck twin beds hugged the bedroom window, and a tiny walk-in closet faced the door. The walls were powder blue, a color dutifully applied every two years by Pastor Price and his crew of foster children. It was a family ritual.

Lonnie's lips twisted into a smile. He had been a reluctant member of that crew and could hear in his mind's ear the Pastor's patient drawl. "Now make sure you just put the tip of that brush in the pail. You don't want to brush the paint on too thick. That's right. Good job, son."

A delectable aroma of homemade biscuits wafted into the room. The combination of bacon, brewed coffee, and buttered biscuits smelled wonderful, shifting Lonnie's thoughts to his foster mother. For the thousandth time, he wondered why he had so few childhood memories of Mother Price's delicious dishes.

He drew his arms up and folded them under his head. His childhood? What a waste. He had spent so much time pushing his family away, and hating Tyler that he had not, as Pastor Price so often quipped, "Counted his blessings." It was amazing to him how he could so clearly see today what he had been unable to recognize then. What an angry and lost boy he had been, so very destructive and malicious.

Lonnie's private admission was the result of a life-altering experience.

He understood now that his mother's act of sacrificing him for her own life had scarred him. The trauma left more than the visible scars that had been removed. The scar was more than skin deep. It was a wound that had stolen his youth—his life. But he wanted it back. He wanted a fresh start. Maybe he could really start over, but he knew, the first step was to forgive—first his mother—and then himself.

Five months ago, Lonnie would have died laughing at the man he had become. But five months ago he'd been a shallow shell without compassion or pity for anyone. Everything changed the night Z pulled out his gun and shot him in the forehead.

The bullet should have killed him, but miraculously Lonnie lived. Instead of entering his head, the slug burrowed through his hair, scraping off skin and parts of his skull. Lonnie had felt a fiery explosion and excruciating pain.

Hours later, consciousness began with a pinpoint of light that grew peeling back the darkness. The light was warm, welcoming, and so luminous it was almost blinding. He ran toward the light. The rays felt like sunshine after a cold winter day. It was the most incredible feeling he ever had, and he desperately sought the radiant heat.

Suddenly, he felt himself lifted and dragged backward. Lonnie fought the invisible force, screaming and kicking in despair. He had to get to the light.

Into the chaos came a soothing voice, so pure it bathed him in orgasmic pleasure. She told him that it was too soon. "No. It is not your time. You have a mission, something that you must do before you can come to me and into the light. It is the only way to reclaim your true essence. Your have been lost."

Lonnie stopped struggling immediately. Defiance was not an option. The force knew all, loved all, and Lonnie was at peace.

CHAPTER SEVEN

The Rebirth

Pastor Price was listed in Lonnie's wallet as the emergency contact. And so, here he lay six months later in the Price home, and at peace. He had walked out over a decade before, and never planned to look back. What a fool he had been. Thank God, he never changed his info, for today, he was renewed, committed to helping, not destroying his fellowman. Washed away was the anger and resentment that had consumed his life until his reckoning with Z.

The days were long, but at the close, he felt fulfilled. Beginning at eight o'clock in the morning, he worked as an intake counselor at a homeless shelter, midday he tutored wayward youth, and late afternoons he mentored foster kids. By seven o'clock, he was at his security job in Beverly Hills.

Few would recognize Lonnie; his transformation was a true miracle. He was very different from the man that had distributed pornography and trafficked in white slavery. That man was as foreign to him as a Chinese rice farmer. The new Lonnie acknowledged there was little he could do about the past. But the new Lonnie was determined to atone for his sins through good deeds.

A week after his release from the hospital, Lonnie accepted Christ as his savior. He stumbled down the aisle with tears streaming from his face, and fell on the floor in front of the pulpit asking for forgiveness. It was a momentous occasion, and both the Prices sobbed in joy. Today Lonnie knew Christ as his redeemer, and believed His resurrection had washed away his sins.

One of Lonnie's first acts as a born-again Christian was to donate five hundred thousand dollars to homeless families, two million dollars to Pastor Price's foster child ministry, and five hundred thousand dollars to an after-school youth program. The balance of his money he entrusted to the Prices. He had given all but $50,000 of his ill-gotten gains away to charities, and he felt the better for it.

He wanted to donate "every last cent of his six and a half million dollars," but Pastor Price had admonished him, "Keep something for a rainy day, son. Mother and I are proud that you have accepted Christ, but there is no reason for you to beggar yourself, and anyways, you can't buy redemption. You must walk the life with *hind feet*. Besides, the chances are we will go to our maker long before you. You never know. You may need that money some day."

There was only one thing that threatened Lonnie's idyllic life. Jan. He was terrified that his parents would learn what he had done. He knew no amount of atonement, no monetary gift, would buy forgiveness for him from them. His parents would be sickened, just like they had been horror-struck when Sophie, Tyler's cat, was discovered on the barbeque grill.

Oh, he could argue that he was mentally ill, consumed with hate, and that he had not meant to do it. But the reality was that Jan was gone, cut down before she had a chance to live, and worse, he had no beef with Jan. He murdered her because of Tyler just as he had destroyed Susie, killed Sophie, and attacked Bobby.

Well, he could not resurrect Jan, and he could not rewind time. His only solace was his belief in the everlasting grace of Jesus Christ, knowing that God the father forgives all—even when man cannot—if one repents.

Z thrust forward with all of his might. It was exquisite. His lover screamed in ecstasy, and his hips pounded into the welcoming flesh. He was on top of the world on an erotic high. The Mueller bitch would never outwit him. Sweat dripped from his forehead and pooled around his mouth. The thought of Tyler's downfall froze in his mind as he hammered into his toy's tight cavern. He strained unmindful of his partner's pleasure.... or lack thereof. He was single-minded, focused on the sensation of the narrow, gripping, gloved flesh pulsating around his cock. Yeah. God! There was nothing sweeter. He looked down into his lovers face all twisted in need; one final thrust. They shouted their release together.

Tomorrow he'd put his plan into action. The bitch would suffer if it were the last thing he did.

"Checkmate." Andre eased back in his chair, and studied his opponent. Tyler's lips were turned up in that particular sensual lift, and he watched her mouth quiver. He suspected she wanted to gloat the win, but held back out of good manners. His suspicions were confirmed when she bit down on her bottom lip, her eyes dancing with mischief.

"What was that you said about male superiority?"

She was good, a worthy opponent. He had to give her that. Their match had been a test of wits, and in the end, he was surprised by her skill. Not only had she avoided his traps, but she demonstrated an intellect far superior to any he encountered before. Only his brother's skill provided an equal challenge. Paul and his chess games could last six months, many times played telepathically from different locations in the world.

Andre beamed silently and continued to study her, mesmerized by the provocative dimple on the side of her...*oh so kissable mouth.*

"No. Surely, you misunderstood me. What I said was men are obviously inferior beings." Andre looked down humbly. False sorrow cloaked his face. "We have a lot to learn from women."

The blatant lie brought a sparkle to Tyler's eyes. "And," Andre continued, tongue in cheek. "I wanted to say that women are truly the masters of the universe, and I, but a lowly man, should prostrate myself at your feet." Andre slid to the floor on his hands and knees, bowed lower and crawled on his belly to Tyler. Removing her slippers, he began kissing her feet with audacious finesse.

The wet smacks rang in the room. The corner of Tyler's eyes crinkled and she strained to hold back the mirth bubbling within. It was hopeless. Andre was ridiculous. A giggle burst from Tyler's trembling lips. She gave up and tossed in the towel. Throwing her head back, she hugged her middle laughing.

Her laughter was a sweet reward, and Andre was charmed anew. He stared up at Tyler appreciatively. He wondered how he had ever resisted her. Mentally shaking his head, he wondered if he would ever regain her trust. He prayed this was a start.

Simon passed a glass of lemon water to his mother. Mercedes' age was glaringly obvious in the morning light. The numerous surgical procedures to her face had done little to hide the excesses of her life. At eighty-four, she looked it. Her hand trembled noticeably as she brought the glass to her mouth. Where had the years gone? Simon could not remember the last time he had spent a quiet moment in his mother's company, and he did not welcome it now. Her bedroom was ridiculously cluttered, and the smell was gross. No matter how often Mercedes' diapers were changed, the suite aired, or the floors mopped, the room smelled of urine. But the interview was unavoidable. The staff was complaining.

They had lost the third nurse in as many weeks, and the veteran retainers refused to go near her, especially Lee. The only one that seemed to have any sympathy for Mercedes was Nanny, and only God knew why, for his mother treated her atrociously. But the task had become too much for the black retainer, and she had called Simon that morning asking for his intervention. There was no other answer.

His mother was going to have to go into a nursing home right away. Homecare was no longer an option. Her dementia had progressed to a point where at best she accused everyone of stealing from her, and at worst she physically attacked her caregivers, punching or biting them. Worse, his mother fingered herself constantly—masturbating in clear sight of everyone. She would remove her diaper and get down to business. She did not care who witnessed the repetitive frigging. It was disgusting.

Today she wanted to talk. In a loud whisper, she mouthed, "Is the nigger still running things?" Simon flinched. Quite frankly, he did not know which nigger she meant until she confided. "The little pickaninny was a real surprise." Mercedes cackled.

"The amazing thing was that tramp Rachel kept the secret so long." Mercedes mentioned her daughter's name as if she was a stranger that one gossiped about, but never allowed close. "Can you believe she brought the little whelp home to me and asked that I be kind to the tar baby? Kind? Kind? Was she crazy when you, my son, were treated like a servant?"

"Mother!" Simon was outraged, not so much in his mother's description, as by the truth in the statement. "Tyler is your granddaughter, and I am her uncle. Why do you insist on being vulgar? Really, there is no excuse." Simon straightened his tie. His long tapered fingers lingered at the base of the knot. "What did you expect? We are not Mueller heirs." He cleared his throat.

"At any rate, that is not the reason for my visit today. I came to discuss your care. I fear that the staff is not providing for you as they should."

"I couldn't agree with you more," Mercedes waved Simon to her side. "Did you know that they steal from me? Just this morning I caught that old nigger sneaking out of my bathroom. I saw a movie the other week where these niggers stole the souls of their masters. Changed places with them, I tell you." She bobbed her head confidently, lowered her voice and whispered.

"They're all thieves, you know!"

Simon mentally rolled his eyes. "Well, yes. I see what you mean."

"Get rid of them. Let's fire them all. Then we can begin again."

"I think that is a wonderful idea mother. I will do just that. Meanwhile, I will move you into a luxury facility until we hire new help."

Simon smiled, dusting his hands mentally. *Well that's that!* he celebrated. *I'll close the house, and you'll rot before you see me again.*

Andre placed a blanket over Tyler, covering her shoulders. She lay on her side with her hand tucked under her chin. Her lips were rosy buds, and her eyelashes formed crescent shadows on her cheeks. He had never imagined someone so perfect. He had merged with her soul many times, and it too was beautiful. She was gorgeous through and through. He watched her, and wondered at the miracle. A shadow of fear entered his mind. If he lost her, life would return to that dark, gloomy, meaningless place that only mimicked life. Immediately, he thought about Hara. How much competition was he really? His mind told him none at all, but his heart was conflicted. Tyler's eyes fluttered. She whimpered and sighed.

"No. Don't."

Andre merged with Tyler immediately. It was a child's memory, a nightmare in which an older boy tormented her. It was Lonnie, he had taken her doll, thrown it on the floor and was using it as a kick ball."

Tyler was crying. "Don't hurt Susie."She could not have been more than five, but she flew at the preteen courageously, fists flying. The older boy blocked her fists with little effort and continued his assault on the doll.

On the bed, Tyler tossed and sobbed. Andre sat down alongside her and took her in his arms. "It's all right; I will never let him hurt you again." Smoothing her hair back from her face, he reassured. "You're safe. I am with you. I will always be with you."

Several hours later, Tyler grabbed a towel and stepped out of the shower. She felt refreshed, even though the uncertainty of Lonnie's whereabouts weighed heavy on her mind. Her stomach was queasy, had been so for days. But she chalked it up to nerves. Newscasters had blasted her return to the helm of Mueller International on the evening news and made a big to-do about her marriage to Andre.

Lonnie, the nemesis, would have to be buried in the mountainous hills of Afghanistan to miss the cable and network broadcasts. She smiled, and shook her head thoughtfully. She doubted that seriously. It would be much too much like right. More than likely, he was out there somewhere plotting her demise. But she refused to cower under the threat.

"Are you ready?" Andre spoke from across the room. His voice was a welcome reminder that she did not have to face the battle alone. He cared about her safety, truly cared. "I'm as ready as I will ever be." Tyler paused reflectively. "I'd like to stop at Starbucks before we get to the office. Do we have time?"

"Of course.

His bedroom smooth voice ignited her senses, and her body leaped with customary response. He knew. Tyler watched as the pupils of Andre's eyes expanded and glowed with passion. She smiled. He answered with a sideways grin that accentuated the fullness of his mouth. He was intoxicating, devastating to the mental peace of any woman. With a superhuman effort, Tyler quashed the train of thought that would have her begging him to return them to Malibu and the seclusion of their bedroom.

I can hear you, baby. We can make love now, if you wish. Andre merged with Tyler effortlessly. His ability to bypass her blocks once again in place. *If you read my thoughts, as I am sure you did, you know that I do not want to indulge myself now, no matter how tempting it may be.* Tyler's fingers floated over Andre's face invisibly.

There are issues we need to address, and we cannot afford the distraction. Distractions...

Her voice was like smooth honey, and it warmed his body, *are what got us into this mess.* He could feel the regret in her voice, and he froze as he felt her invisible tongue run the length of him, hesitate, and slowly take him into her mouth while she sat silently staring ahead.

Andre's eyes swung to her poker face and he growled his pleasure, the sound deep in his throat melting her. By the time they turned into the Mueller subterranean garage, Tyler had regained her calm. Two SUVs, with four security men in each car, flanked their limousine. The moment the cars rolled to a halt, the men jumped out and surrounded Andre and Tyler. It was impossible to get a clear view, or sniper's shot, for that matter, of either of them, surrounded as they were by their giant guards.

When the entourage strolled toward the elevator, two dark brown eyes watched with an unblinking concentration. Lonnie had been staking out the garage for several weeks, hoping to speak with Tyler. But the security was too tight, and he believed they had a "shoot first, question second" directive.

Lonnie was desperate to warn Tyler about Z. He could think of little else. He did not know why the man was so determined to see her dead, but he suspected it had a great deal to do with the magic of *ReVive* and its billion dollar market value.

Initially he had believed that Z owned a rival company, but the man's hatred went deeper. He had a fury of a more personal nature. It was dark and disparaging, and it was an emotion Lonnie could readily identify. Much of his life had been consumed with the same killing rage and explosive dislike of Tyler. The question was how exactly was Z connected to Tyler, and who was he really? He had never seen his face, no one in the porn industry had.

Lonnie watched the elevator doors slide closed, and he hissed with frustration. Another day had passed and he had not been able to warn Tyler. He was becoming anxious. Time was running out. Z would have to put Tyler down soon if he wanted to corner the *ReVive* market.

On the penthouse floor of the Mueller building, Tyler's security entourage exited the elevator. Individually Andre and Tyler were fascinating, combined they were a riveting force, indestructible, and unmatched by any other power couple.

"I hope this will not bore you. I must meet with my cousins to ensure the second phase of ReVive is successful." Tyler apologized with her eyes. Her voice was soothing.

There is no time that I spend with you that I am…how did you put it …bored. Andre's telepathic response was accompanied by a pro-tracted lick on the inside of her upper thigh. Aloud, he smiled and spoke tongue in cheek, "It is no problem, my love. After all, it is my mission as your husband to protect," he paused with preg-nant meaning, "and serve." The second lick was placed higher on her thigh, no more than an inch below her lacy underwear.

Andre chuckled aloud when Tyler, who was exceptionally graceful, missed a step, stumbling over her feet. He reached for her elbow, and steadied her. His eyes danced into hers with amusement. "Let me help you." Tyler's cutting, sideways glance spoke volumes, but she refused to speak to him in their private way.

The day went fast, and Andre was impressed with Tyler's abil-ity to multi-task. She met with her cousins, approved their mer-chandizing proposals, orchestrated a video conference between her attorney, her uncle, and several of Mueller's European ex-ecutives, and reviewed a pile of financial briefs that should have taken days to decipher.

It was after two o'clock when Angela arrived. It was Tyler's last scheduled meeting of the day. Andre was working, on his laptop, which was opened to an aerial map showing a group of remote mountainous villages along the Afghanistan and Pakistani bor-der. Dunn & Burkett were assisting the U.S. government in the search for bin Laden, and Andre was identifying areas within the region that his troops would scout by land.

Andre lifted his head and smiled a greeting to Angela. She was the kind of female executive he both liked and respected, one who did not feel the need to prove her effectiveness by cas-trating her male counterparts. She was a tough cookie, smart, perceptive, with ingenious marketing insight that never ever let you forget you were a man, and she was a woman. He thanked God she was Tyler's mentor.

He watched the two women hug, and then sit down to busi-ness. Twenty minutes into their meeting, Tyler turned to Andre and asked if he would join them at a late lunch. She punctuated the request with a click of a remote. The north wall of her of-fice slid opened onto a spacious courtyard complete with a flora garden fragrant with sweet-smelling gardenias, a cascading waterfall pooling into a rock reservoir filled with giant gold fish, exotic trees, and copper musical chimes.

Andre thought the private garden enchanting, and understood Tyler's love for the Big Bear retreat. In many ways, his cabin mirrored her office courtyard of floral splendor. It was a magnificent marriage of nature and human artistry. St. Julian grass, in deep forest green, was nature's plush carpet. Nestled, unobtrusively into the landscape, was an elegant glass table with three cushioned iron chairs.

A white-jacketed waiter, carrying a water carafe, entered the courtyard from a country lattice door and proceeded to the table. Tyler's private courtyard shared a kitchen with the Executive Dining Room. At Mueller International, you had arrived when you obtained a key to the Penthouse Dining Room.

I must say, you have a way about you. My mother says that the way to a man's heart is through his stomach. But, personally, I feel the way you enslave his heart is through his senses. My senses are totally captivated. Andre sipped at the lemon water. *Did you design this lovely garden?*

"Thank you for the compliment. No, not entirely. My mother was the true architect. I have just embellished on her design." Tyler responded to Andre automatically, as if Andre had asked the question aloud.

Angela had just placed the linen napkin in her lap and looked questioningly between both companions. "Did I miss something?"

"No. Not a thing." Tyler busied herself with her napkin. Andre's poker face was outrageous, and it was all Tyler could do to remain stoic.

The rest of the lunch was uneventful. But at the end, Angela had warmed-up to Andre, convinced that the charming man was the best thing next to sliced bread, definitely worth keeping. Tyler was lucky, she concluded.

Andre was hot, sexy as all get-out, intelligent, humorous, and best of all, personable. He was the kind of man that women dreamed about. Strong. Confident. Unwavering. He reeked of honesty.

Why Simon was so against Andre, Angela could not imagine. But what she did know was that Tyler's uncle had launched a vicious campaign against him, calling Andre an interloper. He drew attention to his millions, and then contrasting them, unequally, to Tyler's billions.

But what concerned Angela the most was Simon's inference that Andre was behind Tyler's disappearance. Just yesterday, after a staff meeting, Simon had called her to his side and confided,

"The entire abduction rescue scenario is ridiculous. It is as clear as glass. He did it to ingratiate himself with Tyler and the family. I find it highly coincidental, convenient that the man has family and property in West Africa. Think about it. Tyler was abducted—supposedly by a Lonnie Jackson—to the same area, and then rescued by Andre. Highly suspicious, I tell you."

Angela studied Simon, and asked with her voice as thin as a wafer, "Just what do you mean by that?"

"Did I stutter?" Simon answered sarcastically. "I do not trust him. I mean, think about it. He marries her in a native ceremony, and then returns to the states for an official wedding—very mercenary, if you ask me. I believe she's got a bun in her oven, and it might not be his, but he will claim the baby anyway. Remember, only blood heirs can inherit. He's an opportunist. She's making a huge mistake, obviously thinking with what's between her legs, and not her head."

"Did you see how she behaves like a puppet on his string? He's cutting her off from her family and friends. I mean, I had to make an appointment through him to get an audience with her. Even then, he was present, sitting in a corner, listening to every word. She is becoming his pawn, I tell you. He'll take over and displace us all."

Angela was shocked with the viciousness of Simon's accusations, but she kept her own counsel.

Simon watched Angela closely trying to gauge her reaction to his banter. He did not like her, had never appreciated her inclusion into the inner circle of his family, but considered her a lesser evil. After all, he conjured, she could be a snoop, and thank God, that she was not. What she was, was bothersome, always acting as if she was Tyler's surrogate mother. He loathed the thought. It was detestable. Simon hid his contempt for Angela well. Whenever he wanted to test a theory or the impact of a lie, he simply planted the seed by confiding in her, and waited for the feedback.

Angela found Simon's speculations to be ugly, and she felt the malicious gossip could undermine Tyler to her managers. She had a nagging suspicion about Simon's confidences, and she had never been as gullible as he had thought. Today, her intuition told her that there was more to Simon's spiteful remarks than simple distrust of Andre.

She was not fooled. Simon had little or no protective instincts toward his niece. She and Nanny Peters were the only real family Tyler had. Mercedes had never taken an interest in her grand-daughter, and Simon, for all his hovering charm, exploited her, and treated Tyler more like a company asset than Rachel's only daughter—his only niece and benefactor. As far as Angela could see, his latent concerns were suspect, and his rumor mangling within the ranks of Mueller were ominous. Shrewdly, Angela lowered her eyelids, deciding to exercise caution and agree with his analogy.

"You might have something there, Simon, but let's keep this to ourselves for the moment. We don't want to excite the other managers before we decide what to do."

It was just before dawn, and Angela sat at her kitchen table sipping coffee. There was an aromatic stream of steam circling the cup, and a hum of pleasure escaped her lips. She leaned back in the chair. Her mouth puckered and she blew softly, cooling the hot brew. The delicious smell of fresh coffee always brought visions of Rachel and their college days to mind, and Angela lost herself in the pleasure of the moment.

It was the time of morning she loved best, the quiet and still-ness centering her as nothing else could. She felt close to God, close to those who had crossed over, close to Rachel who she still talked to on a regular basis. She had even confided to Nanny, "I know it sounds crazy, but there are times, I swear, I feel as if Rachel answers." So it was not unusual that Angela found herself once again in a conversation with her friend.

Tyler is back. It's unbelievable, darling. Miraculous, really! She was returned to us alive, just like you, a feat I never expected, and the surprise of all surprises, darling, is she is married, to Andre Dunn, no less. You must be watching over her, because the man is crazy in love with her, and of course, she loves him. I really didn't think I could live through another kidnapping, but she is back safe. You should have seen Simon's face!

Angela grinned into her cup shaking her head in wonder. When the couple walked into the boardroom, she thought Simon would drop dead on the spot. You could have bought him with a penny.

He had turned into a real otter during the months Tyler was gone, taking control and effected changes at Mueller he would not have dared to do when Tyler was at the helm. The most daring move he made was to remove Juan from head of security and place the security department under a contract agency.

Then, he fired Dunn & Burkett, blaming them along with Juan for Andre's death and Tyler's disappearance. Amazing! The man's motives were insidious. She saw through him, but she had played along, knowing that Simon would eventually expose himself.

Angela took another sip from the oversized coffee mug, enjoying the moment, reflecting on the pleasure she had felt when she had seen Simon's panic. It was worth her shock just to see him speechless. *Oh, Rae, I would have loved for you to have been there. We would have died laughing.* Her musing was interrupted when the phone rang, the buzz jarring the stillness in the quiet of the moment.

Amazed, Angela glanced at her watch, staring at it as if it were a piece of sci-fi technology, and then reached for the phone hesitantly. It was five o'clock. Who could be calling at this time of the morning, she wondered.

"Yes? Oh, it's you. Hello, Nanny." At the other end of the telephone, Christine Peters swallowed and cleared her throat. "Hi, baby-doll." Angela smiled. She was almost fifty, but Nanny would always talk to her as if she was still a young college student. She smiled at the memory, but sobered immediately, asking.

"Is everything OK?" Angela's voice trembled slightly.

"Yes. Of course," Nanny replied and Angela breathed a sigh of relief.

"Pastor and Mother Price called me a few minutes ago. They have a letter for you from Lonnie," Nanny confided.

"For me? Are you certain? Why would he write a letter to me?" Angela asked in amazement, wondering if Nanny knew that Lonnie was responsible for Tyler's disappearance and Andre's injury.

"I don't know, baby-doll—whatever his reason, the Prices want to bring the letter to you this morning. Is that OK?" There was an extended pause. Angela was clearly troubled. "It's Saturday, Nanny. I don't have anything on my calendar. Robert is fly-fishing with the boys, and they won't be back until tomorrow evening. I'm free."

"Good, they want to come right over!"

"Nanny! It's not even six. I'm not dressed."

"I know, I know. But they sounded real nervous."

Angela was tempted to tell the older woman that the letter and its contents could certainly wait another hour or so. However, she reasoned, Nanny's insight and intuition had always proven invaluable. Confidently, she reassured everyone that Tyler would return and that things were not as they seemed?

"OK. Tell them that I will have a pot of coffee waiting." Angela replaced the cordless phone on the base.

When the couple arrived an hour later, she was not surprised to see Nanny Peters in tow. After the hugs and greetings, Angela poured coffee, and when everyone was seated around the cocktail table, Mother Price took the letter from her purse and handed it to the younger woman.

Angela studied each of the cherished faces, thinking of how she had grown to love and trust them over the years, and spoke softly. "Mother Price, I don't have any secrets from you and Pastor, or Nanny either. You read the letter to us.

An hour later, Angela picked up her cordless phone, and selected speed dial. The phone on the other side of town rang for several seconds. Al Rosenthal was in a deep sleep. For a moment, he was disoriented. He fumbled with the phone, dropping it on the bedside table, as he fished clumsily for the receiver. Angela, grimacing, moved her head away from her phone.

"Hello." Al's voice was groggy.

"Al, it's Angela. I need your help. I'd like to lunch with you today. Are you available?"

"It all depends on why we need to meet. Is it something we can handle over the phone?" Al croaked and yawned loudly into the phone.

"It's about Tyler. I don't believe she's out of danger, and I want to run something by you." There was silence from the other end of the phone. Angela waited patiently.

"I'll cancel my lunch date. Can you come to my house at noon? The sleep was gone from Al's voice.

"Yes." Angela hung up the phone and called John Burkett. Unlike Al, John appeared to be wide awake and his voice radiated confidence. "This is John."

"John. It's Angela. Sorry to call so early, but I have an urgent matter to discuss with you. It concerns Andre and Tyler. I believe they're not out of danger, and John, Lonnie might not be the problem." There was absolute silence on the other end of the phone.

"Is it possible for you to meet with Al Rosenthal and me at his house at noon?"

On the other end of the line John Burkett fingered his chin, stroking it reflectively deep in thought. "Have you run this by Andre?"

"No. Not yet."

"I assume you have a good reason for not doing so."

Angela answered firmly, "Yes. I do. You have to trust me on this."

"OK, Angela, I will. But I'm not sure Andre will be as understanding as I am. He's very particular about Tyler, and I'm sure he will not appreciate your holding anything back from him regarding her safety. I won't promise that I will keep him in the dark, because we don't keep secrets from one another. As long as you understand that, I'll be there at noon."

"Thanks, John. You won't regret it."

Angela hung up, and prayed she was making the right decision.

After meeting with Al and Angela, John was in a quandary. Lonnie Jackson's letter had opened a completely new can of worms. But there was never a doubt that he would share the information with Andre. John pressed the speed dial on his cell phone and waited. Andre picked up the phone on the second ring. His voice held his usual confidence, and it was reassuring.

"Andre, I'm coming over. I've got something I think you should see."

Simon sat in his corner office in front of a massive executive desk listening to Mueller tapes—the dailies—as he called them. They were a collection of tapes, which recorded the activities in each of the managers' offices. He began listening in on his colleagues' right after the old man had put him in charge of Corporate Facilities. The bugging of offices started when he became annoyed with one of the managers who made a point of challenging his opinions at the weekly meetings. The final straw came when the man ridiculed Simon after he gave his opinion on an international trade issue.

Listening in on the man's conversations, Simon had learned that the manager was receiving kickbacks from several of the Mueller vendors. It gave Simon the ammunition he needed to have the man terminated, but he had not. Instead, he turned the man into a boy-toy.

The manager was never the same again, and his sexual preference became cloudy. Several times he and the manager had almost been caught when Simon summoned him to his office and ordered him on his knees for a blowjob.

There were two other rewards. First, he initiated his own sweetheart operation, where vendors would pay for his support of their bids. This proved to be extremely lucrative. Over the years, he had stashed millions of dollars of the extorted money in an overseas account. Second, he bugged every office, and every room, in the Mueller corporate offices. He found the conversations to be invaluable, and it was a great way to monitor his allies and foes. No one was exempt, not even old man Mueller. Later, Rachel had discovered the bug in her office and had it removed.

When Adam told Rachel of his impending death, Simon had overheard the entire tête-à-tête. He wondered for years what was in the box the old man had given to his sister. He searched high and low, but he had never been able to discover where Rachel hid it. And when she passed it on, he was sure she had told Tyler the secret of the box, but he had been foiled again.

Oh, but what he would give to get his hands on that box. He could only imagine the secrets it held. Maybe there was a hidden cache of money buried somewhere, or beauty formulas Adam's mother had left behind...like the Coca- Cola secret recipe. Maybe that was where those Seymour brothers got the idea for ReVive. The possibilities were endless.

Tyler's return may have purpose after all, he surmised. *Wouldn't it be a blast to have the old man and Rachel looking down on him while he opened their precious box?*

Simon was in the dark about the box, because Rachel had found out about his eavesdropping system and had her office debugged when she structured her takeover of the company. She never let on that she knew that Simon was the culprit, but before she died, she made sure that Tyler and Nanny were aware of Simon's duplicity.

Simon swiveled in the black leather chair, and stared into the West Hollywood Hills. He felt like an old man. *Hell. He was an old man.* He had grown old at the helm of Mueller International. But in spite of his dedication and devotion to the Mueller empire, he had always been second, first to his sister, and now to her bastard. Simon hissed under his breath, "Unbelievable." A century ago, Tyler would have been relegated to the slaves' quarters. He could have owned her, and her primary service would have been as a bed slave, or better yet, she would have been a broodmare to the master and other plantation owners. Her offspring would have been worth thousands of dollars.

Simon smiled at the vision, reflecting for several minutes on the women in the family. Mercedes' face flashed before him. He grimaced. "God, he loathed his mother. The nymphomaniac! He would never forget the time he walked in and she was pleasuring herself. Disgusting!

She could not even negotiate a prenup to their advantage. Like a lapdog, she had rushed to take the crumbs offered by Adam Mueller. It was ludicrous! Mueller was worth billions, and she had accepted a paltry ten million. Because of her ineptitude, he had been cast in the role of servant. Well, he had finally gotten his revenge. Stuck her in a convalescent hospital where she would rot out the rest of her pathetic life. His shoulders lifted reflectively, and he grunted deep in his throat, *maybe she will frig herself to death.*

His lips twisted into a crooked smile. His plans for Tyler were even better than those he had designed for his mother. He had a perfect solution to his problem, something that would stop the financial probe. Everything could blow up in his face. There was no doubt that Al and several of the board members had become suspicious. The quarterly review of the Mueller financials had revealed serious discrepancies. And eventually, the entire mess would come out.

His skimming off the business, amassing a fortune through sweetheart contracts over the years, had left a trail. There was no doubt that Al was on to him. And there was every possibility that Angela suspected his backdoor deals.

Simon shook his head regretfully. The problem was he had become greedy and overconfident. He grimaced mentally, chiding himself. Adam Mueller had always said, "Humility is a virtue, and arrogance, a sure road to downfall."

Well, the old man had never been more right. Look at Lonnie Jackson. The arrogance of the man, Simon thought, to resurface. What stupidity. What a fool. He should have just disappeared. Security had reason to be concerned. Well, he shrugged philosophically. That was not his problem. His problem, he reflected, was stalling the financial probe.

The phone console buzzed. His assistant's voice came over the intercom. "Mr. Seymour."

"Yes, Steve."

"It's four o'clock. You are scheduled for a game of handball with Mr. Lara. His secretary called to say he would meet you at the gym."

An hour later, sweat dripped from Simon's forehead. His breath came in short puffs and his heart sputtered as he raced to meet the ball. Struggling, he slapped the ball hard against the wall. Juan leaped, and returned the ball. Whack! The ball flew past him and hit the back wall with a loud bang. The game was over, and truth be told, Simon was grateful. There was an unusual tightness in his chest, and he fought the urge to bend over.

He watched as Juan strolled toward him. Juan sported a winner's grin. It was the second time in as many weeks he had beaten Simon at handball and it felt good. He could not help but gloat. "I only hope I'm as good as you are when I get to be your age."

Simon visibly flinched. The age part was like a knife prick, and Juan knew it. For years, the older man had needled Juan about his lack of skill. "It's not always brawn that wins the day; it is skill, young man that ensures the win, skill, mental prowess, and a warrior's spirit. That's what will carry you to victory every time."

Underlining his comment was Simon's confidence that he was inherently superior in every way to Juan, and he never let Juan forget it. Now Juan was on top, and it felt good even if it was only in a handball game.

Juan slapped Simon on the back, cuffing his neck lightly. It was a power move and both men knew it. Simon added a new name—Juan's—to his revenge list, envisioning the man at his mercy.

Back in his office, Simon rubbed his chest. The ache was persistent. Dismissing it, he picked up the phone and walked over to the bar. He dialed his masseur, made an appointment, and buzzed Steve.

"Come in, and bring your note pad."

Simon unzipped his pants, crossed back to the desk and sat down. His request had been a private code to Steve, who understood Simon perfectly. The assistant closed the door softly when he entered the room. Marionette like, he walked over to Simon, sank to his knees, and crawled under the desk. Taking Simon in his mouth, Steve's head began to bob while the executive made several calls.

"Detective Duffy, please." Simon waited for the detective to come to the phone. It had been weeks since they had spoken, but Simon had planted the seeds well. It was time for the *coup de grace*.

"Yes." Duffy's voice was world-weary and gruff. He coughed into the phone, a smoker's raspy noise that grated on Simon's ears.

"Detective Gavin, this is Simon Seymour." Simon paused, enjoying Steve's ministration, looked at the top of his assistant's head, then resumed smoothly. "I'd like to come in to see you. "Aah," Simon's low, half moan of pleasure preceded his next revelation. "I just came across something that might help with the Jan Bellows case."

"Yeah?" The boredom in Gavin's voice was quickly replaced by curiosity. "What is it?" There was a long pause, and Gavin wondered at the deep breathing at the other end of the phone. The man sounded as if he was experiencing a serious gas attack.

"Un...un...aah...It's not something I want to discuss over the phone. I'd like to come to your office. Is tomorrow morning good for you? Around ten o'clock." Simon lifted his hips to better accommodate Steve, thinking there was no power on earth as great as the one he found bending another to his will. He became aware that the detective was speaking.

"No problem. I'll see you then." Gavin hung up the phone and wondered at this new turn of events. Lonnie Jackson was the prime suspect, but Gavin had always felt the man had not acted alone. He had always believed there was a larger plot against the Mueller heir, especially after the attempt on Andre Dunn's life. Why kill him and only tie up the chauffeur? His gut told him there was more, and his gut was rarely wrong.

Simon listened to the click on the other end of the line, and replaced the cordless to its base. He leaned back in the chair. Power surged, infusing him with a sense of absolute dominion. He glanced down. Steve's golden head bobbed between his legs in subjugation. *Viagra was the best invention since the wheel.* It certainly kept him ready. He reached for and found the rhythm that would let him blast down Steve's throat.

Oh yeah, this was the life.

Simon grabbed a fistful of the man's hair and listened to Steve moan, perhaps in pain, or a passionate response. It did not matter to Simon as he grunted his release. His seed spilled forth, thick and bitter, like the man, and Steve slumped back on the floor totally humiliated. *What would his wife think if she saw him, or his son, God forbid?* Steve wiped his hand across his mouth, but the shame would not so easily disappear.

Simon looked down with callous disregard at the man at his feet. He needed privacy for the second call, and he nudged Steve with the toe of his shoe. "That'll be all," Simon dismissed him. He waited until he heard the click of the door, and picked up the receiver and dialed the head of his security team.

After their lunch with Angela, Tyler and Andre returned to Malibu. The ride back to the beach house was peaceful, and for the first time in a several weeks, Tyler felt safe. After dinner, she curled up in a chair with Angela's marketing report. Every few minutes she would glance up at Andre who was working on his laptop.

"Angela was interviewing you today."

Andre looked at Tyler, his gaze thoughtful. "I know."

"You passed the test with flying colors."

Andre was preoccupied. "That's comforting."

Tyler wanted to scream. She wanted his full attention. Agitated, she turned the page of the report with a loud snap and peeked at Andre over the rim of the brief wondering what he found so interesting on his laptop. Minutes passed, punctuated by her numerous sighs.

I can feel your need. It is beating at me. His voice was an inferno of heat as his palm feathered lightly over her stomach, lingering on the slight bulge of life nestled in her womb. He wondered if she knew she carried his child. She had yet to speak to him about it. But he had been inside of her and touched the small life frequently. He turned his head as she responded with a cocky challenge.

What do you plan to do about it? Tyler's voice was provocative, and Andre met her blatant dare with a masterful thrust that merged them instantly.

This. His voice was confidence personified.

Tyler was overwhelmed with sensations, his and hers. Andre's mouth brushed invisibly against the lace covering the triangular curls at her mound. Tyler slid down on the sofa and watched as he crossed to her side. He took her in his arms and nestled her neck, opened his senses and let her feel his need. His lips traveled to her cheek. He loved to watch her respond to him. He caressed her face with his eyes. A red laser dot appeared, hovering in the center of Tyler's forehead.

Lighting fast, Andre flipped them off the sofa, and covered Tyler with his body. Everything happened so quickly Tyler had little time to register the danger. Several shots rang out and the vase on the sofa table behind them shattered. Glass rained around them.

The door burst open and two of Andre's men rushed in guns at the ready, they cautiously circled the room with their weapons. Detecting no immediate threat, the men backed out of the room and ran toward the back of the house. Nothing stirred.

Lonnie is persistent, if nothing else. His tone sounded serious. He pushed himself off Tyler and stood up, assured—as their shouts floated from outside—that his men had secured the outer parameters.

We have to end this. I truly do not believe I will outlast the excitement of his relentless quest.

Andre reached out, seizing Tyler's hands, pulled and crushed her to his chest. He held her close like a priceless jewel. His body hardened. If he lived a thousand years, he knew he would never tire of this woman.

Tyler had come to love their mind merges and the intimacy of telepathy. It was more than the closeness of their private conversations—it was the marriage of thought that could only be compared to sexual mating.

I agree. I believe we can flush him out.

Andre quizzed aloud, "How?"

"I believe we can draw him to us if we participate in the *ReVive* promotions and become more visible, more approachable. Tyler raised her hand to quash Andre's protest. "I know. It will also make us vulnerable, and open to attack. But, I have absolute faith in your ability to keep us safe."

"No," his answer was emphatic. "I will not use you as a decoy to lure our enemies."

"Listen to me, my love." Tyler framed Andre's face with her hands, forcing him to look into her eyes, into her soul. "I cannot go on living this way, and there is more. I am carrying our child." Tyler's index finger pressed against his lips, silencing his protest.

"Our child is more precious to me than my own life. And, darling, we cannot go on this way, in constant fear of an attack from Lonnie, or—God forbid—his plots against our loved ones." She choked. "I tell you, I cannot go on living on edge with an army of men shadowing my every move."

They talked into the early morning. The compromise was hard won, but in the end, both felt they had a game plan that would flush Lonnie out and not put Tyler at undo risk.

Lonnie was desperate. Three weeks had passed since he watched Tyler enter Mueller International's garage elevator. Then he read in the paper that Tyler was going to appear on the Oprah Winfrey West Coast Show to talk about *ReVive*. He knew he must reach her and warn her about Z. He wondered for the thousandth time why the man always hid his face. He did not believe it was Z's participation in the adult movies, and felt that there was a deeper reason for the man's disguise. Various scenarios had run through Lonnie's head, and he wondered if Z could be a married man and did not want to reveal his down-low activities. Whatever the cause, Z had been relentless in concealing his identity.

The crowd in front of the Kodak Theater was boisterous as they awaited the celebrity arrivals. The studio guards worked aggressively to keep the fans away from the theatre entrance. Oprah arrived first and rushed down the red carpet, waving quickly at the crowd as her name was shouted repeatedly.

Shortly after, a long limousine drove up, and Paris Hilton exited the passenger cab. Right behind her, Halle Berry's chauffeur-driven Bentley pulled to the curb. Both women preened and waved to their adoring fans then rushed down the red carpet into the studio.

Lonnie waited, inconspicuous, at the edge of the crowd watching eagerly as more celebrities arrived. His enthusiasm waned after forty minutes had passed, and no Tyler. He began to worry that she was not coming after all, and had begun to debate whether he should stay or not, when a helicopter hovered and began to descend overhead landing on the roof of the Theater. He knew it carried Tyler when he saw the large calligraphy gold M, globally recognized as the Mueller monogram.

He could not believe his luck. The weeks of planning was going to pay off. Lonnie skirted to the back of the crowd, removed his top coat and let it slide unnoticed onto the ground. He turned and walked south on Highland, circled the block and emerged on the north side of Hollywood Boulevard. The Kodak uniform and identification badge was perfect. No one questioned him as he approached the service entrance of the theater and walked to the back of the building.

Security was not as tight as Lonnie had expected. He entered the stairwell, and ascended six stories to the rooftop unchallenged. Lighting was sparse, and the helicopter pad was surprising empty. Only a pilot and two security guards were stationed on the roof. Lonnie watched as one of the guards lit a cigarette, flung his head back, and laughed at the pilot's off-colored joke.

"You got that right."

The guard's voice floated on the night wind. "These Californians are real pussies. I'd like to see them join us in Pakistan, or Northern Nigeria. Ha. There're as soft as a sponge-ball." All three guards snickered. The men's laughter had begun to fade when the door to the roof opened, and Lonnie saw two more guards walk cautiously onto the helipad. Seconds later, Juan and John strolled with military synchronization through the door. Several fully armored guards flanked them. The two veteran soldiers walked out into the open space, and waved to their men to fan out around the helicopter.

Lonnie flattened himself against the generator, his body camouflaged by the structure and black night. He squeezed between the generator and the parameter wall. A guard approached the generator and spoke into his headphone.

Lonnie ducked low, folding his body into a small ball. The guard halted inches from his hiding space. Lonnic could see the guards boot tops, and he experienced an adrenalin rush. His heart pounded thunderously in his ears, and he wondered how the guard did not hear it.

Sweat dotted Lonnie's forehead, and he had trouble controlling his nervous energy. He held his breath and closed his eyes prayerfully. Finally, the guard moved away. Breathing a sigh of relief, Lonnie pushed himself to a stand with his back against the generator. He turned slowly and gazed at the assembled guards.

He was proud of Juan. They were not taking any chances. Security was tight after all. Z would have his work cut out for him to get past the seasoned men surrounding the Mueller helicopter.

His thoughts were interrupted when he saw the door open again. Andre, Tyler, and another man Lonnie did not recognize exited the building. Lonnie focused on the men flanking Tyler. There was something familiar about one of them. His height and the way he carried himself brought about a shadowy memory. Then the man spoke.

"You were great, Tyler. I know sales will jump substantially by end of the week. You did good, kiddo."

The threesome moved toward the helicopter and Lonnie's mouth dropped open in shock. The man standing beside Tyler, flanking her was Z. He would recognized his voice anywhere... and....kiddo? Z called everyone kiddo. Unmindful of his own safety, Lonnie sprang from behind the generator and ran toward Tyler.

"You bastard, get away from her."

Simon stepped in front of Tyler screaming. "It's him. Don't let him get near her." Everyone was shouting at the same time. Andre grabbed Tyler, and pushed her behind him, shielding her with his large body. Shots rang out. Lonnie spun around, hit in the thigh. He reached in his pocket and Simon yelled again. "He's got a gun." Juan aimed, his left hand leveling his right, and shot twice into the human target.

Blood burst from Lonnie's shoulder. He was flung backward, but remained on his feet. He dove, grabbing Simon by the neck and slammed into his body. He pointed his gun into Simon's head. A hush blanketed the roof, and there was an eerie silence.

"Why are you here?" Lonnie's hissed question could be heard by all.

Blood was dripping from the wounded man's shoulder, and it gushed from his thigh, pooling at his feet. Lonnie was weakening, but refused to let Simon go. Tyler twisted in Andre's arms, in a hopeless effort to free herself.

Let me go. I can't let another die in my stead.

"Lonnie. Please no, Tyler sobbed into the night." But he was not listening. Instead, he was focused on the man he crushed fiercely with his body.

"I asked you a question, mutha-fucker." Lonnie jabbed the gun into Simon's head, but the older man refused to speak. "Oh, you want to be cute?" Everyone heard the click as Lonnie pulled the gun trigger back and cocked the handgun.

Tyler sobbed, and twisted out of Andre's arms, stumbling in front of Lonnie. Everyone froze. Tears were streaming down her face. She spread her arm pleading. "You don't want him, Lonnie. You want me. Let my uncle go." Andre moved to Tyler's side taking her hand.

You die. I die. Andre flooded Tyler with warmth.

"You want this bastard?" Lonnie cackled hysterically, recklessly shoving Simon forward. "He's been trying to kill you for over a year. Haven't you, mutha-fucker." Simon flinched and paled as Lonnie jabbed the gun again into his temple.

Simon paled. "Don't believe him. I'm your uncle. He's a confessed murder. Shoot him," Simon's voice remained calm, but it was only bravado. He was filled with dread, and sweat dotted his forehead. Everyone was looking at him and he felt exposed. Naked.

"If I am a murderer, he is a monster," Lonnie's words rang with ominous truth. "He is behind every evil I've committed over the last ten years. This twisted bastard is the world's most prolific producer of pornography. The filth he produces would turn your stomach." Lonnie's thoughts turned inward.

"I'm sorry to say, I helped him."

His eyes focused on Tyler, shadowing her pain. "Forgive me, little sister. I've blamed you for my own sins, and God knows I'm sorry. I hurt you, and I was so wrong. I blamed you for the pain that happened long before you came into my life. You represented everything I wanted to be and have. Everybody loved you." Lonnie shook his head bemused by his errors, "You are beautiful inside and out, but I refused to see it...until now..."

He muttered, speaking more to himself than anyone else, and shook his head again sadly. "My own mother used me as a human shield to save her miserable junkie life, so I blamed you."

Lonnie backed up slowly, dragging Simon with him. The blood streamed from his shoulder and leg. He was growing weaker by the minute, and it was difficult for him to concentrate.

"Lying scum!" Sensing Lonnie's weakness, Simon twisted, almost gaining freedom. But Lonnie had a death grip on the older man, and continued to drag him backward toward the door to the platform exit.

Shocked by Lonnie's accusations, Juan leveled his gun at Lonnie, and spoke softly into his headphone. "Stand down, hold your fire. Repeat. Stand down."

Tyler could not believe her ears. But it did not matter. All she knew was that she did not want another person to die because of her. "Lonnie, please. Let my uncle go. Whatever the problem, I promise I'll stand by you. Just let him go."

Angela began to inch forward. She spoke calmingly, her voice low and soothing. "Lonnie. We understand. Believe me, you are not the only one that knows about Simon. He would have been exposed soon." Lonnie listened doubtfully, and rolled his head slowly from one side to the other side, disbelief written clearly on his face. He was resolute. He knew that even if Simon was exposed there was still a price to pay for his own digressions, and for Jan. That debt was irrevocable, and cancelable only by God.

Andre watched Lonnie cautiously, ready to pounce the moment he sensed a threat to Tyler. Using all his powers, he reached for Lonnie trying to inject reason into his thoughts, but was blocked. The man was in so much pain it was impossible to get past his agony.

"There is no hope, Tyler. I wish there was, but it is useless." Lonnie's speech was slightly slurred. He shuffled toward the door, bending Simon backward, his arm almost strangling the older man.

At the doorjamb, Lonnie halted, memorizing the scene before him, especially the face of his siblings, now appreciated and beloved as he mouthed a silent good-bye. Determination flashed across his face, and it was reflected in his eyes. Two bullets echoed on the roof almost simultaneously. Simon went down like a rag doll and remained motionless. Lonnie collapsed in slow motion, his legs folding into themselves, and he sat down with a muffled thump against the door. Surprised etched on his face.

Andre pulled Tyler's head into his chest. She whimpered into his coat, bunching his lapel with white-knuckled fists. A second later, she twisted out of Andre's arms and stumbled toward Lonnie. He was no longer a threat to anyone. She sobbed, as if he had never caused her pain. Angela pushed past the guards to Tyler's side and wrapped her arm around her waist. Andre hovered in the background.

"Lonnie. Why?" Dropping to her knees, Tyler cradled her foster brother's head and placed it in her lap. His eyes were starting to glaze over. She sobbed again, wanting to turn back the hands of time.

"Sorry..." Blood bubbled at the corner of his mouth. "Had to make amends...protect you...Z...Z...wanted you...dead... kil... yu." He wanted to tell Tyler that her uncle was Z, but he was tired, and the voice was calling to him, telling him it was time to rest. He loved the voice, and the light, the welcoming light. He walked toward it confident that he was forgiven, confident that Tyler was protected. Jan waited in the distance, in the light. Her arms were open, and he knew she offered him something that he had searched for all of his life, something his own mother had been unwilling to give—unconditional love.

EPILOGUE

DECEMBER 2007

The Beverly Hills Court clerk lifted the gavel and lowered it three times. The loud bang garnered a hush in the crowded courtroom. "All rise. The Beverly Hills Superior Court is now in session. The Honorable Joseph McNealy, superior judge, presiding."

Tyler felt the moment surreal. The black-robed judge entered the courtroom and the bailiff ordered all to be seated. She turned her head toward Simon as he was ushered into the room and took his place beside his attorneys. The moment was strangely disquieting. Her uncle's posture affirmed his defeat; he was a beaten man. The months of the trial, the courtroom revelations, and damning evidence had exposed her uncle's treachery and sealed his fate. There was little room for doubt. Testimony from Simon's secretary, Steve, and from his lover of thirty years, Chang, revealed the depth of his depravity.

He had not only masterminded the attacks on Tyler, but Simon had also orchestrated Jan's murder. Coupled with evidence that he had been at the helm of an international pornography ring that was linked to white slavery, his name was now synonymous with heinous sex crimes. The story was covered in all of the international newspapers, CNN, MSNBC, FOX News, and all of the networks carried lurid details of the trial.

At first, it appeared as if Simon's attorneys would successfully convince the jurors that the evidence was only circumstantial, that is, until the state prosecutors presented their star witnesses Steve and Chang. A dropped pin could have been heard in the courtroom when they testified.

Simon's assistant Steve cried on the stand, his rendition of the suffering and degradation he had suffered at the hands of his boss, and the loss of his wife and children elicited sniffles and tears throughout the silent room. But it was Chang that provided the prosecution with irrefutable evidence. He delivered financial ledgers, tapes, and videos documenting Simon's crimes.

In the end, her uncle was convicted of all charges: murder, pornography, pornographic trafficking, white slavery, sexual battery, fraud, larceny, kidnapping and intention to kill.

Chang even assisted the IRS in uncovering Simon's offshore bank accounts in Panama, Switzerland, and South Africa as part of a plea bargaining deal, since there was some evidence that he had known of Simon's duplicities. Considered a flight risk, the court had refused bail and placed Simon in general population until he was cornered and brutally raped. The balance of the twelve-month trial, Simon spent in a solitary cell.

Tyler watched the judge, her hand clasped in Andre's, and experienced a moment of déjà vu. In slow motion, she watched the judge's mouth open and knew what he would say.

"Would the prisoner like to address the court before sentencing?"

Simon moved his head from side to side, signaling to the judge he had nothing to say. This was not surprising. He had not spoken throughout the trial, refusing to testify on his own behalf.

Gone was the proud distinguished gentleman he had appeared to be. His shoulders were slumped, and his head hung low, shielding his eyes. He was a defeated man, stripped of everything he valued, his wealth, his status in the community, his birthright and executive privileges, and his camouflaged persona. The weeks of testimony had exposed him as a Dr. Jekyll and Mr. Hyde, a man consumed by hate and jealousy, masquerading as man of distinction and class, but mired in smut, capable of the most heinous crimes against his fellow man.

"Then, by the power vested in me, I remand you to the State of California Department of Corrections, where you will remain until such time as the state executioner exercises the death penalty in accordance with the laws and regulations of California. May God have mercy on you!" The gavel fell giving a bang of finality. The courtroom buzzed with approval. But after months of anticipation, Tyler felt the verdict was anticlimactic.

Back at Malibu, Tyler leaned into Andre, exhausted. Baby Zak was nestled into her breast snuggled in close sleeping peacefully. Tyler glanced down at the silky waves covering the infant's head and up again at Andre. Her tapered finger smoothed the baby's cheek, his mouth moved, parroting the sucking motion of nursing, and she met Andre's eyes lovingly marveling at their creation.

You have done well my love. Andre's hand joined Tyler's, covering hers as she cupped the baby's head. His voice was a feathered whisper in her mind and she could feel his lips run the length of her neck. If she lived forever, she would never tire of their intimacy. Andre knew what she wanted, when she wanted it, and... *Oh God*, she thought, *how to deliver it.*

Tyler felt his masculine smile. *That is because you and I are chosen, foretold, as one from the beginning of Zankli. Where is the casket love? I want to read our history again. Who would have thought your grandfather was a Zankli...a Zankli, and Zak prophesied.*

The casket is on the nightstand." Tyler pointed to the jeweled box. *It is where we always leave it.* Andre concentrated. In seconds, the casket appeared on the sofa table in front of them.

Tyler's eyes flew to his face in amazement. *How did you do that?*

Andre's eyebrow lifted smugly. Tongue in cheek, he said as he opened the beautifully jeweled case. *Oh, I have my secrets.* He had been practicing levitation for months, his abilities growing exponentially with each passing day. Their marriage and the close proximity to Tyler had increased his powers tenfold. That too, was prophesied, for the union of two chosen fused their gifts.

Andre opened the letter. The paper crackled with age. The handwriting was cursive and in a woman's flowerily scrawl. The story was spun conversationally, in colloquial English that spoke of an era following the Civil War.

"My name is Beatrice Mueller, and I am a child of slavery. My mother and her mother before her were slaves, born on the Mueller plantation outside of Augusta, Georgia," the letter began. "My father owned Mueller Landing, a sprawling cotton plantation that housed over one thousand field slaves, three overseers, eleven drivers, thirty cotton mill labors, twenty craftsmen, and seventeen building artisans. The plantation had shoe cobblers, seamstresses, weavers, cooks, horse wranglers, blacksmiths, midwives, and herbalists.

"My mother told me that when she was a little girl the plantation was like a small village, and the master's house bustled with dozens of domestic slaves. There was row after row of slave dwellings arranged into neat sections of twenty-five, one-room cabins. Each section was named after a Mueller ancestor and each cabin would house as many as four adults and eight children."

"I lived with my mother in the big house, she was the housekeeper and I was a handmaid and companion to my half sister Judith. Of course, in those days, you never ever claimed kinship."

"My grandmother was a mulatto. Her mother was a Zankli, captured in an Efe war in Togo as a preteen and marched in shackles to the Ivory Coast for transport as a slave to America. My great-grandmother Nadu survived the trip from Africa in the captain's cabin and arrived in Georgia a seasoned woman. She was sold under private sale to the Mueller's and renamed Nancy."

"Nancy became invaluable to Master Mueller. Besides becoming his bed slave, she was a healer and herbalist much sought after for her medical skills, and she often traveled miles at the behest of her master to doctor one of his neighbors."

Andre lowered the aged yellow pages. It was at this point that he marveled at his wife's legacy and how Tyler's heritage intertwined with his own. Her Zankli ancestor—Nancy—had become renowned for her medical prowess as well as the beauty potions and creams she produced for the wives of the plantation owners. These things she kept to herself, but secretly taught Beatrice's grandmother how to farm and harvest herbs for the manufacture of lotions that naturally colored lips, cheeks and nails, kept hair silky smooth, and preventing spotting from the sun.

The slaves believed Nancy had the "sight," an ability to see into the future, and they were right. She was a prophetess that foretold the power and wealth her descendants would come to control. She said that there would be a legacy of *lost love*, but in the end, Zankli would join Zankli in the new land to create from love a great leader, and this leader and world unifier would be named Zak Dunn.

Andre replaced the manuscript in the jeweled casket and closed it quietly. He crossed the room to the sofa and gathered his wife and son into his arms.

The Beginning

PREVIEW

Captured Love
Zankli Chronicle
Book Two

M. J. Duffy

Captured Love
Zankli Chronicle—Book Two

PROLOGUE

WEST AFRICA 1781

It was daybreak and a golden orange glow had just begun to peek over the mountainous ridge illuminating the sleepy village. A sweet smell of dew hung in the air, and there was an aura of peacefulness clinging to the misty fog that encircled the cluster of thatched huts nestled in the grassy valley. All was quiet, when the silence of the morning was interrupted by the loud cockle of an ancient rooster strutting proudly across the commons, scattering the clucking chickens in his wake.

In the main compound, Nadu turned on her mat and snuggled deeper into her tie-dyed cotton spread. The twelve-year-old dreaded the day. Soon the seer, a decrepit elder, who Nadu was convinced was a witch, would come for her and take her to the woman's cottage where she would be prepared for the sacred ceremony of womanhood. This was dutifully observed by all women of Zankli.

Cloaked in secrecy and mired in mystery, the Zankli ritual assured prospective husbands of the readiness of the girls for wifely duties and motherhood. On the opposite mat, Nadu's cousin Moza slept undisturbed by the sound of the village beasts, perhaps because at fourteen, she had long since left her childhood behind. But Nadu, who had slept fitfully all night, turned on her back and flung her arm over her face unable to fend off the wakefulness.

Nadu looked at her cousin jealously as a soft whistle issued from her mouth. She stared under her arm at the slumbering girl for several minutes, when irritated and unable to resist, she hissed, "Moza, will you please stop that loud snoring." The small lie made the young girl feel better, if only for a moment, but had little effect on her cousin.

"Are you deaf? Stop snoring, you will wake the dead," she yelled at her cousin.

Jarred, the older girl shot up, looking around in alarm. "What is happening? What is wrong? Has the witch come?"

If Nadu had not been so worried, she would have laughed. It was so comical. By nature, kind hearted, the preteen experienced a moment of shame at her unkindness to Moza.

"No, I am sorry to wake you. Auntie Katu is not come. But I am so nervous. I have not slept all night. I know that you are sworn to secrecy, but can you not tell me just a little of what to expect? Honestly, I will die of the suspense."

Moza's eyes rounded, and she peered into the dimly lit hut fearful of being overheard and spoke in a hushed voice. "You know that is impossible. I will be condemned by all Zankli, and you, you will be banished. What are you thinking? I told you that it is not so bad. I told you that the ceremony is over quickly."

The two girls whispered, their voices low in the morning quiet. Frustrated, Nadu sat up, gathered the spread, wrapped it around her slight body and with a natural grace, knotted the yellow and blue material in the middle of her budding breasts. She was a beauty, and was considered one of the loveliest girls in the village. Her skin was a warm brown, smooth and rare like the sweet chocolate and exotic spices delivered by the caravan every year. Her eyes were large and shapely like almonds. Her nose was long, flaring beautifully at the end, each side of her nostrils perfectly matched. But it was her lips, so flawlessly centered on her face, so full, so beautifully flushed with nature's deep magenta that beckoned with promise to the village men.

And she walked with a sway that said come hither, between my legs, at the apex of my thighs, you will find paradise, joy, and unparalleled pleasure. This was the promise from a twelve-year-old. The elder women of Zankli shook their heads in wonder, and mocked among themselves. "She has not been breached," they snickered. "Yet the old men's roots rise-high and leak like a water jug that has been filled to its brim."

Yes, Nadu was the talk of the village for one reason or another. Her father was king of all Zankli, and her mother, his youngest wife, was a child of Zankli born of Zankli. Nadu was the promised child, foretold to be the bearer of a line of great leaders who would amass wealth and fortune beyond measure. This was prophesized by the keeper of their history, the *holy of most holy*, the native doctor of all Zankli, at the time of her birth. Her entire life she had been feted and spoiled as *the Chosen One*.

As so, on this morning of ceremonial rebirth, Nadu stood in the doorway of the holding hut and looked out upon her village, wishing herself away. She had begged and cajoled, promised and threatened, but to no avail. Her usually tractable father and malleable mother could not be moved. She would have to undergo the same rite that all Zankli women had experienced since the beginning of time.

With fear overriding all reason, Nadu decided she would take a calming walk to the river. She turned to her still dozing cousin and announced with mild irritation, "I am going to relieve myself and bathe. I will be back soon." Moza snuggled back into her mat, pleased to have more time to sleep. The ceremony was not scheduled until midmorning. The girl's deep breathing resounded in the small hut.

Nadu walked slowly, her small hips swaying gently in the quiet morning. She envisioned Kwame Zankli, the young warrior whose parents had spoken to the king to declare their son's interest in his youngest daughter, and she calmed. Kwame was a prize. All of the eligible girls in the village desired him. He was tall, broad shouldered, fast on his feet, an admired hunter, a feared warrior, and most importantly, he was unsurpassed in the mating dance. None of the other young men could even compete with his towering leaps, shoulder snaps, or chest rolls.

"By the God of her great-grandfathers," Nadu gushed, "he was a prize and she had no doubt he would keep their mat warm through many nights. Plus, she would be wealthy. Kwame's father was on the high council, chief of one riches of the twenty villages surrounding Zankli with almost as many cows and pigs as her own father.

Nadu began to hum a maiden's song, her voice floated up and mingled with the sounds of the tree monkeys that swung overhead. She looked up and smiled to herself. Even they knew that this was a special day, and their job joined her own. Why should she fear the gifts of the God of her great-grandfathers? She had been told from as far back as she could remember that she would bear great leaders of eminent wealth. *What should she fear?*

She had been walking for twenty minutes, and the river was just ahead. The morning was beautiful and she trilled to the sounds in the bush, confident and surefooted on the well traveled path. When she reached the river, the nimble girl stripped from her wrap, slipped into the chilled water and waded into the river until it covered her breasts.

Nadu reverently lowered her head, kicked off and swam deep, diving down toward the sandy bottom and then back up again. When she rose, water rained down her face and hair in a shimmering cascade. She was the picture of Eve, high uplifted budding breasts, wasp waist, flaring hips, and a curved buttock of classic proportions.

Her hair was braided close to her scalp framing her face. Red and crystal beads were woven into the ends of the short braids, which dangled enticingly across her forehead, accentuating her large eyes. The same colorful pattern of beads covered her head in a neat cap of extensions that grazed the nape of her long elegant neck. Her ears were pierced and from the delicate holes hung gold woven earrings made by Quazi Owusu, Zankli's finest jeweler.

Several feet away, Kwame watched Nadu. The thick bush surrounding the river bank cloaked his hiding place, but allowed a clear view of his intended as she bathed. He had noticed her as she strolled from the village and followed to see where she was going.

The eager youth had been staking out the holding hut for hours, so obsessed with the girl, and the completion of her rite of passage, was he. The ceremony was all that was keeping him from claiming her as his bride, and it was all he could think about. Everything else was in order. The contract had been made between their fathers and the cows readied for transport to his village. He and several of his brothers had arrived that evening to take the beasts for delivery to his father as her bride's levy.

Ayiii, by the Gods of his great-grandfathers he would die from the waiting. Kwame rolled his eyes toward the heavens and watched as Nadu disappeared beneath the water, marveling at her beauty. He had vowed to take her as a single wife, although it was not a widely practiced custom among his people. But Nadu was *the Chosen One* and deserved his undivided attention. His mind wandered and fantasies of their wedding night caused his body to clench, and he grew heavy, his manroot stretching and thumping enthusiastically, when suddenly, from the other side of the lake he saw three flesh-colored men running at Nadu. Time slowed, the water splashed high and seemed to hang in the air with each of their booted steps.

Kwame shook his head at the vision that would not go away. He burst from behind the bush with blood curdling shrieks and dashed toward the intruders with his spear raised. With the might of years of training, he hurled the razor sharp weapon through the air and it landed with deadly accuracy. The flesh colored man, who had been in the lead, plunged into the river sightless. The spear had severed his aorta artery, and he had died instantly.

Startled, his two flanking companions paused. A second later one of the men raised a dueling pistol, took careful aim and fired. Kwame melted into the river with blood pouring from his chest. There was an eerie silence as he floated ominously face-down in the river. The entire incident had taken but seconds, and Nadu frozen with shock, had not moved from her river perch. She could hear the splashing of feet entering the river and viewed the men closing in on her as if in a dream.

The view of Kwame's body floating in the river jarred her and she opened her mouth to scream, but was lifted out of the water before she could issue a sound. The hairy arm circling her body squeezed mercilessly, and the air was smashed from Nadu's lungs. Laughing, the man dragged the kicking girl out of the water and flung her onto the river bank, kicking her in the side when she continued to struggle.

The men had been pushing the caravan hard, traveling at a breathtaking speed across the West African interior toward the coast. They had been walking for days; their human cargo shackled one to another in a double line of men, women and children, all captured by the Yorba in a fierce war between neighboring tribesmen. They were a cargo of defeated Ibo and Calaba—war prize—fated for enslavement in the New World.

The girl was an incredible boon. When they came upon her at the edge of the river the guards froze, struck dumb by the otherworldly apparition rising from the river. In seconds, they regained their composure in spite of the attack by the male and rushed into the river, grabbed the woman-child, and hustled her onto the grassy bank.

Clutching her side the terrified girl spoke through tears. "I am Nadu. What is the meaning of this? My father will kill you, string you from your fingernails, and skin you alive. I am Nadu, I tell you, daughter to King Kintu of Zankli. Imbeciles! Jackals! Sons of diseased baboons. I am Nadu of Zankli. Aaaah, aaah, let me go!"

The girl's screams filled the empty riverbank, disrupting the quiet of the morning and the natural sounds of the birds and tree monkeys. But no one understood her. They were people from Niger and Nigeria and there was no one among these men, captives or masters who spoke her language. And truth to tell, it would not have mattered if they did. They were in the flesh trade, these caravan drivers. Slavery was an indiscriminate equalizer. Chief, chief's wife, or tribal wiseman, all treated equally as human commodities, non better or worse than the other.

One of the men—a man that Nadu would learn was particularly vicious—grabbed her by her hair. Beads rained down and pelted the ground as he drug her to a small group of exhausted women and children. Nadu fought every step of the way, kicking and gouging, scratching and spitting, to no avail. She was soon shackled at the end of the line next to a young mother clutching a toddler to her breasts.

The bruised and battered preteen—whose face was caked with dirt and mud—looked at the other woman sympathetically. Her feet were blistered and bleeding, and it was obvious that the young mother had been pushed to her limit. No one seemed to care, especially the drivers, as they prodded everyone to their feet. Nadu offered her hand to the young mother who looked at her in surprise then grabbed the extended hand.

Three hours later the group stopped. Nadu fell to her knees, too tired to speak, now understanding the other captives' exhaustion and insensitivity to another one's plight. The drivers had set a back-breaking pace, and her head hung into her chest as she gasped for air spent. But she was a King's daughter, taught from infancy that she was responsible for the survival and welfare of her people. So, when one of the two water boys passed his pouch to her, Nadu waved the boy on to the young mother indicating he should allow the fatigued woman to drink first.

The young mother grabbed the pouch, and with a disbelieving glance at Nadu, jammed it into her mouth. She gulped one mouthful down. Her cheeks bulged with the second. The boy regained the pouch and started on toward the next set of captives. But before he could take a step, Nadu pulled the boy's leg, motioning that she wanted to drink. Saddened, and only slightly irritated, the boy pointed to the young mother and then at Nadu. He raised two fingers, and then place his hand over his mouth and shook his head.

The boy's eyes were old and world weary. At nine, Azu had witnessed horrendous crimes and cruelty, and it had left him hardened to the pain of others. He had five minutes to finish the watering of his line of captives. The iron rule was only one swallow of water per captive. If he took longer than five minutes, or gave a larger portion of water to one of the captives, it would earn him and his twin brother Olu, a severe beating.

Nadu's shoulders drooped. She had not meant to forego her water. But when she watched the mother dripping the extra portion into the toddler's mouth, she was glad of the sacrifice. She watched the precious liquid spill over the baby's cracked lips and wondered about the monsters that had captured them. The mother looked at Nadu, and for the first time on their journey, humanity spill from her eyes. Teary, she stared at Nadu and smiled faintly while she hugged the baby to her breasts. She pointed to her chest and said, "Naomi," and looked at Nadu inquisitively.

"Nadu, my name is Nadu." Naomi smiled and returned to feeding her baby. Too soon they were being driven to their feet again, and the caravan started back into the slow trot.

Kwame pushed through the bush with iron resolve, a picture of Nadu firmly imprinted in his mind. Every step was a struggle, bringing with it a twisting stab of pain to his shoulder. He had packed the hole with mud and leaves in an attempt to stunt the flow of blood. He knew that every tortuous step brought him one foot closer to Zankli and Nadu's rescue. It took him over an hour to retrace his steps from the river to the village, a journey that would normally take fifteen minutes. But he had lost time when he had taken a path curving away from the river.

Ebagbe had just finished feeding the chickens and was preparing to cook the King's waking meal, when Kwame stumbled into the commons and collapsed at her feet. Startled, the old woman jumped back and threw up her hands at the sight of the pool of blood seeping from Kwame's leaf covered chest.

"Ayeeee," the old woman yelled dashing about. Oooh! My goodness!"

"Ayeeee, come see—they have killed him. Come see. Wha ta? Wha tas happen here! Nadu's intended is dead, oh." The woman shouted over and over rushing from one hut to another, until she reached the king's sprawling dwelling.

King Tete Zankli, who was closeted with his latest concubine, did not appreciate the disturbance and, turning over, complained, "Ah. What is this? That screeching is enough to raise the dead. What is that crazy woman talking about?" No sooner had he asked the prickly question than villagers began pouring from their huts alarmed by Ebagbe's noisy outburst. Even Moza, who was still dozing, jumped from her mat and hurried outside. The girl rushed over and added one more body to the human circle crowding around Kwame.

Still enjoying the amble posterior of his bedmate, King Zankli sent one of his slaves to investigate the commotion. When he learned that it was Kwame who was injured, the King hastily pulled the spread from his mat, callously flipping the girl off the pallet onto the packed dirt floor.

The villagers were gawking and whispering to one another from behind their hands—with subdued interest—but not one soul moved to help the young visitor. The king pushed through the crowd, but made no attempt to aid his daughter's intended.

Several seconds passed and then there was a hush, as the crowd became silent and parted like the Red Sea. The village healer walked toward Kwame. His steps were confident, and he moved with unhurried dignity. He bent down and examined the unconscious suitor by raising first one eyelid and then the other. He stood and placed his finger under Kwame's noise to measure the movement of his lungs, shaking his head in satisfaction when he felt the warm breath.

The healer was overjoyed, though he would never allow that emotion to show on his face. *He is alive,* he thought with a mental sigh, thanking the God of his great-grandfathers. The healer was aware that the matter was very grave. Especially, if it were found that one of King Zankli's people was responsible for the young man's injury.

Shifting his medicine bag to ride the front of his large stomach, the healer opened the pouch and pulled out a tiny bag filled with herbs meant to revive and placed it under Kwame's nose. The fatally wounded young man began to roll his head from side to side while batting the pouch with his hands. Spitting, he gagged and released a hacking cough as his lids fluttered, showing the whites of his eyes. His voice was thin.

"Nadu...they have taken her..."

"What did he say?" At once, the crowd began to buzz, the crescendo very much like a large beehive that had been disturbed by an unwanted intruder.

The king, who pushed through the crowd, bristled. "What? What was that he said about my daughter?"

With herculean effort, Kwame opened his eyes and focused. He had heard the king's question through a thick fog, but he had understood that his reply was vital. "She has been taken by slavers...I saw them...killed one...different man ...flesh color..... at river...." Kwame's head rolled as he lost consciousness.

King Zankli was an imposing figure on any day, but with the knowledge that his favorite daughter had been taken, his six-foot frame became huge, his voice a voluminous baritone that could be heard throughout the village.

"To me, Zankli arms to me." Over two hundred seasoned hunters responded to the booming call.

Within the caravan, Nadu had been taken from the main group and chained alone. She did not understand the guard's language, but she feared his intent. She had seen the spark of lust many times openly reflected in the eyes of village men, but was always confident that she was safe. After all, she was the king's daughter—*the Chosen One*. No man, if he valued his life and family, would dare touch her. But these flesh-colored men did not care of her Zankli linage or bloodlines. Nadu had long since decided that they were heathens, low-lifes, and the worst of humanity.

Watching them out of the corner of her eye, Nadu melted into the ground with the shrinking feeling that she was the object of their discussion. When one of the guards raised his fist and pointed at Nadu, clutching his manhood with vulgar intent, her worst fears were confirmed. But the guard, who appeared to be the leader, moved his head from side to side signaling he did not agree and turned to walk away. Incensed at being denied and then dismissed, the guard attacked the leader knocking him off his feet and viciously kicking the side of his head repeatedly until the man stopped moving.

Then, with evil intent, the guard moved toward Nadu. The petrified girl drew her knees into her stomach, locked her arms around her legs, and huddled into a ball. She wanted to scream with terror, but before he could reach her an ear splitting bang was accompanied by a white-silver spark that illuminated the skyline of the campsite. The advancing guard fell with a loud thud and landed inches from Nadu's curled toes, his eyes open, staring sightlessly into the large campfire.

Seconds later, the leader stood over Nadu. He had a jagged cut on his forehead, which dripped blood down the side of his face, but he seemed oblivious to the wound as he reached down and grabbed Nadu's roped wrists and lifted her to her feet. In a loud baritone voice he cried, "This is my slave—anyone touches her, dies."

The next day the weary party reached the seashore where a transitory camp where makeshift pens of bamboo was erected to house the captured slaves. Hundreds of men, women and children were cramped into the tight barracks, and the stench of humanity was overwhelming, combining sweat, excrement, body fluids, and death into one mouth gagging odious cesspool. Nadu and Naomi slipped to the ground thankful of the rest in spite of the malodorous cramped quarters. No sooner had they sat down than they were prodded to their feet and ushered toward a large house, which floated on the water.

Separated into two groups—male and female—the human cargo was marched toward the beach where dozens of large rowboats were banked. Nadu's heart sank. Until she saw the beach, the stark reality of her capture had not truly sunk in. She believed all along that her father would come for her...bring his massive army of seasoned hunters and rescue her from these filthy jackals. But as the group of women was driven closer and closer to the rowboats, Nadu's heart sank.

Too soon, she found herself in a rowboat moving toward the great house on the sea. She was still anchored to Naomi who had managed to keep her baby clutched to her breasts in spite of several attempts to take it away from her. Nadu worried for Naomi. She did not believe the guards would allow her to keep the infant once they reached the floating house, and she feared for her newfound friend.

One by one, Nadu and the other captives were lifted onto the deck. There were several men with the long firing sticks stationed on board, which brought to Nadu's mind her last vision of Kwame. She had not had any time to think of him since her capture, but now her heart became heavy with grief and tears began to roll down her cheeks.

When Naomi noticed Nadu's distress, she placed a sympathetic arm around the young girl's shoulder and in doing so, exposed the baby's legs dangling underneath her breast scarf.

"Hey! What do we have here?" a flesh-colored guard yelled from his station above the deck. Both girls looked at him as he descended the stairwell with dread in their eyes. Nadu's arm crept around Naomi's waist and the two girls clung to each other pathetically, in their attempt to protect the baby between them.

The guard reached the girls and flipped the scarf over Naomi's shoulder. The baby whimpered, frowned, and squinted her eyes at the brightness of the sun. He grabbed the child, wrestling with the frantic mother and laughed as she clutched the child fiercely in her arms.

Naomi's wretched screams filled the bow when she lost the tussle, and the man laughed as he dangled the child by her arm above her mother's head. The child's cry joined her mother's and chaos erupted. Nadu entered the fracas with a fierce blow to the man's back, followed by screams of her own. Without regard for her personal safety, she flung herself on the man digging her nails into his back.

"Jackal, pig's dung, son of a baboon, I will kill you! Let that baby go!" Though no one understood her, there could be no doubt that Nadu was cursing the driver and damning him in her language. Two guards, one a Yorba native and the other flesh colored, attempted to drag Nadu and Naomi away from their human target. They had little success.

The two days of abuse and uncertainty had taken its toll on Nadu. She fought like a wounded tiger, scratching, gouging, and spitting her anger at the devils that had killed her intended and robbed her of her family. Naomi had lost everything except for her baby, and she was willing to die to keep this last vestige of her former life safe. Both girls battled with heroic strength, and the guards feared the wrath of the captain if they damaged either one or destroyed his human cattle.

Captain Callahan heard the screams from his cabin, and could not believe his ears. In the ten years he had skippered the

Black Pearl, he had never been interrupted during one of his meals. "What in damnation?" he blustered, pushing back from the table and rising to his feet quickly in spite of his tall frame.

At forty, Joshua Callahan had spent the better part of his life at sea, first as a cabin boy and finally as owner of his own fleet of cargo ships. In addition to the *Black Pearl*, which he personally captained, there were four other vessels—two slavers and two china clippers.

He could have retired from the sea years before, but found life on land boring to the extreme. His wife, Matilda, a rotund heiress, who had doubled his fleet of ships and tripled his wealth, did little to inspire more than an obligatory visit every two or three years—just long enough to get her with child and then off again he would go. If Matilda was not satisfied, she never complained. And while Joshua knew little to nothing of his six daughters, other than they were carbon copies of their mother who reminded him of a long-eared, brown hare, they too appeared content.

No, Joshua Callahan loved his roving seaways. He was a happy man, unencumbered by the demands of a discontented wife and family. His wants were simple, good food, good company, and good sex. He kept a nimble cabin boy to relieve himself on lonely cold nights, and Joshua had his pick of female flesh at various ports around the world. However, his life was about to change drastically.

What the captain saw when he gained the deck caused his mouth to fall open. The deck was in bedlam. Several of his veteran guards were prone on the deck, tugging at two black sluts who refused to be separated. The girls were kicking and screaming, while one of his men was dangling a mass of rags above their heads. As Joshua watched in amazement, one of the girls broke free and snatched the rag from the guard's hands. She ran toward the end of the ship and scampered up on the rail at the ship's bow looking about frantically, her eyes huge saucers in her face. Suddenly, everything was quiet as Naomi poised like a dancer at the top of the ship's rail. Time stood still. Everyone felt that the girl was only a hairsbreadth away from flinging herself with the rag into the ocean.

"Nee!" The other girl had broke free, and the captain watched struck dumb as the most beautiful apparition he had every envisioned rushed toward the bow. "Nee!" Her voice was satin, the smoothest velvet he had ever heard, and Joshua Callahan felt he would die of need if he could not hear it again.

Nadu spoke quickly. Her voice sounding like a blending of musical rhythms, she pleaded with Naomi, telling her that all was not lost, that she Nadu and the God of her great-grandfathers would protect her and the baby. "This I swear by all that I hold dear—and on the blood of all Zankli, I promise to never abandon you or yours."

Naomi did not understand her friend's words, but she felt Nadu's sincerity and something inside of her shifted subtly. The foreign words moved her as nothing else had in her short life and she turned away from the water suddenly afraid of her precarious perch on the rail. Nadu recognized the panic in Naomi's eyes, and moved slowly toward her friend with her arm extended and her hand open.

The young mother paused, looked at Nadu for several seconds and accepted her hand. Years later, she was never able to answer exactly why, but that day she knew that she had placed her hand into a safe haven.

No one spoke as the two girls stood at the edge of the ship. The captain's presence on deck was enough to silence even the boldest of his men. The captain was not in the habit of tolerating defiance or a challenge to his authority, no matter the circumstance. Every member of the *Black Pearl*, from the cook to the cabin boy, from the first mate to the doctor expected the captain to order a severe punishment for the disruptive and disobedient slave girls. All awaited the outcome.

Joshua Callahan walked toward Nadu, feeling as if he was carried on another's legs. He was aware that his authority and his iron-fisted reputation were under scrutiny, but he did not care. He had eyes only for Nadu. Everything else paled in comparison, and he wanted the beautiful girl in his cabin, at his command, with an urgency he had never felt before.

Shamelessly, Joshua walked up to both girls. Staring, his eyes roamed the young girl's face without seeming to do so. "Do you speak a civilizanguage?" Nadu stared at the flesh-colored man and knew that his words did not matter. He wanted her, and that was all she needed to know. She smiled, her full lips trembling slightly, and Joshua was lost.

Turning to his men, he flicked two fingers and motioned his first mate to his side. When the man reached him, Joshua lowered his voice. "Continue loading the cargo. The slut with the baby," he pointed at Naomi, "let her remain topside. I am going to conduct an experiment. Let's see if the child will survive the ocean trip." The captain hesitated, and he spoke as if in afterthought. "Add a live goat to the beasts below." He turned. His fingers picked at a nonexistent speck of lint on his dark navy sleeve before he looked up at Nadu. "Bring the other slut to my cabin, but see that she is washed first." He sniffed. "They do carry such a musty smell."

Joshua turned back toward his cabin. His casual movement was meant to belie his true emotions. In truth, Nadu's woman smell had filled his nostrils from across the bow making him heavy with need. He jealously searched the face of his first mate and the other men, wondering if they too felt her siren call. As for him, his seed was weeping like a misused virgin, and as he rushed toward his cabin, he was fearful he would stain his codpiece with desire and disgrace himself before his men.

"We will set sail at dawn when the tide is in."

Joshua looked over at the cabin boy. "Billy, come with me!" The boy's eyes fell to the captain's codpiece, and he turned reluctantly, his feet dragging as he moved toward the man's cabin.

Harry Wyle, the first mate, smirked as he watched the boy pass. Well did he know how the boy would be plied over the next hour? The captain would bugger the boy, there was no doubt, but he would drain himself first. Harry's own mouth watered, remembering his days in that very same cabin. Fifteen years before, he had served as cabin boy when he was just a lad. It had been an enlightening experience, one he had never forgotten—and one he enjoyed today with many of the young black captives.

Well it was not for him, at least not at this moment, he thought gingerly. *Best get about the captain's orders, for the man could be vicious when crossed.*

He gathered the girl, taking her by the arm with an ungentle squeeze and marched her below deck. He looked at her with a scowl, his breath as sour as his face. "Now don't you give me a problem, little girl, or I'll smash you good." Nadu did not need any translation for the look or sound. She knew the man was threatening her, and Nadu took heed.

Opening the door to the bath closet, he shoved her inside and locked the door. Nadu looked around, knowing that escape was impossible. The room was small and windowless. The only furniture in the room was a large wooden tub that was built into the floor. In the tub were seawater and a bar of scented soap. The bar smelled like the vanilla nut that grew in the bush surrounding Zankli, and unwanted tears formed at the corner of Nadu's eyes as she was reminded of all that she had lost. Everything she loved, her village and her family, seemed a lifetime away, and yet it had only been three days since she had been taken.

She swallowed her tears, and with a deep sigh, looked up at the ceiling of the bathroom. The young girl was a realist, her shoulders straightened in silent resolve. She realized, even at twelve, that living in the past would be self-destructive and a waste of time. With the wisdom of a seasoned woman, Nadu decided then and there to live in the present. Slipping from her dusty and torn wrap, she stepped into the tub and vowed that she would survive and by doing so return to her family someday. But for now, she thought, *By the God of Zankli, I will take all that is given, no matter how sour, and make it into sweet bread.*

Kwame watched, as the large house floating on the sea became a small spec against the golden horizon. They had arrived too late, and as the morning dawn herald in the new day, his heart sank. They had followed Nadu's trail of red beads to this very spot. She had left them with strands of her hair, a path for them to follow unerringly.

Chief Zanki stood beside Kwame, and the younger man knew the father joined him in heartbreak. The chief spoke in a hollow voice of a prophecy that had been given to the Zankli at their beginning.

"She will follow her destiny, as this too was foretold. I did not understand it, did not fathom that my child would be taken by the sea, but—yes, I see—it all was foretold in the annals of time." The tall man stared at the ship as it floated away, part of him leaving also. "Go, my *lost love.* Go with the blood of Zanki and the God of your great-grandfathers."

Watch for the release of
Captured Love
Zankli Chronicle—Book Two
Coming in 2011

Zankli Prayer

"The God of the Great-Grandfather of Zankli, giver of life, creator of the heavens and earth is forever with us. God always was and always will be."

"Ve Tuk ya ve mein-gutool ya Zankli, toli ya ethvenu, yiftul ya ve vul ti gull e yulto cee utivi. Tuk tultoo vii m tultoo tuki tuke."

THE ANCIENT

LANGUAGE

English / Ancient Language
Always = tultoo
And = ti
Anomaly = Tibooqee
Baby = panta
Ball = plu
Be = peke
Beautiful = putu
Beauty = pui
Before = piti
Bless = pulvi
Blessed = polu
Blessing = poluii
Bountiful = patui
Bring = pui
By = pi
Children = tukvi
Chosen = tukvihi
Chilly = tuulu
Come = tar
Commitment = yivulti
cold= tuu
Creator = yiftul
Cry = tamii

Candy = tiblo
Deliver = biko
Desire = bitae
Devotion = bituk
Earth = gull
Eternal = gultuku
Fish = yala
Forever = yulto
Foresight = yukki
Give = tol
Giver = tolo
Giver of Love = tolelmi
Gifted = totii
God = Tuk
Goodness = tukini
Great-grandfather = mein-gutool
Have = vivne
Heavens = vul
Healer= vituk
I = T
Irrevocably = enutuk
Is = e
Joy = hi
Justice = hituknik
Kiss = mul
Life = ethvenu
Light = etmivi
Longevity = egonii
Love = elmi
Man = io
Mantool= iovo
Marriage = iluki
Mated = itukti
My = iku
Native Doctor = telmik / Tuk-Kawu
Night = tie
Nice = taul

Notice = tibul
Ocean = yulu
Of = ya
Off-spring = yatukvi
Oh = Avi
One = yaya
Onto = yi
Pledge = wetuku
Provide = wevimi
Quiet = smi
Quite = stoo
Run = flki
Responsible = fotuk
Save = oulu
Salvation ouliti
Said = otpi
Say = otpu
Seer = oey
Ship = oblo
Sky = omy
Skyship = omyolu
Soul = oolu
Star = olit
Stay = onli
Supremacy = ofti
Testament vhtukni
The = ve
Their = vtuki
Them = veti
Through = vee
To = vi
Understand = uoo
Unto = ut
Us = utivi
use = uti
united = uoloo
Visitor = dulli

Was = vii
What = qitimi
Who = qiti
Will = tuki
With = cee
You = Tu
Your = Tuu

GLOSSARY

the Ancient Language: A language distinctly different from any other language know to humankind. The idiom is so ancient that it can only be spoken while in trance and understood during a sacred ceremony of the Zankli.

the Anomaly: A Zankli descendant who has become twisted and evil. Usually focused on destroying goodness in humankind, the Anomaly is dedicated to the elimination of the Chosen. The Anomaly is known in ancient language as Tibooqee.

the Chosen One/s: Zankli descendants with special gifts and powers that allow them to move through time and space, speak telepathically, self-heal, and contain extraordinary leadership qualities. Gifted with amazing sexual prowess, the Chosen are usually pure-bred Zankli and incapable of malice or wrong doing.

the First Generations: Zankli offspring who are the children of the first union of earthlings and celestials.

the God of the great-grandfathers: A trinity of one, the messenger affirms GOD is, and always has been the Father, the Son, and the Holy Ghost.

the Healer: A Zankli capable of self-healing. In modern day, the healer is a gifted doctor, surgeon, or researcher. In the days of yore, the healer was an astonishing herbalist, midwife, or remarkable chemist, sometimes persecuted as a witch or warlock.

the Light: An illuminating light with a voice so pure that it instills joy and willingness in the listener to do as commanded. The directives of the voice are so compelling they cannot be ignored.

the Native Doctor: Know as the most holy, Tuk-Kawu, is an ageless sage who is capable of hibernation. Tuk-Kawu evokes reverence. He is the earthly portal for Zankli gifts, language, and powers. He resides in the West African bush and can only be reached by invitation. His dwelling is cloaked and inaccessible under normal circumstances.

The Pure Bred: A Zankli born of Zanki (both parents are Zankli) that can trace his/her ancestry back to the *first generation* and the celestials.

The Savior: Know to the Zankli as the Messenger, he visits Togo around 6 AD with a message of affirmation from the GOD of their great-grandfathers.

the Tuk-Kawu: Translation = God Gifted. He is known as the native doctor and the most holy by Zankli. A mysterious sage, he only appears at the time of Chosen marriages and births. He is thought to be as old as time.

the Zankli Celestials: Mysterious visitors from elsewhere that interbred with indigenous West Africans bestowing on them remarkable talents and skills that include telepathy, out-of-body travel, healing, longevity, and exceptional allure and beauty.

the Zankli Earthlings: Descendants of Zankli Celestials and the indigenous people of West Africa, they have extraordinary intelligence and extra-sensory powers. Gifted with long life and youthfulness, they are physically superior – beautiful/handsome – sexually alluring individuals who bring about positive change to humankind.

However, there are Zankli Earthlings that are Anomalies – men and women – who have embraced evil as a way of life. These

Zankli stunt their gifts and mire their powers in malicious acts against their fellow man. The Anomaly can only be deflected and/or defeated by the Chosen.

the Zankli Gifts: Extra-sensory perceptions and telepathic powers that include mind reading and control, self-healing, teleporting, levitation, longevity, youthfulness, shape shifting, and hibernation.

the Zankli Prayer: A prayer evoked during sacred ceremonies, usually by the native doctor or the Chosen One, in which powers of the Zankli celestials are gifted to their earthly descendants.

> *Oh God, I bring before you your children who you have gifted with the light. Bring onto them what is yours to give, yours to provide, and yours to understand. Bless them with the joy of goodness, and deliver unto them longevity, wisdom, and foresight.*
>
> *They are the Chosen, offspring of your heart and a testament to your supremacy. They pledge eternal devotion to you and through you, they irrevocably vow life and honor to one another in everlasting unity.*

Made in the USA
San Bernardino, CA
09 July 2016